~Inspector Masters Investigates~

PERSONS OF INTEREST

Michael Joll

"Making Literature see the light of day."

This book is a work of fiction. While certain incidents are taken randomly from historical records, the names, characters, places and for the greater part, situations, are either the product of the author's imagination or are used fictitiously, and any resemblance to actual persons living or dead, events or locales, is entirely coincidental.

Library and Archives Canada Cataloguing in Publication

Joll, Michael, author

Persons Of Interest

ISBN 978-1-9991365-0-5 (soft cover)

Cover Photograph courtesy "Freeimages.com/Griszka Niewiadomski "

Cover design by Ken Puddicombe

Praise for PERSONS OF INTEREST by Michael Joll

"Michael Joll's new collection is a must-read for lovers of classic detective murder-mystery stories. He has succeeded in combining story-telling in the tradition of Arthur Conan Doyle and Agatha Christie, with exotic Southeast Asia locales and the mindsets of their early twentieth century British Colonial administrators."
Raymond Holmes, author of *Witnesses and Other Short Stories*

"As a poet, I most enjoyed the metaphors and imagery in Joll's stories…" Debbie Okun Hill

"With consummate skill and passion, Michael Joll weaves eight tales of conspiracy and murder, providing enthralling insight into British police operations in the far-east in the early decades of the twentieth century. These are not just clever who-done-it mysteries. They are stories of a way of life, carefully researched and crafted, of a colonial empire at its peak, and Michael pulls no punches as he lays bare an era filled with bigotry, intolerance and prejudices. Every ex-colonial—loyalist and opponent, will find these stories fascinating."
Ken Puddicombe, author of *Racing With The Rain*, *Junta* and *Down Independence Boulevard and Other Stories.*

"Exotic and intriguing! Joll brilliantly captures the reader's interest with vivid imagery and a relentless sleuth."
Phyllis Humby, short story writer, poet and novelist

"When constabulary's duty to be done,

A policeman's lot is not a happy one."

The Pirates of Penzance, (1879)

W.S. Gilbert.

CONTENTS

		Page
1	Death By His Own Hand	1
2	Only One Shoe	32
3	To Serve And Protect	61
4	Death By Krait	94
5	The Dean Vanishes	124
6	King Tukurahman	154
7	The Headless Bootlegger	186
8	The Commodore's Sea Chest	217
	Afterword	249

DEDICATION

To Honest Coppers.

ACKNOWLEDGMENTS

My thanks to my editor, Ken Puddicombe, whose dedicated use of the red pencil kept me focused on the task of writing these stories. Thanks also to my brother, Richard Joll, who hacked his way through the jungles of early drafts and gave me endless encouragement.

To MiddleRoad Publishers, as always, my thanks for taking the chance on a previously unpublished writer some years ago. To my former colleagues on the police force with whom I worked many years ago, especially Dick Coulthard, Len Favreau, Dave Richards and the late K.G. Greenwood, my gratitude for their guidance and recognition of my shortcomings as an investigator. To Brian Henry for his painstaking tutelage as a writer. To Nancy Kay Clarke for publishing some of my earlier stories in her e-zine, *CommuterLit.com.*

And, of course, to my wife, Linda, who had to put up with me during the writing, revisions and umpteen rewrites that proved necessary before Ken was as grudgingly satisfied as an editor ever is.

1. DEATH BY HIS OWN HAND

The powers that be in Kuala Lumpur sent me down to Singapore in the Straits Settlements during the monsoon season of 1924 to look into a suicide. I had only recently arrived in K.L. and at that time I was the most junior Inspector in the Colonial Police in Malaya. I was naturally as anxious as most young Inspectors are to make a name for myself as an outstanding investigator, hopefully destined for greatness and honours, and to reach the pinnacle of the profession.

I had yet to make my first arrest.

As the perpetrator is deceased, a suicide does not generally lead to an arrest, so I anticipated my arrest tally would not advance. An investigation such as this is generally regarded as straightforward and so quite why they needed an investigator from K.L. to assist the local police, I didn't know. I had thought to ask, but four years on the London Metropolitan Police before arriving in Malaya had taught me it was prudent not to swim against the stream of thought held by those placed above me.

For a suicide, which is what the death of the Englishman, Charles Richardson, concert pianist and one-time temporary resident of Singapore, appeared to be, all one generally needs is a body (deceased), a time of death (approximate), a method used to end life (usually gained from a post mortem) and an absence of motive that might indicate foul play by a third party. A suicide note is often helpful.

I checked in with the Straits Settlement Police, headed at that time by a Chief Superintendent on the cusp of retirement and possessing the florid complexion and expanded waistline that suggested an absence of physical exercise beyond bending the right elbow. The whites of his eyes were of a jaundice yellow tint. I never discovered why his skin, where it was exposed to view, was sallow, and wondered whether it was from too many years in the Tropics or from a liver ailment. His balding head and the backs of his hands were covered with liver spots as one might expect in a man of his age. How he had risen to his present position remained a mystery. He was known throughout the local Force, however, as a master of the art of delegation.

After a cursory handshake and a curt nod, the Chief Superintendent fobbed me off on one of the junior Inspectors. While waiting for the Inspector to tear himself away from whatever had seized and occupied his attention since my arrival, I happened to glance at the large, wood framed clock of the type favoured by railway stationmasters and which hung on the wall opposite his desk. I noted that it was a few minutes before lunchtime.

"Inspector Masters," I said, shaking the hand of the Inspector with whom I would work. "Kuala Lumpur," I added in case further explanation were needed. Detective Inspector Claude Ashton-Browne—A-B he said to call him as they had at school, was a tall, thin and languid young man. He possessed an expensive accent and affected a distracted air, as if everything was a bit of a bore and beneath his English gentleman's dignity, investigations into dead bodies being at the top of the list. So much for a first impression, gained in a brief introduction in the Chief Super's office before the latter burst out on his way to his appointment.

"He'll be back around three, I expect," Ashton-Browne said. "A good mind gone to waste. It happens so often around here. He's been on the job for thirty years. I'm told he was good at it once but now he's just hanging in, waiting for his pension to kick in next year."

I recognized the man mirrored in my own Chief Superintendent in Kuala Lumpur, a man of similar age and experience likewise treading water and hoping to keep afloat long enough to draw his pension. During my years as a policeman I have observed that the cream rarely rises to the top. Perhaps it's because outstanding investigators are too valuable as policemen to have their ability wasted in the ranks of senior management.

"He can't go home to retire, you know," Ashton-Browne said.

I must have looked blank.

"He's been out here too long." He sighed, as if an explanation were needed for someone who had yet to finish primary school. "Not that he's gone native or anything. But England passes you by. Five years, maximum, that's all it takes to realize one no longer fits in when one goes back on one's second home leave. By then it's usually too late."

I regarded him questioningly.

"I've done two years here," he said. "Home leave next year. Don't say anything, old boy, but I don't expect to return. This," he swept an arm around to indicate the police station, or Singapore, or perhaps the entire Colonial Service, "is just something to keep me amused until something more my line turns up. Or my father pops off and leaves the lot to me."

In common with many of his type—upper class, public school educated and moneyed, the art of the not-too-subtle put down came naturally. In contrast to Ashton-Browne, I finished my (free), day boys only, grammar school education at eighteen and was on my way to London University to read French and German when the Great War broke out. In a moment of not completely sober patriotism, I volunteered for the artillery. In addition to proficiency in French and German, uncommon among the mostly unilingual English, I was good at maths. My ability to calculate ranges for gun laying purposes was quickly noticed and in most un-army like fashion, made use of. For once, the army hammered a roughly square peg into a mostly square hole.

By the armistice, the army had unexpectedly recognized my overlooked ability to speak German with reasonable fluency. They dragged me away from my no longer needed guns, bumped me up to Lieutenant Colonel (temporary/acting) in the (well-intentioned but badly misnamed) Intelligence Corps and instructed me to lead the interrogation of senior German prisoners-of-war. Two years and a salute later I was out the door, back in civilian clothes and in need of a job. With no rich father to fall back on and an intended career as a German teacher barred by an understandable general aversion to the German language and an overabundance of men with better credentials, a career with the London Metropolitan Police beckoned. I joined. Four years later I found myself in the Colonial Service as an Inspector in Malaya, which I found a generally more comfortable and far less onerous occupation than being a London Bobby.

Which brings me back to why I was in Singapore that summer—it being a time of year on the calendar that has nothing to do with the weather, which is unvarying in its temperature and stickiness, the only measurable difference being the amount of daily rainfall. I still hadn't a clue why I was needed here, so I did the first thing that came to mind—I asked Ashton-Browne as soon as the Chief Super was out of earshot.

"I knew him," Ashton-Browne said. "Richardson. The deceased. The Chief Super has a policy that we don't investigate people we know personally except possibly for background. 'Without fear or favour' I think the expression is. Not that I think I have anything to fear from Richardson, and it's too late to do him any favours now, or vice versa."

"But why me?"

"Search me, old boy. All the others here are tied up on other stuff, I expect, so tag, you're it."

"I see," I said, none too clearly.

"The body's at the morgue. Single gunshot to the head. Temple. Apparent suicide. Shouldn't take too long to untangle the usual who, what, when, where, why and how of the matter, then back to K.L. There's no room here in the inn so we've put you up in Raffles Hotel for a couple of nights."

"The inn?"

"The police accommodation," he said with a sigh, as if talking to a halfwit was simply too much and beneath his pay grade. "There's a chap lives in the hotel who also knew Richardson. English fellow. A writer of sorts. Greenwood's his name. They say he's quite good—good enough to earn a living at it, anyway. Popular back home. You might want to talk to him and see what he has to offer by way of background." He sighed again.

The effort of speaking so many sentences one after another seemed to exhaust Ashton-Browne.

"I've heard the name," I said, "although I can't say I've read any of his stuff."

He shrugged. "Well, don't burst a blood vessel over this. It's pretty cut and dried, but all sudden deaths have to be investigated. Usually nothing to them, but you never know until you look and ask a couple of quick questions. Two days should do it. There's a car and driver at your disposal while you're here." He glanced at the Chief

Super's clock. "Lunchtime. The bar's open in the mess. The beer isn't up to much, but it's more reliable than the water and doesn't need to be boiled first. And the Chinese curry's not bad most days."

I took that as an invitation to join him. It would have been impolite to insist on getting the investigation under way immediately, and boys educated at grammar schools mostly possessed manners, if not quite as polished as public school types.

I knew better than to broach the matter over lunch. "No shop talk in the mess," had been the rule in the army and not a bad one all told, even if what was left to talk about always seemed to revolve around Labrador Retrievers, horses and cars, the last of which none of us had but which we all coveted. Women were off limits as a topic of conversation too, though I never did discover why, which probably explained why conversations in the mess were as boring as Ashton-Browne's.

"The Chief Super lunches at his own club," Ashton-Browne said. "He says the menu's better and more varied. Translation—a longer wine and whisky list. Still, it means we don't have to be on absolutely best behavior all the time."

I kept my thought to myself. Somehow, I couldn't quite see A-B horsing around in the Inspectors' mess after an evening of beer, debagging the most junior member and running his trousers up the flagpole. But I could be wrong.

Back in his office after lunch I asked him how he knew Richardson.

"Small world. We were at school together for five years, in the same House, the same dorm, everything. Most people need to be good at something and he was always very good at the piano. I wasn't surprised to hear he carried on with it after school. Then of course, the war."

"He served?"

"He couldn't get out of it. Conscripted. Spent a bit of a rough time in the infantry before he cracked up rather badly and got sent home before he could do anything silly. It looks as if things caught up with him in the end."

"How do you mean?"

Ashton-Browne sighed, one of those long, painstaking ones with visible eye-rolling, reserved for boys consigned to the Remove form at school. "It stands to reason his lack of moral fibre caught up with him and he blew his brains out rather than face up to facts like a man."

I thought that a rather cruel assessment of someone he knew from their schooldays. I had known and served with, many who had suffered shell-shock. What reasonable, sane man wouldn't after all they had had to endure in the war? At least in the artillery you don't actually get to meet the enemy at bayonet point. Killing Germans with a long-range shell was not personal, not like it was in the infantry.

"How did you get to meet him here?"

"Bumped into him quite by chance. He was playing at Raffles Hotel one evening and I was propping up the bar with a couple of chaps. I turned around when I heard the piano start and couldn't believe my eyes. When he finished playing, I went up to him. He recognized me straight away in spite of the years apart."

"When was this?"

"A few months ago. Six, eight perhaps. I'm not quite sure. I don't keep a diary."

He sounded cross, as if I was questioning him as a key witness and should mind my own business.

By the time I reached Singapore I had been in Malaya a few months and was slowly adjusting to their style of police work. It's different from being an English Bobby. In England there are the criminal classes: Saxons mostly. Then there are their victims, sometimes members of the same class as the villains, but more often considered a better breed of men and women; the Normans. In Malaya, where the rule of English law largely applied, with allowances for some native customs on a case-by-case basis, there were two distinct categories of individuals—those who committed crimes, and white men. White men, almost by definition, did not commit crimes of any sort and it was important for the Colonial power to show the superiority of the white race as being above low criminality. It was equally important not to embarrass British Colonial Institutions, such as the Church and the Law Courts, by charging white men with the kind of atrocities normally only associated with the depravities of the natives.

All hogwash, of course, but in 1924 it was determined that in order to keep those parts of the world map shaded pink properly subjugated, peaceful and its populace grateful to be citizens of the most gracious Empire ever to rule such a large part of the world, white men and women would enjoy a status well above that of native people. Any sins committed by white men and the occasional white woman, were written off as errors of good judgement, minor peccadillos at worst and easily forgivable. At the very worst a repeat offender might be persuaded to return home to England.

"I'd start at the morgue," Ashton-Browne said, as if he wanted to be rid of me, which no doubt he did.

I took the hint.

The Medical Examiner, Dr. Morton, was there when I called on the morgue, all glaring bright lights and white tiled walls with a pervasive aroma of death, disinfectant and formaldehyde. A morgue attendant pulled open a refrigerated steel drawer with some fanfare and drew back the cover from Richardson's face with a dramatic flourish.

"I will let you have a photographic copy of my report," Dr. Morton, said. "I think you will find it succinct, but thorough."

"Cause of death?"

He pointed to a small hole in Richardson's left temple. "A single bullet wound angled slightly upward and at almost ninety degrees to the side of the skull. I recovered a lead bullet from the inside of the skull, lodged against the bone above the right temple. There was no exit wound. I examined and weighed the brain. It was of normal size and weight and showed no sign of cognitive deterioration or evidence of alcohol abuse."

I examined the skull closely. I had seen many dead bodies over my years in the army. Too many. Some had been shot. Some blown to atoms by a shell or a mine. Some lay in bits and pieces, picked up and shoved unceremoniously into piles or laid out in rows to be buried later. Sometimes a *body* comprising parts from several different individuals was buried in the same hole and a name ascribed to it on a marker as temporary as the cemetery immediately behind the line. Richardson seemed like most of the bodies I'd viewed in Flanders—peacefully at rest, whether willingly so or not, his skin smooth as if the wrinkles caused by the pain of living had been wiped away by death. Someone had closed his eyes and pulled the skin back over his head where the top had been sawn off for the post mortem.

A trace of dried blood surrounded the bullet's neat entry wound and the narrow circle of skin tissue immediately around it had turned a purplish-blue from post mortem bruising. I noticed the pinkness of the tissue on the underside of the body caused by morbid lividity as the blood had pooled by gravity to the lowest level of the supine body.

I examined the hands. "Did you wash off powder burns or residue from his hand?" I said. "There doesn't seem to be any."

"No. We haven't touched him other than to remove his clothing and to conduct the autopsy. As far as I know, he's in the same condition as they found him."

"When was he discovered?"

Dr. Morton checked his notes. "Eight days ago."

"Were you able to determine a time of death?"

"Between one and three a.m. the same day. Someone heard a gunshot, but the caller had no watch. I gather it took him a while to find a phone or a policeman to report it. You've seen the police report?"

I was embarrassed—I hadn't. "It's in my briefcase." A small, face-saving subterfuge, but one I felt necessary if I wasn't to appear a complete clot. "I just came from the police station. I was hoping to catch you in before you left for the day."

"I leave at five," he said coldly, implying that I'd had ample time to read the report before disturbing him and asking foolish questions.

"And before you ask, he was discovered by a native police officer doing his rounds at 3:18 a.m. It was raining and had been raining hard for several hours before the body was discovered. Consequently, the hands and face were clean of powder residue and burns, as were the clothes."

I searched in vain for a cave deep enough and black enough to crawl into. So, for something to do, and possibly to cover up my mortification, I examined the hands again. The fingers were long and bony and the palms soft. Slight calluses at the base of the fingers of his right hand and absent from his left suggested he had probably been right handed. His fingernails were cut short and showed no dirt on, or under them, which I did not find out of the ordinary for someone who made his living by playing the piano. I spread the fingers with some difficulty—not from rigor mortis which had long disappeared, but from being in a freezer drawer—and noted a wide span that would encompass an octave on a piano without difficulty. A bruise and a graze on his right wrist raised my interest and my eyebrows.

"Probably when he fell," the pathologist said. "I doubt if he was sitting when he shot himself, particularly out of doors at one or two in the morning. A gentleman would shoot himself standing up, if he's a gentleman." I sensed a barrier just slammed down. Dr. Morton's accent reeked of public school, like Ashton-Browne's. I sensed the doctor looked down on a mere Grammar School-educated copper questioning his findings, or his suppositions, but he had the grace not to express his distaste to we *hoi poloi.*

Something about the corpse bothered me. It was something one of my lecturers at the London Met police college had said on examining dead bodies, but I couldn't place my finger on it. I examined Charles Richardson from head to toe, searching for some clue to suggest that, although death came from a single gunshot to the head, there was more to it than appeared on its face. It didn't make sense that Richardson, being right handed, would shoot himself in the left temple. And I didn't buy into the notion that the rain must have washed away any trace of powder burns from his hand or clothing.

I stood back and nodded to the attendant to close the drawer. I heard it slam shut, the noise echoing around the white-tile-walled morgue. "His clothing?" I said.

"At the police station, presumably in the evidence locker."

Why hadn't I thought of that?

"Robbery does not seem to be a motive if it wasn't suicide, which in my professional opinion after twenty-five years as a Medical Examiner, is what it was." Dr. Morton enunciated each syllable clearly for the benefit of the hard of hearing and the borderline lunatic. "Suicide," he repeated. "No question."

"Any suicide note on him, or at his lodging?"

"It's in the report."

I sensed the meeting was effectively over. I thanked him for his time and expertise as sincerely as I could and beat a tactical retreat to the hospital car park where I found my driver nonchalantly smoking a cheroot while leaning against the Wolseley's gleaming black coachwork and chatting with a young woman in a nurse's uniform.

He stiffened, then snapped to attention when I hove fully into view. The nurse disappeared without a word.

"The police station," I said. "Then you're done for the day."

"Sir!" He cranked the motor and we were off, beating the afternoon thunderstorm and cloudburst to the police station by a few minutes. Looking to find the property of the late Charles Richardson, I checked with the native duty Constable on the front desk. He examined a ledger at considerable length. He must have sensed my impatience, or tacitly admitted he couldn't read English because he turned the ledger upside down so I could read it. I pointed to an incident number. He grunted something at me in what I took to be Mandarin and went off to fetch an English-speaking Sergeant.

"Bagged and tagged and in the evidence locker, Sir." The Sergeant took me to a locker in the secure exhibits room, unlocked the door and withdrew a cloth bag. I went straight to the outer clothing, such as it was; a lightweight tropical linen jacket, cotton shirt and white duck trousers. The trousers revealed mud stains but nothing else of interest. I checked the cuffs of the long-sleeved shirt.

"Cufflinks?"

"Yes, Sir." The Sergeant handed me a small bag containing a wallet, a watch, a signet ring and a pair of cufflinks.

One cufflink appeared slightly scuffed. I held it up to examine it in better light. I picked up the wallet. "Contents in the police report, I take it?" I said.

"Yes, Sir. Not much. A little money. A couple of business cards in the name of Charles Richardson. A letter from England, dated eight months ago and signed by his mother offering him his old room back if he wants to come home and the piano for as long as he wishes to stay."

"Any identification?"

"His passport was in his jacket pocket. The photo is a good likeness. Inspector Ashton-Browne also confirmed his identification. Folded in two in the wallet was this ticket for the Orient Line passenger liner leaving Singapore for London, Tilbury docks, sailing six days ago."

So, nothing I didn't already know. Not robbery. Not an accident. A single gunshot to the temple. The gun not found, probably stolen by a local and which would have found its way into a gangster's hands within hours. Like Ashton-Browne said, and Dr. Morton confirmed, a run-of-the-mill suicide for reasons not yet apparent.

I thanked the Sergeant and picked up a copy of the police report from Aston-Browne's deputy. I ascertained that A-B had left for the day and had not extended an invitation to drinks or dinner. I retrieved my valise and hailed a rickshaw to take me to Raffles Hotel where I intended to go through the police report with the proverbial fine-tooth comb. Looking for what, however, I had no clue.

My luck changed back at the hotel. I enquired at the front desk about Aubrey Greenwood and discovered that not only did we have rooms on the same floor, but that he was also in.

I dumped my valise in my room and found my way along the corridor to Greenwood's room. I knocked on the door.

I heard a voice muffled behind the door. "Who is it?"

I gave my name. A few seconds later the door opened. Through the crack between door and jamb I caught a glimpse of a four-poster bed with standard mosquito nets occupying part of one wall. The door opened further. I saw a long sofa against the opposite wall and an armchair in a corner by the French door to the balcony. Next to the sofa was his writing desk on which sat a typewriter and an empty glass tumbler. Greenwood's body and the low level of lighting—a single lamp on his writing desk—obscured most of the rest of the details. All in all, a bachelor's suite in a better hotel, I decided and little need for more spacious accommodation with other amenities downstairs.

"Mr. Greenwood?"

"Yes. And how can I be of assistance to the local police?"

"I'm actually down from Kuala Lumpur," I said to clarify my position. "I need to ask you a few questions about Charles Richardson."

At the mention of Richardson's name, I saw a muscle tick in Greenwood's face. He quickly recovered.

"I gather you knew him."

"I wouldn't exactly say I knew him, Inspector. Certainly not well."

"How well then did you know him?"

Greenwood stuck his head round the door and glanced up and down the hallway. "Could we discuss this somewhere other than in the hallway of a hotel, Inspector?"

"In the bar?" The tip of Greenwood's tongue flicked over his lips.

"Anywhere's better than here. Give me five minutes to change into something more suitable and I'll meet you there."

Wearing a dinner jacket and black tie, Greenwood met me in the bar. He made me feel quite shabby, dressed as I was in my working uniform that I had worn all day, and my shave the night before I left Kuala Lumpur was starting to feel bristly. We made our way to a quiet corner of the lounge bar and sat down in padded bamboo armchairs at a round mahogany table. The waiter brought gin and tonics for both of us and I ordered a second before he returned to the bar. Greenwood drank his as if it were a tumbler of water.

"How well did you know Richardson?" I said, when the waiter brought the second round of drinks to our table.

Greenwood swallowed a generous amount of his gin and tonic before he answered. "He came in from the Solomon Islands a few months ago. He'd been an assistant to the Assistant Commissioner in Honiara for a couple of years. A complete fish out of water in that kind of work, but it sufficed to keep body and soul together until something more up his street came along."

"What do you mean?"

"He had his head in the clouds most of the time I knew him. It was music and especially the piano, where his sole interest lay, so hardly the most suitable background for an admin job. How he got it, I don't know. I can only imagine the most important qualification was the colour of his skin. I can't see him getting the job otherwise. He went to a decent school and he was a very good pianist, but..."

Greenwood left the sentence unfinished while he disposed of the rest of his drink.

I pushed my untouched second drink across the table. "I learned a long time ago in the officers' mess that if you can't say *no* to the second drink, don't say *yes* to the first," I said, then realized he'd probably take it as a rebuke. "On my first night in the mess after I received my commission," I said hastily, "they got me horribly drunk. When I woke up behind the mess covered in vomit, wishing I were dead, I discovered I was without my trousers. How I got there and in that state, remains one of my life's unsolved mysteries. If nothing else, it confirmed that I have little tolerance for alcohol."

By now Greenwood, who seemed uninterested in either my

explanation or anecdote, had started on his third gin and tonic.

"How did you meet Richardson?" I said before he could finish the drink. I needed to move the questioning along—the police hosteling expense account only covered so much and a junior Inspector's pay only stretched so far. However, if gin fuelled Greenwood's loquacity then I would bite the bullet out of my own pocket. It wasn't as if I was supporting a wife or anything on my salary.

"I met him here. There's a grand piano in the lounge. You've probably seen it. It lends the hotel an air of sophistication that it might not otherwise earn. Richardson was playing it one evening. People were leaving tips in the glass on the piano in appreciation. I could tell right off the bat he was really good. At the end of the evening we chatted for a while."

"What about?"

"Oh, the usual."

"The usual?"

"You know. Where he was from. How come he got to be so good at the piano, what he did for a living, although that's not the sort of thing gentlemen discuss openly, even here. It turned out that he'd received a medical discharge from the army after Passchendaele. Shell shock, I expect, though it wouldn't do to ask and he didn't volunteer the information. After recovering somewhat, someone had pulled some strings and he found himself in the Colonial Service trying to appear useful."

"Did he say why he was in Singapore?"

"He told me he'd resigned his position and was on his way back to England. He didn't like the job. Singapore was a stopover. I'm surprised he stayed as long as he did. He was flat broke. I don't think he even had the price of the cheapest cabin fare back to England."

"How did he live while he was in Singapore?"

"Like I said, he played the piano for tips. He didn't drink much. The rest went on food. I can't think he ate much either. He was as skinny as a rake. I think he only owned two suits, his dinner suit which he wore for playing and his day suit."

"Where did he live?"

"Here, in the hotel."

"How did he pay for it?"

Greenwood squirmed in his chair. "I took pity on him," he said. "I am a man of not inconsiderable means. With the royalties from my novels and such I can indulge in a few whims. You have no doubt heard of me."

I nodded, without wishing to appear fawning in the presence of self-confessed greatness.

"I had to go up country for a while, Rangoon, Calcutta and Darjeeling. It was research for a new novel. I keep my room here by the year. It was going to be empty for a couple of months. I offered it to Richardson so he would have a place to stay and bathe and get his laundry done while I was away."

"And he took you up on your offer?"

"He jumped at it."

"How long ago was this?"

Greenwood hesitated, then picked up his glass and stared at the contents, the gin, tonic water and ice now a diluted, watery memory. I looked behind me and saw the waiter hovering. I held up two fingers and within seconds two fresh drinks appeared. The first disappeared in double quick time.

"You were asking something, Inspector?" Greenwood said with the innocence of a babe as he wiped his lips with a paper napkin.

"How long ago did you offer Richardson your room?"

"Quite a while ago. Two months at least. Three? I don't remember the exact date."

"Did you share the room before you left for Burma?"

He hesitated, then picked up the second, or more accurately, his fifth drink and took a delicate sip rather than his usual glass-draining gulp. "He had nowhere else to stay. There is a settee in my suite. He slept there for a few nights before I left, then he had the run of the room."

"Was he still there when you returned?"

"Yes. I got in late off the *Vollendam*. Richardson was in bed and already fast asleep. I didn't want to wake him, so I took my turn on the settee. He left in the morning. I've not seen him since. I heard he shot himself. He seemed down in the dumps when he left, so I'm not entirely surprised."

"Have you any idea why he might have taken his own life?"

"As I'm sure you well know, Inspector, the war did strange things to many men. He was one who survived death in the trenches but who still lived in its constant shadow. The war was never over for him. He escaped, if you like, to the Solomons, but he could never have found a home or even a reprieve there."

"And he was on his way back to England, you say."

"He told me the morning he left he intended to resume his concert career. He was very good, Inspector, but I don't think good enough to make a real go of it. It takes more than hard work and talent to succeed in the arts, which, as an oft-published author I know only too well. Even the best serves a long apprenticeship and must pay homage to those who have gone before." He offered a smug smile of self-satisfaction in his assessment.

"Is there anything else you can tell me about him?"

Greenwood hesitated once more. "I discovered after he left that morning, that my old service revolver, a Webley, was missing from my desk drawer. I assume he took it. I can't think it was for self-protection, so the logical presumption was that he planned to take his own life at some point. I don't think his suicide was a spur of the moment decision. If he used my revolver I feel guilty that I unwittingly provided him with the means."

I gave him silent credit for not wringing his hands. "Did Richardson know anyone else in Singapore?"

"He knew Inspector Ashton-Browne of the Straits Settlement Police. Apparently, they were at school together."

"Do you know if they saw each other here?"

"I know they met in the hotel once, early on. Ashton-Browne recognized him and introduced him to me. I pretended that Richardson and I had never met. I had met Ashton-Browne a few times. It's a small social world in Singapore, Inspector. You know how it is."

I did. It was no different from Kuala Lumpur.

"I'm staying here, Greenwood," I said. "For a night or two. Until I've finished my investigation and signed off on the paperwork. Perhaps we can meet for dinner before I leave?"

"Of course, Inspector. And if I can be of any help in your investigation, you will let me know, won't you?" He raised his gin and tonic in some kind of salute and downed the remnants in one long, open-throated swallow.

After breakfast the next morning I summoned my driver and went back to the hospital. I met Dr. Morton, who scowled at me as if he were still cross at my wasting his time.

"You recovered the fatal bullet," I said.

"I did. I have it here," he said, and fetched it from a box in a locker in the morgue.

"Did you identify the caliber?" I said, holding up the squashed lead bullet.

"Not officially."

"What do you mean?"

"It hasn't been submitted to a ballistics expert. Not yet. No urgent need."

"Do you have an opinion on the caliber and the make of firearm used?"

"Subject to confirmation, I believe it is either a thirty-two or a thirty-eight-caliber bullet, fired from close range. I have no opinion on the type of firearm used, other than most probably a revolver or semiautomatic kind of pistol."

"Not a four fifty-five caliber bullet fired from a Webley revolver of the type used in the war?"

"No. You can see it's too small just by looking at it."

"I've seen what a bullet fired from a Webley can do to a skull. Richardson's skull showed no exit wound, correct?"

"Correct. Although it made a real mess of the brain tissue it did not penetrate the bone."

"So, not possible for it to have been fired from a Webley service revolver of the type used by the British and Empire army or the Straits Police?"

"Not in my opinion as a pathologist." He barely stifled the kind of impatient sigh used when humouring the feeble-minded. "That caliber of bullet would unquestionably have penetrated both sides of the skull leaving a large exit wound."

"One last question, Doctor."

Dr. Morton raised his eyebrows but said nothing.

"Why is this bullet not with Richardson's property in the police lock-up?"

He regarded me as if I were a specimen of mucus in a Petrie dish and about as intelligent. I was beginning to believe it myself. "It is the cause of death, Inspector. It is here, along with the deceased's brain and organ tissue samples. Photographed in case of need at a

Coroner's Inquest and sealed with a file reference number."

"Good. I wouldn't want it to go missing for any reason. However, I will sign for it and place it in police custody with the rest of Richardson's effects. One can't be too careful with an unexplained death. It's still a police matter."

Dr. Morton's face turned red. I had just accused him, in a roundabout way, of being careless with forensic evidence, so I could hardly blame him for his reaction. However, it suggested he had a human side after all, something I'd not considered possible in the make-up of a pathologist. Not that I warmed to him in any way. I still thought he had the personality of an undertaker minus the false sincerity.

I took the bullet, signed for it and left the chilly morgue. In the police Wolseley on my way to the Hill Street police station I examined the bullet. It had clearly been washed clean as no human tissue clung to it. The business end was squashed, as would be expected having come into direct contact with the skull bone on entry and on being stopped by a skull bone before it could exit. I could see marks—striations—on the side of the bullet caused, I assumed, by the rifling inside the firearm's barrel. But what kind of weapon had fired the fatal shot? Not Greenwood's Webley for sure. It had not been recovered at the scene. If Richardson had indeed taken it as Greenwood claimed, he more than likely had sold it for what he could get for it. A man must live, if only by beggary or thievery.

I was no expert on ballistics. If Richardson's death was a suicide, it begged a question: How had he acquired the smaller caliber firearm? And another: From whom? And a third: When? And even a fourth: For what purpose, if not to kill himself? Would it not have been simpler to have used Greenwood's Webley? Why go to the trouble of acquiring a different weapon when one already lay in his hand? Perhaps he hadn't wanted to leave behind a mess of his head worse than a dog's dinner, though why he should care was beyond me.

If Greenwood was lying about the missing Webley revolver, and I only had his word for it, then why? What was the truth beneath the relationship between Greenwood and Richardson? Could they have been illicit lovers? I shuddered at the thought. I could not dismiss the notion, however, no matter how much it made me squirm. It might be common in better Regiments, particularly those with fancy dress uniforms, but I couldn't imagine a conscripted Richardson had been a Guards officer. I doubt if he rode, not that he would have needed to in the infantry. Had Richardson taken the revolver, intent on killing Greenwood for some reason as yet undiscovered? Or had Greenwood fabricated the story because it suited his own current or past purpose?

At the police station I checked the incident log at the front desk. They had no record of a report of a lost or stolen Webley service revolver belonging to Aubrey Greenwood. I wondered why he had not reported the loss or theft. He was under no obligation to declare ownership of the firearm to the police, of course and I had no reason to suspect that he possessed it illegally. So why mention it otherwise? As I could safely rule it out as the weapon that caused Richardson's death, I set the matter aside.

I sought Inspector Ashton-Browne but was told he was out on an investigation. I went through Richardson's possessions again but found nothing new. I placed the bullet in a small box with the rest of his belongings, closed the locker and handed the key to the Sergeant in charge of the evidence room.

What had driven Richardson to kill himself? The aftermath of shell shock? General unhappiness with his situation? Or some deep-seated pathological or psychological reason that he had kept suppressed for some time, years perhaps, and which surfaced for one final time eight days ago? The question kept nagging me. Greenwood had not provided a reason, other than he had not been surprised, given Richardson's background and war history. Ashton-Browne had not advanced a theory. 'Took his own life while the balance of his mind was disturbed' was a convenient conclusion, one which fit the bill and did not raise too many awkward questions, but which I felt rang hollow in this case. The police seemed only too happy to write the death off as suicide and have me rubber stamp their suspicions as confirmed.

Absent motive, I was less sure.

I checked in with the duty Sergeant at the front desk. "What type of firearms do the men carry?" I asked.

"A six shot Webley four fifty-five revolver, Sir," he replied immediately.

"What about officers of Inspector rank and above?"

"The same, Sir."

"And those in plain clothes? What do they carry?"

"Detectives carry a variety, Sir." He seemed puzzled, as if wondering why I wanted to know.

I pursued my line of questioning. "What, typically?"

"Snub nose—two or three-inch revolvers for the most part. Smith & Wesson thirty-eights are the most common. They're standard issue for undercover work. I've seen one or two carry Beretta semiautomatics. They fit a little snugger under the armpit or in a pocket than a revolver."

"Thirty-two caliber semis?"

"I believe so, Sir."

"Rather them than me," I said, tapping the holster on my belt and feeling the solid bulk of my Webley beneath the black leather. "I've never been convinced one of those toys could stop a man in his tracks."

"They tell me they're just as effective as the four fifty-five, Sir. After all, dead is dead, no matter how big the bullet is."

I smiled at the Sergeant. "I suppose you're right. I hadn't thought of it like that."

I spent the afternoon in Ashton-Browne's office, drafting and redrafting my initial report. By the time A-B returned from whatever he was investigating I was no further ahead than when I arrived the previous day. All I could conclude with any certainty was what they already knew, that the deceased, Charles Richardson, late of Honiara, Solomon Islands, was dead of a gunshot wound to the head, which was not enormously helpful.

It has been my, admittedly limited, experience, that all suicides have a reason, a motive beyond a disturbed mind. I could find none here. Richardson, if Greenwood were to be believed, was an unhappy man, a man not fully recovered from shell-shock, who found himself as much a square peg in a round hole in the Solomons as he had probably been in the army. Let's face it: an infantry platoon was no place for any sane man in wartime, least of all a concert pianist.

"Anything to report?" Ashton-Browne said as he hung his Panama hat on a peg behind the door and wiped the sweat from his forehead with a handkerchief.

"Not much that we didn't already know. Greenwood told me that when he returned to the hotel from India, Richardson was asleep in bed. Richardson left in the morning, before breakfast, I gather, and took Greenwood's old service Webley with him. Greenwood didn't discover the theft, if that's what it was, until later. He didn't report the revolver missing and he hasn't seen Richardson since."

"You've uncovered more than we have in a lot less time," he said, and sat down behind his desk. "He stole Greenwood's revolver, took himself off into a dark corner and blew his brains out."

I didn't reply. It didn't make sense.

"Right?"

"No," I said, and immediately regretted it.

"Why on earth not?" Ashton-Browne snapped in a tone that mixed incredulity with defiance and not a little anger. "It stands to reason he killed himself. It obviously wasn't an accident. The man was clearly unhappy with his lot in life. He was so overwrought at the futility of it all that he topped himself. Any sane man would come to the same conclusion."

"All I can safely conclude as of this moment, is that he's dead. A thirty-two or a thirty-eight-caliber bullet entered his left temple, traversed his brain and became lodged in his skull bone above the right temple. The bullet did not come from a Webley service revolver. The bore of the Webley is too large. There were no powder burns on Richardson's temple around the entry wound. He was either shot from several feet away, or from closer range and the powder burns you would normally expect possibly washed away by the rain. We have no known specific motive for his death. No suicide note. There were no signs of a struggle and his cash, along with a steamer ticket to England, a watch and his cuff links were still with him when his body was found by a police officer on patrol an hour or two after a gunshot was reported heard. We can therefore rule out robbery as a motive. The time of the gunshot has not been confirmed. He could have been dead a few minutes or a couple of hours when he was found. We don't know if he killed himself where he was found, or killed elsewhere and his body dumped there post mortem by person or persons unknown. The post mortem could only place the time of death to within one to two hours."

I took a breath. "It wasn't suicide. He was murdered."

"Murdered?" Ashton-Browne's face turned red. He took in a deep gulp of air. "Murdered?" he repeated, as if I had lost my mind.

"Almost certainly by someone he knew well enough not to be suspicious by that person's presence." It was my turn to draw a deep breath. I decided to take a flyer. "All the physical evidence points a death that is more than suspicious."

"In your opinion as a junior Inspector." Ashton-Browne emphasized the word 'junior.'

"That is the only rational conclusion I can come up with." I hesitated, then took another flyer, as much to justify my time in Singapore as for any other reason, including solving the riddle. "I know who did it and why. I'm in the process of putting the evidence together to make a provable case in court before I make an arrest."

Ashton-Browne's voice rose. "Richardson took his own life for reasons unknown while the balance of his mind was disturbed. And we move on to more important, dirty and dangerous matters such as opium smuggling and territory wars by Chinese gangs resulting in multiple murders. That's what I and my colleagues spend our time investigating."

He refrained from thumping his desk with his fist, though I think he was tempted.

"Write your report, then get out and go back to K.L. Stop wasting our time, and yours, with fanciful, unprovable theories. Richardson killed himself. End of story."

He stood, rounded his desk and after throwing me a withering look of contempt, jammed his hat on his head. He slammed the door on the way out.

I had overstepped the mark. I had proposed a theory without proof, or even circumstantial evidence to back it up. I had committed the police officer's number one mistake: Postulate a theory, then gather the evidence to back it up. It should be the other way around — gather evidence, then let that evidence guide the investigator to a conclusion. I was sure Richardson had been murdered. My mistake was in mentioning it to Ashton-Browne. Little wonder he was angry. And no doubt a report would be on its way to my superiors in K.L. in the morning. I wondered if I was in the wrong profession and how long I was likely to remain in it.

I returned to Raffles Hotel by rickshaw, too dejected to have my police driver drive me there. I felt like I was an imposter, that I had no right to claim to be a policeman.

Greenwood was perched on a stool at the bar when I arrived, nursing a gin and tonic. His flushed face suggested it wasn't his first. He nodded to me and headed towards a pair of lounge chairs in a quiet corner. I ordered a Scotch and soda and a gin and tonic for Greenwood and joined him.

"How goes the investigation, Inspector?" Greenwood said after our drinks arrived.

"I think we're onto something."

"What might you have unearthed?" He raised his eyebrows and furrowed his brow.

I leant forward. "It wasn't a Webley he used."

Greenwood leaned back. I thought I detected a sigh, possibly of relief or even thanks. He took a long pull of his drink, examined the nearly empty glass for a second and then finished it. He cast a longing look at the Scotch I had bought. I saw his hand twitch as if he was fighting the temptation to reach for it sooner than good manners deemed appropriate. I declined to offer it to him. I needed to make him sweat a bit. How much more he knew than he had let on, I needed to find out.

"We believe it was a smaller caliber bullet. There was no firearm found with the body, but we have retained the fatal bullet for forensic examination." It sounded good. It might even occur in my eventual report if circumstances suggested it was necessary.

An eyebrow twitched this time, but Greenwood made no comment. I tried a different tack. "How well did you really know Richardson? I think there's more than you told me last night. He was more than a casual acquaintance to whom you acted the Good Samaritan, wasn't he?"

Greenwood's face turned a darker shade of red. His lips narrowed as he compressed them. I watched him fiddle with his fingers, and waited for the lie to unfold.

"Unlike most Englishmen, I am a Roman Catholic. I attended Downside School, a Catholic Public School and St. Catharine's College, Cambridge, where I read English as you might imagine. Psychology would have been a far more useful degree had I known I would end up scribbling for a living, but that is by the way. I make no apology for my faith. I find it a quiet refuge in times of trouble." He paused and looked away.

I was about to remind him that there were two of us in this conversation when he returned his attention to me.

"Times of trouble like these, Inspector. Charles went to Downside as well. You probably didn't know that."

I shook my head. Ashton-Browne hadn't mentioned which school he and Richardson had attended. That was something else I had failed to ask during my investigation.

"I came down from Cambridge in '03. Charles would not have been in his preparatory school then. We had never met until that evening here." He looked away again, peered at the ceiling and then focused his attention back on me.

"I trust this will go no further, Inspector. Without your word as a gentleman I will say no more."

"I have been called many things, Greenwood," I said, "but I don't recall gentleman being among them. However, though I may not share your faith, you have my word that whatever you say I will regard as no less sacrosanct than the confessional."

"Confession is good for the soul, Inspector, if our priests are to be believed. But one must remain guarded in the quantum as well as the factum of our confession."

I smiled. Was Greenwood about to confess to Richardson's murder? If that were the case, I should at least have a notebook and pencil to record it. The wherewithal lay in the breast pocket of my uniform tunic, but I let it remain there. The sight of a police officer's notebook often had the effect of drying up the well of information about to spring into an investigator's lap. In this case, more specifically into my ears.

"In the short time I knew Charles I came to know him well." He hesitated, laced his fingers together and unlaced them before cracking his knuckles. "I believe you understand what I am hinting at without me coming right out and saying it."

I nodded. I had wondered how deep the relationship might have been. Now I knew.

"You know how inappropriate our kind of relationship is viewed by the law and by society in general. It was all well and good for Charles to stay in my room while I was away, but I could not allow it to continue on my return. Reputations are so easily damaged and so hard, even impossible to repair. My room upstairs has been my home for a couple of years. If I allowed it, eventually my reputation would catch up with me, as it has in every other anchorage I've called home this past several years and I would have to move on. I made the decision to deliver the news to Charles the morning after I returned. Only the *modus* was up in the air until he let me off the hook."

"How did he do that?"

"He told me about the offer he'd received from his parents to return home, to Sussex and resume his concert career in England. He'd obviously made his decision to leave me, and Singapore, while I was in Burma and India. Possibly even earlier. It must have eaten his insides all the time I was away. He was in quite a state when he delivered the news. I tried to pretend to be upset, but he cut me off. He left me on the balcony of our room—I say *our* because we shared it for several month, not days as I said before and I hope you will forgive that small subterfuge—and packed his few belongings in a small case. I stayed on the balcony until I heard the door to our room click closed. It was some time later that morning, when I sat down to write, that I discovered my old service revolver was missing."

We sat in silence for several minutes. I held my hand up and within a few moments two fresh drinks arrived. If any time was appropriate for a second drink, I decided this was it. I downed my first in two swallows.

"Where did you serve, if you don't mind my asking?"

"My mother was Swiss. I speak fluent French and German. His Majesty's Government found me suitable employment in Geneva and Montreux during the war years. I reported to London. More than that I am not at liberty to divulge unless I wish to go to prison for violating the Official Secrets Act." He turned silent again before he picked up his drink and studied the glass as if he had never seen one before. "I was spared exposure to heroics," he said in a husky voice. "Poor Charles wasn't as lucky. I'm only glad I wasn't responsible for his death."

I sipped my Scotch and waited. When nothing more seemed forthcoming, I took the plunge. "Did you know if he had any other entanglements while he was in Singapore? Anyone else he might have been seeing?"

Greenwood shook his head. "I wondered at first, but I found nothing to suggest anything might be amiss. He had very little money, but always just enough to scrape by with his piano playing. He left

Honiara with the clothes on his back and his last paycheque. I don't know how he managed to pay for his passage here. Perhaps the service paid for it." He shrugged.

"It will go no further, Greenwood," I said. "You have my word."

I lay in bed that night seeking a thread, a clue as to the direction the investigation might turn before I was forced to call it quits. Richardson had very little money on him when they found his body, but that would be in keeping with his earnings and his kept life in Singapore. He had a ticket for the passenger liner which had sailed without him a week ago. If he refrained from drinking, he would not need money on board. It was always possible he could have picked up tips by playing the piano in the ship's lounge. What he had in his wallet might have been enough to buy him a train ticket from London to wherever his parents lived in Sussex.

Who killed Charles Richardson? And why? Whom did he know in Singapore who might want him dead? Who had he met here who felt so threatened by the presence of this young concert pianist that he found it necessary to put a bullet through his brain? The mathematical, rational side of my brain refused to function at four in the morning and I gave up. I managed three hours sleep before the sun shining through my bedroom window directly into my eyes woke me. I admit to being obtuse at times, a dullard in many respects and almost devoid of whatever it is that drives people to write, to compose music, or play an instrument. But I had no excuse for overlooking the blindingly obvious.

I knew with certainty who had murdered Richardson, if not the entire reason why. And I also knew I had no way of proving it short of a confession which was unlikely to be forthcoming. I needed to bounce my theory off Ashton-Browne before I did anything else. The doubts started to surface during breakfast. They gnawed at me during the ride to the police station. By the time I arrived there I was almost a gibbering wreck.

Ashton-Browne was out.

I spent the morning stewing, waiting for him in his office while pretending to work. He had not appeared when the lunch hour arrived. I went to the officers' mess and asked around. No one had seen him since he went off duty the previous afternoon, which was also the last time I had seen him.

I waited until three when the Chief Superintendent returned from his lunch, looking a bit ragged around the edges. "I'm looking for Inspector Ashton-Browne, Sir," I said, wondering if A-B had perhaps joined the Chief Super for lunch and then gone home to sleep it off. "I wondered if you had seen him, or if he left word of his whereabouts."

The Chief Super hung his head and gave me a tired old dog look. I resisted the urge to reach out and pat him. "Not since yesterday," he said. "He works erratic hours. He tends to come and go, depending on what he's working on. Give him a couple of days. He's bound to turn up by then. Friday's pay day. Anything else?" He looked hopeful that there was nothing else that should demand his time or his brain. I shook my head and shut the door quietly on my way out.

When I checked the bar at Raffles Hotel that evening, Greenwood was nowhere to be seen. I had dinner sent to my room while I spent the evening with a pencil and paper jotting down all the information I had gleaned to that point and where it led me. I had to admit there were huge gaps in the evidence. Any half-witted defence lawyer could drive a London Transport omnibus through the case without touching the sides. I decided that I might have been hasty in my pronouncement of murder. Perhaps it really was suicide as everyone connected with Richardson believed, or even insisted.

It was the entry wound to the left temple by a right-handed victim that bothered me. Someone else had pulled the trigger, someone who needed to shut Richardson up permanently without casting suspicion on himself. The police force in Singapore, as does almost all police forces the world over, instinctively closes ranks to protect their own from outsiders. Such was the nature of the beast. Policing is a hard enough job at the best of times—there was no need to make it any more difficult by hanging one of their own out to dry, unless absolutely necessary. And when that rare event did occur it was usually done on the quiet, without fanfare and almost always to protect the good of the force.

I knew I could not rely on anyone in the Straits Settlements Police Force for help. It was their entrenched position that Richardson had killed himself and that was what my report should find. But Richardson had been murdered and the culprit still moved among us. I turned to the best remaining source of information about all things

Singapore—Greenwood. He was in his room when I phoned through, writing, he said. We met in the bar a few minutes later, the prospect of a free gin or two being enough bait for him to swallow.

We took our habitual table and chairs in the corner of the lounge. The lighting there was less harsh than closer to the bar and the grass-cloth wall covering and the swish and clank of the overhead fans absorbed much of our conversations and those of other patrons. Without revealing my suspicions, I said to Greenwood, "Delicate, I know, but you knew Richardson more intimately than anyone in Singapore."

Greenwood's lips compressed into a thin line. Using a paper-napkin, he dabbed at perspiration beading on his upper lip then wiped condensation from the side of his tumbler. "Probably," he said, eventually.

"Who else might he have known, other than Inspector Ashton-Browne, who also went to Downside?"

Greenwood looked blank for several seconds then swallowed half the tumbler of gin and tonic. "I don't know many on the Straits Police. None much better than nodding acquaintances. I know the Chief Superintendent probably better than most. He went to Downside as well, quite a bit before I did and I'm surprised he ended up in the police. He doesn't seem the sort, any more than you do."

"I'm not sure if that's a compliment, or a backhanded one."

"Merely an observation, Inspector. Some people seem to fit into their occupations and professions like a hand into a bespoke glove. Others seem fish out of water, no matter how good and successful they become. Ashton-Browne is no more a policeman than the Chief Superintendent or I are, no matter how well he acts the part."

"I assume Ashton-Browne comes from a wealthy family and is merely treading water until the time comes to strike out for shore and take over the family firm. But I may be wrong."

"I think you're pretty close to the mark."

"How well did you know Ashton-Browne at school?"

Greenwood hesitated, then took another long swallow of his drink. This time he placed the almost empty tumbler on the cork coaster with a satisfied sigh. I raised my hand and two more drinks appeared in seconds. "I wasn't aware you knew that, Inspector."

"Picking at loose threads, hoping to find enough to darn a hole in my shirt," I said.

"I must remember that expression and find a use for it in one of my forthcoming novels. In answer to your question, Inspector, I know Ashton-Browne better than any other member of the force. Old school ties, I suppose. We tend to stick together wherever we find each other."

"He introduced you to Richardson, you said, but by then you were already acquainted."

"Ashton-Browne still doesn't know Charles and I had already met, unless Charles told him."

"The secrets of the confessional still apply, Greenwood," I said. "But I have to ask you this." I lowered my voice even though there was no one close enough to hear anything over the background chatter from the cocktail bar. "Were you or Richardson intimate with Ashton-Browne?"

I sat back in my lounge chair and waited for the reply. I did not have to wait long. Greenwood beckoned me forward. "It is against the laws of England and most other countries that regard themselves as civilized," he said as quietly as he could while still making sure I heard. "But yes, Ashton-Browne and I have had an ongoing relationship, shall we say, for most of the time since he arrived here, about two years. Does that answer your question?"

"Did he also have a relationship with Richardson at any time?"

Greenwood's face turned a deeper shade of red. He put his hand over his mouth then reached into his trouser pocket and pulled out a large white cotton handkerchief. He mopped his forehead and wiped his eyes. "Charles told me he and Ashton-Browne had had a relationship for most of their time at school. It only ended when they went their separate ways after their schooldays."

"Did they rekindle their relationship after Richardson showed up here?"

Greenwood let out a heavy sigh. "I believe they did. I tried not to be jealous, but it was very hard. Charles was a distraction. He kept me from my work when I was here, and I couldn't stop thinking of him when I was away in Burma and India. I don't know what he and Ashton-Browne did while I was away, and I don't ever want to know. Charles and I ended our relationship the morning I got back. I admit I'm a coward, Inspector. I'm not proud of it. Quite the opposite, but I didn't want to hurt Charles by forcing the break-up. I was more than fond of him but I was afraid of commitment to anyone or anything except my writing. I think something must have happened while I was away. I don't know what. You'll have to ask Ashton-Browne, but a dog cannot serve two masters."

I ruminated on this for a while. Greenwood finished his drink. I pushed my untouched second drink across the table to him. He gulped half of it down immediately.

"I believe we can both draw the same conclusion," I said. "Richardson was desperate for money. You were away. The letter from his mother seems genuine enough from what I can tell. It was dated many months ago, well before he left Honiara. His life was a mess and he wanted to go home. The only way he could get enough money to buy a passage back to England, if it was not an outright gift, was to borrow it from someone he knew and who would trust him to repay it. Or blackmail. And that person, I take it, wasn't you?"

"He never asked me, but I knew he was desperate for money."

"And when the hoped-for money wasn't forthcoming?" I raised my eyebrows.

Greenwood said quietly, "I think he may have resorted to blackmail."

"He no doubt confronted his old school chum and lover and threatened to expose him and his activities to the police if he didn't come across with the amount he needed to buy a ticket. If what he had in his wallet when it was recovered by the police is an accurate reflection on the honest character of the man, Richardson didn't ask for more than enough to pay for his fare. He had the ticket in his wallet when he was killed. I don't know who bought the ticket, but I suspect it was Ashton-Browne. I can check with the travel agents and see if I can get a description. According to the report, the police weren't able to lift any fingerprints from it other than Richardson's, which suggests the ticket might have been wiped clean before it came into Richardson's possession."

'*Never pay blackmail.* How many times has someone said that and not only in my novels?"

"Blackmail never stops until the blackmailer is no longer a threat. Permanently in this case, if my suspicions are correct."

Greenwood sat back and gave me a look I couldn't decipher. "You are correct, Inspector." The smug look returned to his face.

"How do you know?"

"I have said farewell to two of my closest, most intimate friends this past several days. Charles you know about. Ashton-Browne came to my room around midnight last night and told me everything, on condition that I told you nothing for twenty-four hours and then, only if you were to ask."

I glanced at my wrist watch. "You broke your promise by three hours. Why?"

Greenwood took a drink. "It doesn't matter now. He sailed first thing this morning. He wouldn't tell me where, but you can check with the shipping news and passenger manifests and take your pick of likely destinations."

"I think we can safely rule out England."

"Wherever he goes, I'm pretty certain it will be next to impossible to have him return for trial."

"Did he tell you what happened?"

"Only that he couldn't risk letting Charles spill the beans. Charles still had my old Webley. He had it on him when they met that night. I don't know what happened after that, other than Ashton-Browne admitted to me that he shot Charles, deliberately and at close range with his own service revolver and left him where they found him. He took the Webley and disposed of it."

"I wish you had come to me earlier with this," I said, somewhere between cross that Greenwood had deliberately withheld this information, and secretly pleased I would be spared the necessity of arresting a brother police officer.

"We Catholics find ourselves in the trenches of life together and tend to look after one another, Inspector. Something the majority of heathens and Protestants will probably never understand." He flashed me a smile as if to remove the sting. I did not take offence in any case, having lost what little allegiance I owed to any faith during the war.

I signalled for another round of drinks. Two gin and tonics appeared. "I'll have a Scotch and soda," I said to the waiter. "You can leave both these drinks here. No doubt we will find a good home for them. "

In the final analysis, Ashton-Browne got away with murder. Not the first to escape justice, I know and he almost certainly wouldn't be the last. It certainly isn't fair, but then what is in this world?

I reported my findings to the Chief Superintendent in the morning and we issued a warrant for Ashton-Browne's arrest. Not that it would ever be executed, unless A-B were stupid enough to return to Singapore, but stranger things have happened. I must say the Chief Super took it well, in his stride and promised to write, if not a glowing report, at least a letter of commendation to my superiors back in Kuala Lumpur. He was good to his word.

During my train journey back to K.L. I kept pulling at a thread, an unanswered question. The Chief Superintendent, Greenwood, Ashton-Browne and Richardson had all attended the same Roman Catholic Public School. I wondered which school Dr. Morton had attended. Downside as well? As Greenwood had said, Catholics tend to stick together, no less than the police. How much did the Chief Superintendent know before I gave him my report? I decided to stop pulling the thread before my whole suit unravelled.

Some things are better left unknown.

2. ONLY ONE SHOE

I stood over the body, suppressing the instinct to be sick which often overtakes me whenever I come face to face with death, especially of the violent and intended kind. The corpse, for there was no doubt that this was a corpse, what with its stillness and the flies already settling on it, lay partly on its side with its leg drawn up and the knee bent, rather like a large question mark. I didn't need to see the face: I knew from the fact that the corpse lay in Judges' Chambers in the Kuala Lumpur courthouse and that it only had one leg, and consequently only one shoe, who it was—His Honour, Judge Faulkner. The solitary shoe belonged to a man I had known, and thoroughly disliked, for the best part of fifteen years.

For most men who have been involved directly in the wholesale slaughter of our fellow beings in a full-scale war, there are matters about which we are reluctant to speak. I am no exception and have long maintained my silence, not that many were curious, until now, as it pertains directly to how I came to know the recently deceased.

It was the early spring of 1916 and by then I had been on the Western Front with my Royal Artillery battery of medium guns for a year. I had even earned a second pip on my shoulder, denoting the rank of First Lieutenant and marking me as one step up from the lowest of the low on the officer totem pole. I had just turned twenty and my enthusiasm for war and its associated heroics had become blunted by my exposure to, and by my distaste for my battery commander, Colonel Faulkner.

The Colonel was something of a martinet, renowned for his medal-winning derring-do as a subaltern in the Boer War. Between conflicts he had followed his father's footsteps and become a barrister of considerable and forceful reputation while maintaining his part-time connection with the City of London Battery of the

Royal Horse Artillery. It was not only his reputation that caused me, and most of the other young officers in the battery to quail in his presence and avoid contact with him at every opportunity, walking in fear and trepidation of the man as if he were a school prefect and the school bully rolled into one. He also had the ability and the authority to make or break any one of us at a whim. None of us wanted to become a rank private in the poor bloody infantry.

After dinner one night, and with a broad beam on his face, Colonel Faulkner addressed his cadre of young officers in the mess tent.

"It's the twenty-third of April, Gentlemen, which, as you will all know, is St. George's Day. It's high time you all did something for St. George, King and Country, other than lob shells at Germans." I remember a ragged cheer going up as we each probably wondered what alternative dangers he had planned for us. "As we're in reserve," he reminded us, "it's not like we can go out on a trench raid and debag some unwary Hun, so I've arranged for a raid of a different sort. Bars and brothels. I've snagged a lorry for the evening, and we're all going in to town to check out the local night life."

A few cheers erupted. I glanced at a couple of my fellow officers, smiles of lecherous anticipation lighting up their faces. I was not what you might call experienced with women and the last thing I wanted was for my formal introduction to the fair sex to take place in a French brothel. A gurgle and a feeling of queasiness clutched at my lower innards.

I have never been able to hold my drink. Consequently, after a couple of glasses of *vin ordinaire* and one of the local *pastis* at a filthy bar with a beaten earth floor I was forced to admit that, if not actually drunk, neither was I entirely sober. The C.O. and the six eager young officers, including, I'm ashamed to say, me, stumbled out of the *estaminet* and into the brothel next door. We, the junior officers, expected leadership by example from our Commanding Officer, along the lines of some appropriate dash to show us baby-faced and, for the most part, still downy-cheeked subalterns the way forward. It occurred to me that someone would have to drive us all back to camp afterwards, and judging by the state of insobriety of most of my brother officers, I was the one most likely to be tagged with the honour of sorting out the gearbox and operating the clutch, neither of which I had ever done before.

Without hesitation, in full view of all the men, our Commanding Officer chose the least repulsive of the prostitutes on hand and led the way forward as we all looked on, offering encouragement. Then it was our turn. I watched my brothers-in-arms make asses of themselves until one of the women finally turned to me. Through the fog of cheap wine and *pastis* I realized with horror it was now my turn to be the object of ridicule, and in the days ahead would have my performance critiqued by those who had been present as well as by those who had never witnessed my degradation. I balked at the thought of becoming a temporary legend and shamefaced, slunk out the door with a figurative tail between my legs. I made my way to the lorry and waited.

"Not good enough for you, Masters?" the C.O. said when he climbed up into the cab and settled noisily into the passenger seat, breathing wine and *pastis* fumes over me. "A bit squeamish? Or are you queer?" He laughed, an unpleasant, grating sound that sounded more like a snarl. I heard it echo from the body of the lorry behind me as my brothers took up the jeer.

I counted myself fortunate for, by the beginning of May one by one, all except me had to see the Dr. Archibald, the M.O., complaining of various ailments ranging from crabs to gonorrhoea and syphilis. My caution, or perhaps my lack of bravado, had spared me a lifetime of embarrassment, ranging from apologies and explanations to potential marriage partners, to agony, blindness and raging madness. Not even the C.O. was spared, though there was a dark, unconfirmed rumour that he had been harbouring a secret in his underwear that not only his wife, but several London prostitutes knew about.

After the war, when I was a police officer in London and he a one-legged barrister—he had left the other one behind courtesy of a German shell on the Somme battlefield—with a reputation of chewing up witnesses and their testimony and spitting out the bones, we crossed paths frequently at the Old Bailey. Whether he was prosecuting or defending, he employed every tactic at his disposal to discredit witnesses, whether the police or the public, using character assassination, bullying and badgering until the unfortunate and by then unnerved wretches wavered in their evidence. Then he went for the jugular, his version of a mercy killing.

After one particularly merciless grilling by him—he was defending a well-known local villain on a charge of receiving stolen goods that I had investigated in Camberwell—he approached me after the charge had been thrown out for lack of evidence.

"I'm not surprised to see you as a copper, Masters," he said quietly, but with the same undertone of menace I always associated with him. "You always were a bit of a bloody Boy Scout." He granted me the benefit of a withering, icy stare from his water-pale blue eyes, replaced his papers in his briefcase and made his way out of the courtroom on his crutches with his junior carrying his case. He steadfastly refused every attempt to use a prosthetic leg. I heard him once snarl at someone in court, "I'm a cripple. I live with it. It's who I am. Nothing's going to change it. I neither need nor want anyone's sympathy any more than I need or want a false leg."

When I heard he had been elevated to the bench, trying cases in the London suburbs rather than at the Old Bailey, I breathed a sigh of relief. As no longer a barrister acting for the defence, at least he would not be trying to shred my evidence and cast aspersions on my memory, my intellect, my competence or my integrity. I only once had a case tried in front of him as a judge—it didn't turn out well for the Crown—and shortly thereafter I left the London Metropolitan Police to take up policing as an Inspector in the Colonial Police in Malaya, which was about as far away as I could get from His Honour, Mr. Justice Faulkner, short of going to New Zealand.

How wrong I was.

Without warning, one morning in 1928 Judge Faulkner showed up in court in Kuala Lumpur, wigged and gowned on his first day as a trial judge, waiting to hear a case for which I was the lead investigator. Before I had recovered from my shock, my nemesis had sent my airtight case down the drain, "for lack of credible evidence."

Although it is a small world in Kuala Lumpur, he and I managed never to meet socially for the nearly two years he was there. When I came across his bludgeoned body in Judges' Chambers on the ground floor of the two-storey courthouse that morning, with the police photographer having trampled much of what physical evidence there was into the judge's rug, I knew without doubt whose corpse it was. But, I still had no clue who had committed the foul deed. Or equally importantly, why.

By now, recently promoted to Chief Inspector, still among the lowest of the low on the Officer list, it would normally fall to me to head the team investigating a murder, particularly one of such prominent a figure. But here I was in somewhat of a dilemma.

"Bit of a bind, Commissioner," I said, later that morning.

"Why?"

"Judge Faulkner and I have a history. We've disliked each other intensely for fifteen years. I served under him at the Somme, which was where he got his leg blown off. That did nothing to improve his temper or his opinion of me."

"I see." Although I didn't think the Deputy Commissioner saw what I was getting at, I let it go.

When he said nothing more, I said, "Perhaps I should disqualify myself from the case, Sir."

"And why's that, Masters?"

I decided an explanation was in order. "There's probably a list of people as long as the cast of a Shakespeare play who would be neither surprised nor particularly distraught to see Judge Faulkner in this predicament. Given our past relationship, one could suggest that I might find it difficult from a personal perspective to pursue the investigation with my customary vigour. But rest assured, I will, of course, give the case my fullest professional engagement, if you think I'm the best person to do it."

I watched the Deputy Commissioner toy with a fountain pen for a moment before taking it up and using the clip of the cap as a drumstick on the edge of his desk. I listened to the drum solo, wondering which Duke Ellington or Count Basie tune might be running through his mind, while my silence put pressure on the Deputy Commissioner to make a sober decision. This ought not to have been difficult, given that he was a lifelong teetotaller, but he still took his time.

"Perhaps you could fill me in with some of the more pertinent details."

I threaded my way carefully through the minefield of my relationship with Judge Faulkner, omitting the bar and brothel raid and his consequently low opinion of me.

While the Colonel was in hospital in Boulogne recovering from the loss of his leg, I told the Deputy Commissioner, I was bumped up to Captain and sent home on leave before taking up new duties as adjutant of a heavy battery operating near Ypres. I dropped in on the hospital to see my former C.O. and to wish him well, secure in the knowledge that I would thankfully never see him again in this world or the next. I had been brought up to believe one should not hold grudges, even when deserved, but it was more than usually hard to be magnanimous to Colonel Faulkner.

He greeted me grumpily, sitting in a wheelchair contraption with his crutches by his side, and as usual I withered beneath his icy gaze.

"On your way home, Masters," he grunted, "drop this letter off to my wife. I've been meaning to post it for some days, but if you deliver it to her it will get there much the quicker. Here's the telephone number to let her know when to expect you." No, 'Please.' Or, 'Would you mind?' As gruff, blunt and terse in hospital as he was in the field. I wondered what his wife must think of him, and why she consented to marry him in the first place, unless she was as hard, determined and as disagreeable as he. Without a word of thanks, I took the envelope and scuttled out of the hospital.

"You're probably right, Masters," the Commissioner said when I finished. "A bit too close to the woods to see the trees, is that it?"

"I would be happy to help in any way I can, Sir. But perhaps someone a bit more senior might be better. I mean, the Chief Justice in Malaya deserves more than a newly appointed Chief Inspector to investigate his murder, it that indeed is what it was."

"From what you say it doesn't seem like an accident or suicide, which really leaves us to draw only one reasonable conclusion."

"I agree, Sir. I don't know whom you might have in mind, but perhaps someone more objective. A bit harsh to say this, I know, but I would have shed crocodile tears had the shell taken his head off rather than just his leg and his chance at fatherhood. If you know what I mean."

The Deputy Commissioner winced then grimaced. "Losing a leg is one thing. But to lose the bits and pieces as well?" He shook his head and noisily sucked in a draft of air through puckered lips. "That would put anyone in a bad mood. Not sure I'd want either, but given my druthers…" He glanced around his spacious and comfortable office then placed his hands on his desk, palms down. I listened to the ceiling fan drone on with a quiet clack once every revolution of the blades. "Right," he said. "I'll have someone else take over." He nodded his dismissal and I left.

From a personal perspective, I was quite content that Faulkner's head had received the benefit of a good bash over the crown with a knobkerrie, a golf club, or something similar of the hard and unforgiving kind. Which pointed to premeditated murder rather than a wayward golf swing and uncontrolled follow-through by the deceased, practicing his putting on the office carpet while balancing on one leg. But, I reminded myself, Faulkner had been a fellow human being, a hard driving leader of men under the most trying of circumstances, and one who never considered his own safety, preferring to lead by example, as he had on St. George's Day nearly fifteen years ago. And as much as I may have disliked him, or indeed have feared him with the same awe as the ancient Israelites feared Yahweh, I could not wish another human being to die violently, and probably needlessly, as Faulkner had. Except Germans in the war, of course. And even then, I never relished the job assigned to me by His Majesty.

As I thought fleetingly of the late, but unlamented Mr. Justice Faulkner, an image of Evelyn Faulkner flashed through my mind. More than fifteen years had passed since our only meeting when I delivered her husband's letter to her, she would be in her late forties or early fifties if my arithmetic was correct. She would be long past the bud rose of her youth, or even as she was, a rose in full bloom, in those few, all-to-short days we spent in each other's company before I had to return to Flanders and she to her husband.

Colonel Faulkner maintained a country estate near Romsey, in Hampshire, which was relatively well placed for my journey back to my parents' home in Bournemouth. I caught an early train from Waterloo Station and changed at Southampton for the Romsey branch line. A taxi from the station brought me to the Faulkner home at Mottisfont, a rambling building of honey coloured stone beneath its ivy-covered walls, Queen Anne I guessed, with later additions. The taxi's tyres crunched the circular gravel drive as it rounded the formal rose garden in front of the house and the driver came to a stop by the wide stone steps leading up to the porticoed front door. Suitably awestruck at my first impression of my most recent Commanding Officer's home, I alighted and, suitcase in hand, mounted the steps.

A liveried manservant greeted me at the top of the steps, took my valise into the marble tiled and columned hall and set it aside behind the door. "I shall inform Her Ladyship that you have arrived, Sir," he said. "I shall have one of the servants take your case to your room directly."

This was the first I had heard that I was expected to stay overnight. I tried not to let my surprise show as I followed the footman into a large, informally furnished and sun-flooded morning room. Lady Faulkner—I had no idea that she had a title until that moment—turned from where she was fiddling with her flower arrangement to greet me as the footman closed the doors behind him on the way out of the room. I was acutely aware of her smoky, blue-grey eyes inspecting me as if I were on passing out parade after my officer training course. My uniform was as clean and tidy as could be expected after two hours travelling by train and taxi, and my tunic and trousers had received a sponge and press at the Artillery Club where I had stayed overnight. I must have passed muster, as a smile crossed her face and reached her eyes. She put down a half-opened pink and white rose on the table top, crossed the intervening gap and offered me her ungloved hand.

"Lady Faulkner," I said, as I kissed her fingertips. "I'm delighted to meet you." I could think of nothing more original to say and I'm surprised I managed to say even that, consumed as I was by her poise, elegance and beauty.

"Evelyn, in private, Captain Masters. And you?"

"I have a Christian name, of course, two in fact, but I dislike them intensely and never use either. I go by Masters to everyone but my parents. And Captain, naturally, when I'm working, so to speak." I knew I was uttering gibberish. I told myself to keep quiet and speak only when spoken to as a good and dutiful child, which is how I saw myself in her presence.

She was younger than I imagined—barely thirty at a guess, probably a good ten years younger than her husband and ten years older than I—and possessed a pale complexion enhanced by a hint of powder and perhaps the merest touch of rouge on her cheekbones. She had a small nose and full, red lips beneath straw coloured hair which I thought was cut unfashionably short. Her hand lingered in mine for several seconds before she released it. Her watered silk morning dress rustled as she turned and headed for a settee. She sat and patted the cushion next to her.

"Do sit down, Captain. Coffee and biscuits will be here in a moment. And while we wait you can tell me why you're here and to what I owe the honour of a visit from one of my husband's gallant officers."

While we sipped coffee and nibbled on chocolate covered digestive biscuits, I explained the nature of the Colonel's injuries as delicately as I could, omitting the bit she would no doubt discover in good time and in private. "He was in good spirits when I left him," I said, trying to put on a positive face. "He should be home before too long."

"The army doesn't seem to have much use for one legged officers," she said in a matter-of-fact tone of voice. "I suppose he'll content himself with the law in due course. He's quite good at it, you know." She offered another smile.

I felt like rolling over on my back and have her pat my tummy like she might a spaniel puppy. Instead, I gulped, and said, "I hear being a barrister is quite cutthroat."

"I suspect that's why he likes it," she said. "Still, the offer of a place on the bench may be more to his liking as he grows a little older, although I can't ever see him losing his competitiveness."

"It has served him well thus far."

The small talk dried up after that until Evelyn suggested a stroll through the garden before lunch. I jumped at the chance and listened to her patiently while she told me all about the plants and flowers and bushes and trees that grew there.

"There's even a grape vine," she said, "although the grapes can be a bit on the tart side for the table and not suitable for making wine."

Botany was never a strong subject of mine at school and consequently Evelyn's narration left me impressed although slightly bewildered by her knowledge of flora.

I must have left something of an impression with her, though goodness knows how or why. A grammar school boy of no great family or connections, a recently promoted Captain, one shallow step above a Subaltern, and of no income other than my army pay and a quarterly cheque for £50 from my father—which he could ill afford—to help defray the cost of my mess bill and uniforms, would not attract more than a second glance from a shop assistant. Evelyn, however, whom I discovered during the course of that afternoon, was the younger daughter of the Earl of Bury St. Edmunds. Not moving in such rarified social circles, I was blithely unaware there was one such Earl. Evelyn cast my humble background aside as being as inconsequential as gossamer. Her expression, not mine, but I remember it distinctly.

She touched my hand—the lightest of brushes rather than a touch, but deliberate—before lunch that day, and by mid-afternoon had her arm linked through mine during our second, long, slow stroll through those parts of the grounds which we hadn't visited before being interrupted by the lunch gong. With afternoon tea dispensed with and before my bath and change into clean clothes before dinner—I had to apologize for not having evening clothes, but they seemed unnecessary at the front—she insisted I spend more than one night at her home. I was initially taken aback at the boldness of her suggestion but managed to stammer my agreement before biting the tip of my tongue in anticipation of what her invitation might imply.

I was not disappointed. I spent probably the three most memorable nights of my life at Mottisfont.

Her father's Earldom, however, carried prestige and a considerable income, much of which trickled down to his daughter, and Colonel Faulkner was intelligent enough to understand that to abandon his wife on the grounds of her adultery, whether it was the first, or only, or one of frequent such occasions, would not be in his best interests, financially, socially or professionally. I was consequently surprised to read in the Times society column that their marriage ended in divorce, the details of which the editor chose not to disclose. You may imagine my relief when I was not cited as a co-respondent or even mentioned in the column. I questioned how Judge Faulkner would make ends meet in Malaya without his wife's income, her social standing and her influence. Of one thing I was certain, however, was that his love of the bottle would do less damage to his reputation in Kuala Lumpur than it might in London.

I wondered whether the years had been kind to Evelyn, or harsh, physically and emotionally. She had seemed content at Mottisfont, surrounded by her rose gardens and sunshine, the elms and the copper beeches and the huge Cedar of Lebanon on the close-cropped front lawn, a green expanse the size of many a meadow with that single tree gracing the centre. How would she have reacted to the presence of her invalid husband night and day? A full-time nurse would have attended the first few weeks or months as he adjusted to a new life without a leg and his manhood. What would Evelyn have done? Taken a lover? Or soldiered on, stiff upper lip as if nothing had happened in the finest tradition attributed in fable to the English aristocracy? "Don't write," Evelyn had whispered before my taxi drove me away from her house to Romsey station. "Nothing will ever come close to what we shared these past few days. Don't spoil the memory." I had nodded, tongue-tied and glum. I kept my word. Fittingly, it rained that morning, matching my gloom at parting. Evelyn, however, had seemed as happy and serene as ever as she waved at the back of my taxi as it crunched down the drive. For her, it – the affair – I – was undoubtedly over, ended as if it had never begun. I realized that I was a footnote on the bottom of a page of her life, to be shared with a reader, or not, as she willed. For me, our parting was a supreme wrench, but events overtook me the next few years, both in Flanders and in London, and my memory of her, and that time together, faded peacefully like old wallpaper until my first encounter with her husband that day at the Old Bailey.

No. That time at Mottisfont was not something the Deputy Commissioner needed to know, even if it possibly had some bearing on the investigation.

The newly-appointed Commissioner, as dour a Scot as ever hailed from that country's soot-stained, grey granite capital, called me into his office early that afternoon. The purplish veins in his nose betrayed evidence of his liquid lunch, as did the filigree of red blood vessels, as fine as silk threads, in the whites of his eyes. But he could hold his Scotch well, given the amount of time and practice he devoted to the task, and could speak without slurring his words until late in the evening.

"I'm not keen on playing pass the parcel, Masters," he sniffed and looked down it at me, pronouncing each syllable of each word with a slight Edinborough accent as pinched as his nose. "But under the circumstances I can understand your reasons. I've compiled a list of suspects. It's a very short list at the moment" He hesitated. "Yours is the only name on it."

I stood aghast, open-mouthed. I snapped it shut pretty quickly. "I disliked Faulkner," I said, trying hard to quell the quavering in my voice. "But not enough to want or need to see him dead." I added the Commissioner to the list of people who did not need to know about Evelyn. I took a deep breath and steadied my voice. "I would have had plenty of opportunities in Flanders if I'd wanted to and no questions asked about how he was killed in action." I watched for a reaction, but the Commissioner gave nothing away. "If I had killed the Judge, I would have remained on the case as the lead investigator, removed or destroyed evidence and obstructed the investigation in any way I could to divert suspicion from myself. The fact that I immediately brought our relationship to the attention of the Deputy Commissioner only points to my complete non-involvement in the crime."

I was seething, but I hoped my calm delivery overrode my anger at the Commissioner's suggestion that I was complicit in Faulkner's death. Had he somehow stumbled upon my relationship with Evelyn, brief though it was, and considered it motive for murdering her husband fifteen years later? Unlikely, I decided.

"Perhaps, Sir, you might like to add the names of his clerk, the Crown Prosecutor, any defence lawyer who recently lost a case in front of him, any innocent person wrongly convicted of a minor crime since the Judge's arrival and who has since been released from jail, and any security personnel who had access to chambers after hours and who may have granted access, actually or implicitly, to the murderer. It would seem that this case is a matter of revenge rather than a domestic dispute that got out of hand. Most wives and girlfriends don't resort to bashing people over the head with a blunt instrument, and to the best of my knowledge he had neither here. They have ways of killing a reputation with a word in the right ear. It doesn't even have to be committed to paper."

"Point taken. And don't think I haven't thought of all those. I merely wanted to gauge your reaction."

The Commissioner might be a good drinker, but he was a poor liar. I refrained from pointing this out. "If you like, Sir, I can make some enquiries and come up with a list of names we should be ticking off."

He took off his eyeglasses and pinched the red marks on the bridge of his nose. When he spoke again, his accent was more pronounced than usual. "I can't have you directly involved, Masters. We need an outside investigator, someone who doesn't know the

Judge. We must not only be impartial but be seen to be impartial by the people of Kuala Lumpur, indeed the whole of Malaya. The reputation of the Force is at stake. I'll get Superintendent Sutcliffe up from Singapore to handle the investigation on the ground."

"But it will take a day at least for him to get here. We can't afford to waste twenty-four hours. If the cowboy films are correct, the trail will have grown cold by then. We need to get cracking immediately, before witnesses inexplicably go missing or suffer memory lapses."

The Commissioner sighed. "I'm still calling in Sutcliffe. In the meantime, be very discreet in whatever enquiries you make and keep the Deputy Commissioner posted at every turn. Understand?"

"Yes, Sir."

At least the Commissioner had chosen the right man for the job. I had known Graham Sutcliffe since the first form at our grammar school in Bournemouth. The morning after the war broke out in August 1914, and in a moment of hungover patriotism, we had volunteered for the army. We had drunk far too much beer in an evening-long pub crawl and reported at the recruiting office in the morning, green-faced and barely able to stand. I volunteered for the artillery. Sutcliffe chose the infantry, the Royal Hampshires, our County Regiment. That was the last we saw of each other until the war was over and which, against the odds, we both survived physically intact. Sutcliffe joined the London Metropolitan Police immediately after being demobilized in 1919 and had the leg up on me by a couple of years. He went out to the Straits Settlements, to Singapore, not long before I arrived in Malaya and maintained his one jump ahead of me in the promotion sweepstakes.

A lot of chaps didn't take to life, or policing in Malaya, and often quit the force early. Promotion was fairly rapid therefore and didn't always go to the best man for the job. It often went by default to the last man standing in the rank, filling dead men's shoes. Sutcliffe had bucked the trend and had been recently appointed Superintendent, entirely on merit, which I thought was fitting, as he had been a copper longer than I had and he seemed to be in it for the long haul. He had always been brighter than me at school, which I never held against him, though I was better at French and German, and sometimes at Maths.

On my way back to the scene of the crime I churned several questions over in my mind. In the absence of any real suspects, for example, or even an obvious murder weapon left at the scene with an identifiable set of finger prints, I looked for motive. Who stood to gain by Faulkner's death? And who would risk the gallows to bring it about? The list was long, and I wondered where I should start.

The love of money is the root of all evil, had long been drummed into me as the prime motive behind most crimes, and it certainly seemed to fit in many cases. My first Sergeant, however, took me to one side not long after I joined the Met and said to me, "Never mind money, Masters. Mark my word, there's usually a woman at the bottom of it, the missus or the girlfriend. She wants something and the poor sap feels duty bound to provide it." He gave me a conspiratorial wink, as man to man, and tapped the side of his nose. "A little bit of larceny follows to provide the means to bring about the lady's wishes, and the next thing he knows there's a tap on his shoulder, a finger in his collar, His Majesty's bracelets are around his wrists and he's off to the nick before he can say Jack Robinson." The Sergeant being normally a man of few words, I took to heart what amounted to a lengthy speech from him.

With his advice in mind, I decided to order a background check on the Judge's female companions since his arrival in Kuala Lumpur. Someone must know if he was seeing a woman on a regular basis. There are few secrets in K.L., and late-night visits at flats or hotel rooms by members of the opposite sex were front and central in the rumour mill. It was a shot, and one I could ill afford to overlook.

'Meanwhile, back at the ranch,' as the captions read at the bottom of the screen on the silent pictures which we still regularly received at the club, there was a crime scene to go over with a fine tooth comb in search of evidence overlooked at the first inspection, and a post mortem report from the aptly named Dr. D'Eath, the pathologist.

A native police constable stood guard on the door to Judge Faulkner's chambers when I arrived, very thoughtful of whoever had ordered it. When I showed him my warrant card he stepped aside and let me enter the room. Chambers is rather a grand word for the Judge's rather cramped office, his robing room and private toilet and wash basin.

"How long have you been here?" I threw over my shoulder at the guard after I had crossed the threshold into the crime scene.

"Since the last detective left this morning, Sir."

"Makan tengah hari?"

He frowned. "No Sir. No lunch yet."

"*Membawah setengah jam,*" I said, telling him to take half an hour. A broad smile replaced the frown.

He bowed. "*Terima kasi banyak, banyak,*" he said, offering his effusive thanks and backing out of the room as if in the presence of Malay-speaking royalty.

I shut and locked the door and took my bearings. From my memory it looked as if nothing, apart from the Faulkner's body, now lying on a slab in the hospital morgue, had been disturbed. His crutches leaned against his large mahogany desk in much the same manner as I had observed earlier that day. His pen and ink set and leather framed blotting pad sat four square in front of his chair. The chair was pushed in under his desk, all neat and tidy as if he was preparing to leave for the day. I crossed his office and checked his robing room. His gown hung from a coat hanger behind the door and smelled, like chambers, of pipe tobacco smoke. I opened the door of the wardrobe and looked inside. A change of shirt of white silk, a charcoal, tropical weight, worsted three-piece pinstriped suit and a Royal Artillery tie hung inside, which I presumed allowed him to travel to and from the courthouse without attracting attention to himself or his position. A pair of onyx and gold cufflinks sat on the flat wooden surface below where the suit hung. I closed the door and turned my back on the wardrobe.

Something didn't quite fit, and it took me a while to put my finger on it. Everything was so neat and tidy that it looked as if someone had cleaned up the place after the attack. Faulkner had always been careful about his appearance and required his officers to reflect his self-image, but he had never been one to dress as if on King's Parade, although he could probably afford to. His uniforms came from Gieves and Hawkes in Saville Row, a standard to which, as the son of a middle-class bank manager, I could only aspire in my dreams. I reopened the wardrobe and checked the label in the suit and was not surprised to see the name of the same London tailor. The shirt, however, was without doubt locally made, the silk threads fine, almost thin enough to see through, and fitting for the temperatures in K.L.

I looked around the robing room. Nothing seemed out of place, not even a scrap of lint on the rug. I made a note to enquire whether the cleaners had been in the room after the court closed for the day.

The Judge's chamber was likewise immaculate in its appearance—a place for everything and everything in its place. The thin canvas blind over the only window was pulled down but I could see through it the outline of the shutters, closed over the window pane. Which, I congratulated myself on, explained why the electric ceiling light was still on in mid-afternoon. Why no one had thought to turn it off I could not guess. I stood in the centre of the room and examined every square inch of the walls, ceiling and floor from a distance. The ceiling, I noted, had been recently distempered and had not started to flake nor yet taken on the yellow hue so prevalent in the tropics. The walls were panelled in teak and, for the most part, lined with substantial bookcases crammed with leather-bound volumes of the law. I crossed to the nearest case and examined the spines of some of the books. Wigmore's *On Evidence* had a different cover from the rest of the books on the shelf. I pulled it out, opened it, and read the inscription inside: *To my beloved Edward. May you never stray from my heart and from Mr. Wigmore's well-trodden path. From your ever-loving Evelyn. August 1919.*

Reading those lines hit me: They reminded me vividly of her. Notwithstanding her exhortation to her husband not to stray, by the time she had written those words she had shared her affections with not only her husband, but with me, and with how many others? It seemed clear that her words were a lie, as, I suspected was her life all the time she knew Edward Faulkner. An uneasiness fell over me as I replaced the book on the shelf, certain that Judge Faulkner would never again read those words and wonder if his wife's evidence had ever been true. It left me feeling unclean, like a peeping Tom, or a man who rummages through a lady's handbag.

I examined the desk. Not a speck of dust lay on its polished surface. I bent down level with it and cast my gaze along the surface. Even the residue of the fingerprint dust had been wiped clean away, destroying with it any clue as to the identity of the late incumbent or his assailant. I made another note to question the officer who had taken the photographs of the scene and the body and who had dusted for prints. Who had passed the order to clean the room before we had declared it no longer a crime scene and ready for habitation? Had the order been a deliberate attempt to destroy potential evidence? Had it been carelessness on someone's part? Police methods being somewhat haphazard in Malaya, and certainly not up to the standards of the Met, I would have put a couple of shillings on the latter.

I leaned against the edge of the desk and cast an appraising glance around the room from a different angle. I walked around the desk and clutched the corner on my way past. My hand came away sticky. It felt like blood—clammy, with a strand of black hair—stuck to my fingertips. Whose was it? Faulkner's? His assailant's? How long had it been there? Once again, I had more questions than answers.

The guard returned at that moment and I gave the room a final once-over and asked myself why a one-legged man would leave his crutches leaning against his desk while he hopped around it, only to meet his death in the centre of the room. It made no sense. I had never seen Faulkner without his crutches since the day I left him in the army hospital in France. I picked them up and examined them without great hope of finding anything significant. That's when I noticed a fleck of what seemed to be dried blood with a very short strand of black hair embedded in it stuck to the wing nut that held the handpiece in place. Could this be the murder weapon? I went over the rest of the crutch, and its twin without finding any more blood or hair. To be on the safe side, I took the crutches with me to the path lab at the hospital.

Dr. D'Eath, a morose, gloomy and usually taciturn individual about whom rumour persisted that he was a pathologist only because he was an abominable healer of the living, met me with his customary downturned corners of his mouth. I handed him the crutch and pointed out the speck of dried blood.

"Can you get a match with Faulkner's blood type?" I said.

"You want the impossible," he grumbled, and reminded me of Winnie-the-Pooh's friend, Eeyore. "Next thing you know, you chaps will expect me to lift fingerprints off running water. Wait here. It'll take me a few minutes."

"You might like to look at what's on my fingers, too, and let me know if we have a three-way match." I held my hand out.

"Where did you get this?" he said.

"From the corner of his desk a few minutes ago."

Dr. D'Eath scraped the residue from my fingers and transferred it to a glass slide which he placed under a microscope. He fiddled with the focus and looked up a few seconds later.

"What do you want me to say?"

"Is it Faulkner's?"

"How the hell would I know? It's a blood smear. Probably human, with a black hair in it. Faulkner had black hair. Put two and two together, Masters, and what do you get?"

"Four."

"Or twenty-two. Your guess is as good as mine who this sample belongs to."

I'd hoped for something positive to go on.

"There's no point in badgering me for an answer to your riddles, Masters," he said in a voice falling somewhere between petulant and belligerent. "I don't have them. It'll take some time to get a tissue match, assuming what was on your hand matches what's on the crutch and either or both match the deceased. Leave it with me."

Game, set and match to Dr. D'Eath, it seemed.

"Any definitive cause of death yet?" I asked hopefully.

"Preliminary only."

I raised an eyebrow, hoping to elicit a titbit of information on which to base a case.

"He suffered a massive stroke. There is also a fracture near the base of the skull consistent with a blow from a solid object. The blow, with or without the fragments of bone splinters penetrating his brain, could also have been the cause of death, before or after the stroke."

"Could he have tripped, or otherwise have fallen onto the sharp corner of his desk?" I hadn't meant to sound so exasperated and he obviously picked up on it.

"Toppled over backwards? Or pushed? I couldn't rule either out."

"Or been struck with a crutch, a golf club or some other wooden or metal object?"

"I couldn't rule out any of those possibilities either." This answer was no more helpful than the first. I tried again.

"Which do you think killed him? The blow or the stroke?"

He sighed the sigh of the longsuffering Latin master confronted by the pupil impervious to instruction in the conjugation of even the simplest verbs or the declensions of nouns. His mouth formed a thin line before he finally parted his lips and spoke. "The blow to the head would have been enough to render him unconscious and if left untreated would probably have led to his death within hours at the most. There was a large blood clot on his brain, possibly something left over from his war wound that had remained undiagnosed for a long time and which caused the stroke. That on its own would have probably killed him, perhaps in as little as a few minutes." He looked at me as if for the first time. "Which came first, Chief Inspector? The chicken or the egg?"

I thought for a moment. "One is murder, Doctor. One is natural causes."

"And until I have exhausted all the tests at my disposal, I can't say definitively which it is. But if I were you, to err on the safe side, and particularly if you are interested in protecting your backside from a caning by the Commissioner, I'd treat it as suspicious and look for motives. Or at least look for a black-haired person. Your hair's black, as is mine and Judge Faulkner's. You can probably rule the judge out as a suspect in his own murder. Apart from you and me, there should be about a million others in K.L. to choose from. You can always rule out murder later, after you have exhausted all avenues of investigation, but you might finish your career in a matter of hours if you don't regard the death as suspicious. That's my advice." He gave me what he probably thought was a smile. "Now, if you don't mind, I have work to do and it's getting on for teatime." He hesitated, and I thought he may be about to toss a tit-bit my way. I raised my eyebrows.

"He also had syphilis, quite advanced. And gonorrhea. Both well beyond any physician's ability to treat effectively."

I suppressed a smirk. So, the rumours were well founded. I thanked the pathologist and as I took my leave, he said, "His liver was in pretty poor shape too."

Although the court was closed indefinitely due to the untimely and unforeseen death of the Chief Justice, the staff were there when I returned, as they had been all day. I sought out Faulkner's clerk, an elderly Indian with a law degree from the University of Madras according to the heavy framed and browning, red sealed document hanging on the wall behind his desk in his small office adjacent to the judge's. The clerk's main attributes seem to have been his fluency in English, Malay, Mandarin and Malayalam, which is nothing like Malay, in spite of its similar name, and is a language spoken in southern India and by a sizeable portion of the Indian population of K.L. The clerk's other attributes were a reputation for knowing everyone worth knowing, who everyone was and how everything worked.

I had not met the man before although I had often seen him in court, preceding His Honour from the door leading from the court room to chambers as a sort of Master-at-Arms, and remaining with him until all were seated.

I knocked on his door. He opened it and squinted at me through a pair of pince-nez. Recognition must have sunk in fairly quickly as he opened the door wider with a flourish and indicated with a half bow that I should enter.

"Chief Inspector," he said. "To what do I owe this unexpected pleasure?"

He sounded like he had rehearsed this short speech which he had perhaps remembered from a Victorian melodrama.

"Mr. Chandrasekhar," I said, as I entered his cramped office. Every flat surface lay buried beneath a pile of books, briefs and other papers.

"Alas, Chief Inspector, it is only Chandrasekhar. I have no other name, not even a Christian name. It serves as both. I think my parents had run out of names by the time I was born. To my lasting shame and embarrassment, even the title Mister is superfluous."

I glanced at the law degree above his desk. It indeed contained only one name, Chandrasekhar, one of the commonest Indian names. It was entirely possible that the document was genuine. It was even possible it had been awarded to the man standing at my side. Or the opposite might also be true. I had no way of telling, and it was probably irrelevant in any case. I squinted at the date at the bottom of the document—1891—which suggested the issuance of the degree, or at least the document, coincided with the approximate age of the stooped man with the black, ill-fitting toupee with tufts of white hair visible below it.

"I need answers to perplexing questions, Chandrasekhar," I said.

"Fire away, Chief Inspector."

I marvelled at the man's command of the English vernacular.

"Who was the last person to see the judge yesterday?"

"That would probably have been me, after the afternoon docket was finished, although I don't know with absolute certainty."

"Probably?"

"I believe so. His Honour usually pokes his head around my door to say good night on his way out to the car park at the rear of the court house where his taxi awaits him. That's usually around 5:30 in the evening. He didn't do that last night, but I thought nothing of it. When I finished for the day it was a little after six. I called the night watchman as I always do to accompany me, as the last person out of the building, and lock up after me. The watchman has a hut where he spends the night watching for mischief. He came and I knocked on Judge Faulkner's chambers door. There was no reply. I tried the handle but the door was locked. As there was no light coming from under the door I assumed the judge had left for the day without saying good night."

"Then what happened?"

"I arrived for work as usual this morning. By eight-thirty, well before the judge usually arrives, I called the daytime security wallah to open his door so I could make his chambers ready and lay out his court clothes for him. The lock was jammed, locked from the inside as it turned out, with the judge's key left in the lock. When we finally managed to get the key out and the door unlocked we found Judge Faulkner lying on the floor. The security wallah felt for a pulse in his throat. He shook his head and said the judge was dead. We closed and locked the door and I telephoned for the police. The rest you know, Chief Inspector."

Which was very little, I thought ruefully. "Did either of you touch anything in the judge's chambers?"

"No, Sir. We left it exactly as we found it."

"When you went in this morning, was the blind pulled down?"

A puzzled look crossed Chandrasekhar's face for a moment, then cleared. "The room was quite dark, so the blind was probably still down."

"How about the punkah? Was that on?"

He looked to be concentrating, then shook his head. "I don't remember."

The ceiling fan had definitely been on when I attended the scene, and police officers have it drummed into them from their first day on the job never to touch anything at a crime scene unless told to do so by a senior officer. Was Chandrasekhar lying? Or did he genuinely not remember?

"And the light?"

"That was definitely off, Chief Inspector."

The light had been on when I arrived. "And you didn't turn it on?"

"No. Nor did the security wallah."

Someone then, probably a police officer who should have known better, had turned the light on before I arrived. Either that or Chandrasekhar was lying. If so, why? Would the security guard corroborate Chandrasekhar's story? It was time to find out.

"I need to speak to the security wallah. Is he still here?"

Chandrasekhar pressed a lever on the box on his desk. A tinny voice replied a moment later. They conversed in Malay before Chandrasekhar flicked the lever back up.

"He will be here in a minute, Chief Inspector."

Good to his word, the security guard showed up within thirty seconds. I addressed him in English. He turned a blank face to Chandrasekhar, who translated. "He speaks Malay, Chief Inspector, and only a few words of English. I will translate if you wish."

I thanked him, but I wanted to get the story from the horse's mouth rather than at second-hand and possibly manipulated by Chandrasekhar. I had developed a suspicion about the judge's clerk. I don't know why. Policeman's intuition, perhaps, but I thought his answers too pat, too prepared. You can't convict and hang a man on a suspicion, although I'm sure it must have happened countless times in our less enlightened past. I had barely a suspicion. More of a dislike than anything. So, I played a hunch, which is rarely a good thing and I had little hope that it might work.

I pulled my handcuffs from their leather pouch on my Sam Browne and before either man knew what was happening, I had them over the security guard's wrists. The startled man looked at me, then at Chandrasekhar.

"Please inform this man that I am arresting him on suspicion of being an accessory to murder and taking him to the police station for questioning."

Chandrasekhar translated and a few moments later the man was in the back seat of the police vehicle. I sat in the front next to my uniformed native Malay police driver and turned to watch the security guard as we drove through heavy rain in the dark to the police station. I needed to gauge the man's mental state at being arrested for murder before deciding on a line of questioning. We couldn't hold him indefinitely without charging him formally, but an early arrest set the minds of the population at ease and provided a feather in the cap of the Commissioner. It was quite possible the guard had helped in the murder in some way, and if he did, he should pay the price. If he hadn't, then my fishing trip would have been in vain. I would dust him down, release him unconditionally, thank him for doing his civic duty in helping with the enquiry and assure him that his job was not in jeopardy. All through the intermediary of a qualified police interpreter, naturally.

I interviewed the terrified man in a holding cell away from any other prisoner. Through a police interpreter he essentially repeated what Chandrasekhar had told me and, try as I might, I could not get him to change his story. I decided he was either an extremely accomplished liar or telling the truth. By late evening I had drawn the conclusion that he had nothing to do with the death of Judge Faulkner. I released him with my effusive thanks for helping with our enquiry and I had my driver drop him off in a police vehicle a short distance from his home to avoid embarrassment.

On his return, I had the driver take me back to the court house. I needed to speak to the night watchman. When we drew up at his hut the rain was still teeming down and the court house lay in complete darkness. Huddled under a large umbrella he came to see who had interrupted his night and seemed to be taken aback at the sight of two police officers in uniform in an otherwise unmarked police car.

The hut was barely big enough for the three of us—a little larger than a guardsman's sentry box but not much—but it had a rattan and bamboo chair and a small charcoal stove for brewing tea. Through my driver I told the man to sit down and relax, that we were not here to arrest him. Word had undoubtedly had time to get out about the arrest of the security guard that evening, so I assured the watchman his daytime counterpart had only been assisting the police with their enquiries and he had been most helpful, that we had personally taken him home only a few minutes ago and he would be back on the job as usual in the morning. He seemed to be more at ease but still eyed us warily.

"I need to know exactly what you did last night," I said in English and waited while my driver interpreted, "from the moment Chandrasekhar asked you to accompany him to the judge's chamber until he left the building." The driver said something to the night watchman that my Malay didn't catch.

The man looked terrified, his eyes darting around the cramped hut with only the glow of the charcoal stove to shed any light. "Chandrasekhar called me almost as soon as I came on duty," the interpreter said. "It was only a few minutes after six and I had just completed my first tour around the building."

"It was dark by then?"

"Oh, yes, but there were lights on in the building."

"Anyone or any cars still in the car park?"

"Two or three cars, but no one in them."

"Was there a taxi waiting for the judge?"

"No taxi. Gone."

"You went with Chandrasekhar to Judge Faulkner's room?"

"Yes, Sir."

"And what did you find there?"

"Nothing."

"What do you mean, nothing?"

"The door was locked. We couldn't get in, so I went with Chandrasekhar to the side door and let him out. Then I locked the door from the outside and resumed my rounds."

"Was the light on in Judge Faulkner's room when you tried to open the door?"

"There was a light coming from under the door which doesn't fit well in the monsoon, so a little light…" He shrugged, as if it were nothing.

"Did Chandrasekhar say anything about the light?"

The night watchman took his time while he regarded each of us in turn. Eventually he said, "He said it looked like the judge had forgotten to turn his light out. But we couldn't get in to turn it off. Then Chandrasekhar left. I saw him again when he left tonight. He didn't say anything to me. We passed the judge's office and I let Chandrasekhar out the side door like always and watched him cross the car park to the road and wait for the bus. He got on the bus when it came and that's the last time I saw him tonight. It was the same as last night, as every night. It never changes."

I thanked the man and we left. We crossed the car park in the pouring rain, in spite of the umbrellas getting soaked in the process and stopped by a ground floor window.

"Why are we here, Sir?" my driver said when my curiosity had drifted on in silence for half a minute.

The outside shutters were hooked flat against the wall. I tried to pull the top half of the sash window down. It would not budge. With both thumbs and forefingers, I tried pushing the bottom pane upwards from the sash above the glass. It slid up soundlessly. Gingerly, I pulled it back down until it was firmly closed. The *modus operandi* started to form in my mind, even if the *who* continued to escape me.

The police driver drove me to my small flat after that and I lay awake half the night turning over different scenarios in my mind. Dr. D'Eath had yet to determine a single cause of death. We had not turned up a definitive murder weapon, if indeed it were murder. And I had no motive. That Chandrasekhar had lied to me about the light under the door I had no doubt. But why? The Judge's crutches had been left leaning neatly side by side against the desk with the Judge's one-legged body at least a couple of paces away with the crutches out of reach. Someone had placed them against the desk after Judge Faulkner had fallen to the floor. Why? To make it seem like an accident? Unlikely. Someone who had a tidy mind perhaps? Again, why? It made no sense. The most obvious suspect was Chandrasekhar, but to judge from his cluttered and untidy office, he was far from neat and tidy. Besides, I had not uncovered a motive, if it were the judge's clerk. I made a mental note to add my suspicions to everything else I had to give Sutcliffe when he arrived in the morning.

"No rumours in the rumour mill about affairs or other liaisons," I told Sutcliffe over a late breakfast. "I can't absolutely rule out an affair of the heart or blackmail by a jilted lover, as salacious as that may be, but I think it unlikely. Faulkner was one of the most disagreeable customers one can imagine."

Sutcliffe made a note on a scrap of paper and looked up. "Thirty-six hours after the event," he said. "Who do you suspect? And why?"

I shifted uneasily on my seat. "No known motives have come to light. We can't rule anyone out, except for the day security guard at the court house, whom we've already interviewed and released."

"Who else, then?"

Sutcliffe had always managed to focus on one thing at a time, which probably went a long way towards making him a good policeman. Now it was my turn to feel the unwavering gaze of the investigating officer.

"Chandrasekhar," I said. "He lied to me about there not being a light on in chambers when he and the security guard eventually managed to get in before court was due to start yesterday. I don't know why, but it's all I have to go on. No one else springs to mind."

"Let's bring him in and have a friendly chat, shall we?"

"And see what he has to say." I pushed my plate of unfinished toast to one side and rose from the table. "No time like the present."

I summoned my police driver and within minutes we were at the court house. We found Chandrasekhar as expected in his office. I introduced Superintendent Sutcliffe. The clerk rose and extended his hand in greeting.

"We need a quiet word, Chandrasekhar," Sutcliffe said. "In private."

"Certainly, Superintendent. Please take a seat."

"Not here. At the police station."

Chandrasekhar's head jerked up and his mouth gaped. I saw fear flick across his eyes as his gaze went from one of us to the other. "As, as you wish, Superintendent," he stuttered and staggered to his feet. The polish of the previous day melted like candle wax beneath a flame. "Am I under arrest?"

Sutcliffe glanced at me. "No," he said, turning back to Chandrasekhar. "We are hoping that you will help us in our enquiries into the murder of Judge Faulkner." He paused. "As a material witness only at this time."

Chandrasekhar looked as if someone had pulled the rug from under his feet.

I sat in the back of the police car with Chandrasekhar while Sutcliffe sat up front with the driver. Chandrasekhar was silent all the way back to the police station. After searching him thoroughly we placed him in a holding cell and closed the door.

"We'll leave him there to stew on his own for an hour or two," Sutcliffe said, "while we decide on a course of questioning. If it is murder, we have to make it stick, otherwise we'll all lose face and risk becoming a laughing stock all the way from Burma to Singapore. Anything new from the pathologist?"

I went off in search of someone who might have intercepted incoming reports from the hospital, only to be informed by the desk Sergeant that the report was on my desk. I hustled to my office, grabbed the report and glanced at it on my way back to Sutcliffe and the cells. He looked up as I breezed into the anteroom and handed him the report.

Sutcliffe read it through without interruption from me, then once again. "Blood samples from the deceased, your fingers and the crutch all match," he said. "The hair is horse hair, not human hair. Cause of death almost certainly was from a stroke with trauma to the skull a contributing factor."

"So, not murder," I said. "Manslaughter?"

"We'll see. Let's hear what our suspect has to say first."

When we opened the cell door it appeared obvious that Chandrasekhar had wet himself. The room stank of urine and Chandrasekhar did not rise from the seat in front of the desk where we had left him. He swivelled around on the seat, his eyes wide with fear, pleading. His toupee sat askew on his bald head with tufts of white hair peeking below the edges.

"We will need to seize your toupee as evidence," Sutcliffe said without preamble, and lifted it from the man's head. He came around the desk and sat at the investigator's chair. "We have received the pathologist's report. Judge Faulkner received a violent blow to the back of the head, fracturing the skull and causing bone fragments to lodge in his brain. What, if anything, can you tell us about the incident?"

He sat back and waited. Chandrasekhar shuddered, wiped the tears from his eyes with the backs of his hands, sniffed loudly then blew his nose on a large white handkerchief. With a voice quavering with fear, he said, "Judge Faulkner threatened to expose me as a fraud and have me dismissed."

"How are you allegedly a fraud?" Sutcliffe said.

"The law degree on the wall in my office is a forgery. I obtained it years ago, before I started working at the court. My real name is not Chandrasekhar. I don't know who that person is, or was, or if he ever existed. Everyone, even my wife knows me as Chandrasekhar. My name is Ram Gupta and I am from Bangalore. I needed the paper to obtain my position. I don't know how, but Judge Faulkner found out and confronted me in his chambers that evening after the court had closed for the day. I begged and pleaded but he refused to back down. He came around his desk and pointed a crutch at me. He was very angry. He told me I was dismissed as of right then. His voice was slurred. I think he had been drinking. I knew he drank a lot, even during the day and between cases, but he didn't smell of whisky." He ran his tongue over his lips. "I didn't know what to do. I need the position. I retire in less than two years and I will receive a small pension, but nothing if I am dismissed. He advanced towards me and levelled a crutch at my chest. I felt threatened. I pushed the crutch aside. The Judge tottered over backwards and hit his head on the corner of the desk. Then he crumpled in a heap at my feet on top of his crutches. I think I blacked out because my head was dizzy and when I came to I found myself on the floor next to him. I felt for a pulse but I couldn't find one. I didn't know who else he'd told about the degree. I realized that it looked bad for me. I panicked. I locked the door and left the key in the lock to make it would look as if he had locked himself in his office. I don't know why, but I propped his crutches against the desk and left him on the floor. I opened the window. The car park was deserted. Everyone but the security guard had left for the day. I pulled the blind down behind me when I climbed out. The outside shutters were open and I left them like that. No one saw me come around to the side door and let myself back in. It always remains unlocked until I leave for the day. I gathered my composure and called the security guard to lock up after me. The rest you know, Superintendent."

He slumped back in his chair. I looked at Sutcliffe and he raised an eyebrow.

"Your toupee, Mr. Gupta," I said, pointing to the black hairpiece on the desk top. "How did two hairs from your toupee become lodged in the crutch and under the desk top?"

"It became dislodged when I fell. I replaced it on my head when I rose. It is quite possible that a hair came unglued from the backing and became stuck on the crutch either when I blacked out and fell, or when I pulled myself to my feet. I remember using the desk to help me. I have no other explanation, Chief Superintendent. Judge Faulkner was meticulous in his habits, quite fastidious, and demanded that chambers be cleaned daily. The office is cleaned every day while court is in session. It would have been clean and tidy when I entered that evening. I left it like that. It seemed fitting somehow."

"You failed to summon help when Judge Faulkner collapsed," Sutcliffe said in a reproachful voice. "You left him to die if he was not already dead. You failed to notify the police. You obstructed justice at every turn, and we have only your word that he fell, rather than you pushed him against the corner of his desk, causing the skull fracture that ultimately led to his death."

"It's the truth, I swear," he gasped. I looked at Sutcliffe. He was putting the squeeze on the man, hoping for more than an admission—a full confession. He turned to me with tears in his eyes. "It's the truth, Chief Inspector," he gasped between sobs. "There was no pulse. He was already dead. There was nothing I could do to help him. He fell. I didn't push him. I swear." He put his hands over his face and wept.

Sutcliffe rose. "You will be remanded in custody, Gupta, while we decide on what charges to bring against you." He called for a guard. "Book him and place him in a single cell away from any other prisoners," he told the Malay officer when he appeared. I followed Sutcliffe to my cramped office.

"Sometimes all it takes is a stranger in a senior officer's uniform to open the floodgates, Masters," Sutcliffe said. "Having come all this way I was hoping for a confession. We have nothing to disprove what he said." He sighed. "And we probably never will."

"And no serious reason to doubt him," I said. "We have the pathologist's report showing the cause of death as a massive stroke. What do we have to gain by charging Gupta with obstructing our investigation?"

Sutcliffe shrugged. "Nothing, really. It's your manor, Masters. It's your beat. My suggestion is we go with the path report and rule it as death by natural causes. Nobody loses that way. The pathologist maintains his reputation and you and I can go on our merry way knowing that justice was served in a roundabout and totally mysterious way."

"Like God, it's wonders to perform."

"After what we've been through, Masters, you don't seriously believe that, do you?"

I gave him what I hoped he would interpret as an enigmatic smile. "And Chandrasekhar? Or should I say Gupta?"

"I think a quiet caution for obstructing police might suffice. We all need a pension, however small, to show for a lifetime's work, don't you think?"

3. TO SERVE AND PROTECT

The man in front of me had the build of a middleweight boxer gone to seed. His nose had obviously been broken more than once. His dark eyes were sunk deep in their sockets, surrounded by sallow skin which bore several small scars. A touch of grey infused his temples and his narrow, matinée idol moustache. What might have passed for a fleeting smile gave me a glimpse of his bad dental work, some of which may have been done by a dentist.

Whoever he was, he didn't impress me at first sight.

I rose to greet him and extended a hand. He ignored it. "Detective Chief Inspector Masters," I said affably, ignoring his offhand rudeness.

It was May 1931, and I was barely a month into a one-year detachment from Kuala Lumpur to Malacca heading up the Criminal Investigation Division. A native constable from the front desk of the police station had shown the man into my office just in time to cause me to postpone my lunch. The man surveyed my office with an appraising glance then, without being invited, pulled up a chair and sat down. He grabbed the heavy glass ashtray on my desk and pulled it towards him. He fished out a pack of Chesterfields from his jacket pocket, selected one and straightened it between thumb and forefinger. Without a further word exchanged he lit the cigarette, inhaled deeply and exhaled, blowing the smoke towards the ceiling.

He waved at the office walls. "This used to be mine, you know." He turned his attention back to me. "Bart Falconetti's the name."

Although I'd never met the man, as soon as he mentioned his name, I knew who he was, and the reputation that preceded him. Inspector Bart Falconetti had indeed occupied this office at one time, but that had been several years and at least a couple of predecessors ago.

"Don't believe everything you read in the newspapers or in a police file," he said. "You wouldn't believe the truth if I told it to you."

"You'll bump into him, I'm sure," the Chief Superintendent had warned me as he placed Falconetti's file on my desk a day or two after my arrival in Malacca. "Just keep this under advisement for when you do." A wan smile crossed his face as he pushed the dossier towards me. My immediate thought was that he had basset hound somewhere in his genealogy.

"It's interesting reading, considering the short time he was here. A copy of his letter of resignation is the last item in the file. I'll leave you to it." I detected a certain lightness in his step as he left my office. According to his file, Falconetti cleaned up Malacca, his way, as he had in the East End of London, the Military Police during the war, and in Canada where he started his one-man crime-clearing police career.

In spite of six years in the army, rubbing shoulders with officers and other ranks from across the Empire, I had never met a Canadian. My first impression was not favourable. Falconetti blew smoke in my direction and placed the cigarette between two nicotine stained fingers. He leaned forward, as if to share a confidence. I did the same and wished I hadn't. I received the dubious benefit of cigarettes and last night's supper.

"Perhaps you'd better start from the beginning," I suggested. "You know how it works." I leaned back and listened.

"From the beginning, which is this morning," Falconetti said.

His speech had a distinctive American twang which I recognized from the steady diet of Hollywood films we received in Kuala Lumpur. I assumed the accent was Canadian, but I'm no expert.

He told me he heard the door to the hall outside his office open. A client, he hoped. "Business can be up and down at times," he said, waving his hand with thumb and little finger extended like an aeroplane waggling its wings. I got the point first time.

A moment later, he said, the door slammed shut and the glass pane rattled. Footsteps thumped across the floor of the outer office and stopped. He heard words, "Some guy getting mouthy with Stella, the receptionist, and Stella giving it back as good as she took like the good Aussie she is. I made a mental note: Needs to work on customer relations." He looked at me with a faint grin as if expecting me to share the punchline of his joke about Stella. He heard more footsteps across the floor coming towards his office and the door burst open.

"A guy the size of a Buick," Falconetti said, spreading his arms far apart in case I underestimated the size of his visitor, "Plugs the doorway. Must be seven feet tall and weigh three-fifty if he's an ounce. I've never seen him before, or anyone that size. He pulls a small howitzer from the waist band of his pants and waves it in my direction, stroking it with his thumb like it's a puppy." Falconetti pointed two fingers at my face in case I needed actions to understand what he was getting at. "Could have been he was searching for the safety. Maybe not. I wasn't about to ask. He's got a large brown envelope in his other hand."

By now what I assumed was a Canadian accent had taken on what sounded like Edward G. Robinson in the American gangster films.

Falconetti took a breath. "The gun looks like maybe a nine-millimeter semi-automatic. He maybe had a permit, but I didn't like to enquire. I get a close-up of it, closer than I want, but I'm not good with guns." That didn't exactly jibe with what I gleaned from his service file and I wondered why he thought it necessary to deflect the truth. My eyebrows twitched. He raised his hand like a traffic policeman. "I told you not to believe everything you read. Anyways, whatever it was, it was big and black and mean-looking." He took a long pause while he dragged heavily on his cigarette.

He waved an arm around, doing Swedish aerobics but indicating what, I couldn't guess. "Malacca," he said, blowing smoke and taking another drag. "You get used to the place after a while. And it's a helluva lot warmer than Hamilton. That's where I'm from. Hamilton, Ontario. Canada."

"I can imagine," I said, as if I hadn't read that bit in his file and before the conversation drifted sideways into a reminiscence of how cold it is in Hamilton, Ontario, Canada.

"The office is on the third floor of what's gotta be the oldest building in Malacca. Who in Christ's name needs twelve-foot ceilings? No elevator. I don't think Otis was born when they built the place. If you need to come to my office, take your heart pills first. The building's a fire trap, probably doesn't meet any code ever invented, but the rent's cheap, which I like."

"Then what happened, Mr. Falconetti?" I said, swallowing my dislike of this particular member of the public whom I'd sworn to serve and protect.

"The guy points the business end of the piece at me and asks if I'm Bart Falconetti. He looks puzzled. So I ask him what it says on the door, like maybe FALCON DETECTIVE AGENCY. And maybe INVESTIGATIONS in big friggin' capital letters? The guy still looks puzzled so I put him out of his misery and tell him I'm Bart Falconetti, proprietor of Falcon Detective Agency, Investigations."

Falconetti leaned back for a moment. "My name's not on the door. The sign writer didn't ask if I wanted it there. I didn't think to tell him." Falconetti leaned forward again as if he's about to share a secret. "Then, at the bottom of the panel, there's the phone number. I don't know why. Anyone standing outside the door don't need to phone. The sign writer must have gotten the number off of my business card. I wasn't going to pay him to take it off."

Falconetti said he asked the man what was on his mind. "The guy's voice rises a couple of octaves. I wanted to laugh, but I choked the impulse in time. He's still holding onto his gun." He lit another cigarette from the butt of the first and sat back. "His boss's wife's apparently gone missing and the boss wants to hire me to find her and the guy she's living with. The guy tells me his boss will take care of the rest. That's none of my business. So I ask the guy if he's got a photo of the boss's wife. He throws this brown envelope on my desk. I slide the photo of his boss's wife out—it looks like a publicity shot for an acting agency—and examine it for several seconds. White woman. Drop dead, friggin' gorgeous. Straight out of a Hollywood magazine. Blond hair, salon job, not like Stella's. Deep cleavage, the whole nine yards." He took a breath. "And my blood froze like it was friggin' February out on Hamilton harbour with the wind blowing straight outta the North Pole."

"What made you react like that?" I said.

Falconetti blew more smoke at the ceiling. He didn't look quite as self-assured as he had only a few minutes earlier.

"I know her. And I know who the guy's boss is."

I was on the point of asking how he had come to know her when he interrupted my thought.

"But obviously I don't let on. The guy seems friendlier, now the introductions are out of the way and we're into the business part, but he doesn't relax his grip on his hardware. At least by now he has the business end pointed at the ceiling. I didn't want to be the accountant in the office upstairs if the piece goes off. Accidentally or not."

I nodded to encourage the flow of the conversation, and perhaps find out what Falconetti expected from the police.

"The guy stops smiling. Flashes an inch or two of shirt cuff, exposing a cheap gold chain bracelet and an imitation Rolex. I decide to cool it for a while. If I take the case, his boss is paying me, not him."

Falconetti smiled without humour. "I point at the blond in the picture and ask if the broad was his boss's wife. That might have been the stupid question of the day, but I had to ask, for clarification. He gives me another of his dumb puzzled looks. I put two and two together.

"If the blond is who I know she is, I figure his boss would need a lot more than one clip of ammo to take care of all the guys she's seeing on the quiet. But I didn't tell him any of that. I like breathing." He paused for thought. "I'd been with her." He hesitated. "But only once," he added quickly. Perhaps a bit too quickly. "Not my type even on a dark and stormy night. I make do with Stella, if you must know."

I didn't, and could hardly have cared less about Falconetti's private domestic arrangements. He might have been reading my thoughts.

"Anyhow, I plays it cool, like I'd never seen her before and I'm not interested in her hobbies. The guy gives me the details I need—the basic stuff, her name, address, make, model and plate number of the car she drives—it's a friggin' Cadillac a block long, for Chrissakes. I quote a fee. He gives me an odd look. I don't know if the fee's too high or too low.

"I told him it's twenty per cent up front. Cash. Or leave a cheque with the girl out front."

Falconetti snorted. "Girl. Stella. She's forty if she's a day but she's used to being called a girl, and I'm not changing now. She's been with me since I started in this business." He shrugged. "She's not expensive to maintain.

"The gofer wants to know when I start and I tell him as soon as the cheque clears and I'd report in daily. He gives me a phone number and tucks the cannon back in his waist band. A few minutes later I hear the outer door slam. If he pays my bill, a client can slam the door and bang around in the outer office as much as he likes. I give it a couple of minutes before strolling into the outer office, looking nonchalant, like it was just business. I wanted to impress Stella." He paused. "She rations her favours and it's been a while since the last time, know what I mean? Infrequently. That's one word, not two, eh?" He gave a coarse laugh.

I liked him even less than I had when he walked into my office. I decided no reply was needed. Falconetti resumed his tale.

"Stella explodes and wants to know who the asshole is, only not so politely. I tell her it's a new client if his cheque clears. She hands over the cheque, drawn on The Malacca Trading Bank. Business account. MalImpEx. Illegible signature. I still don't know the gofer's name. Maybe that's deliberate. Then she wants to know if the cheque's for twenty per cent. I assure her it is.

"Stella does the arithmetic. She's not the swiftest pony in the race but this time she gets it right first go. She looks up and tells me for that kinda dough the asshole can pitch a tent in her office and she'll bring him coffee every hour, on the hour."

I nodded. "And why have you told me all this?"

Falconetti sat back abruptly in his chair. "Isn't it friggin' obvious?"

"So far you've made no request for service and I'm not about to jump to conclusions."

He waved his arms about as if exasperated. "I need protection."

"From whom?"

"The woman's husband."

"And who is that?"

Falconetti bit his lip. "Do you really need to know?"

"Yes. We need to know who to protect you from."

"Okay. You know the guy who got in front of the accidental ricochet in his boat a few years ago? The incident on my file?"

I nodded.

"Yeah. The one and the same. Farooq. I didn't have a warrant to search, and when the bastard tried to stop me from searching his boat I emptied my service revolver into the bottom of his hull. He got in the way of the first round. With him out the way I finished the job and watched the boat sink under him. Then I hauled him out before he drowned, and wrapped a towel around his leg as a tourniquet before I drove him to the hospital. He didn't have the courtesy to thank me. You know how that ended. Anyway, I never knew until this morning we had a connection."

I suppressed a smile. I'd heard an expression from some American soldiers at the end of the war—What goes around comes around. Now I knew its full implication. "It looks like you have a couple of choices to make," I said.

"Such as?"

"Earn your fee, omitting the minor role you admit playing. Or book a passage on the first ship out of Malacca. It might be advisable to do both, in case the first option doesn't go too well."

"Taken under advisement. Isn't that what the Chief Super always says?"

I rose and offered my hand. This time he took it. I read genuine fear flicker in his eyes. In my opinion he deserved it. But I had a job to do, which was to make sure nobody ended up dead on my watch, Bart Falconetti included. "Let me know when the cheque clears and I'll find the manpower," I said to his retreating back. "Somewhere." He didn't acknowledge me.

Before I made up my notes of the interview, I thought about Falconetti's story. I admit that even after six years in the army and eleven more as a copper, I have to work on skepticism and sharpen my suspicions, both of which tend to lie close to the surface of good policemen. The events of the morning as told by Falconetti did seem a bit far-fetched, though not altogether impossible and I could think of no reason why he should fabricate them. Besides, that was all I had to go on at this point. I crossed my fingers and hoped the cheque bounced or something else cropped up to cause Falconetti to withdraw his request for protection.

I had a couple of days to spare before I had to take any action but in the event that it became necessary to follow through, I decided to put Inspector Squires from the uniform branch on notice to make up the other half of my team. Squires was a man of medium height and build and quite unremarkable features which made him perfect for surveillance. Malacca was Squires' first posting and he seemed keen. He obviously had no idea how stultifying boring a surveillance detail could be. However, given Falconetti's temper and service record I had a feeling this one wouldn't break any marathon records before something erupted.

I called Squires into my office and gave him the glad tidings, absent the great joy. "No one's getting a promotion over this," I told him to cool his enthusiasm and to wipe the pleased Labrador puppy look off his face. "But if we mess up, there are likely to be several dead bodies to account for, two of which could be ours, and a month's worth of paperwork if we're still around to tell the tale. We don't let him out of our sight for a minute. I'll let you know when I need you. Any questions?"

If he had any, he kept them to himself.

Two days later, a Friday, Falconetti was back in my office, unannounced.

"The cheque cleared," he said. "I'm on the job."

"I have my team assembled," I said. "I won't introduce you. It's best if you don't meet them. They're quite inconspicuous and I wouldn't want you to give the game away if you recognize one of them at a crucial point."

He seemed to ponder this snippet of intelligence for a moment, then nodded. "Okay, *Tuan*. Out of sight, out of mind. Just keep close. He's a mean, unforgiving son of a bitch."

Falconetti gave me his office and home address and phone numbers at both places. "I drive a nineteen twenty-two Studebaker, black, four door," he said. "Needs a wash but what the hell. It don't stand out. No one makes it as a private investigator's vehicle."

I made a note.

"We work half day Saturdays and off Sundays unless it's a rush job. I won't have anything of use for you before Monday so start then. Besides I have a date this Saturday night and I don't need anyone snooping around, eh?"

"Gotcha," I said. I'd heard the expression in a Hollywood film.

He seemed on the point of leaving when he hesitated. "This shouldn't be a long job," he said.

I arched my eyebrows, which elicited a response that I didn't expect.

"When I dated her, Brenda Littlewood her name is, I checked her out. Old habit and a good one. She had four guys strung in a line that I knew of. A guy who owns a nine-year-old Studebaker don't run with a broad who drives a Caddy, which is why I ducked out of the running real early. Like I said, once and done. The other guys are Country club members. Play golf on Sundays instead of going to church. Local big shots. Lotsa dough. I don't think they pay taxes on any of it, know what I mean? But if you look the wrong way, they'll be dead big shots." He pointed two fingers at me in case I missed the point and he blew imaginary smoke off the end. "I'm getting a good payday for this. I'll string it out as long as I can to make it look like I'm working hard and earning my fee. But it should be a wrap in a week." He grinned. "I don't know where Brenda is but she won't be hard to find. Dime to a dollar she's with one of them and I know where they all live and work."

He saw himself out.

An hour later, rather than come into my office, Falconetti telephoned.

Before I could get a word in edgewise, he said, "I phoned the client's gofer, the guy the size of a Buick and just as smart? I told him the cheque cleared. He squeaks something. If it was meant to be menacing, I misunderstood. It's hard to take a squeak seriously, even when it's backed up by nine-millimetre semi-automatic. So I don't laugh. That woulda been bad for business. And probably for my life expectancy. So I put on my professional voice.

"'Seeing as we are now in business together,' I says to him, 'perhaps you could give me your name and contact information.'

"I try not to show I'm exasperated, but getting information out of the Buick's like pulling wisdom teeth.

"'What is your name, then?'

"'Raul.'

"'Raul.' I write it down. And your last name?'

"'Castro.'

"You Spanish or something? I figure that's a good bet, even if he does work for that Lebanese, Farooq. Besides, it didn't sound Lebanese or anything.

"After a while, as if he's digesting the information and formulating a response, he says. 'Filipino.' I wonder what the hell he's doing in Malacca before I remember people from all over the world wash up here. Why not a Filipino? I'm tempted to ask how he spells the name, but I refrain. I have this vision of a nine-millimetre slug travelling down the phone line and burying itself in my skull. Brain all over my office carpet. Bone fragments splattered over the wall. Stella having to find a new job and somebody else to brighten her Saturday nights once in a while. You get the picture."

I tried to interrupt this flow of verbal effluence but to no avail.

"'Right,' I says. 'I'm your man, Mr. Castro. I start work right now. Any questions before I begin?'

"I wait for the silence to end. I can almost hear the cogs and flywheel turning in his brain.

"'No,' he says at last. The line goes dead. Not a born conversationalist, I'm guessing. Maybe that's a good thing. Maybe not. I put the receiver down, pondering my next move. 'Lunch time,' I tell Stella. 'And after I gotta earn my fee.'" He paused and turned his attention to me. "So that's where at. How about we meet at Fernando's place in the bazaar for lunch and plan our next moves?"

I agreed, reluctantly.

He was already there and didn't stand when I entered the restaurant. He had curry sauce on his shirt front. He must have caught me staring at it because he tried to rub it off with a handkerchief. It only made it worse.

"Sorry," he said. "This isn't the kind of place they give you table napkins with lunch."

I looked around the restaurant. Most of the other diners were busy spooning curry into their mouths and didn't spare us a second glance. None of them had table linen either. I said 'No' to the water offered. I have an aversion to water-borne diseases. I don't even trust the locally bottled soda water.

"At least I'm not going to have to meet prospective clients this afternoon and impress them with my charm, good looks and table manners," Falconetti said.

Over lunch Falconetti gave me a run-down of his plans while the ceiling fan clacked overhead, making no difference to the temperature inside. He gave me a list of the names and addresses of the four men he knew currently were or had been seeing the woman. "They're all successful. This one's the Dutch Consul-General, Henk Boersma." He pointed to a name and went down the list. I didn't recognize any of them. "This one's in cement. Roopinder Singh Bansal. Major construction projects. This one's American, Stanley Burge. I don't know what he does, but he has lotsa dough. And this one runs the Malacca Trading Bank. Indian fellow from Dacca, I believe, or Calcutta, somewhere like that. Name's Tariq Malik. No coincidence the client banks there. I'll get up close and take a couple of photos to please the client." He pushed a manila envelope across the table. "This is Brenda Littlewood."

I glanced at the photo. The smiling blond came exactly as Falconetti described, and she certainly was beautiful. And if Falconetti was right, she was also certainly a dangerous woman to become entangled with.

"English. Kept her name when she hooked up with Farooq. You'll recognize him from the bullet scar on his leg." Falconetti laughed. "He runs Malacca Import and Export, a cover for a drug business, importing raw opium from Burma mostly, but they've never been able to pin anything on him. He refines it and exports the finished product. Again, he's never been caught. He's careful, like he should be in his line of work."

I made a non-committal noise in my throat.

"He's also the biggest pimp in Malacca, and that's saying something. He specializes in white women but he'll bring in Siamese when there's a demand. Young girls mostly. Children, some of them." He wrinkled his nose. "Not uncommon in these parts, but then you'd know that, eh?"

I didn't know whether he was implying that I had personal experience or professional knowledge, but I let it drop. My opinion of the man took another step towards the cellar, but I couldn't afford to let personal likes and dislikes interfere with the job.

"I can't confirm it," He said without missing a beat. "But I believe Brenda was one of what he calls his hostesses, but he decided to keep her for himself. I've no idea why he decided to marry her. By all accounts he didn't have to, know what I mean?" He snorted, which I took to be a man-to-man laugh. I imagine he'd have dug me in the ribs if we'd been sitting side by side.

The veneer of Englishness that he showed briefly at our first meeting had vanished. By now I was starting to take a real dislike to the man and wondered if all Canadians were like that and how he had managed to convince the powers that be in London to take him on in the Colonial Police. I knew some fish manage to slip through the net. Perhaps he was one of them. I no longer had an appetite for food, or for Falconetti's company. Still, I had to work with the man to prevent anything unpleasant happening to him.

"I'll post a man in your office during business hours," I said. "He'll be in plain clothes and armed. I'll have him pose as a client waiting to see you. He'll follow you to and from your home and whenever you're out of the office. There'll be someone outside your home twenty-four hours a day. You won't see him, but he'll be there. Let me have your home and business addresses before we leave, and any photos you may have of Farooq and the Filipino."

"I'll see what I can do." He rose from the table and walked out of the restaurant, leaving me to pay the bill.

I parked the unmarked police Austin 7 well down an alley a few yards along from, and out of sight of Falconetti's tiny house. To judge from the exterior of the house he certainly lived modestly. I doubted if there was room inside to swing a cat. I shuddered at the bachelor living conditions that must exist within his four walls. I was glad he hadn't asked me to conduct our surveillance from inside.

Squires had taken one look at me when I entered the CID office and almost arrested me on the spot.

"Good God," he laughed when I showed him my warrant card. "I'd never recognize you like that."

I had on a pair of ragged and filthy trousers that I'd bought that afternoon in the bazaar near Fernando's restaurant. The shirt came from the same stall and had probably once been white or cream but was now a dingy grey with a rip down the front. I was shoeless, my feet dusty, and I sported a dun coloured turban wrapped loosely around my head. I'd used a brown vegetable dye to darken my exposed skin. I had a pair of cheap sunglasses perched on my nose. I pushed them up to cover my eyes. From under the shirt I produced a tin cup and scrap of cardboard on which I'd scrawled, *BUTA TOLONG BANTU.*

"What does that mean?" Squires said, pointing to my makeshift sign.

"Blind Please Help. At least I hope so," I said. "Indian beggar. I tried looking like a Malay but I couldn't come close."

"Well, there are enough Indian beggars on the street to go round."

"I'll be out in the open most of the time. I need to pass unnoticed. I could hardly stand on the street corner in uniform with a pair of binoculars around my neck insisting I was an eccentric bird watcher. Hopefully, this get-up will let me keep tabs on the place without attracting attention. If no one remembers anything about me, I become invisible, part of the landscape, which is best of all."

The alley lay deserted. No one saw me park the car so no one wondered why a blind Indian beggar was driving a fairly new vehicle. I chose a spot in the shade at the opening of the alley and sat down to wait. The sun was almost down when Falconetti drove by, turned into the narrow alley across the street from me and parked beside his house. He looked around as if searching for something, or someone. He shrugged, put the car keys in his pocket, took out another set and unlocked the front door. A light went on. Several hours later it went off and the house, like the street, lay in darkness. Falconetti's was the only car I counted on the street all evening which, given the neighbourhood, was hardly surprising. I settled down to cat nap the night away in the deeper shadows of the alley. I reckoned it was too early in Falconetti's investigation to place him in danger of reprisal by Farooq, or the Filipino, but I couldn't take a chance.

Almost a week of complete inactivity passed. Falconetti had no visitors at his house. Squires reported the same lack of interest in the office. "I don't know how he makes ends meet," Squires said at the start of our morning briefing. "He hasn't had a client in three days and only two all week."

"I'm not sure he does, unless he's doing something dodgy on the side. Another day and I'll have to call the whole thing off. We can't spare the manpower much longer." It didn't pay to admit that this might be a wild goose chase but I was beginning to contemplate the possibility.

The phone rang.

It was Falconetti. "I've given the gofer the names to pass on," he said, without the customary greeting. "He says Farooq's going to invite the four to dinner at his place. A black tie, friendly get-together. More than that he wouldn't tell me. I won't be there. Farooq obviously doesn't extend invitations to the hired help. If anything goes down, especially if it's of a terminal nature, I'll have to be silenced too. I know too much. That's where you come in."

"I see." I ran some thoughts through my mind. Who stood to

gain from the death of any of these men? How could their deaths possibly stay hidden? How many witnesses would remain alive after the smoke cleared? How would he dispose of the bodies, from Falconetti to the Filipino to any of the household staff who might have witnessed anything? An image from a Hollywood gangster film flashed through my mind, then as quickly vanished: A group of hoodlums on the running boards of some high-powered American car firing submachine guns at an unseen target. It didn't make sense. This was Malacca, not Chicago with a corrupt police department and mayor in the pockets of the gangsters who ran the city. And the Colonial Police Force was as far removed from its Chicago equivalent as the far side of the moon.

"Then our first priority is the prevention of any violence," I said.

"How do you plan to do that? You're obviously not on the invitation list. If you tell the four not to go, Farooq will find another time and place to settle his score, assuming he plans to kill them. I don't even know if that fits into his plans. Maybe he reckons a bit of extortion will work. You know—leave my wife alone, hand over a large amount of money as well, or else something unpleasant will happen to you and some people you know, like maybe your wife or kids. That sort of thing."

"You have a point."

"Taken under advisement?" He wheezed a cough and a laugh down the line.

"We obviously can't simply show up in force and gatecrash the dinner party."

"No. But I'd love to see the look on Farooq's face if you did."

"If Farooq connects you with us…" I let the thought hang.

"I'm going to need police protection for as long as Farooq's alive."

"Then I suggest you go for Plan B."

"Remind me."

"Take the first train or ship out of Malacca and don't come back until you hear he's dead or serving a life sentence."

He mulled this over for a moment. "Now what?"

"We call off the surveillance and protection detail as of right now. You've done your bit and earned your exorbitant fee, which you no doubt received in cash."

"Cheque. I deposited it before the bank closed yesterday."

"It'll clear today, or tomorrow at the latest. You close your account, lock the office door and take Stella on the trip of a lifetime."

"Sounds too easy. What's the catch?"

"There's nothing to keep you in Malacca. Take your money and ride off into the sunset. Isn't that what they say in the Westerns?"

"You're giving me the bum's rush, Masters."

"You catch on quickly. I hear Australia's looking for a few good men. Perhaps Stella will jump at the chance to go home. And you'd save me weeks of paperwork of the 'Herewith the reasons why I discontinued the surveillance and protection detail on the deceased' variety."

"Heads you win, tails I lose?"

"That's about the sum of it. Any luck finding Brenda?"

"I didn't really look very hard. She'll show up once whoever she's holed up with isn't around any longer."

"Have you checked their driveways for her car?"

"Yeah. It's not parked in any of them."

"Have you checked the port and the train station?"

"No. I'll get on it."

"My guess is she's probably skipped town, heading for healthier climes. When you've found her car let me know. If you report back to Farooq perhaps he'll give you a bonus."

"Good idea."

"I'll be over after lunch to pick up all you've managed to dig up on the four men whose lives I'll be responsible for saving, whether they know it or not. They're all squeaky clean on police files."

"See you then." He hung up.

I turned to Squires. "Back to your regular duties," I said. "And I can have a shower and a shave and put some decent clothes on once I've washed this dye off me."

"I was rather getting used to seeing you as a blind Indian beggar, Sir. Perhaps you could reprise it for the next fancy-dress party."

"Cheeky young pup. Go away before I box your ears."

Back at my desk and feeling more like myself after my shower and lunch, I pondered my dilemma. A policeman's first priority is to prevent a crime taking place. If I couldn't do that, then I had to solve it with the limited resources at my disposal and bring the perpetrators to justice. Prevention was only kicking the ball into touch. The game would be far from over. Farooq could wait for another opportunity at a time and place of his choosing. If Falconetti took my advice and left town, he'd be the least of my concerns. Intervention rather than prevention seemed the order of the day.

I went to his office. Stella was everything Falconetti said she was, including the dark roots in her hair. She greeted me warily but brought me a coffee anyway. Falconetti was behind his desk when Stella showed me into his office. He waved at the only spare chair and lit a cigarette.

"The car's at the docks. I checked around. Brenda left a week ago on a steamer to Singapore. Used her own name and a British passport. She could be anywhere by now."

"England might be the first place Farooq would look, if he can be bothered."

"He holds grudges for a long time. It wouldn't surprise me if he sorts Brenda out, permanently, once he finds her."

"Australia?"

"Could be."

"I hear they're not too particular who they let in," I said.

Falconetti laughed. "Don't let Stella hear you say that."

"You know I can't let them walk into a trap."

"You'll warn them off?"

"I have to. I can't have four bodies landing on my desk when I can prevent it."

"Too much paperwork?"

"And too many questions from the Chief Super begging answers. And the Commissioner in K.L."

"A pity. A chance for community improvement wasted." He uttered a short, hoarse laugh.

I winced. I have never liked violence and its use in the prosecution of the law I considered particularly reprehensible. "I can't guarantee your safety. Farooq can wait us out. And if he ever connects you with Brenda…" He winced this time. "I can justify one body," I said, turning the tourniquet a little tighter and looking directly into his eyes. "Five might prove impossible, even if we take down Farooq and the Filipino."

He sat silent for several moments then placed his palms on the desk top. He held the position for a few seconds, as if deciding on a course of action then pushed his chair back and stood. "You're right," he said. "There's nothing in Malacca, or Malaya, for me. It's time to move on. There's a ship leaving tonight for Port Moresby and Darwin. I checked. There's a spare cabin. I'm sure there'll be something for me to do in Australia."

He didn't offer to shake hands. He looked around the small, grubby office with its few pieces of worn furniture and filing cabinets, stared out of the window for a couple of seconds as if imprinting the view on his memory, and strode past me into the outer office. I followed a few seconds later and heard Stella say, "Yeah, it's still valid. Why?"

"'Cause were outta here as of right now. We're going to Australia. I'll explain on our way back to your place." He looked at me. "You can thank him," he said. "If you feel like thanking anyone."

I felt like telling Falconetti he'd made the right decision but decided not to say anything. If he was as astute as I thought he was, he'd figure it out for himself. Instead, I said, "Don't leave a forwarding address for your creditors. It'll be all over Malacca in a day or two and I'm sure you don't want anybody finding you."

I saw myself out of the office and almost floated down the three flights of stairs with the Falconetti problem now off my shoulders. I picked up Squires at the police station and during our short drive to the Malacca Trading Bank put him in the picture.

"The Chief Super will be most impressed, Sir. He's been trying to get rid of Falconetti for years without luck. How did you do it?"

"I made it clear he'd probably be digging his own grave before Farooq pushed him in it if he stayed, literally."

The president of the bank saw us straight away. A clerk of some sort closed the door of the dark office behind us and the president invited us to sit down. A ceiling fan whirled slowly. The shutters were in the closed position allowing only a little light to bleed in around the slats. The whole office gave me the impression that Malik was a man obsessed with privacy. "Mr. Malik," I said once I'd made the introductions. "We have information that your life may be in imminent danger."

His head jerked back. "Where did this information come from?" he said, after a moment.

"From police intelligence sources. We have cross-checked and we have no doubt it is accurate."

"I see." He seemed to regain his composure. "Do you intend

telling me who is responsible for these threats? And why?"

"Syed Farooq. You have, or you will shortly receive, an invitation to dinner with Farooq. I understand he's one of your banks' biggest customers."

I was about to continue when Malik quickly said, "I cannot comment on confidential bank business, Chief Inspector."

"Of course not, but an invitation from one of your biggest customers would not come as a complete shock, would it?"

He shook his head. "I have not yet received such an invitation. And tomorrow is very short notice. I have a busy calendar tomorrow."

"I gather the dinner will be to honour you and three other prominent members of the Malacca business community."

"I see," he said, but his puzzled frown clearly indicated he didn't.

"You all have one thing in common."

"We do, Chief Inspector?"

"You all know Brenda Littlewood."

Malik's head jerked again. I knew I had hit the target. Beads of sweat appeared on his forehead. "Can I get you a glass of ice water?" he said, and half rose from behind his desk.

I shook my head. He sat down again. "It is our information that you all know Brenda Littlewood better than Mr. Farooq appreciates. Furthermore, he not only disapproves of your relationships but he intends to end them and to ensure that they stay ended permanently. The timing is inexact but our informant indicates that he will use the dinner party tomorrow as his opportunity to dispose of you all. We strongly advise you not to attend."

"And if I don't go?"

"We can't protect you forever. We have no doubt he will find another opportunity and take matters into his own hands at that time. In the meantime he'll probably let you dwell on it and sweat."

"You haven't told anyone…?"

"No. We have yet to warn the other three." I checked my watch. "We don't have a lot of time."

His shoulders slumped. He shook his head briefly. He exhaled loudly and he seemed to diminish in size before my eyes. When he looked at me, I saw genuine fear in his eyes. "I can assure you, Mr. Malik that Farooq wouldn't think twice about killing you, or anyone else, if it suits his purpose. He doesn't need blackmail money. We don't think he wants to expose you or teach anyone a lesson. We have reason to believe he wants you all out of the way."

"Brenda is a whore," Malik spat.

"I have never met the lady," I said calmly, "but from what I have heard I'm rather inclined to agree with you."

Malik looked first at me, then at Squires, then back to me. "I need protection."

"That might be harder to provide than to agree to. We don't have the manpower even if we took every police officer off his other duties and had two men with you night and day until Farooq is locked up for good."

"But I demand it," he shouted.

"I can spare one man for each of you for the next twenty-four hours, and only if you do exactly as I tell you."

Malik licked his lips. His eyes darted back and forth. He took a handkerchief from his pocket and dabbed his forehead.

"Leave here at your normal time today. Go straight home. Inspector Squires will meet you at your home and remain at your house overnight. Do not let anyone in under any pretext. Inspector Squires will follow you back here tomorrow morning. I will have another officer remain here with you all day tomorrow. We will let you know where we go from there once we have your consent and cooperation. Otherwise, you're on your own. Do you understand?"

He nodded. "Yes," he rasped.

Once we left the bank, Squires turned to me and said, "What's the plan for tomorrow, Sir?"

I stopped on the pavement with one hand on the car door. "I don't know yet. I'm hoping something will come to me after I've slept on it."

We paid a visit to the other three on our list, Stanley Burge, the American, Henk Boersma, the Dutchman, and Roopinder Singh Bansal, the contractor. Burge blustered his emphatic denials of anything and everything to do with Brenda Littlewood or Farooq, declined our offer of protection and showed us out of his house within minutes of our arrival.

Henk Boersma, as we discovered on calling at the Consulate, was in Kuala Lumpur at the Dutch embassy and not expected back for a week, so he was one potential problem we wouldn't have to worry about immediately.

Our next stop was at the cement plant on the outskirts of Malacca. Bansal greeted us with a lifeless handshake and refused to make eye contact the entire time we were in his dusty office. Yes, he said, he knew Farooq – "Who doesn't in the business community?" I decided the question was more rhetorical than if expecting an answer. He denied knowing Brenda Littlewood—in my opinion an obvious lie to judge from his body language—and avoided answering my questions whenever he could and evaded straight answers when he couldn't. I took a dislike to him which I found hard to suppress. But I had a duty to warn and protect him. He declined my offer of police protection in his home or office, for which I was grateful and he assured me he would not attend the dinner.

"His loss," Squires said as we made our way back to the car. "Our gain."

I had to agree.

Squires turned up at the office the following morning, baggy-eyed and unshaved. I sent him home and told him to be back at four. Meanwhile, I needed to come up with a plan of action, and to be honest I hadn't a clue what my next move might be. At least two potential problems were out of the way—Falconetti was on his way to Australia and Boersma was in K.L. That left Malik, Bansal and Burge. I phoned Burge, the American. His house boy answered. *Tuan* Burge had left for Kuala Lumpur by train the night before. No, he didn't know when he might return but he had taken a large suitcase with him. I put the phone back in its cradle. That made three out of the way. I wondered if I could persuade Malik and Bansal to take an extended trip somewhere, anywhere, as long as it was outside Malacca, and better still out of Malaya.

I phoned Malik at the bank. No, he had not received an invitation either at home or at the office. Yes, there was an officer in plain clothes in the outer office trying to look inconspicuous among all the Malay staff but who only succeeded in arousing attention from the bank's customers. They had agreed on a cover story—the bank was expecting a large shipment of cash later and the police officer was there, just in case. "That should satisfy curiosity," I said, and I could almost imagine Malik's smile at the other end of the telephone line. "Go home at the end of the day as you normally do," I told him.

"Lock the door and stay in until you hear from me by phone. Don't let anyone into the house. Do you understand?"

"I understand."

I phoned Bansal. He told me he had yet to receive an invitation. I asked him not to attend if he did receive one. He agreed and abruptly hung up, leaving me holding the receiver and feeling puzzled by his apparent lack of concern. The Chief Superintendent chose that moment to interrupt my deliberations.

"Anything new?" he asked.

"No invitations yet, Sir. I starting to wonder if our informant got the date wrong."

"We can't keep up the surveillance indefinitely, Masters."

"There are only two we have to worry about, Malik at the bank and Bansal, the cement man. I can't for the life of me think what Farooq's wife could possibly have seen in Bansal, other than perhaps money."

"You never know what lies in the hearts of the most mild-mannered of men, Masters. Keep me informed." He wandered out of the office. I glanced at the government-issue wall clock. It was lunch time. No doubt the Chief Super had an appointment to keep at his club where the whisky list was both long and varied.

What could any woman find attractive in Bansal? Or Malik for that matter. That Brenda Littlewood was, in Falconetti's word, a hostess, a high-class prostitute, at least at one time, I took as a given. Perhaps she'd had a falling out with Farooq and had left, possibly penniless and in need of an income, which could explain dalliances with four relatively well-off men. The more I thought of it, the less sense it made but I couldn't figure out why. We had nothing on file on Malik or Bansal and went through my notes again, looking for something, a remark, a note, anything that might give me a clue to my uneasiness. And not sure I would recognize it if it hit me in the face.

I was no further forward when Squires returned at four looking refreshed, shaved and smelling clean. "What next?" he said.

I had to admit I hadn't any more to go on than I had twenty-four hours earlier.

A few minutes before five the phone rang. I answered, uttered a single word, and hung up.

"You look like you've seen a ghost," Squires said. "What's up?"

"Did you notice a private entrance to the bank when we were

there yesterday?"

"Now you mention it, I did see a door, but I thought nothing of it. I thought it probably led to his private bathroom and toilet. I didn't notice another, not even to a cupboard. Why?"

"The chief clerk has just discovered Malik in his toilet, dead."

"Oh, Christ. How?"

"When he didn't answer the intercom a short while ago, a clerk went into the office. It was empty. He called the chief clerk and the officer who was supposed to be conducting surveillance. I'll have his job and his pension for this."

"Was it natural causes? Or what?"

"They found Malik bound and gagged, naked from the waist down with his genitals cut off. He was lying on the bathroom floor in a large pool of blood and with his femoral artery severed. He bled to death."

I looked over Squires' head to the outer office where the detectives worked and bellowed, "Brady." A middle-aged inspector rose from his desk and hurried over. "There's been a murder. Take four men, get down to the Malacca Trading Bank and secure the scene. Then bring Inspector Young, who's already there, back to this office. I don't want him looking like John the Baptist with his head on a platter. Not until I hear what he has to say. Go!" I thumped the desk top and clenched my teeth. I should never have said that, least of all to a subordinate. I'd let my anger overtake me, which was unpardonable.

The office cleared immediately. "Squires," I yelled, and almost jumped when he replied from right behind me. "Call the identification team and have them attend. Then phone the Chief Super at home and put him on notice. Use a phone from the office. I want this line left clear."

I fumed while I paced with Squires watching my every step. Forty minutes later Inspector Brady returned with a white-faced Inspector Young trailing him.

I suppressed the urge to throttle Young. "Let me see your notebook," I said brusquely. He handed it to me without a word. I could see his knees shaking beneath his trousers. He had every reason to be scared out of his wits.

"Every person who entered or left the office and the times are there, Sir," he stammered.

"Where were you?"

"I stood by the office door the whole time. No one passed me without my recording it."

"You never left your post?"

"Not once, Sir."

"Not even to go to the toilet?"

"No, Sir. I deliberately didn't drink coffee this morning. Or anything else. Not even a glass of water. I've done surveillance before, Sir. I know the drill."

"Well, Young, someone slipped by without you noticing which is why you're here. How the hell could you let it happen and lie to me about it?" Young's whole body quaked.

"I didn't, Sir. No one passed me. I stayed where I was told. I recorded each entry and exit to the office with the name and time. No one went in after three o'clock until the clerk at four fifty. He came out a moment later. A few minutes later he and the chief clerk entered and almost immediately summoned me. There's a private entrance to the office from where the victim parks his car. It's disguised as wood panelling. I was unaware of its existence. My fault, Sir. I should have checked. Mr. Malik came into the bank through the front door at ten past nine. We spoke briefly, agreed on the cover story, and he went into his office. He was in there all day. I never saw him alive again, Sir."

I digested this information. Yes, he should have checked, or at least have asked, but then again how many people have a private entrance to their office? I had to admit the thought hadn't occurred to me or to Squires, although he did notice the door to the bathroom, something which had failed to register with me at the time. Even now I couldn't picture it in my mind.

"I don't doubt there'll be the devil to pay before this is over, Young." He squirmed. "But I'll go to bat for you. It's my responsibility to make sure nothing goes wrong, though goodness knows if it can, it will."

"I believe it's called Murphy's Law, Sir. It happens all the time in the army. You'd know that."

"You served? I didn't think you were old enough."

"Royal Marines Light Infantry. I lied about my age. I volunteered in time for the Zeebrugge raid. April, nineteen eighteen." He pulled a face.

"I heard about it. Nasty show. Well done."

Young stared at his feet and fidgeted. "This must be a bit quiet for you, after that," I said, realizing I knew nothing about him.

"I like it, Sir. Being a policeman was all I wanted to do, growing up. My father was a station sergeant in Bristol."

Bristol would explain the bit of a West Country accent I detected. I warmed to him. A good man, I thought, and I had rushed to judgement. That was egg on my face. I cleared my throat. "Now, you'd better go to the toilet before you leave a puddle on my floor. Then, before you go home I'm going to need a full statement from you, including your instructions, from the moment you arrived at the bank until the moment you were relieved of your duties. Leave nothing out, understood?"

"Yes, Sir."

The Chief Superintendent arrived and called me into his office. "It doesn't look good, Masters," he said with all the cheerfulness of a gravedigger with lumbago.

"It's my responsibility, Sir. I'm not playing pass the parcel."

"Is there possibly more than this than meets the eye? Some extenuating circumstances?"

"It's a long story, Sir and once the smoke's cleared we'll get a better view."

"It's going to require some fancy paperwork for the Commissioner before it's over," he said. The gloomy basset hound-look returned.

I nodded. There didn't seem to be anything more to say. The phone rang as I was about to leave. The Chief Super picked it up and grunted into the receiver. He took a pencil and a piece of paper from his desk drawer and made notes interspersed with a series of grunts. He grunted a last time and put the receiver down gently into the cradle. I looked at his ashen face.

"Another one," he said. "A man named Bansal. At his home in the north end. A neighbour saw a man running from the house. He checked the house as the door was wide open. He found the body in a pool of blood next to his genitals."

I felt the blood drain from my face and held on to the door frame for a moment. "He was one of a list of four men we believed to be at risk of…" I searched for the word I wanted. "Of reprisals by Syed Farooq. Bansal declined our offer of protection. It's in my initial report, Sir."

"Who's still in the office?"

"Squires, Sir. And Young. He's writing up his report on the Malik murder."

"Not any more he is. Grab them both and get over to the Bansal house. Keep me posted. I'll be here all night if necessary. God knows what I'm going to tell the Commissioner."

I turned and left him alone in his office.

Bansal still lay where they found him. I stood back while the police photographer's flash bulbs popped one after the other and waited for him to finish his work.

"Get him down to the morgue," I said to Squires as soon as the photographer packed up his equipment. Squires grabbed the phone in Bansal's drawing room and placed the call. The ambulance arrived within minutes. I told the native sergeant to secure the scene with his men until further notice. I didn't know what else we might find at the scene but the fewer policemen traipsing through the place before we wrapped up the investigation, the better.

Young and I got in the car with Squires behind the wheel. "Where to, Sir?"

"Where do you think?"

"I don't know, Sir. The morgue?"

"Where the pathologist will tell us what we already know. That the two men had their genitals cut off while bound and gagged. That way they couldn't cry out for help. Then a single knife slash through the femoral artery. Death within minutes, ten at the most. What does that tell you?"

"The perpetrator's a sadist, Sir?"

"And what else? Motive?"

"Revenge," said Young. "An opportunity to settle a score."

"Four men threatened. Two died. Who wants them dead?"

"Farooq?"

"Who else?" No response. "At the very least he's got some serious explaining to do." I gave Squires the address. We arrived a quarter of an hour later at an opulent mansion in spacious grounds on the outskirts of Malacca. A voice squawked through a tin box on the gate pillar.

"Police," Squires said.

The gate slid open as if Farooq was expecting us. Farooq stood in the open front door when we pulled up. I made the introductions.

"Do come in, gentlemen," Farooq said, and gestured to the inside of the house.

The door closed behind us. If this was a Venus flytrap, we had just flown into it in search of nectar in the form of an admission of complicity, if not an outright confession. Or perhaps, like the fly, we might never emerge and our bodies never found.

"The sun's over the yard arm, I think they say in the Royal Navy. May I offer you a drink? Bombay gin and imported tonic water? We boil the water before we make the ice."

I licked my lips. I hadn't realized how parched I was. I could murder for and gin and tonic. "We're on duty," I said. "Otherwise I'm sure we'd be glad to accept."

"Then please sit down and tell me how I can help you, Chief Inspector." He indicated a sofa and several voluminous arm chairs surrounding an enormous circular brass coffee table on intricately carved legs. It looked strangely out of place in the otherwise very much Malay furniture and furnishings—mostly bamboo, rattan and mahogany. He must have seen me admiring it. "It's from the country of my ancestors, Lebanon. It was my grandfather's. It's the only piece of his I still have. The top is brass, the legs are cedar."

"It's very beautiful," I said. I turned to him. "A link with the past, another time, another place and another person. Priceless. I have nothing of my grandfather's and I don't think my parents have either."

He nodded.

I decided on the direct approach. "Two men died this afternoon, Mr. Farooq. We believe you have a connection to both, as well as two others. A third left Malacca hurriedly last night without leaving a forwarding address or any indication of when he might return, if at all. A fourth is away on business and won't be back for a week or more. They are alive, as far as we know."

"Who has died, Chief Inspector? And what is my connection to any of these men?"

"The first is Tariq Malik."

Farooq squinted at me. "Malik? I saw him only yesterday at the bank. He seemed perfectly healthy."

"He was murdered in his office this afternoon. Stabbed to death rather gruesomely."

"Oh, my goodness."

"The second is Roopinder Singh Bansal, owner of Malay Fabrications and Construction."

"I know him as well, Chief Inspector."

"He was murdered in his home in exactly the same way later this afternoon."

"We did business. That's all. I didn't like him but one doesn't have to be friends with those with whom one does business. Are you sure you wouldn't like a gin and tonic?"

I wasn't too keen on Farooq's smooth, almost supercilious tone of voice and manner of speaking, and wondered fleetingly where he went to school to learn how to speak like that.

"No to the drink, Sir," I said. "Thank you all the same."

Farooq leaned over the table and rang a brass bell. A servant appeared almost immediately. "Cold lemonade," he said. The man disappeared and returned seconds later with a tray on which balanced a cut crystal pitcher of lemonade and four glasses. Farooq turned to me. "I'm sure that you gentlemen must be thirsty after a long hard day doing whatever it is policemen do. And non-alcoholic, as you can taste." The servant poured, I took a mouthful and the others did likewise.

"Excellent," I said. "The gin and tonic can wait a while longer."

"And the other two gentlemen you mentioned, Chief Inspector?"

"An American named Stanley Burge. And the Dutch Consul-General Henk Boersma."

"I know both men," Farooq said. "Not well, but we've met several times."

"Two are dead. You are the link. It begs an explanation, Mr. Farooq."

"I'm sure it does, Chief Inspector. But have you considered that there may be other links to these men apart from me?"

"Of course." I didn't want to admit that the possibility was not only plausible but potentially damaging to my case, but I could hardly deny the obvious, least of all to the main suspect. I changed tack, hoping to catch Farooq off guard. I pulled out the photograph of Brenda Littlewood from the envelope and slid it across the table to him. "Do you know this woman?" I said, and sat back ready for the denial. I wasn't expecting him to laugh. Out of the corner of my eye I saw Squires and Young scribbling away in their notebooks like policemen the world over are trained to do and which I have made a practice of avoiding. I saw their heads jerk up at the outbreak of laughter.

"What's so funny, Mr. Farooq?"

"Of course I know her, Chief Inspector. I expect half the world knows her. It's Jean Arthur, the Hollywood film star."

"I've never heard of her," I snapped. "Are you sure?"

"Yes, I'm sure. You should get out more often, Chief Inspector. Take in a film occasionally."

I heard the mockery in his voice. I resented that immensely. Right then I wanted to snap the handcuffs on him and drag him down to the police station and interrogate him properly. I suppressed the urge, with difficulty.

"Do you have a servant or an employee named Raul Castro?" I said.

"No."

"A big man. Perhaps seven feet tall, twenty-five stone, not too bright?"

"Let me ask you a question by way of a reply, Chief Inspector. How tall are you?"

"A little over six feet two inches."

"And how long have you been in Malaya?"

"Seven years."

"The let me ask you this. You've seen Malay men. They're not very tall, are they?"

"No."

"In your seven years here, how many men of the size you describe have you seen?"

"None. Nothing close."

"And neither have I."

"He's Filipino."

"A Filipino would be even harder to hide in this country. I assure you in all my life I have never met anyone that big or tall. I can only think he is a concoction of someone's imagination."

Unless Farooq was lying, there was no seven-foot-tall Filipino by the name of Castro. I suspected my case had just taken a torpedo through its hull.

"Do you know a man by the name of Bart Falconetti, a private investigator in Malacca?" I said, realizing that by now I was clutching at straws.

Farooq's face clouded. "Yes." He almost spat. "Your former colleague. The one who shot me and sank my boat."

"I gather it was an accident, a ricochet."

"It was no accident. He deliberately shot me in the leg then emptied the rest of the chamber into the bottom of my boat."

"And you would like to see him out of the way permanently."

"He is merely a minor nuisance now that he's been drummed off the force, Chief Inspector, but I would not shed tears if he came to a nasty, and hopefully painful end. I'm sure someone will take care of him one day, but it won't be me. I have bigger fish to fry. Isn't that what you English policemen say when you let the minnows go free?"

"Which brings me to Brenda Littlewood, your wife, Sir."

A muscle in Farooq's cheek twitched. "I have no wife, Chief Inspector. My wife died of cancer many years ago. I have not remarried, nor do I intend to dishonour her name by taking another wife."

"Then who is Brenda Littlewood, your supposed wife?"

Farooq threw his head back and laughed.

"What's so funny?" If I had inadvertently cracked a joke, I didn't get it.

"Brenda Littlewood, Chief Inspector, is in real life Bertram Littlewood, a female impersonator on the London stage. He has been here for about a year one step ahead of the London police who want him on a morals charge. He stayed with me until about a week ago when he told me he was going to try his luck in Singapore. I wished him luck. I've not seen him since."

"We found his Cadillac abandoned."

"My Cadillac, Chief Inspector. I didn't report it stolen. I considered his need greater than mine. A small price to pay to be rid of him. He was an embarrassment."

"What's his connection, if any, to all this?"

"While he was here I introduced Littlewood to the four men you named. They were not ladies' men, if you understand my meaning. I understand Littlewood had relationships over a period of time with them all."

"And with Falconetti?"

Farooq stared hard at me. "I would put nothing past him, but I rather think not. If my information is correct, his receptionist provides all the comfort he needs once a month at the Commercial Hotel in the centre of Malacca."

I could almost hear and see the cogs turning, whirring and clicking in my mind. I no longer knew who, or what to believe, except that Falconetti had played me for a fool and set me up. I had fallen for it. Farooq was the real target. I'd arrest him, make a watertight case against him, a jury would convict him and he would hang. Falconetti would gain his revenge and I would come face to face with the low point of my police career. But, angered at my foolishness I still wasn't prepared to call it quits.

"Did Falconetti ever threaten you after the incident with the boat?"

"No. I don't doubt he hated me. I cost him his job and his pension, but I don't ever recall him saying he'd get his own back." He hesitated. "You might want to have a word with him, Chief Inspector. He's not a stupid man intellectually but an idiot emotionally. I'd put nothing past him."

"It's too late for that. He caught the boat for Port Moresby last night. He'll be in Australia in a week."

"Really? I saw him this afternoon coming out of his office. I didn't think anything of it. I don't know if he saw me but I rather think not. He had his back to me. He turned down an alley."

Splat! My dead brain hit the floor. Farooq had just confirmed that I was an idiot. The Chief Super would have my resignation on his desk in the morning.

I finished my lemonade. "Thank you, Mr. Farooq. You've been most helpful," I said, as I rose.

Squires and Young closed their notebooks and followed me out to the car. With the door firmly shut, I swore.

"Where next, Sir?" Squires enquired.

"The docks," I snapped in a fit of petulance. "And whatever you have in your notebooks concerning our interview with Farooq, I want torn out. If I decide that interview ever officially took place, I'll tell you what to write. Understood?"

"Yes, Sir," they chorused. It didn't make me feel any better and I chided myself silently on losing my self-control.

Twenty minutes later we pulled up at the Port of Malacca docks. The night supervisor in the port authority office came to the car as we skidded to a stop outside his building.

"There's only one ship leaving port tonight, Chief Inspector," he said in answer to my enquiry. The *Taku Maru*, outbound for Jakarta and Manilla."

"Is she still in port?"

"She's at anchor in the roads, waiting for the tide to rise so she can clear the harbour bar." He paused. "It's common practice. Demurrage."

I hadn't heard the word before. Before I could stop myself from showing my ignorance my eyebrows arched.

"It costs money to tie up alongside," the night supervisor explained.

"Did a passenger by the name of Bartolomeo Falconetti board the ship?"

"Let me check, Chief Inspector."

He returned a moment later. "Yes. See? Canadian passport. He came at the last minute and paid cash for his ticket."

"Was he alone?"

"Yes, Sir."

I thought for a moment and decided to take a flyer. Not much else could go wrong with this investigation. I had little to lose but my job and my pension which were only hanging by a thread, as it was. "He's wanted for murder. I need a launch to take us to the *Taku Maru* before she sails."

"Immediately, Sir." He turned and blew a whistle. A sailor came running. After a brief but noisy exchange of Malay, the night supervisor pointed the way. "Follow him. I have instructed him to stay with you while you conduct your business and bring you back."

I thanked him and a few moments later we were speeding across the inky water of Malacca harbour towards the twinkling lights of the only ship riding at anchor. The officer of the watch spoke rudimentary English and together with hand signals we conveyed our wish to speak to the ship's passenger, Falconetti. The officer showed us to a cabin and knocked. The door opened and Falconetti stood in front of us, blocking entry to the tiny cabin. His shoulders sagged. He took a step back without saying a word then reached behind his back and in the same movement whipped at semi-automatic pistol from his belt.

I saw a blinding flash and heard the gun go off, the deafening sound reverberating around the steel cabin. I felt a searing pain simultaneously burn my left shoulder. I staggered back and hit my head on the steel door frame. I slumped to the floor with my head reeling, fighting blackness and stars as I tried to maintain consciousness. I heard more gunfire, two, three, possibly four shots that left my ears ringing. I threw up violently.

Falconetti fell to the floor, bleeding from his chest. I reached for the door frame and hauled myself to my feet. Squires and Young stood over Falconetti, each holding a service Webley revolver with wisps of smoke still trickling out of the barrels. I heard Falconetti rasp something in his throat. With one hand steadying myself on the side of his bunk I knelt down and placed my ear close to his mouth.

"I know I'm dying, Masters. This is my dying declaration." He coughed, spraying foamy blood over the side of my face. "You know how it works." I nodded but didn't say anything. I'd never received a dying declaration before. There's a first time for everything, I thought. I hoped I wouldn't cock this up as badly as the rest of the investigation.

"Go ahead," I said. "I'm ready." I glanced up. Squires stood over us with his pencil poised over his notebook. Young had his revolver aimed at Falconetti's chest.

"I killed Malik and Bansal," he rasped. "I killed Brenda too, when I found out. Same way. You'll find the body in the woods near the railway station if you look. I left the car at the docks to throw you off the scent. Like I said, I only went out with her, him, once. He fooled me." He drew a shallow breath. "They're all queers, Malik, Bansal, the other two. Farooq. I hate queers even more than I hate drug dealers. I decided to pin the murders on Farooq. That way he'd get what he deserved." He coughed more blood and froth. "I figured no one would believe he was innocent. I figured they'd convict Farooq and he'd hang, but I couldn't take the chance of being around much longer in case it went wrong. I knew my time was up in Malaya. It was time to move on."

He grimaced and took another breath. "I chose you to put the noose around Farooq's neck." He drew me close to his mouth and whispered, "Because you're not as smart as they think you are." He turned his head away.

"Stella," I said. "Where is she?"

He looked back at me with a blank expression on his face.

"Stella," I persisted.

"She left on the boat yesterday," he gasped. "She knew we'd never be together again. I'll miss her. She had a great body, know what I mean, eh?" I think he laughed but his head flopped to one side and I couldn't hear to be sure. I felt for a pulse. He still had one, not very strong, but he was still alive. Squires and Young threw a blanket over him and bundled him in it. The crew by now had flocked to the cabin. I got four of them to take a corner each and between us we got Falconetti into the launch.

An ambulance took him to the hospital and emergency surgery.

I'd like to think Falconetti hanged, but he died on the operating table. A pity. Hanging would have been a fitting end.

The surgeon cleaned my wound—only a surface scratch but it hurt like hell—and a nurse bandaged it and gave me a tetanus shot. "The bullet damaged a lot of nerve endings but didn't kill them," she explained. "It wouldn't hurt as much if it had gone into you and stopped at the bone." She didn't mention that I might have lost my arm in the second scenario.

My hands shook and my teeth chattered.

The nurse looked at me. "Shock," she said. "I'm not surprised after what you've been through. I'll make you a nice cup of tea."
I couldn't bring myself to tell her it wasn't shock but funk. In twelve hours, I'd be out of a job and looking for work in England in the midst of a depression. I felt pathetic, wretched and undeserving of an ounce of sympathy.

The Chief Superintendent, however, was pleased that I—we—that is the police, and not a jury or a commission of enquiry would word the final report. When he left the hospital late that night after checking on my wellbeing the basset-hound-look had vanished from his face. I'm not sure, but he might even have smiled.

In the end I didn't resign. I buried the full story deep inside me instead, always afraid the truth might surface in an unguarded moment. No matter how one looks at it, this was not a sterling moment in the annals of British policing. I wanted to refuse the medal they awarded me for police bravery but I knew it would raise suspicions if I did.

Sometimes you get what you deserve.

4. DEATH BY KRAIT

Lady Millicent, Countess Tenbridge greeted me at the top of the steps of the Official Residence of the Acting British Resident in Malacca as if I were her long-lost brother even though it had only been a few days since out last meeting. Her wide smile lit up her face, her even white teeth gleamed and her lipstick was perfectly applied as if a Hollywood makeup artist had done it. Her hand touched my forearm as part of her greeting and lingered a second or two longer than I thought necessary. As I was there on official police business, she refrained from linking her arm through mine as we entered the Residence, though I wouldn't have minded if she had, not that she ever did, or ever would. But one of the most beautiful women I had ever met had that effect on me.

It was in the early part of 1932; April I believe without checking my notes. The worst of the winter rains were over by then and Malacca was returning to its normal state of perpetual dampness rather than being on the verge of floating away into the Bay of Bengal like an overcrowded Noah's Ark. I was nearing the end of a one-year detachment from Kuala Lumpur, heading up the Investigative Team in the Straits Settlement Police Force in Malacca as the Acting Detective Superintendent. In spite of its abundant sunshine, Malacca is not a cheerful place. For the most part its teeming hordes live in noisy squalor on either side of the sluggish Malacca River which meanders through the city, cutting it in two and providing a sort of filthy water thoroughfare-cum-sewer, though any similarity to Venice would be beyond fanciful.

On this occasion, Lady Millicent and I stood in the rather magnificent hall of the Residence making small talk. Except for the circulating ceiling fan, we could have been in a fine house in England. The floor was all black and white marble tiles, the walls covered in faux silk wallpaper and the few items of furniture looked as if they had been borrowed from the Victoria and Albert Museum. Classic Greek and Roman statuettes, or very convincing copies, occupied niches in the walls and several enormous English landscape paintings hung prominently on display. The effect, almost certainly designed to impress and intimidate the locals with its Great British Empire theme, looked like a cross between a miniature National Gallery and the British Museum.

Lady Millicent seemed reluctant to move on but, once the small talk dried up, she enquired into what had brought me there.

"The usual." I smiled in an attempt to remove any misunderstanding she may have read into my accompanying sigh. If her husband, the Acting British Resident, were to be believed, the native staff regularly pilfered spoons, food and other small items from the kitchens, pantries and sideboards. He refused to speak to any police officer except me (a fact for which my Chief Super was effusively grateful), believing that all natives, the *mata mata*, the local police constables included, were untrustworthy and in league with the staff, helping their friends and family members employed in the Residence get away with larceny.

Over the months I developed a trusting relationship with Iqbal Ibrahim, the head bearer, a tall, turbaned, former member of the Indian army cavalry, the Bengal Lancers, who had served in the same sector of Flanders as I during the war. He had impeccable manners and dressed as if permanently on parade in front of the King. Having once gained my confidence, he confessed that he heartily detested his employer, the Acting British Resident. The longer I knew Iqbal Ibrahim, the more I was inclined to share his feelings towards his employer. But, as any professional soldier or police officer will admit, the instinct to obey runs deep and the option of deserting one's post does not exist, even under the worst of circumstances.

Iqbal Ibrahim kept a detailed inventory of every item of silverware, ornaments, photographs, bed linen, towels, chairs, tables and lamps, in short anything not actually screwed down, in the Residence. He and the head cook kept track of every food and drink purchase down to the last block of ice, grain of rice and lump of turmeric. If anyone was stealing, it was the mice. No native employee of the Residence would dare pilfer anything. The punishment was public flogging, of which I heartily disapproved, but the British Resident was of the opinion it deterred petty crime.

On the rare occasions when I was able to connect a minor theft with a real culprit, the individual was dismissed from his or her employment, usually without a charge being laid. Without the culprit's knowledge, the theft would then be pinned on the next criminal due to be flogged and the punishment reported back to the Resident who would offer a dusty smile in acknowledgement. On almost every other occasion, the 'stolen' item would be 'found' and returned to its original place from which it had been inadvertently moved during cleaning and dusting. To keep the Resident happy a totally fictitious native member of staff would be dismissed and publicly flogged *in absentia*.

I don't believe the Resident ever suspected that it was all a ruse.

"Your husband says a silver sugar dredger from the sideboard has gone missing," I said. "One of the servants no doubt, needing to supplement his or her wages. It won't take long to flush out the culprit."

Which was mostly true.

"I won't keep you in your investigation, Superintendent," Lady Millicent said, and rang for Iqbal Ibrahim. "I'm sure between you and Iqbal you'll get to the bottom of the mystery in no time." Mr. Ibrahim appeared in seconds, almost as if he had a sixth sense and anticipated us needing him as, indeed, the head of the household servants in any properly run house would. English butlers are like that, too, so I'm told although with my humble upbringing such tales were rumor and not based on any firsthand experience. With a smile, Lady Millicent left us to our task of ferreting out the culprit.

When I enquired, Ibrahim told me that the sugar dredger in question had not been on the table at breakfast. In the opinion of the British Resident it therefore must have been stolen by a light-fingered member of the staff.

"Any ideas?" I said.

"It is in the kitchen, Superintendent Sir. It is being cleaned and polished at this moment. One of the servants removed it from the table before breakfast this morning as it appeared tarnished and not up to His Lordship's standards. If you will wait here I will bring it to you."

"Cleaned and polished like you said?"

"Exactly, Superintendent Sir."

"No indication that it was about to make its way out the back door when nobody was looking?"

"No, Sir. The person concerned brought it straight to me and offered to clean it. For some reason no one thought to inform His Lordship."

"I shall inform His Lordship as soon as he takes a break from his duties, Mr. Ibrahim."

One might wonder why I addressed the head bearer as Mr. Ibrahim and not as Iqbal. The answer is quite simple: I was a policeman. To be effective all policemen need reliable sources of information and therefore I needed well placed people like him on my side. To cultivate this relationship of mutual trust I treated him with the same respect I reserved for my equals. The British, with their haughty and superior airs, were not hugely popular in Malaya in those days—they still aren't, for that matter. The relationship between the native Malay and the British was very much one of overlord and servant, or in police terms, them and us. I have found that mutual trust is not the natural outcome of such relationships. Over my time in Malacca I relied heavily on Iqbal Ibrahim to make my job as easy as possible *vis à vis* the Resident. There was no point in breaking out in a sweat over some petty incident, usually a sooterkin of the Resident's imagination. Besides, sweating in public is most undignified.

Peregrine, Viscount Tenbridge, the Acting British Resident was a man nearing sixty, certainly not old, but more than old enough to retire from working in the unhealthy climates of the Far East if he chose. The Chief Superintendent of the Straits Settlement Police detachment in Malacca had introduced me to him when I first arrived and I had attended several social functions at the Government Residence over my time there, thereby relieving the Chief Super of what he undoubtedly regarded as a chore.

With my investigation satisfactorily concluded and the stolen sugar dredger 'recovered' and put back in its proper place, Lady Millicent asked me to dine with them that evening.

"Just the three of us," she said, pointedly. "Strictly informal. I believe Perry has something on his mind he would like your opinion on, in an unofficial capacity. Black tie. Seven o'clock for drinks first?"

She rested her hand on my sleeve. I will admit to a flutter in my stomach and a tingling in my spine. Millie had grown on me considerably during my time there and I knew I would miss her when my time was up, or hers, whichever came first. She was a few years older than I, a year or two either side of forty was my guess, but unlike her husband, the years had been kind to her. Good genes and the financial means to afford the best clothes, make up and grooming left her the envy of every white woman in Malacca.

"I'd be delighted, Lady Millicent," I said.

She shot me a stern look. "It's Lady Millicent in public. Millie in private, Superintendent. I've known you for a year. You should know by now I don't stand on ceremony."

The horse-drawn carriage dropped me at the entrance to the Residence at seven precisely. Millie as usual was there to greet me. Her hands twitched and for a moment I thought she was about to clap in her excitement at seeing me. Then the good manners of a proper upbringing prevailed and she hid them behind her back. I took the steps as slowly as I could, not wishing to appear too eager to greet her. Millie met me at the top of the steps, let her hand linger on my sleeve, something I had not seen her do with any other visitor, male or female. I admit to suffering from a little vanity at this apparently preferential treatment and it was often as much as I could do to prevent myself from taking her in my arms and carry her unprotesting to a secret hideaway. Not that I had ever done anything like that in my life, nor was ever likely to, but we all fall prey to harmless fantasies from time to time, don't we?

She led me into the formal drawing room where Peregrine, Viscount Tenbridge stood next to the liquor cabinet with a large cut crystal glass of whisky in hand. His florid face beneath his normally sallow skin suggested that this was not his first drink of the evening. He approached me and stuck out his right hand. I took it as an invitation to shake hands. I got it right first time.

"Ah, Masters," he said, and I could hear the slurring in his voice. "Good of you to come."

Until that moment Viscount Tenbridge had always addressed me as Superintendent. By addressing me by my surname he had conveyed the information that this was indeed an informal occasion, as Millie had said, but not informal enough to use my Christian name. I disliked both my Christian names intensely and never offered either except when forced to include them on official forms. I doubt if either he or Millie actually knew them. But his greeting left me in somewhat of a quandary—how do I address the Viscount in his own home?

I must have appeared a bit at sea and in something of a fog. "Tenbridge," he said, sparing me embarrassment, and gripped my hand. "Millicent insisted we invite you, seeing as you have been most diligent in running so many unscrupulous members of the staff to earth. Flogging's too good for most of them but that's what the local Poo-Bah wants and who am I to suggest otherwise? Scotch for you?"

Iqbal Ibrahim, impeccably turned out as always, poured a generous amount of Scotch whisky into a glass and added a single ice cube. How Ibrahim knew how I took my whisky I never discovered. I read abhorrence in his eyes when he handed me the drink with a slight bow. As a Mohamadan—I have always disliked the British way of referring to members of the Muslim faith as that—he must have disapproved of handling alcohol. I wondered why the Viscount insisted on a Muslim serving him. Was it ignorance? Hardly, not after all his years in India. Perhaps it was to put Ibrahim in his place and keep him there as a member of an inferior race, a reminder that we British ruled and that the Malay should not only know, but keep his place. It is small wonder why the British in their colonies failed to head up the popularity list. I allowed the tiniest of smiles to flick across my lips and the faintest nod of my head in acknowledgement of receipt of the drink.

"Millicent generally confines her pre-dinner drink to tonic water," Tenbridge said. He held his glass up in salute, perhaps in acknowledgement of his wife's choice of pre-dinner sobriety. "Her choice, of course. We can't all be perfect." He snorted, or perhaps it was a laugh. I couldn't tell, never having heard him utter either before. "Parasites can't live in alcohol, but they say the quinine water staves off malaria. Probably nonsense, of course, but who am I to disagree with the medical bods?"

Viscount Tenbridge was a slight, balding man no longer enjoying robust health, if indeed he ever had. I knew him as a man of fussy habits, one who could not help rearranging ornaments and bric-a-brac then berating the servants for moving them in the first place. He could not stand dust, which he said contributed to his asthma. He ordered the building be constantly cleaned by a small army of native staff. He suffered from repeated attacks of malaria and dengue. His world-weary face reminded me of the old basset hound I had as a child when he stared gloomily at staff and guests, probably wondering if or when he had ever set eyes on any of them before. Tenbridge avoided social functions whenever possible, snapped at staff and barked at anyone who dared make a suggestion with which he disagreed. To his credit he worshipped Lady Millicent, (his second wife, having been widowed some ten years before remarrying and who was considerably younger than he) as if she were a Greek goddess on a temple pedestal. However, she seemed as devoted to him as he to her, which I thought rather odd.

The Viscount consumed two more large whiskies before dinner. "That makes at least five," Millie whispered when he turned his back to top up his glass. "Probably six. I know he's upset but he rarely drinks this much."

I nursed the one drink, making small talk until the dinner gong sounded. Tenbridge held his arm out and Millie took it. They sailed ceremoniously into the dining room with me acting as a Supernumerary, a sort of scruffy tug weeping rust from every rivet and porthole, to their posh ocean liner. I hoped the liner was not another 'Titanic' and I the iceberg.

Claret followed a chilled, bone-dry Chablis with the fish. Tenbridge drank most of both bottles. By the time we had finished the beef I wondered when the real reason for my invitation might be forthcoming. I know one doesn't discuss business at the dinner table with ladies present but I needed at least a hint before he passed out from the effects of the wine and whisky.

By now his face had turned a dark shade of red, the colour called either 'Carmine' or 'Scarlet Lake' in a child's box of water colour paints. I wasn't sure which. What little he said over dinner made little sense as his speech had become so slurred that each syllable required an enormous effort of concentration simply to fathom it. I wondered if he had had a stroke but dismissed the thought and put it down to too much alcohol in the empty stomach of a slightly built man.

With difficulty he pushed his chair back before the dessert course. Iqbal Ibrahim hurried from his position by the sideboard to help him.

"I am not feeling well," he said, breathing heavily. "I do apologize, Masters, Millicent, but I think I should retire to bed." He turned to the bearer. "You may assist me, Iqbal." He held his arm out and Ibrahim helped the Viscount from the room.

"I also apologize," Millie said, as soon as the two left. "I don't know what got into him tonight, but Perry's behavior was completely unacceptable. I'm so sorry you had to see him like this."

I offered Millie a watery smile in return. It had been an embarrassing performance though the Viscount had one enormous advantage over me—reports of tonight's show of poor judgement would not make their way back to London. "Perhaps I should be going too," I said. "I don't want to keep you up." I rose.

"Nonsense," she snapped. "It's barely nine thirty. It's certainly nowhere near time for me to go to bed." She looked directly at me. "Unless I choose to, in which case…"

I felt my face heat as it turned red. I opened and closed my mouth several times in an attempt to say something intelligible, let alone intelligent, at the obvious implication. Although enjoying my bachelor years, as much out of choice as circumstance, and being of a somewhat cautious type by nature, I did not count myself among the eligible bachelors of Malacca (some of whom were neither strictly eligible nor bachelors). What the Countess could possibly have seen in me, a Colonial policeman, I did not know. Unlike her husband, I enjoyed neither independent wealth nor title. If my nearly eight years in Kuala Lumpur and environs had been any signpost, I did not appear to be on the road leading to any definition of greatness.

"Surely you must have guessed my feelings towards you," she said, and touched my sleeve.

I felt my legs go wobbly, the once sturdy bones now pliable and no longer able to hold me upright. I put my hand on the table to steady myself. I would have flopped over like a dying fish otherwise and made a complete ass of myself. The way things were going I was in danger of doing that, in any case. My pulse raced. In a split second of clarity, I had a vision of my pension floating downstream while I lay in bed with the wife of the British Resident of Malacca in my arms. I sat down again.

With Millie being married, if not ecstatically, then at least conveniently to a man of wealth and prestige, it would have been career suicide to blot my copybook by throwing my hat into the ring of potential suitors, temporary or permanent. A man in my position had to be sure his behavior was beyond reproach. Should word of an indiscretion reach the Commissioner in Kuala Lumpur I would most likely find myself on the next liner out of Singapore and heading for

England. I could kiss my pension *arrivederci* and with the unemployment situation in England looking grimmer by the minute, I might be lucky to find a job mending holes in the road for the local Council.

"You flatter me, Millie," I managed. "And there is no question that I…" I ran out of words.

"How blunt do you need me to be? I want you, not just tonight, but for the rest of my life. Can I be clearer than that?"

I took stock of the situation, in short order weighing the pros and cons of an affair with perhaps the most beautiful woman I had ever met, more beautiful even than Evelyn, my former Commanding Officer, Colonel Faulkner's, wife. Lucidity, like ice water, succeeded in drenching and cooling my ardor. "The only way that can happen is for me to be cited as co-respondent," I think I said, not trusting my tongue to render into formal speech what my overheated brain wanted to convey. "I have no private income and no friends in places of influence who could possibly help me if I am dismissed from the force for conduct unbecoming of a police officer. You'd be consigning yourself to a life of poverty to which you are not accustomed."

"I doubt that," she snapped. "Once Perry and I met, I couldn't shake him off. I had no idea he was a Viscount and loaded with money. When he finally came clean, I changed my mind. He paid off my then lover and helped himself to me. I don't love him. I never have. I never will, no matter how rich he is or high up the aristocratic ladder he climbs. It's all a show, an act for public consumption."

I put my hand up to stop her but she brushed it aside.

"But I will tell you this—since the day I married Perry I've not shared my bed with anyone else, and for the last few years not even with him. We sleep in separate rooms, if you must know. The choice is mutual. He no longer seems interested, perhaps no longer capable. I don't know." She shrugged. "I have spurned all offers of a liaison, as the French say. Then I met you. I've racked my brains ever since trying to find a way out of this marriage, but nothing comes to mind. But poverty doesn't scare me. I've been poor and I've been rich. If you must know, being rich is better. Wealth, and the creature comforts money buys are attractive and help one put up with a lot, but it's true—it can't buy happiness, as trite as that sounds."

She sat back, seemingly exhausted by her speech which I thought might have come from near the end of Act 3 of a school play in which she acted. Did I buy into it? Could I? As much as I would have given my right arm to spend the rest of my life with Millie, I knew the sensible thing would be to turn down the offer of a lifetime. How much could she possibly get in a divorce settlement when her husband was the aggrieved party? Enough to compensate for my lost income and pension for decades? I shook my head.

I saw her eyes flash. Anger? Disappointment at being turned down? There was no way I could tell. Then I saw her eyes brim with tears.

"Don't you see?" she said. "I love you, and I don't even know your name."

"It's because I never use it," I said, trying to make light of a serious situation while being thankful that I had had only the one Scotch, a small glass of Chablis and one of Claret. I am a big man, appropriately built for my profession, though not known for my ability to handle alcohol. What I had drunk that night was about my limit before I ran the risk of saying, or doing, something silly and probably regrettable come the morning. It had happened before. I spent six years in the army as a result.

I rose and took a step towards the dining room door. Millie followed. A servant held the door open for us. I don't know what, if anything, the man understood of our conversation. That Millie spoke so freely in front of him suggested he didn't understand English but I couldn't be so sure. Trust ran both ways, and the Malays had no reason to trust the English. What might get back to her husband before the next day was over remained to be seen, but I wanted no part of whatever eruption would certainly result.

Millie stood with me in the hall while I waited for my carriage to arrive. "Something to drink before you go?" she said.

I shook my head. She touched my sleeve, momentarily, then removed her hand.

"I don't know what came over me tonight," she said. "I was so certain you felt the same way towards me as I did for you, that I thought we had a silent understanding. I came out and said what was in my heart. In a way I think you did too."

I heard the catch in her throat. I thought I had the same feelings for her but an alarm bell kept ringing in my mind. As much as I would have liked, I resisted the temptation to fold her in my arms, kiss her passionately and swear everlasting fealty to her. However, a nagging little voice kept saying, *Damned if you do, Masters. Damned if you don't.*

How could I ever be sure of a beautiful, older woman, one who admitted to having had many lovers? How could I be certain I wasn't more than a passing whim, a plaything to relieve the boredom of a woman emotionally imprisoned for life with a man twenty years her senior? I realized I couldn't, and at the risk of antagonizing her I could never be sure she hadn't been shedding crocodile tears. And what might become of me when we approached the end of a relationship?

Against my wishes, for once I listened to the voice of reason.

"I'm not a particularly brave or bold man," I said. "But I have learned circumspection in my job. And this I know with certainty—neither of us would emerge unscathed if we were to take a relationship any further. Honestly, I can't afford the risk. And if you think about it seriously, I don't believe you can either."

The phone rang in my office shortly after nine the next morning—the British Resident had died in his sleep. As all unexplained deaths should be regarded as at least faintly suspicious until medical evidence confirmed otherwise, I would have to investigate. After all, we had dined not twelve hours earlier without any indication that Millie would become a widow between then and now.

Millie was in a state when I arrived. For once she did not greet me on the steps or touch my sleeve. Her red eyes told even the blind that she had been crying, and I was sure these were genuine tears. She kept clasping and unclasping her hands. Her face, normally immaculately made up, bore the channels of tears down her powdered cheeks. Her mascara was smudged where those same tears had run. Her hair, normally so carefully groomed, today flew away from her scalp in disarray. Even her lipstick seemed to have been hastily applied. In her present state she was no longer the most beautiful woman in the world. For once she looked her age, plain and ordinary, as if this were how she would normally appear to the world were it not for an expensive wardrobe and a case full of cosmetics. This, I decided, is what a husband or lover would wake up to every morning, and not the prettiest sight imaginable.

She collected herself as I crossed the floor of the drawing room.

Iqbal Ibrahim hovered at her side, awaiting orders. "Thank you for coming," she said.

I straightened myself to my full height and pulled my shoulders back, my bearing all stiff and military. "I came as soon as I heard, Lady Millicent," I said. "I am here in both my official capacity, and as a friend. May I express my condolences?"

"Thank you, Superintendent. It was sudden and unexpected. I certainly wasn't prepared for it. I'm not sure what I'm supposed to do next."

"No doubt Viscount Tenbridge left a will. Perhaps it contains instructions for his funeral arrangements and for the disposal of his estate."

"His personal papers are in a filing cabinet in his office. I should look there first." She turned to the bearer. "Coffee for Superintendent Masters, if you would Iqbal. And a few biscuits. I'm sure the Superintendent would enjoy something to nibble on while he conducts his investigation."

"Is your husband's body still here, Lady Millicent?"

"No. It was removed first thing this morning when Iqbal discovered him…" She put her hands to her face and wept quietly while I stood, feeling embarrassed, shifting my weight from one foot to the while I waited for my coffee to arrive. I did not have to wait long. The bearer brought it in on a silver tray and set it on an occasional table.

"I gather you discovered Viscount Tenbridge's body this morning, Mr. Ibrahim," I said.

"Yes, Superintendent Sir."

"How did you find him? In bed? On the floor? In his bathroom?"

"He was in his bed. I thought he was asleep. He was very tired when he went to bed last night. I decided to let him sleep a while longer. I returned at eight and he was still asleep. I knew he had an appointment at nine, so I shook him gently to wake him but there was no response."

"Then what did you do?"

He looked at Millie, who had stopped crying, before he replied. "I realized he had died. His body had started to stiffen so I was of the opinion he had been dead for some time, a few hours at least."

"I see." It all looked pretty clear to me. An older man, not in good health, had suffered a life-ending heart attack in his sleep. A good way to go if one had a choice.

"Then what did you do?"

"I notified Her Ladyship who instructed me to call the doctor. He arrived in half an hour and confirmed the death. His Lordship was taken to the hospital a short time later."

He would be lying in the morgue, I assumed, awaiting a post mortem, standard procedure with an unexplained death.

"Was there anything about the bedroom, or the bed, that may have given rise to suspicion that the death might not have been from natural causes?"

"No, Superintendent Sir. I escorted His Lordship to his room from the dinner table last night, helped him undress as is my duty and saw him get into his bed. He closed his eyes immediately and I had to pull the mosquito nets closed and tuck them in under his mattress. He was breathing noisily, snoring, when I turned out the bedside lamp and closed the bedroom door. His room looked perfectly normal, as I had left it when I went to wake him with his morning cup of tea at seven."

"Has anything been touched since, Mr. Ibrahim?"

"Yes, Superintendent Sir. The servants have stripped the bed and taken the mattress downstairs. It is the custom to burn the mattress in circumstances like these." He wrinkled his nose in what I took to be disgust. "They are superstitious. They believe fire kills the demons responsible for the death." He spread his hands, as if to say, *What do you expect?* "Hindus," he said, as if further explanation were called for.

He took a couple of steps back when I thanked him but stayed nearby. I turned to Millie. "When you find his will, see if a local solicitor is mentioned. If not, I can make a recommendation if you wish. Will you be all right on your own? Is there anyone I can call to be with you?"

She collected herself and perched rather primly on the front of the velvet seat cushion of the chair. "No, Superintendent. I shall be fine. You will keep me posted on any developments, won't you?"

"Certainly, Lady Millicent," I said, as formally that morning as I had been informal the night before, largely for the benefit of Ibrahim whom I did not wish to read something into a relationship which didn't exist. I left the Residence and instructed my police driver to take me to the hospital near the centre of the city. There I met the pathologist, Dr. Herridge, who had already conducted the post mortem.

"Let me show you the body, Superintendent," he said, all bustling and eager, almost excited to show me the gruesome remains.

The mortuary attendant pulled back a sheet covering the naked body of the late Viscount Tenbridge on the mortuary table. The skin had been pulled back over the face and top of the head where the pathologist had sawn off the crown and removed the brain and the pituitary gland. The long Y-shaped incision over the chest and breastbone and down the torso to below the stomach looked garish in the harsh light, the clean scalpel cuts tinged red. I glanced at Dr. Herridge, who was almost hopping up and down. I raised an eyebrow.

"Signs of a congestive heart condition, but not fatal yet. Lungs had partially filled with fluid, similar to pneumonia. We have yet to conduct toxicology tests on his blood and vital organs."

"I was with him last night, Herridge. He was drinking heavily and didn't eat much at dinner."

"So a preliminary examination of his stomach contents would suggest, Superintendent. But you've missed something."

"I have?"

He pointed to a spot on the calf a couple of inches above the ankle.

I peered closely at the two minute pinpricks. "Snakebite?" I said.

"Almost certainly." The pathologist could scarcely contain his glee. "Krait or cobra are the two most likely suspects. If I'm right, we'll know which when the toxicology report comes back. I've had the lab people put a rush on it."

"But wouldn't he know if a snake had bitten him?"

"Not if it was a krait that bit him. It's no more painful than a mosquito bite, and often a victim doesn't even know he's been bitten. A cobra's different. He would know if that bit him, unless he had already passed out from drinking."

"I've heard said a krait bite's the worst, the most excruciatingly painful way to die."

"Quite the opposite, in fact, might be closer to the truth. A krait bite is quite painless, as is the outcome, though probably not the way most people would choose to exit this world if they had their druthers."

"How long from bite to death from either?"

"The krait is one of the deadliest snakes out there, considerably worse than the cobra. It's also smaller and harder to see. It prefers undergrowth and damp earth, ponds, slow moving streams, rice paddies and such. The British Residence is near some pretty marshy ground, perfect for mosquitoes and kraits. Not quite so good for the cobra. As for how long from bite to irreversible mortality?" He spread his hands apart. "How long is a piece of string?"

"I gather in Viscount Tenbridge's case the piece of string won't have been very long."

"If I were an insurance underwriter I would decline him. I wouldn't have given him five more years in his present condition. He was a man whose body suggested he was ten to fifteen years older than his birth certificate probably indicated."

"He could have been bitten by a snake, a krait for example, without knowing it even if he had been sober?"

"Quite possibly. A stroll before dinner, what appears to be a mosquito bite and a few hours later, six at the most, the neurotoxins in the venom attack the central nervous system. The organs begin to shut down. The muscles controlling the diaphragm stop working, the lungs take on fluid and he asphyxiates. He will have lost consciousness by then and won't know a thing about it. The alcohol only serves to hasten death."

"Have you determined a time of death?"

"From his core body temperature when I started the post mortem, between two and four this morning. Had he been bitten around dusk, when the krait is waking up after a day spent dozing, he would have died eight to ten hours later."

"Not sooner, in your opinion?"

"You've probably heard the krait called Five Step Charlie, as in bite, five steps and you fall down dead. Nothing could be further from the truth, unless the victim succumbs to a heart attack brought on by fear. Six to forty-eight hours is the normal range, but that depends on the victim's age, weight, state of health and the amount of toxin delivered to the blood stream."

I mulled these variables over for several minutes while Dr. Herridge busied himself in the morgue. "In his condition," I said, interrupting him, "could he have died quicker than even the six hours at the low end of the normal range?"

"I can't rule it out, not in his case."

"He wasn't a well man, Herridge. Almost frail in my opinion. If it was a krait rather than a cobra, and the bite came, not at six, say, but a few hours later, say at nine or ten, could he still have died between two and four in the morning?"

"Feasible, yes. He weighed a little over nine stones when I put his body on the scales. A full shot of krait venom could easily have killed him in six hours, quite possibly less, if he didn't suffer a heart attack first."

"If that were the case, he could have been bitten after dinner and before he went to sleep. He left the dinner table around nine thirty. The bearer says he went to bed straight away. He even had to turn the Viscount's light out for him, as if he was putting a child to bed."

"Kraits almost never enter buildings, Superintendent. They like to live in rat holes. If they bite humans it's usually at night, when someone's sleeping outdoors and rolls over on one of the buggers. They've only just become active after semi-hibernating for most of the winter. They're at peak venom right now, and hungry." He grinned. I was at a loss why.

"Don't you see, Superintendent?"

There are times when I feel like the dullest knife in the drawer. This was one of those occasions. "No," I said, admitting defeat.

"If he was bitten indoors, it almost certainly was no accident. You could have a murder on your hands." The grin this time was one of satisfaction.

"In which case, make sure you don't throw anything out," I said, completely unnecessarily.

"I'll let you know what the toxicology results are later today, Superintendent. Expect the worst, hope for the best and start searching for motives is the only suggestion I can make."

I took that as my cue to see myself out.

I shared the pathologist's suspicions with my Chief Super when he returned from lunch, '*Tiffin*' he called it, having spent the first half of his service with the Colonial Police in India.

"Good God, Masters," he said. "We can't have that sort of rumour doing the rounds. For Heaven's sake, keep it under your hat. The last thing we need is a murder on our hands, particularly of the British Resident. If there's no other plausible explanation, we'll have to face facts and bring the murderer to trial. One can only hope it's not a white man who hangs."

That was quite a long speech for the Chief Superintendent. He slumped back in his swivel chair behind the uncluttered wooden desk; indeed, clear of any indication that he did anything more than drink tea or coffee in his office. If his worst fears proved to be true, and a white man were responsible, then the Chief Superintendent would be filing reports until past his retirement date, dealing with an angry local populace, the chain of command in Kuala Lumpur, perhaps even the Colonial Office in Whitehall itself. It would be an inglorious end to an unremarkable career.

Reading between the lines, I understood my mission.

The phone rang in my office a little after three.

Dr. Herridge sounded exultant. "Krait venom," he almost bellowed down the line. "Enough to kill a healthy man of your size, Inspector. More than enough to kill the Viscount twice over."

"Keep it under wraps, Herridge," I said. "We don't want this getting out. Should anyone ask, heart failure is the cause of death, which is not that far from the truth. After all, his heart did stop beating."

"Can't have the natives getting restless knowing the truth, you mean, Superintendent?"

I didn't like his attitude but had the presence of mind not to say so. I saw no point in antagonizing the man when I had to rely on him to keep the truth suppressed. "I'm sure you're aware the Resident was not a man greatly admired by the Malaccans. We don't need a cause for jubilant celebration with fireworks followed by general unrest. As for motive, I can think of close to a million people who would quite happily have seen the Viscount in an early grave, but I will look closer to home, and very discreetly."

"I'll let you have my report in the morning, Superintendent. In the meantime, mum's the word."

I hung up before he could complain about being complicit in a conspiracy of silence and passed on the good news to my Chief Super.

"Damn," he muttered.

"I think we can rely on Dr. Herridge to keep quiet, Sir," I said. "It would be unprofessional to blab his mouth off."

"I hope you're right, Masters. Any ideas who it could be, if it really was no accidental bite while out for a short stroll at dusk?"

"I'll gather the facts first, Sir, before I draw any hasty conclusions. If it really is murder."

I think he caught the underlying meaning of the words. He sighed anyway and seemed a little less despondent when I left his office.

I telephoned Millicent—it was strange, I thought, but I had already started thinking of her by that name rather than Millie—from my office and asked how she was coping.

"As well as can be expected, Superintendent. You were right about the will. Perry had one, recently updated with the name of the solicitor in Malacca who redrafted it. Perhaps you'd care to go over it."

"Certainly."

"Tonight? Come for dinner. We can go through it afterwards."

"I'm honoured. I mean that sincerely."

"I know you do." She hung up before suggesting a time.

I arrived at seven, hoping that was neither too early nor too late. She met me on the top step, as impeccably dressed, groomed and made up, as always. She wore jet ear rings in place of the precious stones normally in her lobes but otherwise no other outward sign of mourning. As she didn't drink before dinner, we skipped cocktails and went almost straight into the dining room.

"Perry hated Malayan food," she said. "So tonight we're having a *rijsttafel*."

I raised my eyebrows.

"I know," she said. "A celebratory meal in Sumatra. I have nothing to celebrate but I needed something to lift my spirits. But relax, only six or eight dishes tonight. And I don't want wine with mine."

"Then I won't either. It'll keep my head clear for later."

She gave me a funny look.

"Going over the will," I said, to clarify my intent.

Over dinner, I quizzed her as delicately as I could about her husband's last few hours on this earth.

"He usually took a walk around the grounds before dusk," she said. "He said it calmed him after a difficult day dealing with the locals and Whitehall. He liked to breathe in the scents of the flowers and the damp earth after a rainfall. I accompanied him sometimes, if he asked. If he didn't, I assumed it was because he had something on his mind he needed to sort out without burdening me with it."

"And last night?"

"He was out for about an hour, alone. I don't know where he went. I was in my room, getting ready for dinner." She shot me a look as if to remind me that, as it turned out, her preparations had been a waste of time. I felt the blood rise to my face. I had dashed her hopes in order to save my pension. Not very gallant of me and sitting across the table from me, she was still probably the most beautiful woman I had ever met. But she had been a widow for fewer than twenty-four hours and ought to be crying her heart out in her darkened bedroom. I wondered why she wasn't.

"Did he appear in normal spirits when he left for his walk? And when he got back?"

"He had been out of sorts for some time. Weeks at least, a month or two perhaps. He wouldn't tell me what was eating away at him. I was hoping he might unburden himself to you last night. Unfortunately, he overindulged." She stopped and I saw her jaw tighten. "Any cause of death yet?"

I felt my heart beat harder and faster. I was always a terrible liar and that night was not one of my better attempts at obscuring the truth. "The preliminary report by the pathologist says he succumbed to a heart attack while he slept. I don't expect anything more in his final report."

Millicent seemed to take it in her stride. "I think it was bound to happen," she said. "It came sooner rather than later. At least he didn't suffer. It could have been something horrible, like cancer."

I thought for a second she was going to say, *Like a snake bite.* Perhaps I looked somewhat relieved because she smiled at my reaction. "If any of us could choose, I think it would be like that," I said.

We continued the meal, discussing matters of small consequence, until I asked, "Did he complain of any mosquito bites last night?"

"He was always complaining about them. He had this thing about malaria and dengue. I've never had either and seeing how they affected him, I certainly don't want them. But yes, now you mention it, he did complain about getting bitten around the ankles and said he hoped he wouldn't go down with another attack. He said nothing more about it. He went to change for dinner and then you arrived."

"Did you go to his room before you went to bed last night?"

"No. I never do. You know we sleep apart. I have no reason or desire to tuck him in like a mother would her child." She snorted. "I'm sorry. That wasn't very ladylike. But the truth is, sleeping in separate rooms was a bit of a godsend. I shall mourn him officially, but privately? No. That embarrassing exhibition you witnessed this morning wasn't grief. It was not knowing what to do next. I was scared. I've never been a widow. Thank you for calming me down with your steadiness and advice."

I didn't know what to say, so I did the right thing and kept my mouth shut.

When we finished dinner, we went to her husband's private office. She took the will from the filing cabinet and I read it. It was not as I expected. The Viscount had signed this will in late February, declaring him to be of sound mind, and leaving the bulk of his estate to the only child of his first marriage, a son. The estate consisted of the family seat north of Sterling, in Scotland, a large number of stock certificates, and his bank accounts. To Millicent he left the sum of £5,000. That was all for fifteen years of marriage.

I gave her an enquiring look.

"I know," she said. "Not much to show for it. He told me when he made the will. He said I was a gold digger, only after his money and the title. I think he probably mentioned the lifestyle, as if living with him in India and Malaya was a lifestyle to which I aspired."

"Did this come as a surprise?"

"Not really. I thought five thousand pounds was a bit measly." She caught her breath before continuing. "But we'd drifted too far apart over the years for either of us ever to want to patch things up and continue with the charade once his time was up in Malaya. I think he may have contemplated divorcing me but I've never given him grounds."

"And you hoped I might oblige and you would be free of him?"

Twin red spots appeared on her cheeks. "I'm sorry," I said. "That was completely uncalled for. I'm embarrassed I even thought it possible."

"What I said last night was from my heart," she hissed. "I meant every word. Perry's death changes nothing."

In spite of my misgivings, I reached over and held her hand. She looked uncomfortable at first and I thought she was about to pull her hand away when she squeezed mine in return.

"I suspect he would have written me out of his will completely, had you taken me up, and I would be five thousand pounds worse off. We would have had nothing. I still don't think that's a very good trade."

"Did you know about his son?"

"Yes. Perry told me before we became engaged. I've never met him. I know his name but I have no idea where he lives or what he does for a living, or even if he has to."

"Sit down, Millie," I said, reverting to her more familiar name.

"Why?"

I raised my eyebrows in what I hoped was a *Do as I say* look without having to say it.

She obeyed. "All right. What's the good news?"

"There isn't much."

"What do you mean by that?"

"You might be lucky to see five hundred pounds, unless it's sitting in his current account as we speak."

"What do you mean?"

"Your husband was as good as bankrupt."

"What?" The surprise seemed genuine.

"I don't know the extent of his liabilities," I said, "but I do know the stock certificates he cites in his will are virtually worthless. I've been watching the stock markets closely for months. New York crashed in late October twenty-nine. London followed suit within days. These investments are in companies which either no longer exist or are on such shaky financial footing that they will probably follow the rest to the junk yard in a matter of weeks, months at the most. Even the best of them aren't worth a shilling on the face value of a pound. After his son has paid the death duties on the estate, if he can, he'll be as broke as his father. Did you ever wonder why he accepted a transfer to Malacca? He must have been close to retiring."

"Because he needed the income the position paid?" she said.

"It seems more than plausible."

"I think he saw Malacca as a demotion," she said with a sigh. "Not even a sideways transfer. It left him in a bad mood ever since we arrived."

"I don't want this to sound like a harsh judgement," I said, trying to sound soothing. "But I suspect he faced up to the truth." I paused, but she didn't look me in the eye. "A man in his state of health would hardly extend his stay in the Far East unless he had no viable option." She shook her head. "How much longer before his term here was due to expire?"

"Another year at least, if he'd lived that long. Poor Perry. He's never been in good health since I've known him. If it's not the mosquitoes, it's the flies, or the dust or the dirt, and goodness knows what might get into the water to give him…" She left the sentence unfinished, the subject of the Viscount's internal workings not being the sort of thing one discussed outside a medical examination room.

"Perry dreamed of retiring," she continued in a faraway voice, speaking as if I weren't there and she was talking to herself and needed reassurance. "It couldn't come soon enough for his liking. He couldn't wait to get away from here and back to somewhere he called clean and civilized." She sighed, rather dramatically. "But he's been away from Scotland for most of his adult life. I doubt he'd last a month back home before he froze to death or got eaten alive by midges. He talked about going stalking and grouse shooting again." She snorted. "It's been years since he did either. I don't think he'd have remembered how." The laugh seemed brittle. She shivered. It was too hot and sticky to be chilly. I wondered if she might be coming down with malaria.

"Are you all right?"

"I'm fine. Just a passing thought of Scotland. It's not my idea of fun." She stopped and looked around the room as if she were a stranger there, while she seemed to gather her thoughts. "We've only been in Malacca for a year but I like it here. I'd have been quite happy to stay." She paused again, this time only for a moment. "Malacca's not Bombay or Delhi, however hot and dusty both places are. And there's no Raj here." She sighed again, perhaps to emphasize her point in case I'd missed it. "Perry had more to do in India. He certainly had more status there."

I digested this information and paused for thought before taking a deep breath and letting it out. I could find no way to put this to her kindly. "In the circumstances, Millie, my only suggestion is that you persuade his bankers in England to write you a cheque for five thousand pounds before your step-son gets there first."

I saw her face turn white and her body tremble. Tears welled in her eyes. She dabbed at them with a handkerchief. Then she uttered a word I have never heard come from a lady.

"Five thousand pounds," she spat. "I could have bought a really nice house with that, somewhere in the Home Counties, Surrey or Kent, or in the Downs, and started a small business, a tea room or something to see me through. I could have enjoyed that, being my own boss, working hard like I used to when I was on the stage."

My mouth gaped at the revelation.

"I'm from Reading, in Berkshire. It's only an hour from Paddington Station and the West End shops. And the stage. I was an actress before I met Perry. It's not the sort of thing one admits to, given the reputation we have. Does that shock you?"

I must have had a strange look on my face without realizing it. The West End Stage. That, I surmised, was where the polished accent came from, learned for the stage, not one cultivated in the nursery, then a good boarding school followed by a Swiss finishing school before being presented as a deb.

"Bournemouth, myself," I said as cheerily as I could. "Closer to three hours from London, not that there's much in town I can afford when I go back on home leave. Not on a policeman's pay." I left it at that. I had nothing to gain by pinning down her probably fairly humble origins in Berkshire or her professional career prior to becoming a Countess.

She held her hands out, palms up but turned her head away from me and fiddled with her fingers. "It's almost as if I can see the sand slipping through my fingers." She spoke as if she hadn't heard a word I'd said.

Then she turned back and looked at me. I would like to think it was beseechingly, but I doubt it. And even if it was, I wasn't about to bite. One snake bite was one too many.

"I'll miss Malaya," she said. "I've liked it here. Iqbal is a dear. I could tell he loathed Perry but he was devoted to me. I will miss him particularly. Still, what was it the poet said, *Oh, to be in England, now that April's there*? Only it will be May before I'm back there. I really can't leave until after the funeral and the other details are taken care of. And it will be so much easier to settle Perry's affairs in London than from here."

"I'm only so sorry to be the bearer of such bad news, Millie, especially on a day like this."

"It's not your fault. Still, I suppose I should call the solicitor in the morning and start things off. If what you say is true, I don't have much time to waste."

I bid her goodnight and made my way back to my lodgings.

Lying in bed after a large Scotch I thought about what Millie had said. She seemed genuinely surprised about her change in circumstances, if not over her minute legacy from her late husband. So, what if she was an actress, good enough to ply her trade on the stage in London's West End? Still, I couldn't bring myself to believe she had been acting the past twenty-four hours. What convinced me was the way she spoke about her modest ambitions, a house near London, and a tea room. It seemed more in keeping with the real Millicent than the falsehood of the life she had led with the Viscount for the last decade of their fifteen years together.

As I tossed and turned, I kept coming back to the snake bite. Had a krait bitten Viscount Tenbridge while he was out for his evening stroll around the grounds of the British Residence and he remained unaware of it? The symptoms I observed that evening over cocktails and at dinner could easily have been those of a man in the early stages of respiratory failure and not merely from having drunk too much. He had retired to his bedroom around nine-thirty. Iqbal Ibrahim had seen him into his bed and turned out the light. Approximately six hours later he died in his sleep. Ibrahim had discovered him the next morning, as dead as the proverbial doornail.

Dr. Herridge had been quite emphatic about kraits not coming into buildings. But what if one had? What if one had made its way into the Viscount's bedroom and bitten him while he was asleep? The Viscount was unquestionably drunk when he went to bed. He would hardly be likely to feel the bite. According to Ibrahim, he fell asleep straight away and had to have his mosquito net tucked in and the light turned out by the bearer.

I thought some more while the effects of the whisky diminished and greater clarity seeped into my brain. What if the krait had been placed in the bed by someone wishing to see the Viscount dead? Dangerous, I knew, but I had seen men in the bazaar handle kraits in their bare hands. Admittedly, that had always been in what passes for winter in Malacca and during the daytime when the snakes were at their most sleepy, but still… It was certainly possible. But surely no one would walk through the home of the British Resident holding a krait or two in his bare hands and plonk it in the Resident's bed. Someone would see him and report this strange occurrence. It's not as if the servants weren't afraid of snakes. They would know full well what a krait that got angry at its treatment could, and probably would do to the handler if not to some other innocent bystander.

If the Viscount had deliberately fallen prey to a krait, without question it was murder. Which led to hypothesizing who had done it, when, where and why. Millie had not left my sight from the time I arrived until I left around ten. I doubt if she knew how to handle a deadly snake without being bitten herself. If she was like most women, she would have turned tail and run from a snake of any sort, assuming she didn't faint first. Millie, however, seemed quite content with her husband's death—at least not upset by it other than having to deal with its aftermath. She stood to gain a relatively small amount of money from the estate, enough to enjoy a modest lifestyle back in England. That is, if she could ever get her hands on the money before her husband's creditors helped themselves. And even then, she may not be able to keep it if the courts decided otherwise. She was in a pickle and might end up with nothing. At her age could she return to the stage after all those years with her name out of the limelight? Unlikely, no matter how much she might need to.

Who else might want the British Resident dead? The locals? Mostly native Malays with a sizable population of Chinese and Tamil Indians who generally lived apart from each other in their own closed communities. They kept to themselves and distrusted the other, only coming together to conduct business out of the sight of the ruling British against whom they were united in their dislike. Too many possibilities to be helpful.

I turned my thoughts to Iqbal Ibrahim. A possibility, but other than loathing his employer, he had no real motive that I could see, and would he cut off his income to see the man dead? Jobs didn't grow on trees in Malaya, the same as everywhere else. I placed him in the unlikely category. If it was murder, the method, the murder weapon at least, was known. That left two question marks—where were the overwhelming motive and a failsafe opportunity?

By three in the morning I was not further ahead in finding a plausible answer and I gave in to a fitful sleep.

Over a pot of coffee in the office the next morning I had not changed my opinion. If it really was murder, what did either Millie or

Iqbal Ibrahim stand to gain? Nothing that I could see. And if it was an accidental snake bite, everyone was in the clear. The Chief Super would breathe a hearty sigh of relief, could afford to relax a little longer over *tiffin,* and I would finish out my term in Malacca with an unblemished record—'Everyone a winner'—as the fairground barker cries.

Except. Except what? The more I sniffed, the more like murder it smelled. My Chief Super would not be happy. No one would be, least of all the culprit. I called for my driver and the car to take me to the Residence. I did not call first to advise them I was coming.

Iqbal Ibrahim met me on the steps. The *jamadar* at the front gate must have alerted the main house as soon as he lowered the barrier after I had passed through.

"I need to speak to Lady Millicent, if she's at home, Mr. Ibrahim," I said. "It is somewhat urgent, enough that I didn't have time to phone first. If she can see me, please tell her that I apologize for inconveniencing her."

Ibrahim left on his errand and a few minutes later Millie appeared, as immaculate as she usually was.

"Perhaps we could go somewhere quiet where we won't be disturbed. His private study?"

"Certainly. Can you tell me what this is about?"

"In a minute, when we won't be overheard."

She turned to Ibrahim. "Iqbal, would you bring us a pot of coffee, cream and sugar in the Resident's private study." Her voice sounded tart, unlike the Millie I had come to know. She normally spoke to Ibrahim in a kind manner, saying please and thank you as a courtesy and as a matter of course.

I let the matter drop, writing it off to the stress of the past two days. We sat on a leather settee in the study. The fan clanked overhead, swirling tepid air around us. Bright sunlight streamed through the window, casting aside the gloom of the occasion.

"Well, Superintendent?"

"I'm convinced your husband was murdered."

She gasped and I wondered if she was acting, or genuine. With Millie I could no longer be quite sure.

"We know the means. It was a snake bite, a krait. The pathologist found two pinpricks on your husband's calf just above the ankle. That's why I asked about the possibility of him saying he had been bitten by a mosquito while he was out in the garden. He might have thought that. Had he known he had been bitten by a krait he might have died of a heart attack on the spot, or shortly thereafter."

I watched her face and hands carefully for any telltale sign that might give her away as the murderer. Her cheek twitched a couple of times but her hands remained calm, folded in her lap as she turned to face me.

"What a horrible way to die," she said.

"Apparently not. I'm told it's quite painless. The bite, if felt at all, is a mere pinprick and no pain as the venom goes to work. Your husband would have passed away quietly in his sleep without knowing a thing. The questions remaining though are, who did it, and why?"

Millie drew in a deep breath and exhaled noisily. Was she angry at my suggestion that she may have had something to do with her husband's death? Was she about to confess to his murder?

"I didn't like Perry very much, but he gave me status and a more than comfortable life. That his death will probably leave me virtually penniless is unfortunate, but nothing more. I bore him no ill will. He never mistreated me. Rather the opposite. I think he almost worshipped me. The fact that we rarely slept together over the past ten years worked to both our advantages. I had no desire to become pregnant. Motherhood was never on my list of priorities. And if Perry was capable, which I suspect he was no longer, then he would be spared the need to redraft his will, which circumstances beyond his control forced him to do anyway."

There came a knock on the closed study door. "Come in," Millie called out, and Iqbal Ibrahim entered bearing a tray with coffee which he set down on the oval mahogany coffee table in front of us. He bowed and was about to make his way out when I told him to stay. He looked puzzled.

"Mr. Ibrahim," I said. "I have some questions I must ask you." I saw the frown furrow his forehead beneath the brim of his turban.

"You may answer, Iqbal," Millie said.

"Viscount Tenbridge was murdered the other night." I watched Ibrahim's face for some response. I saw his eyes widen. "It was not an accident, or a heart attack. We know the method, a snake bite. The pathologist at the hospital conducted blood tests and determined that the Viscount received krait venom into his leg, probably before ten o'clock that night and he died about six hours later. There is no question with respect to the cause or time of death."

"But I put him to bed myself, Superintendent Sir. He was not capable of undressing himself. He had drunk too much alcohol, so much he could barely stand. I helped him in every respect and left him in his room asleep before ten o'clock. I have already told you that."

"I know. I simply wanted to confirm some details." I caught myself holding in my breath. I was on shaky ground here. I was pretty sure I knew who had killed the British Resident, but not why. I took a flyer.

"It was you who put the krait in his bed, Mr. Ibrahim." I saw a look of horror cross Millie's face. This time I was sure it wasn't an act.

"I didn't, Superintendent Sir. I swear." He looked wildly around, then fixed his gaze on Millie. "I didn't. I swear."

I sat back in the settee. If my hypothesis were correct, I could make the arrest and have my number one suspect back at the police station for further questioning within minutes. If it wasn't, I was stuck with no other plausible suspect and a lot of explaining to do.

"You bought a krait from a snake handler in the bazaar. You had him put the snake in a sack and you brought it back to the house. You had planned to kill your employer in this way, so that it would look like an accident. Only the opportunity was missing. Then came your chance. You knew Viscount Tenbridge had drunk too much that evening and that he would need more help than usual in getting to bed. You had already placed the snake in the bag in the bed. When you helped the Viscount get into bed, you untied the bag and let the snake loose. You then tucked the bedclothes and mosquito net tightly around him so the snake couldn't escape except by wriggling to the top. The snake would be angry and you could count on it biting the Viscount. A thick pair of leather gloves would have kept the snake from biting you as long as you were careful to hold it by the neck. After it had done its work, you snared the snake and shoved it back in the bag and disposed of it. All that remains to be known, is why you did it."

Iqbal Ibrahim looked desperately from side to side, from Millie to me and back, as if searching for—what? A means of escape? Divine intervention? A convincing lie that might divert suspicion onto some innocent party? His eyes widened and he gulped down shallow draughts of air through a slack jaw. Perspiration beaded his forehead beneath the lower edge of his turban.

With a loud exhalation of air, he finally looked at me, eye to eye, then hung his head. "You are correct, Superintendent Sir. I used the snake to bite the Resident, but I will never tell you why. I will take that to my grave. I was a soldier as you know. That I have lived is only because others died in my place, ordered to their deaths by their British officers. I have hated the British ever since, but a man must live, even under the thumb of the British. But that is not why I killed the Resident."

He looked over at Millie. "I am sorry, My Lady, for bringing shame on your name."

I stood and reached in my pouch for my handcuffs. "I'm sorry, too, Mr. Ibrahim, that I have to do this to you, but I have my duty to perform."

"The snake is still in my quarters," he said. "I have not fed it for several days. It will be dangerous if someone finds it."

"Then take me to your room and we will dispose of it."

I dropped my hand to the butt of my revolver sitting snug in the leather holster on my belt. I decided there was no need to demean him by handcuffing him and parade him in front of the household servants. I followed Ibrahim out of the study and through the house to the servant's quarters.

On his bed lay a canvas bag. I took my revolver out and cocked it.

Ibrahim untied the neck of the bag and thrust his hands inside, thrashing them to and fro. For a moment I froze in horror, unable to prevent Ibrahim from committing slow suicide. He turned and looked back at me. He nodded, once, and tipped the snake onto the bed. I gathered my wits, took careful aim and shot the krait through the head. Ibrahim replaced the dead snake in the bag, tied the neck tight and together we left the room. There was no need to handcuff him.

A crowd of chattering servants had gathered in the servant's hall. He handed the bag to the gardener and told him to bury it in the garden. The gardener took the bag and held it at arm's length. He looked at Ibrahim enquiringly.

"A snake," Ibrahim said to the man in Malay. "The Inspector

shot it dead. You have nothing to fear. Do as you are told."

Ibrahim turned to me. "We must be going, Superintendent Sir. We have work to do."

I followed him out of the house, down the steps and into the waiting police car.

"I am in better health than the Resident," he said in English to be sure that the Malay driver would not understand. "Perhaps twenty-four to forty-eight hours for me. I will never tell why. But I will say that you are not like the rest of the British. You have always treated me well and with respect, and for that I thank you."

"And I have always respected the courage and devotion of the Indian soldier," I said, quietly.

Ibrahim fell silent for several minutes. At last he turned to me. "Do not marry her," he said. "She is not for you. You could never be happy."

Iqbal Ibrahim never said another word to me. He died of respiratory failure in hospital the next evening. There was no call for an autopsy.

I compiled my report, concluding both deaths as accidental snakebites, the British Resident's in the garden and Ibrahim's when he came upon the snake in his living quarters. My Chief Super offered a rare smile and a congratulatory handshake and invited me to lunch with him at his club. I accepted and spent the rest of the afternoon sleeping it off at my desk.

The new British Resident arrived with appropriate fanfare in May. Millie took me aside before she left. "He loved me, you know. In his own way, he loved me. I'll always have that."

I have never been sure whether she meant Peregrine, Viscount Tenbridge, her husband, or Iqbal Ibrahim, her devoted bearer. At the time I thought it best not to ask for clarification.

I still do.

5. THE DEAN VANISHES

He was the kind of man one easily forgets, as memorable as the wallpaper in an art gallery, if one remembers him at all. His physical stature and facial characteristics being completely unremarkable, he would likely have made a good spy, although certainly not one in the mould of Bulldog Drummond.

All I remember about him is that he was probably his early forties, perhaps a little under medium height, slightly built, with fine, even wispy hair receding at the temples and starting to go grey. He had about him an air of diffidence—some said of permanent distraction—as if he didn't really want to belong to this world at all, let alone participate in it.

When I met Howard Wilton, at the start of the monsoon in 1937, he was the organist and choir master at St. George's Cathedral in Penang, and I the most junior of the Assistant Police Commissioners in Kuala Lumpur. The Commissioner must have considered me at a suitably loose-end and, based on my service record to that point, just the man for the job of investigating the disappearance of the Dean of St. George's. I did as I was told, an easy habit to fall into in the Colonial Police, and went down to Penang to conduct the official enquiry. In other words, as the Commissioner hinted heavily without actually saying so before I left, my job was to snoop around and come up with insufficient facts to point a finger at the prospect of foul play. Foul play was frowned upon in the police service, especially if a white man were involved as the perpetrator as it tended tar all white men with the same brush, at least as far as the native Malays were concerned. And that would not do, not at all. Besides, it was necessary for the professions, the government, the law and the Church to be seen as above the daily fray.

Having taken my unwritten instructions to heart, I set about the investigation in such a way that we could mark the case closed without expending too much in the way of time, money or energy.

On my arrival, I set up shop in the small guest bungalow in the local British Resident's compound. The Bishop, the Right Reverend Thomas Fanshawe, introduced me to Howard Wilton shortly after I arrived as, "Our organist and the last man to see the Dean alive. That is, as far as anyone knows," and refrained from further comment, perhaps to avoid tainting the independence of my investigation. Or possibly to lay blame at feet well away from the ecclesiastical world.

When he shuffled his feet and avoided making eye contact with me, I thought Wilton seemed uncomfortable at the Bishop's introduction, and I immediately wondered what he was trying to hide. Or perhaps he was simply intimidated by my navy blue, army officer pattern police uniform, the two rows of medal ribbons from the Great War, or the fact that I stood a good head higher than he and probably weighed twice as much.

"Choir practice starts in a few minutes, Commissioner," the Bishop said in an unctuous, upper class accent. "Will your enquiries take long?"

"A few days I expect. Hopefully no more than a week or two." I turned to Wilton. "Perhaps we can meet at the Club after choir practice? Just to get the ball rolling. Background stuff for my initial report. Supper and a peg?"

"I don't drink, Commissioner, and the Dean's wife, Mrs. Butterfield, has invited me to join a small group of the Anglican Church Women for a light supper. She's very worried, naturally. I do my best to offer support, but between you and me, she's sure her husband's dead."

Unusual, perhaps, for a policeman, I am not naturally suspicious. However, I didn't like his evasive answer nor the way he deferred our meeting, though no doubt his reason for putting me off was genuine.

"Tomorrow, then? For lunch? One o'clock at the Club? Good. I'll see you there."

I spent that evening at the Club and managed to get myself invited to sit in as a fourth for bridge with stakes at a penny a hundred to keep things sensible. Nobody seemed in the least perturbed by the presence of a uniformed and armed policeman in their midst, but then probably no one there needed to be. We were all more or less middle aged and exclusively white, except for the staff, of course, and were presumed to be less inclined to indulge in a life of burglary or embezzlement than the great Malayan public around us.

The four of us made our introductions. "Dennis and Daphne Donaldson, from up Salah Merah way," the male half of the partnership announced. The third member of our quartet, a slim and rather attractive blond woman of about my own age, or perhaps a little younger—I find it always so difficult to tell with women—spoke up. "Loretta Ingles." She offered her hand. "I'm local. You can partner me. There's no point in them paying each other their share of the housekeeping money."

"He's a rum sort of chap, you know," Daphne commented when she established the truth to the rumour why I was in Penang.

"Who?" I wondered for a moment if she was referring to her husband.

"Howard Wilton."

"Ah. In what sort of way?"

She looked at me sideways after glancing at her husband across the card table. "He came back after the war, you know."

They obviously knew what they were talking about. As the outsider, I sought clarification. "Came back?"

"His father was a rubber planter, like most people around here. Successful enough when the price was up." Loretta Ingles gave a small shrug. "You know how it is."

I nodded. I didn't need reminding that the price of rubber, and the fortunes of the planters in Malaya, had been in decline for a decade or more. Nearly twenty years after the Armistice most owners still hung on, running the estates virtually on their own with a skeleton staff of local labour, desperately hoping for a change in fortune, if only because they had no other option. I wondered if the Donaldsons numbered among them.

"His father owned a large plantation up the coast, not far from us," Daphne said. "Howard grew up there, but like most of our children he went home to go to school when he was nine. I forget which one."

"King's College, Canterbury, I think it was, Daphne," her husband said.

"He's very good at music," my partner, Loretta, said. "I'm told he's a terrific pianist, but the organ's really his instrument."

"Which explains his position here," I said.

The three exchanged furtive glances. "Partly. But not entirely,"

Loretta said slowly. "He knew the Dean. They were at school together."

"I see," I said. "But undeniably a musical asset to the Cathedral and its congregation."

"He and the Dean were friendly," Daphne said, now that the gossip had gathered steam. "But not close, not as close as some old school chums. And I think Howard—that's Wilton's Christian name—preferred it that way." She looked around the table for support. "He kept his distance. The Dean was a school prefect. I'm not sure if Wilton was his fag, but they're only a few years apart in age."

"You speak of the Dean in the past tense," I said.

I saw Dennis Donaldson shift his weight on the seat of his chair and wondered if it was with unease.

"He's dead," Donaldson declared. "He went up country with Wilton and didn't return. Is there any other reasonable explanation for his continued absence?"

"That's what I'm here to find out. And if the Dean really is dead, what were the circumstances."

"We all have our theories, but if you ask me, two minus one leaves one. I don't think you'll have to look too far, Commissioner."

Three whiskies and a gin and tonic arrived at that moment, and I let the matter drop.

"If you don't mind my saying," Donaldson said as he shuffled, "Wilton's not the strongest of characters around."

"A bit of a fair-weather sailor," Daphne said.

Loretta lowered her voice. "I heard he was a conscientious objector in the war." The other two nodded in agreement.

"But unconfirmed, and not something a gentleman would ask about," Donaldson said.

"And no doubt he had his reasons," Loretta said, though the manner in which she gave her pronouncement suggested that she didn't really believe he was anything but a coward.

"I met him briefly earlier," I said. "He had to rush off to choir practice before we could do more than exchange pleasantries."

"That's more than he does with most people," Loretta said.

"Until he knows someone well," Donaldson chipped in. "He's not a bad sort really. Just a bit standoffish with certain people."

"As if he has encountered a bad smell. He's friendly enough with the Dean's wife," Daphne said. "And he gets on all right with the Bishop, of course. And the Dean and one or two other people."

"But not with any of you?"

They looked at each other uncomfortably. "We tried," Loretta said after a short pause.

"Especially when he first returned to Malaya," Daphne said. "He seemed lost. After a while we gave up trying. He seemed immersed in his music, and in himself."

"But Daphne and I are only in Penang once or twice a month," Donaldson said. "So we don't know him that well. This is our last visit before the monsoon starts in earnest. We go home tomorrow and hunker down."

I nodded. I'd been in Malaya long enough to know what the roads were like during the rainy season.

We played our hands. Daphne kept score—in my brief exposure to her I thought of her as the type of woman who would always keep score of everything, including her husband—and while the Donaldsons chattered on about Wilton I watched Loretta's reaction. I sensed she blushed. It was warm in the club but the punkahs were pushing the air around, though admittedly without noticeable effect on the temperature. In any case, we'd all lived in Malaya for long enough that we were used to the heat and the humidity so I doubted if it were the heat causing the colour to rise to her cheeks. I looked directly at her and raised an eyebrow. The blush—it was definitely a blush—deepened.

"I knew Howard when I was a child," Loretta said, fanning her face with her cards. "We didn't exactly grow up together, but my parents owned the plantation next to his parents'. I thought no more of it when he went back to England. I must have been five or six then." She looked at the Donaldsons. I caught their 'Carry on,' glance. "Then a few years ago he returned to take up his position as organist." She offered a weary sigh. I raised my eyebrows again, a tactic I have used to good effect when questioning suspects, inviting them to spill the beans while remaining empathetic to their plight and the reasons for justifying their slight error of judgement.

"It's no secret I'm divorced, Commissioner," she blurted out although I hadn't enquired after her marital status, "and it's pointless denying why. Penang's too small a place to keep secrets but more than big enough to start and expand rumours."

"For better or worse, we all know each other's business, I think is what Loretta's implying," Daphne said.

Loretta nodded. "At one time I had a bit of reputation. Overblown, of course."

"Of course," Dennis Donaldson said, hastily, before catching a stern look from his wife.

"It happens sometimes in a bad marriage," Daphne said, quietly and looked directly at her husband. The penetrating stare made me wonder if he had had occasion to seek the company of a divorced woman several years younger than himself. "And rightly or wrongly we women bear the brunt of it."

Loretta nodded. "But when Howard returned I thought he might be my best chance at happiness." She hid her mouth behind her card fan and glanced at each of us in turn before she laid her cards face down on the table in front of her. "Or at least stability of a sort. Security. He's not a bad sort, really. We were both single, or in my case divorced, and white. He had a job, though it didn't pay much as you can imagine, but better than nothing, which is what too many of us around here have to live on."

"Quite," Daphne said. She drew a breath. "I'm sure no one would have blamed you if you had managed to get together." She sounded as sincere in her sympathy as a shark about to eat a turtle.

"He didn't seem interested," Loretta said, with a shrug. "I may be wrong, but perhaps my reputation preceded me and he shied off."

"I wouldn't put it past him if he bats for the other team," Donaldson said.

"I wouldn't go quite that far, Dennis," Loretta said, but her face, if anything, took on an even deeper shade of crimson.

"I would. It's bloody obvious he's not a ladies' man. That leaves us to draw only one plausible conclusion, which could explain why he either chose not to fight, or the army turned him down. For obvious reasons. I can't imagine it was roses and Champagne for him in jail. I've heard about things that happen to conscies and Nancy boys on the inside. Let's leave it at that."

We played our hands out. In the end, Loretta Ingles and I went down rather heavily after some enthusiastic but badly over-optimistic bidding on my part. Fortunately, we weren't playing for the Crown Jewels. With the crowd in the club thinning out, given the lateness of the hour I handed over our evening's losses to the cheerful

Donaldsons and bade them a safe journey home in the morning.

Over drinks with Loretta Ingles at the bar after the Donaldsons left I mulled over what my bridge companions had said, but little more than speculation was on the menu. It was pointless asking Loretta for theories on the Dean's disappearance and probable death. That would have to come from Wilton himself, if he chose to disclose the truth, or fed me whatever he wanted me to believe. It was my job to sift through the evidence, such as it was, and separate fact from fiction if they were not one and the same. I also needed to interview the Dean's wife—often a mine of information in disappearance cases—but it was now after eleven and far too late to go calling on the probably recently widowed doyenne of the Anglican Church Women.

"Not much of a partner tonight, Mrs. Ingles," I said as I pushed myself away from the bar. "Perhaps you'll have better cards tomorrow, or a better player as a partner."

"Part of the fault was mine, I'm sure, Commissioner." She needn't have said it but I admit it made me feel a little better. She wasn't a bad player by any means, about on a par with me, but neither of us a match for the Donaldsons.

"I doubt that, Mrs. Ingles. I should have drawn trumps when I had the chance rather than go two down, doubled and vulnerable." I smiled, playing the role of the good loser. "At least it was only small change."

"It's Loretta, Commissioner." She rested her fingers on my tunic sleeve for a second. "They're good, almost professionals. They don't need the money either. They got out of rubber years ago. They're into palm oil now, though God knows what it's used for, and coining it in hand over fist by the looks of the car they drive."

"Speaking of which, how are you getting home?"

"I don't live far, Commissioner. I walk a lot."

"I won't hear of it. I have a car at my disposal, though alas no driver at this time of night. I'd be happy to drive you home."

I wondered if it was the whisky talking, but by that time I was beginning to look at Loretta Ingles without the scales of early prejudice clouding my eyesight. Still, I cautioned myself that, with her self-confessed reputation as a divorcee, which could only lead one to draw the obvious conclusion as to the reasons, it would only lead to trouble for me if any hint of impropriety on my part should get back to the Commissioner in K.L. He would be unlikely to write it off as a minor lapse in judgement and could easily invoke the morals clause in my terms of service with the Colonial Police. Mentally standing back as I examined the evidence, I doubted if any entanglement with Loretta Ingles would serve much purpose beyond burnishing her *curriculum vitae.* And that, I decided, would not be worth my sailing on an early ship back to England with a stain on my reputation, no character reference from the Commissioner and little chance of employment of any sort at home.

I dropped her off at her tiny bungalow and waited until she had let herself in through the front door before I drove back to my own temporary accommodation. In Penang, as in all of Malaya, like the peacock of Greek mythology, some eyes never close. My employment prospects I did not I care to contemplate, had I accepted her invitation to a small nightcap, and I congratulated myself that I had not drunk enough that evening to let common sense take a back seat.

St. George's Deanery lies only a few steps from the Cathedral and within the precinct itself, and I made my way over there the next morning to call on Mrs. Butterfield, the Dean's wife. As I passed the Cathedral's north door, I heard the sound of the organ. Howard Wilton, no doubt, in full flight with a Bach partita, or something equally complex in both form and execution—and bereft of any tune, so far as I could tell.

Mrs. Butterfield seemed flustered when I called without first announcing my intention to do so. She pushed a stray strand of hair off her forehead and tucked it behind an ear before smoothing the front of her cotton frock. She was a woman in her mid to late thirties, I guessed, slim and quite good looking in an unostentatious sort of way, with skin that still had, for most white people in Malaya at least, an envious paleness to it. It suggested someone who had only recently arrived in the peninsula, or who took great pains to stay out of the sun.

I heard children's voices coming from the darker depths of the two-storey house, followed by a thump and crying.

"Excuse me," she said, and turned her head away to gauge the source of the noise and its potential need for maternal intervention. "I'll be right back, Commissioner. Please come in a take a seat in the drawing room."

She hurried off, leaving behind a trace of perfume in the still air and the slight rustle her cotton dress made with each firm stride. She returned a few minutes later, the domestic crisis smoothed over for the time being and with her light brown wavy hair now held in place with a pin of some sort. I noticed that the ends of her hair were streaked blonder than the rest and wondered if she dyed her hair, but concluded, on little or no evidence that she was not sufficiently vain, nor old enough, to resort to such subterfuge. Besides, it probably would not go down well with the women of the congregation if a clergyman's wife, instead of remaining a prim model of ecclesiastical propriety, sought to pretty herself for only one reason. My mind immediately lit on Loretta Ingles. I forced myself to concentrate on my reason for being in the Butterfield home.

"I'm Valerie Butterfield," she said, when she returned, with the domestic crisis under control, "as I'm sure you already know or you wouldn't be here."

I thought her tone a trifle snippy. We took seats opposite one another in the comfortably furnished drawing room, waiting for the house boy to bring iced coffee. "The Bishop no doubt told you that Edgar, my husband, is the Dean not only of St. George's, but also of all the parishes in the area, including a couple of churches up country."

I smiled encouragingly, hoping she would continue without verbal prompting. My silence succeeded.

"As the organ here needed a little repair work, he and Howard, the organist, decided to pay their annual visit to the most northerly parish in the Diocese much earlier than usual. Howard agreed it would be a good time to go while someone who knows about repairing sticky stops, or a syphon, or whatever it was, fixes the problem." She waved a hand in a dismissive gesture. "Howard's very fussy about his organ, you know. They have a harmonium up there in the jungle—way below Howard's abilities—but no one there knows how to play it, so for one Sunday a year they get a musical accompaniment."

"When do they normally leave for their visit?"

"After the monsoon because of the difficulty getting there during the rainy season. This year they set off in time to get back before the rains arrived in earnest and made the journey all but impossible."

At that point two young boys, perhaps a couple of years apart in age, tore into the room and interrupted our *tête-à-tête* by imitating cowboys and Indians. When she had finished taming the Wild West, I invited Mrs. Butterfield to continue.

"There's a Land Rover that takes them part of the way, as far as the Donaldson's plantation—I gather you played bridge with them last night—then a small launch carries them another day and a half upriver to the village."

"Word travels fast around Penang," I said.

"Just as fast as it does in Kuala Lumpur, I'm sure, Commissioner. I hear the Donaldsons are good players. I hope you didn't lose too much."

"Loose change." I smiled, as if the amount meant nothing.

"They don't need it, but it prevents one side from hogging the cards all evening. But Loretta Ingles can ill afford to lose anything. I don't know why she plays with them. She's not nearly in their league."

"In the final rubber we went down rather badly, thanks to my over-zealous bidding. I made sure Mrs. Ingles didn't suffer as a result of my misreading the bidding convention."

"That's very kind and thoughtful of you, Commissioner, but unless you have a private income, you might want a better player as a partner. That is, if you intend staying in Penang for more than a night or two. Then again, perhaps it's because with her reputation no one's wife will let her husband partner her."

It was time to bring the conversation back on track before the claws raked Loretta Ingles' back any further. "When your husband left for the trip, was there anything on his mind? Anything unusual, strains or stresses that you couldn't account for, or anything he might have mentioned?" I was tempted to ask if she thought the Dean might be entangled in some sort of affair with Loretta Ingles, but thought better of it. I was hardly likely to receive an honest answer in any case and I'd probably be shown the door.

She pondered my questions for a moment. "Nothing I can think of. He has an occasional drink before dinner but otherwise he's pretty abstemious. He might have been a little preoccupied, now that you mention it, but nothing I haven't seen before when he's pushed for a sermon topic and nothing comes to mind. That sort of thing."

"There's nothing you can think of that would make him decide to walk off into the jungle on his own without telling anyone?"

"No. Edgar seemed perfectly normal when he left. He was quite looking forward to the trip. He says these excursions are a chance to escape his obligations as Dean and become a parish vicar again, at least for a few days. And it gives him an opportunity to talk church politics with Howard without being overheard. You know there's not a secret worth keeping in Penang."

I smiled and nodded. "Your husband's been gone for over two weeks, Mrs. Butterfield," I said slowly, licking the imaginary tip of an imaginary indelible pencil and holding it poised over a blank page in my imaginary notebook. "Yet you don't seem overly upset that he may not return."

I saw her take a deep breath and hold it for several seconds before exhaling noisily. Then she put her hands over her face and burst into tears. "I'm trying to hold it together," she sobbed. "But I know in my heart he's dead. He's never going to return. They'll never find his body. He'll never get a proper Christian burial, I know it."

I resisted the temptation to wrap my arm around her shoulders and dry her tears. Instead, I waited until the floodgates closed and she finished dabbing her eyes and wiping her nose with a delicate lace handkerchief.

"I've prayed night and day for Edgar's safe return, but as each day went by it seemed less and less likely I'd ever see him again. Until now. When they told me they were assigning a senior police officer to investigate the case, I knew I'd never…" She burst into another flood of tears which I also took to be genuine, having no reason to assume that Valerie Butterfield had ever earned a living on the stage or the silver screen. I waited her out. I still had almost two hours before my lunch appointment with Howard Wilton.

"Thus far we've established that your husband did not seem overly preoccupied or tense before he left, that in fact he was looking forward to discussing the state of the organ fund and the need for repairs to the Cathedral roof, things like that."

"Yes." She offered a wan, watery smile that matched the state of her eyes.

"Did he leave a letter behind, a note, anything, before he left?"

"Nothing. He kissed me goodbye. He and Howard climbed into the Land Rover with the driver and they set off as if they hadn't a care in the world."

"An indelicate question, Mrs. Butterfield, if I may."

"What's that, Commissioner?" If her eyes had shutters, they just snapped shut.

"A Cathedral Dean is not the best paying occupation in the world. Does your husband have a private income?"

She hesitated. "Yes. And before you ask another indelicate question, it's about a thousand pounds a year. He's the third son, you know. He's lucky even to get that from his father's estate after his two older brothers helped themselves. There's also a trust fund for the boys' education, enough for boarding and tuition fees for the two of them if we don't send them somewhere expensive."

"King's College, Canterbury?"

"Like Edgar? Heavens no. Their fees are far too expensive for us. They're down for Bloxham. Even that might be pushing it unless we can obtain a grant or a bursary of some sort."

"You said a thousand a year, on top of his stipend?"

She nodded. "It's enough to live relatively comfortably here with our housing free." She waved a hand around to indicate the well-furnished drawing room. I assumed the rest of the house lived up to the same standards of creature comforts, though I chose not to enquire. "Heaven help us if we have to move back to England with the cost of everything there these days."

"Have you and your husband been in Penang long, Mrs. Butterfield?"

"Six years. The boys were born here. Edgar's only recently turned forty-five. He has a long time to go before he can retire anywhere, let alone England."

"Does he have any life assurance?"

She looked at me with a puzzled frown. "I'm sure he does, through the church," she said slowly, "but I can't imagine it would be for more than a few hundred. A thousand at most. Why?"

"If you husband decided he wanted to disappear, for whatever reason, he would need money. He could have cashed in his life assurance for however much the surrender value is. Do you have access to your bank account and transaction records?"

"I know he keeps a cheque book in the bureau drawer but he does the monthly reconciliation. I never see it. And what do you mean by disappear?"

"Perhaps he decided to leave the church. A crisis of spirituality. A loss of faith that underscored the hypocrisy in continuing here as Dean. A problem with alcohol. Or debts he couldn't repay. Any one of a number of reasons."

"Including an affair with the Ingles woman, you mean?" I noticed she didn't use Loretta's first name this time.

"A possibility, though having only just arrived and being unaware of who's who in Penang, I hadn't considered it. But now you mention it, I shall file it away for future consideration."

"She's a…, a tarnished woman, Commissioner. And she's as good as broke, financially as well as spiritually. I wouldn't put it past her to dig her claws into any vulnerable man for whatever she can gain. Any more than that I will not say."

"Nevertheless, that's quite the character assessment."

"I think you mean assassination, Commissioner. And deservedly so, in my opinion. And in the opinion of many others." She snorted indignantly and took another of her deep breaths. "Edgar would have nothing to do with her. He wouldn't give her the time of day and he resolutely denied that his disapproval was undeserved and far from Christian."

I rose to leave. "I'm having lunch with Howard Wilton," I said, hoping, and failing, to spur some reaction. "I hope he'll have something useful to say. After all, as far as anyone knows, he was the last person to see your husband alive."

Valerie Butterfield seemed on the verge of saying something, then she put her hand over her mouth. The moment passed. She held her hand out and I shook it. I found her handshake surprisingly firm for someone as slim and as slight as she. I thanked her for the coffee and the conversation and told her that I hoped we'd see each other again soon. I offered her an encouraging smile and walked the few steps to my waiting car. As I took my seat in the rear of the Wolseley, I switched on my police officer's mind and pondered what additional information I might have elicited had I had the foresight to press on with my questions. However, I received the impression she had decided that she wasn't going to say any more at this time. When I had more to go on, I could always return. Perhaps I might catch her in a contradiction in an unguarded moment. Or she might say something unknowingly that could shed new light on my investigation, which I had to admit had not yet progressed very far.

Lunch with Wilton at the Club proved congenial enough at the outset, given our relative positions in the investigation. The place was pretty well deserted at lunchtime on a week day, and I made it clear at the start that I was on a fact-finding mission and needed his help in getting to the bottom of the Dean's disappearance. Nonetheless, he seemed guarded when answering my questions and I gained a new respect for dentists who pull wisdom teeth for their livelihood.

Wilton told me that the Dean had been in fine form the Friday morning when the two of them, plus their driver, left Penang and took the ferry for the short ride to Bukit Mertajam on the mainland. He seemed not in the least tense or worried about anything, domestic or ecclesiastical on the drive to the Donaldson's plantation near Salah Merah. They had lunch with Dennis and Daphne and instructed the driver to return to pick them up around noon on Tuesday. They transferred their luggage to the motor launch they had hired for the return journey and set off later that afternoon. The shallow draught boat was beyond elderly, neither large nor comfortable—probably no more than twenty-four feet from stem to stern—and powered by a wood-fueled boiler which the pilot kept stoked from a dwindling supply stacked next to the door of the firebox. A canvas awning on rickety poles covered all but the foredeck and kept the sun off during the hottest part of the day.

With the launch anchored in mid-stream overnight in an attempt to avoid the worst of the mosquitoes, he and the Dean slept as best they could on thin and lumpy mattresses. The river was quite wide at that point, perhaps a quarter of a mile from the middle to each bank, and still shallow with mud and sand bars plentiful before the rains started in earnest at the headwaters a couple of hundred miles upstream. After another singularly unexciting day spent staring at the river banks and the jungle on either side, they arrived at their destination on Saturday evening, a village of a few hundred native Malays with a small, white clapboard church whose spire rose high above the roofs of the mostly communal huts.

The Dean presided over the Eucharist service the next morning, Sunday, while Wilton played the wheezy harmonium, and the villagers feted their guests with a sumptuous celebratory dinner that night. Wilton and the Dean stayed for a second night in their one-room, thatched roof and rattan walled hut before their scheduled departure for Salah Merah and ultimately to Penang on Monday. "We slept in our clothes," Wilton said. "It wasn't the best arrangement but we had made the trip several times before and decided there was no need to travel with a lot of unnecessary stuff."

He said he fell asleep almost immediately and slept soundly until the Dean woke him briefly when the latter rose from his sleeping mat during the night, "I presume, to relieve himself outside. There's a communal latrine, but I doubt if he would have bothered to cross the compound to use it, especially in the rain, and it's awfully smelly, you know. I heard rain, either on the roof or on the ground, I don't remember which and it didn't seem remotely important at the time. I thought nothing of it and I fell asleep again almost immediately. I only discovered the Dean's absence in the morning. I didn't think anything was amiss. I presumed he had risen early and had business to attend to at the church or with the village elders and had neglected to tell me." After having breakfast with some of the natives, Wilton packed his small valise and prepared to leave.

When the Dean failed to appear by mid-morning, and as no one knew where he was and denied seeing him after he retired for the night, Wilton became concerned. By noon he was decidedly worried and arranged for a search party. With no sign of the Dean by nightfall they called off the search. By this time Wilton had started to panic and hardly slept at all that night, lying awake instead, listening to the heavy rain's muted drumming on the thatch above his head. Another muddy search for the Dean the next morning also failed to turn up any clues.

The villagers combed the area all around the village but with the vegetation so dense on the jungle floor it was all but impossible to see more than a few feet in any direction. A man could remain hidden if he chose for as long as his food and water lasted. But there are a hundred ways to die in the jungle—malaria, snakebite, even blunder into a pit or a swamp. It rained again that night. By now, the launch pilot had become anxious about delaying the return journey any longer and all but threatened to leave without either Wilton or the Dean. In any case Wilton knew the pilot was right—they had to leave before the rains made the river unnavigable for several months. Reluctantly, he loaded his and the Dean's luggage into the launch and they cast off.

"And I have not seen the Dean, or heard a word from the village," Wilton said with a tone of what sounded like genuine regret in his voice. "Though it wouldn't seem likely that word would filter through until after the monsoon in any case."

"What do you think happened?"

"I've asked myself the same question hundreds of times. To be perfectly frank, I don't know."

I hoped he'd been perfectly frank with me up till now but thought better than to admit it. "Do you think he deliberately went missing? Or could someone have made certain he stayed missing?"

I saw Wilton blanch. Then his face turned red. He took a long swallow from his glass of water before responding.

"I don't think he had any enemies, if that's what you're implying, Commissioner."

"I'm keeping an open mind, Wilton, as I must when conducting an investigation. And I must pursue all avenues." I waited for this to sink in. "You don't think anyone was paid to bash him on the head and drag him, or his body, into the jungle where it would rot in a matter of weeks."

"No. And if you're suggesting I did, I didn't. I have no reason to wish him dead. We have a cordial relationship. I've known him off and on since we were at school together."

"King's College, Canterbury, I gather from Mrs. Butterfield. Or perhaps it was the Donaldsons. I forget which. A Cathedral school. And you were his fag?"

"It was King's, Commissioner. And the Dean was in my house at school but I was never his fag, as you call it. I despise the term. It has such unfortunate connotations. I prefer to call him by what he is, a junior boy used by the seniors as a personal servant. I doubt that fagging serves any purpose beyond making a junior thoroughly miserable. In my opinion the system should be banned."

"I remember my days as a house junior without great affection," I said. "The grammar school I attended as a day boy didn't allow fagging, but life was bad enough without that."

It's always important to try to establish a common bond with a witness, or a suspect, early in an investigation. Confession, if one should be forthcoming, is more easily imparted to someone with whom the confessor has a shared experience, a sympathetic ear, and an understanding.

Wilton didn't bite.

I tried a different approach. "How well do you know Mrs.

Butterfield?"

He hesitated. "I've known Valerie Butterfield for a little under five years, basically since I arrived as organist and choir master."

"I asked how well you know her, not for how long."

I saw his face redden, and I wondered if it was from anger at the impropriety of my question, or with shame at being discovered that he had something to hide.

"Not that well, considering how long I've been in Penang. Our paths cross, obviously. They invite me to lunch after the Sunday service from time to time. I would like to reciprocate, but I neither cook nor have a place big enough to entertain. The best I can do is to invite them here."

He eluded the bait and the hook skillfully. I tried again, more directly this time. "Do you not see each other socially? You and the Dean, I mean. With or without his wife."

"Not often. We have a professional relationship. I probably see the Bishop and his wife socially more frequently than the Butterfields, and that's not often. Again, I have a professional relationship with the Bishop."

"And how about Mrs. Butterfield?"

Wilton's face reddened further. "I'm not sure I like your implied suggestion, Commissioner."

"Whether or not you like it, Wilton, it begs a reply."

Wilton cleared his throat and lowered his voice. "I might see Valerie on her own once a month, if that. And only for a brief period of time, a few minutes at most, and never alone. Her children, their amah or their house boy are always present when I call. Tongues wag in Penang. I would not wish to give anyone the opportunity to draw a wrong conclusion, as they might if you were to drive the Ingles woman home again after an innocent bridge evening here. Any hint of impropriety would almost certainly cost me my livelihood and a one-way ticket out of Malaya."

That made me think. Given his position within the church, Wilton's morals clause was obviously understood. Mine, on the other hand, was written into my employment contract. I made a mental note to be cautious about any contact with Loretta Ingles outside my professional capacity as the investigating officer. Not that I had any intention or need to see her socially, but a lie would be believed by the Commissioner in Kuala Lumpur as readily as the truth.

"But you do see her from time to time."

"Yes. I said I do. The Dean knows. I have nothing to keep from him. I doubt if Valerie does either."

It didn't take a genius to figure this snippet to be a barefaced lie, but I suspected the Dean wasn't about to emerge from the jungle to confirm the truth or protest the lie. Perhaps I'm biased, or occasionally suspicious, but I believe it's within our human nature to be devious when it suits our purpose, even with a spouse or loved one. But if Mrs. Butterfield were discovered indulging in a liaison outside her marriage, I had to agree with Wilton that the Bishop would make sure her husband would never preside over another service in his See. And if an affair were with Wilton, he would get the chop in short order too.

"You're probably right," I said with a straight face. "I'm not married and therefore have no one from whom I should keep secrets." I paused, long enough to give Wilton time to think. "I spoke to Mrs. Butterfield this morning. She struck me as being quite a private person."

"She is, though I've no reason to think she wouldn't be open with the Dean. They seem to enjoy a happy and loving relationship. Two fine healthy young sons can attest to that."

"Who seem to enjoy playing cowboys and Indians."

"We get a steady diet of Hollywood Western film shows at the Club. The boys lap them up. It's only to be expected at their age."

Now that Wilton seemed more relaxed, I changed tack again. "What will happen to Mrs. Butterfield if her husband doesn't reappear?"

I saw Wilton flinch, no more than a minute twitch of a facial muscle and a slight uncomfortable shifting of his body on his chair.

"They will appoint a new Dean, and Valerie will probably return to England."

"She has already expressed a wish not to do that," I said. "She says the cost of living there is outrageous. Still, she could always remarry. She's young enough. It's not like she's in her fifties and without prospects of love, or even a second husband for comfort and security. And she's certainly an attractive woman. I can't see her staying a widow, if that proves to be the case, for long."

Wilton sat opposite me with his lips in a tight, straight line. I knew I had managed to needle him. I waited for the pressure of silence to provoke a response.

"She's all of those things, Commissioner," he said eventually. "And if you spend the next few years in Penang you would probably get to know her better. It takes a long time for her to open up. She led a sheltered life as a child. Her father was a Canon. She's spent almost her entire life around the church. I don't see her throwing off those traces in a hurry. But I might be wrong."

"The complete opposite of Mrs. Ingles."

"That woman!" he burst out. I sat back and waited for the water to flow through the sluice gate. "Spreading lies and slander about me ever since I refused to surrender to her questionable charms. I'm not like that, Commissioner. Not what she implies. God forbid that I should ever be so cursed. But the truth is simpler than fiction. I have never found the right woman, one with whom I would like to spend the rest of my life and who will put up with my dedication to the organ and church music. I doubt I ever shall. And the rumour about being a conscientious objector? Also absolutely false. I object most strenuously to violence, as any sensible man would. However, I volunteered to be a stretcher bearer. I served mostly in Flanders. I witnessed so much death there that I long ago dismissed the idea that there was any glory in dying only because a higher authority ordered ordinary soldiers to attempt the impossible."

The Bishop confirmed the existence of life assurance for the clergy, paid for generously, he intimated, by the Diocese. It only amounted to two times the annual stipend, twice as much if the unfortunate clergyman died by accident. Not enough to get excited over, I decided, even with the accidental death benefit, and almost certainly not enough of a return on investment as a motive for murder, if that was the case with Dean Butterfield. The sum assured would only be paid on proof of death, the accidental nature of which would probably remain open to doubt by the insurers. It would be seven years under English law, which applied in Malaya, before the Dean could be declared legally dead if he failed to turn up alive. In my experience, if money were the motive, seven years was about six and a half too many for a murderer to wait for payday.

I questioned the driver of the Land Rover who had taken Wilton and the Dean as far as Salah Merah, and who had brought an agitated Wilton back alone nearly a week later. Yes, they seemed in good spirits on the way out. Wilton, he said, looked dishevelled and hadn't shaved, and had seemed close to tears several times on the way back to Penang. No, he hadn't noticed if Wilton's clothes were unusually muddy. Questioning the launch pilot who lived up-country would have to wait for several months until the start of what passes for the dry season, as would my questions of the villagers who had had contact with either the Dean or Wilton. Such is the nature of investigations in the tropics, and patience occasionally brings its own rewards, though not often enough to be a reliable proverb.

After several days of frequent heavy, but intermittent showers that had started before my arrival in Penang, the monsoon broke in earnest that same afternoon. I spent the rest of that day writing up my report from my notes I jotted down in my room after each interview and passed the evening alone, nursing a Scotch and soda on either side of dinner at the Club. Loretta Ingles failed to make an appearance. So did the Donaldsons, whom, I suspected, had managed to beat a strategic retreat to their plantation that morning in time to avoid the worst of the unpleasant drive home in the rain and mud.

I tried to keep an open mind as I swirled the Scotch and ice cubes around in the bottom of the glass. It was a losing cause. I kept returning to the same questions—was the Dean simply missing because he had decided to take off without telling anyone? It seemed unlikely. Could he be embezzling from the organ or some similar fund which enjoyed only cursory accounting oversight? Possibly. But why steal when he had more than enough to live on reasonably comfortably? Could it be there existed an undiscovered liaison between him and another woman and that he needed money to finance such an arrangement? Someone such as Loretta Ingles? Again, possibly, but if that were the case, he had been extraordinarily careful in covering his tracks. If there was infidelity, could the affair have gone badly, or left him open to blackmail? Could embarrassment over a failed love affair be sufficient reason to take off into the jungle and deliberately vanish? Or could the affair have become known by one or more individuals, possibly including his wife? Or the Bishop? Or Wilton?

If there had been an illicit affair I could not discount the possibility of either blackmail or murder. But Valerie Butterfield was, in my view at least, a pleasant, very attractive and fairly young woman, one who seemed unlikely to drive her husband away from his family or cause him to abandon his faith, his church and his livelihood. Prying into her private affairs might bear fruit and nudge the investigation definitively one way or another. However, scruples aside, questions of that sort in Penang would reach Mrs. Butterfield's ears within minutes and no doubt cause her to close up like a clam.

That Valerie Butterfield had not been fulsome in her truth telling I did not question. But what else she could be hiding, and why, would have to remain her secret for a little while longer. I had no reason to suspect her of any wrongdoing beyond a minor peccadillo of the sort most people are guilty. My mere presence in Penang should prove sufficient impetus to flush out secrets, hers or anyone else's. I was in no hurry to return to K.L., and so had time on my side. Someone, if my suspicions were correct, didn't. It remained to be seen who.

I had more time than I anticipated. I received word two days later that the rains had washed out a section of the railway track connecting Bukit Mertajam on the mainland opposite Penang, with Kuala Lumpur. My stay, therefore, had been extended indefinitely. I made myself as comfortable as possible, expensing my meals and drinks at the Club and compiling reports which I doubted would ever be read, let alone followed up on. The only way that mail could reach K.L. with the railway washed out was by steamer to Singapore, then the ferry across the Johore Strait to Johore itself and by rail north from there. It seemed likely that the track would be repaired before my reports reached the Commissioner by steamer, and less chance that they would be lost in transit if I hung onto them until I could hand deliver them. I took solace in the fact there had not seemed any sense of real urgency when they assigned me to the case, and I was probably now happily out of sight and out of mind.

I had lunch with Wilton again a week after the news about the railway tracks. He seemed unworried about my extended stay and answered all my questions, posed as casually and as conversationally as I could. I learned nothing new.

I spoke to Valerie Butterfield over tea that same afternoon. In contrast to Wilton, she seemed agitated, unable to sit still. The boys were down for a nap in the nursery but she constantly turned her head as if expecting to hear a sound emanating from that direction.

"I don't have any news," I told her. "Like you, I suspect the worst, but I can't confirm it. I have yet to talk to the launch pilot and the villagers but I don't expect much, if anything will come of it. Has Howard Wilton spoken to you at all about the incident?"

Her hand went to her mouth and she coughed lightly, buying a few seconds in which to think and formulate an answer. "He has, Commissioner, but I'm sure he has spared me specific details that I might find upsetting."

"Such as?"

"What, for instance, if anything, he or the villagers found that first day when they formed the search party. A man can't simply vanish into thin air without leaving a trace. It's not a conjuring trick my husband pulled. He must have left something behind, some evidence, footprints, or signs of a struggle. Blood." She wrung her hands and crushed her handkerchief, which I found a bit theatrical.

"What did Howard Wilton tell you?"

"Only that they found nothing." She paused. "Nothing."

"Wilton said it had rained overnight. The village would be a sea of mud when it rains. That might account for not leaving any discernible footprints."

"Howard mentioned there's quite an overhang from the roof. The ground would be relatively dry for a few feet at least. Surely there would be something to find, footprints leading from the door of their hut, for example. My husband didn't just sprout wings and fly into the jungle."

"I'm sure they looked hard, Mrs. Butterfield, and came up empty. After all, they're not trained evidence gatherers." This did not seem to satisfy her, so I changed the direction of my questioning. "Did Wilton bring back your husband's suitcase?"

"Yes." She seemed surprised by the question.

"What was in it?"

She thought for a moment. "His vestments. Two chalices for the bread and wine. A silver serving plate. His shoes. His worn socks and underwear and a shirt. I've washed them." She paused. "His shaving kit and suchlike. Collar studs and collars. I don't think there was anything else in the case."

"The shoes? Were they muddy?

"No. They looked clean. A little scuffed perhaps and unpolished. Edgar was never that fussy about his appearance."

"The unused communion wafers? Any communion wine left in

the bottle?"

A confused look crossed her face. "Only the two chalices. No wafers, and there was no bottle of communion wine in the suitcase. I know he would have taken a bottle with him when he left. Bread without wine would be rather pointless, wouldn't it?"

"Did he have any money on him when he left?"

"A little cash to pay for the launch. The Land Rover belongs to the Diocese and the driver is paid by the Diocese as well. And, as I'm sure you know, barter is the common currency up country."

"Quite. So, if there were a motive for foul play, money would not seem to be it."

Her hand went to her mouth again. "Do you think Edgar was murdered?"

I hesitated. I didn't know, and speculation is pointless so I evaded the question. "If your husband decided to leave you, where would he go?"

"You mean, if he wanted to end our marriage? He wouldn't. We have a lovely, and loving marriage. Ask anyone." She burst into tears. They seemed genuine. I waited her out.

"You haven't answered my question, Mrs. Butterfield," I said when she stopped crying. "If he wanted to, or felt he needed to leave Penang, where would he be most likely to go? Kuala Lumpur? Singapore? England? Not the jungle, surely. Unless he never wanted to be found alive."

"If he were seeing the Ingles woman," she said with cold venom in her voice, "I doubt if he would stay here. Not in Penang. The Bishop would almost certainly sack him if it came to light. I doubt if Edgar would get much of a reference either. Clergymen lacking in morals are not taken on with open arms by other parishes. And that Ingles woman can't keep her mouth shut. If there was anything going on between them, I would know in a heartbeat, half of Penang would know by nightfall and the other half before dawn."

"Why would you think Mrs. Ingles might be mixed up with your husband?"

The nature of her reply caught me by surprise. "I don't. But she's a bitch in heat, Commissioner, and only someone desperate for sex would have anything to do with her. She's desperate for money and security and she'll try and snag anyone with a salary. It's a good job you didn't take her offer of a nightcap when you took her home after your bridge game that night, that's all I can say."

I hadn't mentioned a nightcap. Someone had evidently been watching my movements and the whispers had found their way back to Valerie Butterfield, which served to reinforce my determination not to be seen with Loretta Ingles without a reliable witness present.

I watched her chest heave after her outburst and gave her a few moments to calm down. "He'd go back to England," she said in a small voice. "He likes it here, probably more than I do. But he's not married to Malaya. He has no history here. It's a posting, but he hoped it would be a long one." She paused and looked around her drawing room, seeming to draw solace in the comfort of the familiar. She turned her attention back to me. "Now he may be here forever." She looked away again and stared at a spot on the rush floor mat. "He was a chaplain during the war, you know. Then a vicar in an East End of London parish. That's where we met. Then the opportunity arose to come here as Dean. The Bishop… Edgar knew the Bishop from their days together in the Chaplaincy Corps during the war. Malaya was quiet. A long way from guns and death and shooting, and the grinding poverty of an East End parish. He didn't need to be convinced. But you'd be wrong if you thought I came out here out of a sense of duty as a wife. It was as much my choice as Edgar's."

"What might you do if he doesn't show up?"

"The Diocese will replace him. I doubt if I'd stay in Malaya. It's not home to me any more than it is to Edgar. I'll be living on charity until I can find work, probably in England, no matter how expensive the place is nowadays." She shuddered and shook her head. "But I'll make my way somehow. I have to, though I can't see the boys going to a good school." She turned away again, half anticipating a cry from the nursery to tell her the boys were awake and up.

Seemingly satisfied that all was quiet, she turned back to me. "Do you really suspect foul play, Commissioner? I asked you before if you think my husband was murdered."

"I can't rule anything out, Mrs. Butterfield. But if, as you say, your husband didn't sprout wings and fly off into the jungle, and if he didn't walk there of his own free will, someone took him there, alive or already dead, for a purpose I have yet been unable to discover. But I will get to the bottom of it, I promise you. And if I can prove it wasn't accidental, that person will hang for it."

She sat back in her chair and picked up her tea cup. "Cold," she said. "I can get the house boy to make some more if you'd like another cup."

I shook my head. "Thank you, but I have to leave. I have a report to write up. There is one thing I must ask before I go."

"What's that?"

"If your husband was murdered, can you think of anyone who might want him dead? And why?"

"No one, Commissioner. Not even that Loretta Ingles woman. I don't think Edgar had an enemy in the world."

"If I'm right, it would seem he had at least one. The question remains, who is that one?"

I still thought it unlikely that the Dean of St. George's Cathedral, Penang, the Reverend Edgar Butterfield, had not become disoriented on communion wine, had wandered off on his own into the jungle one rainy night, and become lost. Or that he had committed suicide. And if Wilton's version of the events were to be believed, a sober Dean probably would have chosen to remain dry under the wide eaves of their hut rather than go to the communal latrine in the rain to relieve himself. Which meant that someone had seized on that opportunity to murder him. But who? The most obvious suspect would seem to be Wilton, the last person reportedly to have seen the Dean alive, leaving their shared hut during the night. That is again, if Wilton were to be believed. And if I didn't accept Wilton's version as factual, where did that leave me and the investigation? With a single suspect, and nothing to suggest a motive, means or opportunity. Or a convenient body.

The Dean, by all accounts, was a little smaller than I. Given their disparity in size, though, and with his abhorrence of violence, for Wilton to overpower him in a fight seemed unlikely. To render him unconscious would require stealth on Wilton's part, certainly not an impossible task using a heavy blunt object on the Dean's head while he slept. Wilton could then have hefted the unconscious, or possibly already dead body, over his shoulder in a fireman's lift. That was something Wilton had no doubt done countless times in Flanders twenty years ago, when he was a younger, fitter and stronger man. But if he had managed to render the Dean unconscious, or even dead in their hut, could he have carried him off into the jungle, scooped out a shallow grave away from a path and returned to the hut and feigned surprise in the morning? If that really was what had happened, the Dean would be buried and the world none the wiser.

Alternatively, Wilton could have carried, or dragged, the Dean's body to the river's edge and dumped him in the water. The current would carry the body downstream where it would either be eaten by whatever creatures eat dead bodies in rivers or disintegrate as it rotted. But that would have meant passing through part of the village, albeit probably at dead of night, with a body over his shoulder. Somebody might have seen him.

The more I thought about it, the more improbable either scenario seemed. But, without a body or a confession, how do I prove murder? It would be months before I could get to the village and resume a search for a grave or a skeleton. The village, unless it were one of a kind, would have been built close to the river bank but well above the level the waters could be expected to rise to during the monsoon. If it were the river where he disposed of the body, Wilton would have the advantage of carrying the Dean downhill, which rendered the river the slightly more plausible option. However, by now the river would yield nothing. In several months' time, even less. I made a mental note to check with Wilton on the local geography next time I saw him.

To compound the problem there was the issue of a lack of any obvious motive, even if the means and opportunity held up under closer examination. Why would Wilton want to kill the Dean, a man whom he had known, admittedly off and on, for nearly thirty years, and the man largely responsible for getting him his position at St. George's? That Wilton was not greatly loved by the community in Penang went without saying, but would someone as inoffensive as him commit murder? It wouldn't be the first time such a thing had happened, but if he had, what could possibly drive him to kill the Dean? What could he possibly gain by his death?

I cautioned myself against putting the cart before the horse, of devising a theory before unearthing the facts to prove it. The cart in this case was a rag and bone man's dray, with what little there was on it threadbare and of little use. And the nag pulling it—I, in this case—was in no great shape either, having a theory based on hearsay, no provable facts, and no discernible motive for the sole suspect. Absent a confession, it might prove an insurmountable task to build even a circumstantial case against Wilton.

But there was one thing nagging at the back of my mind that refused to go away—why were the Dean's shoes in his suitcase when Wilton delivered it to Mrs. Butterfield? If the Dean had left the hut to relieve himself outside, either at the communal latrine or elsewhere, why would he not have worn his shoes? It was raining, after all. And white men did not walk around barefoot, especially in front of the natives. It simply wasn't done. Besides, there are nasty little things, jiggers, which crawl under one's toenails and lay eggs there if one is foolish enough to walk around barefoot like the natives. So, against conventional wisdom, the Dean was obviously barefoot when he left the hut over Wilton's shoulder. Wilton then dumped the body either in the jungle, where they searched without success, or in the river where it was less likely to be discovered miles downstream. But if it had happened like that, where was the mud on Wilton's clothes that he would have picked up carrying the Dean to the jungle or the river, or during the searches?

I was still a long way from proof, or even enough to bring Wilton in for questioning with a view to charging him. If it was him, and the signposts pointed in that direction, why would he do it? He had reasonable security in work that he loved, a seemingly excellent relationship with his immediate superior, the Dean, and no apparent problems with the Bishop. Could it be for the one thing that had eluded him all his life—love? Not for Loretta Ingles almost certainly. Nor the Bishop's wife, whom I had yet to meet. That only left one plausible candidate—the woman he always referred to by her Christian name; the Dean's wife, Valerie Butterfield. Was she up to her neck in a plot to kill her husband and sail away into the sunset with the organist? I had to laugh at the suggestion, although stranger things have happened. If it was murder, and if Wilton were the culprit, had he acted alone in the hope he might persuade the object of his love to join him on a trip down the aisle at some future date once the hubbub had died down? Or had she already agreed and they had jointly conspired?

I stood at the window, turning over the possibilities, clutching at straws that probably only existed in my imagination. I watched the rain wash away the filth of Penang, turning its streets into muddy open sewers that would eventually find their way to the sea, and purification of a sort. If only crime could be cleansed in the same way. A knock on the open door interrupted my contemplations. A young man, little more than a boy whom I recognized after a moment as the Butterfield's house boy, stood dripping wet on the threshold, holding a black umbrella uselessly over his head. He handed me a note, and I bid him stay while I answered the unexpected, scribbled invitation from Valerie Butterfield to dinner that night at her home.

I wondered if this could be the elusive break I so desperately needed in the case.

I presented myself at the appointed time, wearing my only set of civilian clothes for an off-duty affair. To my surprise, and somewhat to my relief, Wilton was already there. It is not every day I dined with a murder suspect and his possible accomplice.

"Do call me Valerie," she said when, out of habit, I called her Mrs. Butterfield. I smiled in return.

"Howard," said Wilton. "But you already know that."

The pair looked at me expectantly. "Masters is fine. I don't like my Christian name or my middle name and never use either," I said. "I had no say in the matter when they were foisted upon me, and it's too late and too complicated to change them now."

"If it makes you feel more comfortable, perhaps we'll simply call you Commissioner," Valerie said, and nodded at Wilton.

I watched the pair over dinner, searching for clues as to their relationship. I came up disappointed. They were polite to each other, but no more so than any dinner guest and hostess should be. There was no hint of familiarity, other than the use of Christian names, and no touching in any sort of proprietary way. Not even a smile that lingered a shade too long on the lips, or a facial expression that hinted at more than a platonic friendship. Certainly, they gave no clue that passion simmered barely beneath the surface, passion hot enough for one to kill for his rival's wife, and the other to benefit from it. If what I was witnessing was an act, they were highly accomplished players.

Wilton left before I did. I had half expected him to leave after me, if he left at all that night, but then I realized he would not only have to leave but be seen to leave by the investigating officer. Had he stayed, the house boy would know. So too would the boys' amah, who had not yet retired to her room in the house. Their servants' silence was not a forgone conclusion. With what had happened to the Dean, the scandal would be all over Penang in hours without the help of Loretta Ingles. The finger of suspicion would not only point to murder for love, but Wilton would feel the tap of my hand on his shoulder and my finger on his collar. From there to a confession would be a baby step, and a short one to the gallows.

Just when I thought nothing new would turn up to assist the investigation, Wilton asked to see me at the church after choir practice. Curious, I met him at the foot of the stairs leading to the organ loft after the last of the choir members had left.

"Come with me, Commissioner," he said in the sort of quiet voice I associate with churches and reverence.

He led me to the vestry and closed the door. He took a few steps over to a cupboard and unlocked it. When he pulled the door open, I saw two, possibly three, dozen bottles. "Sacramental wine," Wilton said. "A bottle normally lasts a month. This represents nearly three years' supply." He shut and locked the cupboard door.

"What are you telling me," I said.

"He drank. He kept it from Valerie and the Bishop, but I caught him several times, here in the vestry after a service. Edgar Butterfield was my friend. He was responsible for recommending me for this job. I felt I owed it to him not to say anything. Mrs. Fanshawe, the Bishop's wife, does the books. She's not very good at it. I doubt if she thought anything of it when Dean Butterfield ordered half a dozen cases of sacramental wine at a time."

I watched Wilton's face closely while he told me this. He could be making it up, to lay blame, or at least cast suspicion, at the Dean's feet. Or he could be purging his own soul by betraying a confidence.

"I found two empty bottles in his suitcase when I packed it before leaving. I left them behind. I didn't want anyone asking questions." He shuffled his feet and looked down at them. "I'm sorry I was less than fulsome in what I told you before. I wanted to protect the Dean, and especially Valerie." He looked up. "Can I rely on your discretion not to say anything, Commissioner? As a gentleman?"

I hesitated. "You may," I said eventually. "Neither Mrs. Butterfield nor the Bishop need to know." I neglected to mention my official report to the Commissioner in K.L.

I packed my suitcase and, with the railway still inoperable, took the steamer from Penang to Singapore. After a night there, I took the ferry to Johore and the train to Kuala Lumpur.

"As a result of my inquiries, Sir," I told the Commissioner, "it is my opinion, and in the complete absence of any evidence to the contrary, that Edgar Butterfield became drunk on most of two bottles of sacramental wine one night and became disoriented. In that state he wandered off into the jungle, or possibly into the river and met his death." I handed in my carefully worded report, marked 'Missing—Presumed Dead by Misadventure. No further action required.' I doubt that anyone bothered to read it.

That was, I suspect, the scandal-free outcome everyone, from my superiors to the Diocese, had hoped for. I maintained a continual, nagging doubt about Wilton's innocence and a lasting suspicion that I might have whitewashed his role in the affair. But proof positive of murder proved elusive. In spite of what may you read in detective novels, such is the fate of so many investigations.

The Diocese appointed a new Dean in due course. Word filtered back in the form of a brief letter from Loretta Ingles that Valerie Butterfield and her three children returned to England. The third child, a daughter, had been born about six months after I left Penang. I had not suspected Mrs. Butterfield's condition. I have no personal knowledge as to who fathered Valerie Butterfield's daughter, but in the absence of evidence to the contrary I accept she is the Dean's.

I also learned that Wilton resigned his position as organist and choir master not long after the arrival of the new Dean. The official explanation was that they apparently failed to see eye to eye on church music. I gather that on his return to England Wilton took up a teaching post with the School of English Church Music near London, in good time to endure the Blitz. I almost felt sorry for him.

6. KING TUKURAHMAN

Despite his living in Kuala Lumpur, I had never met the self-styled King Tukurahman until the morning I came face to face with him, or more accurately his corpse, on the large silk Persian carpet in his spacious drawing room. I met him again later that day on the pathologist's stainless steel table in the basement morgue of the K.L. hospital.

The morgue smelled as it usually did, of formaldehyde, antiseptic floor wash and the ever-present cloying aroma that hangs over corpses like a pall over a coffin. I have never liked the smell of death and I doubt if I will ever become accustomed to it. It did not seem to bother the pathologist in the slightest, however, or his assistant who was busily engaged in drawing blood from a vein or an artery—it doesn't seem to matter which when the object of the exercise is a corpse—and syringing it into a glass vial. With a soft grunt the assistant affixed a label and wrote something illegible on it. I wondered if he had acquired his vocabulary and handwriting skills from the pathologist.

When I walked into the morgue, Dr. D'Eath had just sawn off the top of the skull. He then pared back the skin of the face so that it sat on the neck and upper torso of the deceased, and removed the brain which now lay, shining and lifeless, on a scale next to the steel table. I watched D'Eath peer through his eyeglasses at the scale's calibrations and heard the occasional grunt escape his lips. D'Eath ignored our intrusion into his world. I waited while the grunts continued.

"Good afternoon, Commissioner," the pathologist at last grunted over his shoulder without looking up from his work. "I understand congratulations on your recent promotion are called for. I wondered how long it would take you to wend your merry way here."

"Good afternoon to you too, D'Eath," I replied good-naturedly, for the pathologist was never happier than when dissecting a fresh cadaver. "And thank you. I hope neither we nor the deceased caused you to miss lunch."

The pathologist ignored me. He straightened and pointed at the grey mass on the scale. "Smaller than I would have thought," he said, presumably to me. "Under eleven hundred grams. Still, it's within the lower end of the norm, if only barely." He glanced at me. "For your information, Masters, the normal range is 1,300 to 1,400 grams."

I brought my heels together in the mode of standing at attention and bowed stiffly from the waist. "Your Majesty," I said as reverently as I could to the corpse, only barely managing to suppress an unseemly giggle. I turned to Dr. D'Eath. "And how much is eleven hundred grams?"

The pathologist subjected me to a lengthy visible examination before sighing. "About two and a half pounds, forty ounces for you backward non-scientists. When will you chaps ever move into the Twentieth Century?"

I fought down the temptation to wither beneath the penetrating gaze of the chief medical examiner, coroner and pathologist for Malaya. "My compliments to His Majesty," I said, "but perhaps he wasn't as bright as some."

D'Eath ignored my comment and pointed at the brain "There are lesions present. See? Here and here. And a tumour, most probably cancerous. I'll know more when I've done the tests." He turned to Inspector, the Honourable Noel O'Toole, my young charge, whose initial training in Malaya had been delegated to me, "You, too, Inspector. Gather round, you can't see anything from the back of the room."

I turned to see O'Toole's face turn a deeper shade of grey-green. He shuffled forward and stopped well short of the steel table on which the corpse lay. I saw nothing untoward on the surface of the brain's side or top, but then I'm a policeman, not a pathologist. I muttered something by way of a reply which seemed to satisfy the doctor.

"Not to mention the six bullet holes in the back of his skull and their channels through his brain. No exit wounds. Probably of a low velocity, small caliber pistol. I'll extract them when I dissect the brain."

"Don't lose them," I said.

He turned to me and lowered his wire brush eyebrows until they shrouded his eyes. "I've been a pathologist for twice as long as you've been a policeman. I've not lost an exhibit yet and I don't intend setting a precedent today."

I bowed metaphorically to his superior knowledge of things medical and forensic. "The cause of death, I take it?"

D'Eath regarded me with that pathetic look reserved for the use by Greek masters with a particularly obtuse member of the fourth form.

"And given the number and *loci*, I can confidently rule out suicide." He turned back to his task.

"Murder it must therefore be," I said, having mentally declined the Latin *locus,* nominative singular, second, or possibly fourth declension, I couldn't remember which, meaning a place, with the plural being *loci*, places. Latin was not my strong suit. I had discarded both it and Greek after the upper fifth form, finding French, German and maths far more to my liking. Each had served me well from time to time, although admittedly mostly in the army, and all of which I had found of questionable use in my career as a policeman.

"At a first guess, Commissioner," he said once more over his shoulder. "But we cannot be too hasty. There may be other, underlying causes. Leave no stone unturned, I always say, and no one can find fault."

The call had come in to the police station from the king's major domo around mid-morning, the king having a telephone in his home, requesting a policeman as the king seemed to have died. The first officers despatched to the scene, a Malay sergeant and a native *mata mata*, quickly identified the probable cause of death, multiple gunshot wounds to the back of the head, execution-style. The sergeant immediately decided the death fell under the heading of *suspicious*. Inspector O'Toole received the call from the sergeant and held the telephone out to me. "For you, Sir. A possible murder." The blank look on his face told me nothing, though my exposure to the Honourable Noel should have warned me not to expect more than incomprehension.

I sighed. When first introduced to me, Inspector O'Toole admitted having received his education at Eton College where, given his stubborn resistance to learning, his housemaster had enjoined him to take up farming, politics, or enter the army. Having no interest in any of the suggestions offered, I suspect he joined the Colonial Police Force for something to do while he waited for his share of the inheritance.

"Assistant Commissioner Masters," I barked into the instrument and listened to the excited sergeant on the other end explaining the rudimentary details.

We arrived at the rambling, two-storey house in spacious grounds in the best part of K.L. at almost the same moment as the police photographer. O'Toole and I examined the body *in situ* after being assured by the English-speaking head of the household servants who had discovered it that he had not moved the body nor touched anything before calling us. It was as if he had read the novels of Agatha Christie and Dorothy L. Sayers and discovered dead bodies on a regular, if not daily basis.

O'Toole and I waited in the background while the photographer's flash bulbs popped until he had committed to film every angle of the body, his clothing—the body was fully dressed in suit and tie and a pair of highly polished black Oxford shoes—bloodstains, the room, furniture and furnishings. Only then did I step forward and get a close-up of the deceased. Behind me I heard O'Toole retch and heave, but he had the decency to keep his breakfast down.

"How do we know it's a body, Inspector, and not someone asleep or unconscious?"

"It's not breathing, Sir. Or he's taking a very long time between breaths."

"Anything else strike your fancy?"

"What appear to be several holes in the back of his head, Sir?" He didn't seem too sure of that one.

"Have you seen anything in this room that could suggest a means to make these holes?"

O'Toole glanced around. "No, Sir. Nothing immediately apparent."

"No ice pick? No hand drill? No gun, for example."

"No, Sir." He seemed more assured of himself this time.

"Which suggests…?"

"He probably didn't do it to himself before disposing of the instrument and returning here to collapse on the floor where we now find him. Assuming the servant's not lying about not touching anything."

"And the blood splatters on the rug? What do they tell you?"

O'Toole frowned and furrowed his forehead further until his

eyebrows closed in on each other, giving him something of a caveman look.

"I don't know, Sir," he said hesitantly.

"Look closer."

"I don't see anything, Sir."

"Precisely. No blood splatters. He's lying almost face down. There's a little cerebral fluid still leaking from the scalp, tinged pink. None of it on the rug. What does that suggest?"

O'Toole looked blank then ran a hand over his face as if deep in thought. "He was shot, Sir?"

"Is that what you think?"

He shuffled his feet and examined the toecaps. "Yes, Sir," he said eventually.

"So do I, O'Toole, for what it's worth. Though we still have to rule out anything else that could have drilled those holes in his skull. That's the pathologist's job. Have you met him?"

"No, Sir."

"Well, you will this afternoon, after lunch. He should have completed most of the post mortem by then. It will be your chance to impress him with your medical acumen."

"I don't have any," he stammered.

"In which case I suggest you don't say anything. It's better to appear a fool than to open one's mouth and remove all doubt. Meanwhile, turn the body over and see what else there is to see."

There was nothing to see. No blood oozing from a gunshot wound in his chest; no mysterious London Transport bus ticket in a pocket that might send us on a wild goose chase; no strange amulets, signet rings, items of jewellery—in short, nothing to raise the suspicions of Hercule Poirot or Lord Peter Wimsey. We went through his pockets. He didn't have any cash, letters, or business cards, on him, not even a wallet. In fact, he carried nothing by way of identification, almost as if he didn't want anyone to know who he was or his business.

O'Toole left the body on his back and straightened. "Who is he, Sir?"

"According to the major domo our victim calls himself King Tukurahman." I paused to let this information sink in. The pause stretched into several seconds without eliciting a response. I changed the subject. "How are your Malay language studies coming along?"

"Still non-existent, Sir."

"Then you'll have to use the sergeant as an interpreter while you question the household servants. I suggest you start with the chap who discovered the body, the head of the household servants. You might begin by confirming who the deceased is while I arrange for it to be picked up and taken to the morgue."

O'Toole busied himself questioning the servants while I listened in from a discreet distance. My knowledge of Malay had improved with the years of exposure to police work and the day-to-day living in Kuala Lumpur, but though reasonably fluent it was still nowhere near good enough to conduct an interrogation without the help of an interpreter, which was where the sergeant came in. One of a sergeant's job requirements was fluency in English. Not the fluency of the chaps who compiled the Oxford English Dictionary, of course, but still pretty good and more than good enough to write reports in English.

"Abdul Mohammad Umar bin Ibrahim Tukurahman," O'Toole announced with a smug smile of satisfaction on his face. "He calls himself King Tukurahman."

"That's identification confirmed, then. I know of him but I can't say I've ever met him."

"I don't recognize the name, Sir. Is he a well-known villain in these parts?"

"You sound like something out of a bad Victorian melodrama, O'Toole. Where on earth did you learn to speak like that?"

"By watching bad Victorian melodramas, Sir?"

I had to laugh. At least he had a sense of humour which probably meant he was human.

"How do you know of him, Sir?"

"Because I've been here more than a dozen years longer than you. It's a copper's job to know who's who and what's going on in his manor." I tapped the side of my nose rather too theatrically for my liking but I wanted to make my point. A policeman who simply stands around like a stick of celery is about as useless as the said stick of celery. I don't know if O'Toole took it to heart, but I hoped he had.

"But why is he called the king, Sir?"

"It goes back a long way. His grandfather is rumoured to have been the King Mongkut of Siam, who died about, oh, seventy years ago I'd say. Records were a bit sketchy in those days. The king's reported to have had eighty-two children."

I heard O'Toole take a sharp intake of breath. "Busy man, it seems. I hope he had a nanny."

"I'm sure he did. Anyway, the official government records only show eighty-two. Who knows how many others there may have been. He went through a lot of wives, some of whom may have been his rather than someone else's at the time. He was a Buddhist, if that makes a difference, though I can't see how it would. Then of course there are the children of the children, of whom Tukurahman claims to be one, and in his eyes the only legitimate claimant to the throne. Probably nonsense, of course, but we all have our occasional fantasies."

"But why would that get him killed, assuming he was murdered?"

"At a guess it had nothing to do with being the King of Siam, real or imaginary. More likely is that Tukurahman is reputedly the kingpin of the opium trade in South East Asia. His tentacles are said to stretch from Siam and Burma, through Indo-China to Singapore and into the Islands of Sumatra, Borneo and Sarawak and the like. He stayed out of China proper. They wouldn't tolerate him there. If he'd stuck his nose into their business he'd have been dead years ago. He was obviously smart enough to realize that."

I took a last look around the room. There was nothing more for us to see there for the moment. I left a police guard on the locked room and followed O'Toole to the waiting police car.

"An early lunch," I told the Honourable Noel as we set off for headquarters. "You'll need something in your stomach before the post mortem. Liver? Kidneys?" I saw O'Toole pale at the prospect of animal offal before encountering the human variety.

I left O'Toole gnawing unenthusiastically on a sandwich in the officers' mess while I made my way to the records department to reacquaint myself with the slim police file on Abdul Tukurahman. As I suspected, there was nothing new since the last time I had read the reports, most of which were skimpy on detail but heavy on rumour. Tukurahman had never been arrested. He had rarely been photographed in public and seldom left his home from where the reports suggested he ran his opium empire. Although Tukurahman's grandfather, King Mongkut was a Buddhist, Tukurahman, or perhaps his father—there was nothing on file to indicate which—had converted to Islam. Our records showed Tukurahman had five wives, although there was no mention of children. In short, mostly useless speculation and old news which failed to shed light on our current investigation.

As we were at that moment bereft of suspects, no obvious motive for killing Tukurahman and no established opportunity to commit the murder, we faced a blank wall. How nice it would have been had someone crawled out from behind the skirting board unannounced and confessed, provided us with the murder weapon complete with his fingerprints all over it, and explained his motives for committing the deed. That sometimes happens—more often than the detective novels would have you believe—but thus far we had had no such luck. No jilted lover had come forward. No crossed business partner had had a fit of conscience. No wronged spouse or disinherited offspring had thought fit to confess. It looked as if the death of King Tukurahman would have to be investigated the old-fashioned way, by a laborious slog through all possible leads, dead ends, blind alleys and red herrings until we could eliminate all but one and hoped we hadn't overlooked any.

O'Toole and I spent part of the afternoon in the morgue, watching the dissection of the cadaver and the collection of the still warm tissue specimens. The dissected brain yielded six, small caliber bullets, the tips squashed in a variety of mushroom shapes by their contact with and passage through the cranium.

"A ladies gun, Masters, at a guess," Dr. D'Eath said. "Or something a Mafia assassin might use for close work. Definitely not fired from a Lee Enfield three-o-three or even a twenty-two caliber rifle. There are powder burns near the entrance wounds, indicating that at least one of the shots was fired from close range, possible point blank. All except one had a similar trajectory. Any one of the bullets fired would likely have caused instant death. Someone certainly wanted to make sure he didn't pull a Lazarus trick."

One by one he dropped the bullets with a clatter into a kidney basin and placed it on one side. I found the process rather too theatrical for my taste and wondered if perhaps the pathologist had seen the same bad Victorian melodramas as O'Toole.

"As the stomach was almost empty he probably hadn't eaten

breakfast or had more than a cup of tea. All indications are that he had stomach cancer. It probably metathesized from the bowel, which was Stage Four, and into his liver." He held up a jar of turgid liquid and pulled the stopper out. An acrid stench quickly filled the air around us. O'Toole clapped his hand to his mouth and almost sprinted for the morgue door. "I can confirm that the brain tumour was cancerous but was probably a separate entity, unconnected with the other cancers. I'll know more when I've completed my work. Suffice it to say," he said, straightening. "He was a walking dead man until this morning. If someone hadn't pumped six bullets into his brain he might not have lasted a week."

When O'Toole returned several minutes later, the stopper was back on the jar and the jar itself sitting on a shelf with the other exhibits.

"Sorry," O'Toole muttered. "Something I ate at lunch I expect." Dr. D'Eath and I exchanged grins. It was a favorite trick of his with new officers and I knew it was coming.

"Initiation fee paid," I said to O'Toole. "We all go through it." I patted him on the shoulder, but I don't think it made him feel any better.

"Kidneys and liver were in bad shape, apart from the cancer," D'Eath said. "The heart was enlarged as well. We'll know more when we've completed the toxicology, but at an educated guess I'd say it's not alcohol but hard narcotics." He raised his eyebrows enquiringly.

"He's reputed to be a major opium dealer, but we've nothing we can pin on him," I said. "If he was using what he sells, he's a fool."

"He wouldn't be the first. Or the last. I'll know more tomorrow. There's nothing more for you to do here. I'll let you have my report then."

Back in my office I sat behind my desk with the Honourable Noel on the other side looking as apprehensive as a recalcitrant third former in front of his headmaster.

"What do we know so far?" I said.

O'Toole looked blank, one that didn't take much practice.

"Six small caliber bullets to the back of the head, execution-style?" I suggested, trying to emphasize my patience before it dwindled to a vanishing point. "Someone wanted to leave a message, either for us, or more likely for anyone else thinking of muscling in on what they perceive to be their territory. Agreed?"

He nodded.

"Who do you think did it?"

I received the same blank stare.

"I don't know either. That means we have to start putting two and two together until we hit on the right answer, which is probably closer to four than twenty-two. Who wanted King Tukurahman out of the way? Any ideas?"

"Someone who wanted to take over the business? A rival?"

"That would be my first guess, except for the fact that there's nothing in our intelligence that suggests he wasn't number one by a long way. There was no one we know of even close to knocking him off. He owned the opium trade, most of it the raw stuff you can buy almost anywhere if you know who to ask. There's a suggestion he refined some of it as morphine and heroin but we've never found a lab or anyone who'll squeal."

"Perhaps we should question the staff again, Sir."

"A very good idea, O'Toole. Perhaps you might start with the servant who found the body and put the fear of Christ or whoever he worships in him when you question him again. Meanwhile, we'll need a list of all the household servants, wives, children and visitors in the twenty-four hours before the body was discovered. Then we question them, one by one under threat that they will rot in jail for the rest of their lives if they so much as think of lying to us."

O'Toole looked puzzled. "Can we do that, Sir? I mean, threaten them with life imprisonment?"

"No. Of course not. But they must believe we can, otherwise we might never hear the patter of the tiny feet of truth that exist behind those walls."

"I see what you mean. Lean on them, enough to bend them but not to break them. A willow, not an oak."

"How very poetic of you, O'Toole. I didn't know you had it in you."

"I think I learned that in the third form, Sir. I never guessed it might prove useful one day."

I wasn't sure that it had, or would, but I let it pass without comment. "These Malays—they're mostly Muslims and some Hindus and whatnot. Not Christians. And Muslims are not in the least like Christians, sad to say. From what I can tell from experience, they understand brute force and blind obedience to the commands and the absolute will of Allah and the teaching of their priests. They are easily led. Our notion of democracy is an alien concept to them. The rank and file Muslim has no will of his own, and their women are mere possessions and of little use. They'll close ranks against us and lie like Irish gypsies—no disrespect intended, O'Toole, but you know what I mean."

"I know something of Irish gypsies, Sir." He grinned.

"Well, that's the official version of the Malay Muslim, come down to us from on high. Don't take it too much to heart. Some of it may be true but I've found them to be little different from the rest of us, trudging through the daily grind of trying to make ends meet on too little pay and not much hope of a pension at the end of it."

"I see."

"Whether you do or not doesn't matter much. We have a job to do and a murderer to bring to justice. We'll get a warrant to search the premises before we leave. We may be the law around here, but the Rule Britannia still applies to most things and limits what we may desperately want to do."

"Like throttle the life out of some lying little shit." He covered his mouth. "Sorry, Sir. It just slipped out."

"I didn't hear what you said, and it probably wasn't important."

"I said…"

"I don't want to know what you said. I only want to know what you think, and then only if I ask." I caught myself sounding more and more like my first sergeant on the Met.

The puzzled look descended over his face for a moment. Then he brightened. "I understand, Sir. A bit like, 'Speak only when you're spoken to' isn't it? And I'll only offer an opinion if you ask for one."

I'd had brighter lance bombardiers under my command when I was in the Royal Artillery, men who had been in the army since they were fourteen. Why couldn't I have one now?

An hour later, search warrant in hand, we went through King Tukurahman's opulent home with a fine-tooth comb. We found the laboratory used for making morphine and heroin on the ground floor at the rear of the house, the door unlocked and all the raw ingredients and equipment needed for the process in full view. It looked as if Tukurahman, or someone else, had been interrupted and left the room hurriedly.

Through the sergeant, O'Toole questioned the servant who had discovered the body. Although visibly withering under the sergeant's menacing scowl, the man denied all knowledge of the lab. He appealed to me for help. I raised my eyebrows and offered a light cough. The man immediately recanted and admitted to not only knowing about the lab, but also to assisting his employer and master in the refining process. We were at last getting somewhere, but at that moment I didn't know where. We pressed on.

"Ask him about a pistol, Inspector," I suggested, when the well of questions ran dry.

"He keeps a small pistol in the drawer of his desk in his study," the servant replied.

"Show me," O'Toole said, and we followed the servant through the house to the study.

"There," the servant said, and lo and behold, in the top righthand drawer of the enormous mahogany desk lay a pistol with a silencer still attached to the muzzle. I saw plenty of firearms of all shapes and sizes once I joined the army in 1914, but I had never come across one like this. I peered closely at the gun without touching it, a semi-automatic of some sort by the looks of it, with a small magazine in the pistol grip. The manufacturer's name was not uppermost, but I suspected it might be a Beretta, or some similar weapon of European manufacture.

"Find me a manila envelope, Inspector," I said, "and we'll take this little darling with us."

O'Toole found an envelope in a filing cabinet filled with stationery and I slipped the pistol into it by inserting a slim ivory letter opener through the trigger guard. The weapon had obviously not been cleaned recently but I could not tell from the smell when it last had been fired, although there were powder burns on the silencer.

From the wide-eyed and suitably terrified servant we obtained a list of the household servants, the names of Tukurahman's wives and a small list of visitors who had been in the house in the past twenty-four hours. These latter turned out to be two men: Tukurahman's personal physician, Dr. Imran Aziz; and a business associate who had arrived around ten o'clock the previous evening and left a few minutes later. Dr. Aziz had called during the evening and again around seven that morning, and both times had only spent a few minutes with his patient.

We returned to the police station where our fingerprint expert lifted several sets of prints from the flat surfaces of the gun, which did in fact turn out to be a .32 caliber Beretta. The prints, however, were mostly smudges with several overlaid on others and originated from more than one individual, though how many had handled the gun since it was last cleaned was anyone's guess. I took the gun down to the firing range in the basement of the police station. I briefly told the firearms officer about the murder and what I needed. He took the gun apart.

"It's been fired recently," he said. "I can't tell you when, though. It definitely hasn't been cleaned since. There's spent powder all over it, in the barrel and the silencer. It's the first I've seen. They've only just started making them for the Italian army. Nice silencer, by the way. Custom made. You wouldn't hear it go off from the next room."

"Do a test fire. We have bullets from a corpse in the morgue we'd like to compare with these."

He went to his desk, pulled out a cardboard box, and loaded the clip. "Only an eight-shot mag. It's designed for personal use, as a last resort. Low muzzle velocity, short range. Stand back." He took aim at a paper target about twenty feet away and fired all eight shots through a keyhole not much larger than the caliber of the bullet. The sound of the gun firing with the silencer fitted was not much louder than a light cough. He extracted all eight bullets from the sandbag behind the target and handed them to me.

"You'll need a microscope to compare the striations on these with the ones fished out from the brain. I'm sure Dr. D'Eath will be able to provide what you want." He glanced at his wristwatch. "You might catch him in if you hurry."

O'Toole and I beat the record for the dash from the K.L. police station to the hospital and caught the pathologist packing up for the day.

"One more thing before you go," I panted, still winded from my headlong sprint down the corridors and staircases of the Kuala Lumpur hospital.

D'Eath gave me an ill-tempered scowl. I handed him the eight rounds from the Beretta. "Could you give these a quick squint and compare them with the ones you fished out from King Tukurahman's noggin." I paused to catch my breath. "Please," I added. "They may be from the same gun."

I had his interest aroused. Apart from his barely controlled joy at dissecting a fresh cadaver, I knew D'Eath fancied himself as a bit of a forensic firearms expert. He took the bullets from me without another word, crossed the floor and pulled the cover off a microscope. I heard him grunt a couple of times.

"To judge from the striations, these all appear to have come from the same source."

"They did, less than a quarter of an hour ago."

He crossed the floor again, unlocked a steel cabinet and retrieved a small box. "The bullets removed from the brain of Abdul Tukurahman today," he said. He placed one under the microscope and examined it in silence, adjusting the focus several times. He then examined each of the others, one by one. "No question in my mind the eight you just gave me and the six I extracted from the deceased's brain were fired from the same gun." He gave a satisfied smile.

"Certain enough for court?" I said.

"Never absolutely certain, Masters. But I'd say ninety-nine-point nine percent sure."

"Photographs for evidence in court?"

"Coming right up." He fixed a camera to the eyepiece and clicked away for several minutes until he was satisfied with his handiwork. "I'll develop and print enlargements for you if you'd like to wait. Or you can pick them up in the morning."

"We have people to see and places to go, D'Eath," I said. "Tomorrow is fine."

In the corridor, and once the morgue door was closed behind us, O'Toole turned to me. "Who are we going to see now? And where are we going?"

"To the club for a drink. We've earned one. Or more than one if you feel like it. We've got the murder weapon. All we have to do now is find out who fired it, when, why, and why six times when once was probably enough, and six, but not all eight. That can wait until tomorrow."

"But what about the doctor and the business chappie who came last night?"

"Dr. Aziz will still be there tomorrow. As for the business

associate, if he's only half as careful and elusive as King Tukurahman, we'll probably never track down. He may have pulled the trigger, but my guess is he probably left long before Tukurahman died. D'Eath placed the time of death tentatively around seven this morning. Unless the business associate returned unobserved, or the servant's lying, Tukurahman died about eight hours after the visitor left."

"I see."

We had reached the top of the stairs by that time and I stopped to catch my breath. "Besides, I'm thirsty." We walked down a corridor and into the hospitals' main receiving area. I looked through the doors to the parking area in front. "Raining, as usual," I said. "Even more of a reason to have a drink. Go and see if the driver's anywhere near."

The Honourable Noel trotted off and came back a moment later. I saw the black police Wolseley pull up and stop in front of the main doors in the spot reserved for ambulances. Without getting too wet, I slid into the rear passenger seat with O'Toole next to me.

"The Imperial Club," I told the driver.

The sight of two uniformed, armed police officers in the club did not raise an eyebrow. It was where most of us hung out after work. Very few of us were married with wives, children and homes to go to, and the club was as good a place to unwind as any, and better than most. The selection of Scotch was good, if a trifle expensive, the menu as varied and palatable as anywhere in Kuala Lumpur, and the company affable. Unlike the officers' mess in the army, there was no proscription on talking shop or discussing women.

"So far, so good," I said, after we placed our drinks order. It was fully dark by now and I couldn't see the rain through the reflections in the large picture windows behind O'Toole. I could hear it though, and even inside the club, the smell of wet tropical earth and decaying vegetation infused the air. Most chaps get used to it after a while, but those of us who served in Flanders remember it as the smell of fresh turned mud after a bombardment, or the smell of a newly dug mass grave. On the plus side, at least that night it didn't carry the stench of rotting corpses. That was bad enough in the artillery, but I pitied the poor bloody infantryman who had to live in an abattoir daily. I don't think I could have done it but I knew plenty who had, and few were ever the same again.

I raised my glass of Scotch and soda. "Cheers. All we know at this point is how it was done. The rest is an unknown. Time to put our thinking caps on."

"The servant," O'Toole said hesitantly. "Awang, or something. I don't trust him. I don't think he's telling us the truth. At least, not all of it."

"He was only too quick and happy to lead us to what wouldn't incriminate him. What's he hiding? Any ideas?"

"The identity of the trigger man, Sir?"

"You sound like someone out of one of those Hollywood gangster films, O'Toole."

"Sorry, Sir. Do you think he did it?"

"I've no more idea now than I did at breakfast this morning. If he did, then why? We've not uncovered a motive. He has a good job. He runs the household. He's Tukerahman's right hand man. According to him, he's been a household servant there since Tukurahman was a boy. To borrow an expression from your gangster films, he probably knows where all the bodies are buried, literally and metaphorically. He may even have had a hand in some of the more nefarious deeds, whatever they were. But to kill the boss? To kiss his weekly envelope goodbye? If he did, we need an awful lot more to go on."

"How about the doctor?"

"We'll talk to him tomorrow. He didn't come back today, did he?"

"Not that I'm aware of."

"No doubt word got back to him that his biggest client was dead."

"Or he already knew he would be, Sir."

"Aziz slipped his meal ticket a lethal cocktail? Possibly. We'll know more when D'Eath gives us his toxicology report."

"What about the wives?"

"What about the wives?" I repeated.

"We haven't spoken to them yet."

"And what do you anticipate getting out of them?"

"I don't know. But we should at least question them, find out where they were at breakfast time this morning, that sort of thing."

"I shall leave that in your very capable hands, O'Toole, while I pick up the glossies from D'Eath, and hopefully his toxicology report."

The Honourable Noel sat back with a look of satisfaction across his face. The poor chap couldn't tell sarcasm from a compliment. It was like having a battle of wits with an unarmed opponent. Then I was hit by a pang of remorse. I shouldn't have said that, but to take it back or to offer an explanation would only make matters worse. I mentally chastised myself and promised not to do it again.

He leaned forward and dropped his voice to a loud whisper. "It would be convenient, though, Sir, if Awang confessed to killing his boss and told us why, wouldn't it?"

I leaned forward and dropped my voice in return. "It would. Or the doctor. Or the business associate. Or any one of the wives or servants. The fingerprints on the gun match. We find powder burns on the wrist or sleeve of the murderer's clothing which the murderer neglects to wash off before we arrive." I paused, searching my memory. "I didn't smell gunpowder on Awang when we arrived. Did you?"

I watched O'Toole think for a minute before he said, "I can't say I did, now you mention it."

"Which could mean that the servant, Awang, either wasn't your trigger man, or he had time to wash, change his clothes and dispose of them in the laundry or somewhere before he called us."

"Either is possible, I suppose, Sir."

"And if Awang did pull the trigger and pump six rounds into the back of his employer's head, then we need to find out why. Perhaps he'll tell us if we ask politely." I realized I had gone overboard with the sarcasm again, broken my promise and stood to lose a young officer who may yet improbably turn out to be a valuable resource to the Colonial Police. "Another drink?" I said, hoping to turn the Honourable Noel's attention away from my rudeness. I'm normally a long-suffering individual who rarely takes offence, but somehow the Honourable Noel seemed to have the knack of rubbing me the wrong way. It probably wasn't his fault and he likely had no idea he was doing it. But he made me thankful that I was the only child of a bank manager from Bournemouth and not a titled peer of the realm, and Old Etonian.

The morning came, teeming with rain and hotter than Hades. It reminded me of a Turkish bath I once foolishly allowed myself to be talked into taking in a sleazy bath house whilst on leave in London's Soho. Like that occasion, as soon as a break in the downpour occurred steam rose from the paved surfaces and vegetation alike. It was on mornings like this that I pined for Bournemouth, the sea front, the golden sand and the pier where, as a boy in the summer holidays I used to wet a line in a vain attempt to catch my supper. Sometimes it was hot enough on the pier to roll up my shirt sleeves and come home with red sunburn on my arms. But those days didn't happen often and the most I normally got from the Bournemouth weather was a wind-reddened face and ears and salt-caked, chapped lips. How I would have swapped them for a day like this!

I sent O'Toole over to Tukurahman's house immediately after breakfast to make further enquiries. Still in a bad mood over the weather in K.L., I was about to call D'Eath at the morgue for a progress report when the phone rang in my office. With O'Toole out, I had to answer it myself.

"A breakthrough, Sir," O'Toole's excited voice came down the wire.

"Elaborate," I said grumpily.

"I think you might like to come over and finish the interviews yourself, Sir."

"And why is that?"

"It's a can of worms, Sir."

My mind drifted to the Bournemouth pier and my tin of wrigglers waiting to be gobbled up by an unwary mackerel.

"Is that another of your American expressions, O'Toole?"

"I suppose it is, Sir. I hadn't thought of it like that."

"Do go on," I said, trying supremely hard to suppress the impatience in my voice.

"The sergeant's here doing the translation for me. If the sergeant is correct, then the servant has confessed to shooting the king. Then each of the wives confessed to shooting him. I'm sorry, Sir, but it's a bit of a shambles."

I wanted to say something short, sharp and Anglo-Saxon in origin. A word not fit for the ears of ladies or permitted in Parliament, though I'm certain both ladies and Parliamentarians had heard it more than once, and probably used it. "I'll be right over," I assured him, and grabbed a notebook from my desk drawer.

Ten minutes later I was at the late King Tukurahman's home. I took O'Toole to one side. "Tell me again in words of one syllable what they told you."

"Well, they didn't tell me. It was the sergeant who told me. Except for the servant, who speaks English, and the oldest wife, who speaks better English that either of us, none of them speaks a word of anything but Malay."

I suppressed an urge to do a slow imitation of the burning bush in the Book of Exodus. With supreme difficulty I relaxed my jaw line. "I'll tell you what," I said. "I'll question them myself. One at a time."

"Oh, I did that, Sir. With the sergeant's help, of course.

"I'll do it in Malay. No middle man to get in the way of whatever pearls fall at our feet. I'll start with the chief wife, or whatever she calls herself."

O'Toole led the way into a smaller drawing room and closed the door behind us. A stunningly beautiful woman in her thirties, dressed in the European manner of a bereaved widow, rose gracefully to greet me, and as she did so she drew back the black veil covering her face. I took in the flawless, café au lait complexion, her dark brown eyes and the row of perfectly even white teeth when she smiled. She offered me her hand as if she expected me to kiss her fingers.

"I am Fatima, Abdul Tukurahman's first wife," she said with a slight curtsey. I immediately released her hand rather than have it linger in mine, which would have been my overwhelming preference.

"Assistant Commissioner Masters of the Colonial Police Force in Malaya," I said, managing each syllable without my tongue actually sticking to any one of them and making me sound like a complete clot.

"And you are here to investigate my husband's death." It came out as a statement rather than a question and left me with the impression that she was a woman accustomed to giving orders, to being obeyed, and to being respected.

"If you don't mind, I have some questions to put to you, your staff and to other members of your family."

"You have already questioned Awang. I can assure you he has nothing more to offer. If you are referring to my sisters, my late husband's other wives, they have already told your officer all they know. Where would you like to start?"

"With some background. Frankly, everything you have told Inspector O'Toole is a bit too fanciful to believe." She shot me a cross look. "At least, at face value," I added hastily. "And meaning no disrespect."

"Do sit down, Commissioner. This might take a while."

She had that mesmerizing quality that defied disobedience. I sat in the offered chair and accepted perhaps one of the most delicious cups of coffee I have ever had, anywhere.

"I was educated privately at an English-speaking, all-girls school in Delhi. My father was – still is, in fact – the Maharaja of Allahabad. We are not the average, poverty-stricken Indian family. We are Muslims, in a minority in what is now UP."

"UP?"

"The United Provinces, the area around the middle Ganges. You may have heard of it."

"The Ganges, of course. But not the United Provinces."

"It was created two months ago. Good news travels slowly these days."

She had me there. It could have been the far side of the moon for all I knew. I took her word for it. I could always check the facts later. Someone would have an Encyclopaedia Britannica somewhere.

"I married Abdul immediately after I left school. It had been arranged since shortly after I was born. I had no objection. I found India under the British stifling. No offence meant, Commissioner, but you know how it can be."

I did but decided not to admit it verbally. I nodded slowly instead.

"More the case there than here, Commissioner. In Malaya, you advise, we rule. At least that's the way it's made out to be, and why spoil the illusion. But inevitably I discovered that I merely exchanged one suffocating existence for another."

I raised my eyebrows, hoping she would take the momentary twitch as an invitation to continue. She took a sip of coffee and replaced the cup in the saucer.

"Abdul, my late husband, was very controlling. Thanks to my British education and my refusal to become a secretary, clerk or school teacher or, Heaven forbid, that lowest of the low, a governess, I was a more determined and independent thinker. He wanted me to conform, to bend to his will. I did at first. Then I grew bored. Not long after that he took a second wife and repeated the process. Then a third, and a fourth and a fifth."

"Not uncommon, or so I'm led to believe among wealthy Muslims."

"None of us has children, Commissioner, which is a source of great embarrassment for him, and a source of anger which he directs to each of personally in the form of regular beatings for our barrenness."

"But that can't be your fault, surely. Not all of you."

"You are absolutely correct. Not one of us is barren. We are all capable of bearing children. Believe me, we have no secrets among us. I think you know what I'm getting at."

I felt my face grow red. I was not in the habit of discussing the more intimate workings of the female human body, and least of all having them explained to me by a woman, and a beautiful one at that. Fatima must have guessed at my discomfort. She smiled at me. A nod's as good as a wink to a blind man, so my old sergeant used to say, and a nod accompanied her smile.

"I'm sure you do, Commissioner. The plain truth is that Abdul was incapable of fathering a child, no matter how hard he tried. The spirit was willing but the flesh was weak? I think that's an expression people sometimes use."

"I see." At least I thought I did.

She gave me another smile, this time a coy one. "I'm pregnant."

I didn't know what to say. "Congratulations," sprang to mind, but might have been inappropriate coming from the senior investigating officer in a murder case to someone who had, according to O'Toole, already confessed to shooting her husband.

"And as I already implied, it's not by my husband, overjoyed as he was when I told him. Then he realized the truth. We have not slept together for three years, for which I thank Allah. The doctor confirmed it a week ago. That would have been the last straw if the truth had ever leaked out. My husband was very weak and the light bruises he left have vanished, thanks to arnica and ice."

"What did you do?"

"I told him if he kicked me out, I would tell the world that he was not only impotent but incapable of making love to a woman."

"How did he take that?"

"He told me he was going to kill me to cover up the cause of his shame. An honour killing would absolve him and leave me and my memory tarnished as a common prostitute. We went back and forth in a similar vein for some time. I'm sure, as a man of the world, you know how these things go."

"So, with or without the help, or perhaps I should call it the connivance of the father of your child, you plotted to kill your husband, which you successfully managed to do sometime before breakfast yesterday." I could not help a note of triumph creeping into my voice. The Commissioner of Police would be thrilled, as would the deputy commissioner and my fellow assistant commissioners, of which I was one of the more senior. My star, which had been on a horizontal trajectory of late, might once more be in the ascendance.

"Not exactly." She arched her eyebrows. "More coffee?"

"I'd love some," I said. It really was excellent coffee. At a nod from Fatima a servant poured, added a sugar lump and cream and handed me the cup and saucer.

"Not exactly, you said, Mrs. Tukurahman," I repeated slowly after taking a couple of appreciative sips.

"The other wives and I had long since playfully planned what we would do should a tragic event such as this occur, not dreaming that it might become a reality. He treated us all rather badly, you know. Poor Mumtaz, the youngest. She was barely eleven when he married her. She hadn't a clue, poor lamb. She's still not sixteen and she's terrified of him."

"I see," I said, although I didn't really. I resorted to the script. "Would you please tell me in your own words what happened yesterday morning." I was on pretty firm ground there, but to be on the safe side I left my notebook and pencil in my breast pocket. I didn't want to ruin the moment when the truth was supposed to come out by making the affair all formal and police-like. I hoped O'Toole had the presence of mind to take notes discreetly somewhere in the background.

"Perhaps I should start from a bit nearer the beginning rather than at the end and have to work backwards, if that's all right with you."

"Perfectly," I said, which seemed to be the way to go, especially as she had suggested it. She reminded me of She Who Must Be Obeyed, the title character in the popular H. Ryder Haggard novel *She*. Command seemed to come second nature to her, and who was I to disagree? Or disobey?

"Dr. Imran Aziz is my late husband's personal physician. He is also my lover and the father of my unborn child. He attended my husband twice a day for various minor and major ailments. More recently he treated my husband with pain killers for inoperable, terminal cancer. My husband has used opium for many years. When Dr. Aziz diagnosed cancer, he prescribed morphine, and most recently heroin, both of which my husband, with Awang's help, made in his laboratory. In the last few days of his life, my husband was a walking dead man. There's no other way to put it."

"Was this a mercy killing of some sort? It's still murder, you know, even if you can justify it in your own mind." I waited for the confession to tumble out where it could be recorded verbatim, and in triplicate, for use in court.

"No."

"Oh," I said. I gathered my disassembled wits bit by bit. "Then this wasn't a mercy killing?"

"I think we've already covered that possibility, Commissioner." I detected withering scorn in her voice which could only be directed at me. Suitably chastised, I tried a different tack.

"It therefore leaves me to believe you deliberately shot and killed your husband."

She hesitated, and I knew I'd got her. All I had to do was reel her in, the elusive mackerel for my supper.

"Yes, and no, in that order."

She had me there. "Perhaps you could offer a fuller explanation, madam," I said rather too huffily.

"Yes, I deliberately shot my husband in the back of the head. But no, I didn't kill him."

"But the pathologist's report at the post mortem clearly showed six bullet tracks through your husband's brain, any one of which would undoubtedly have killed him."

"We all took turns shooting him, from me, the oldest, down to Mumtaz, the youngest. He was lying face down on the carpet when I shot him. He already had a bullet in the back of his head. You can ask the others. None of us killed him. He was quite dead before any one of us squeezed the trigger." She seemed quite unmoved by the telling of this grizzly turn of events.

"Then who fired the first shot?"

"Alas. I can't help you there. You're the policeman, Commissioner. Isn't that for you to find out?"

Did I believe her? I didn't know, but at least it was plausible. If she was telling the truth, then an imminent arrest was starting to look more like a long shot in the Grand National. I was sure there was something somewhere about committing an indignity to a dead body, which might fit the firing of five bullets into the back of the head of a dead man. But the more I pondered the question, the less certain I became. I would have to look it up back at the station.

I finished my coffee in two rather unmannerly and noisy gulps and put my cup down in its saucer. "You've been most helpful," I said, with a smile. "I have no further questions at this time." I feared I sounded altogether too pompous and rather much like a lawyer ending a cross examination in court. I stood. "I shall question the other wives as a matter of course, with the aid of a police interpreter." I turned to O'Toole. "To the morgue, I think, to gather the forensic evidence." It sounded good and it may even have the effect of her begging us to stay with a more detailed confession. We were not so lucky.

"Will I see you again later, Commissioner?" she said with another of her coy smiles.

"Perhaps later this afternoon? Say, around four?"

"In time for afternoon tea."

In the police car O'Toole turned to me. "A bit rum, what?" he said. "I mean, admitting to everything but insisting she didn't kill him. I don't know how you even got her that far."

"Technique," I said. "It comes with practice and experience." And left it at that. The plain fact was that I had uncovered little more than O'Toole had a couple of hours before. We still had an unsolved murder with multiple suspects, five of which either had, or soon would, confess to firing a bullet into the back of the head of their already dead husband. Two unused rounds remained in the Beretta when we examined it. Six had entered and failed to exit the head of Tukurahman. It didn't take a genius to do the arithmetic without the aid of a slide rule. So, who fired the first round, the fatal shot, if Fatima were to be believed?

We interrupted the pathologist enjoying an early sandwich lunch at his desk.

"My report is right here," he said, pushing a government form across the desk. "Take your time." He bit into the sandwich and chomped away unhurriedly without offering further explanation of his findings.

I glanced at the report and passed it to O'Toole, who read it with a furrowed brow.

"The toxicology report could be Egyptian hieroglyphics for all I know," O'Toole said. "Can anyone translate?"

D'Eath wiped his mouth with a linen table napkin. "He had enough heroin in his system to kill most men, but I suspect it didn't. His body, scrawny as it was, had probably become accustomed to ever increasing doses. His arms are covered in needle track marks. Virtually every vein in his body has been pierced at one time or another."

"How did he die, Doctor?" O'Toole asked.

"Heart failure almost certainly. You didn't find blood on the floor, did you?"

"No," I said.

"Because his heart had already stopped beating and couldn't pump any blood out through the wound site."

"Is it possible he still had a faint heartbeat when the first bullet penetrated his brain? And that would be enough to stop the heart?"

"Masters, you're clutching at straws. You desperately want a murder to solve and I can't oblige. Have you any idea who fired the shots?"

"We have a pretty good idea, D'Eath. A confession of sorts that should stand up in court even with a good defence lawyer."

"Well, whoever it was, he almost certainly didn't kill our victim, and I'll testify to that if called upon to do so. Sorry to disappoint."

"It wouldn't be the first time. But the truth must be served. Thank you for your time and expertise. May I take a copy of your report?"

"By all means."

"That's not very helpful, if you ask me," O'Toole said after we climbed into the back of the police Wolseley. "We have a dead body full of heroin and bullet holes, the chief widow who admits to firing one of the shots, a servant who aids and abets the manufacture of an illegal drug, four more widows who most likely shot their husband at least once, and no charge laid. It's a Hollywood gangster's dream."

"Abandon hope all ye who enter, O'Toole. Dante Alighieri. We have yet to meet Charon and cross the River Styx. All is not yet lost." Unsurprisingly, the literary allusions flew unimpeded over his head.

"Where to next, Sir?"

"To visit Dr. Aziz and see what he has to say." I gave the driver the instructions and half an hour later we pulled up in front of the doctor's private surgery in Bukit Bintang.

We waited briefly before Dr. Aziz welcomed us into his office. The doctor, a smartly dressed, good-looking youngish man of above average height and a slim build greeted us with, "Word reached me yesterday," he said. "There was nothing I could do. I saw him on my way to do my rounds in the hospital as I do twice a day seven days a week. I gave him his medication – morphine – for the pain, to keep him as comfortable as possible during his final days, and I left him in an armchair in his drawing room. That was shortly before seven in the morning."

"The pathologist's report states that Mr. Tukurahman probably died of a heart attack between seven and nine that morning. Terminal cancer and a large quantity of both morphine and heroin in his blood stream were contributory causes."

"I was not aware of heroin. I certainly did not prescribe or administer it, Commissioner." He sounded huffy, as if I had accused him of medical malpractice or some other form of impropriety.

"He was shot with his own gun. He had six bullets in his brain," I continued, "but apparently none killed him as he was already dead. We know who fired five of the bullets. We hope you can tell us who fired the first."

The doctor frowned. "It wasn't me, I can assure you, Commissioner. The Hippocratic oath prohibits me from taking life."

"An oath honoured more in the breach than the observance, as Shakespeare once said."

Dr. Aziz shot me a dirty look, tightened his jaw, but said nothing.

"You could have hastened his departure with an overdose of morphine, Doctor. With what was already in his body it would hardly raise an eyebrow."

"Nevertheless, I did not, Commissioner," he said through tight, thin lips. "Nor did I shoot him. I didn't even know Mr. Tukurahman had a gun. Perhaps you might address your enquiries to Awang, his major domo."

"We already have, Doctor Aziz." Which was true, although the questioning had only been cursory.

"You might wish to speak to him again, then, Commissioner. I suspect he knows more than he has let on, even if you don't." He rose from behind his desk and smiled politely. He held out his hand which I took. "I'm sorry I couldn't be of more help."

"I should offer my congratulations on your upcoming parenthood, Doctor. I hope your wife doesn't disapprove."

He snatched his hand from mine with fury in his dark eyes. "I am not married, Commissioner. One day, perhaps, if Fatima will have me. That will be her decision."

"I did get the impression she makes good decisions. I wish you both well when the time comes."

Standing in the sunshine outside the surgery, O'Toole said, "I didn't much like him either, Sir. A bit too self-assured and smarmy. He probably never received a good thrashing for impertinence from a prefect. I can't understand what she sees in him."

"Everything her late husband didn't possess. Youth, good looks, virility. All the things she's been missing all her adult life. I can't say I blame her."

"Each to his own, Sir. She's not my type. Too much of the tar brush."

"I could see that the moment I saw you in the room with her when I questioned her. Your open hostility was apparent in your body language even if you didn't utter a word. You should work on that. People talk to us out of fear or because they like and trust us. They won't talk to us otherwise and we'll get nowhere with an investigation."

Which was rather where we stood right then, but if he realized it, he had enough gumption not to say anything. I had blown the interview with Aziz, allowing my dislike for the man to cloud my thinking and consequently my line of questioning. I had given Aziz every reason to dislike me, and I suspect trust had flown out of the window. In spite of my immediate and unreasonable dislike for the man, however, I couldn't bring myself to believe that he had pulled the trigger on the first shot or deliberately given his patient an overdose. Tukurahman was dying, in a matter of minutes or hours as it happened, rather than days or weeks. I couldn't see Aziz risking losing his licence to practice medicine, or even go to jail, over his patient. An accommodation with Fatima, even marriage, if that's what she wanted, would only be a matter of time. Or a dissolution of their relationship if no accommodation could be reached. It was their problem to resolve and neither the Medical Licencing Board nor the Malaya Colonial Police really had any business interfering.

O'Toole and I returned to Tukurahman's home. With the help of a police sergeant I questioned the other four wives separately. All told me the same thing: Fatima had shot first. They had each taken it in turns to fire one round into the back of their husband's head in order of seniority, finishing with Mumtaz. She was the one who broke down crying. "It was awful," she wailed. "I didn't want to do it, but Fatima said it would be symbolic if we all did it to rid ourselves of a horrible man. So I shot him, once, just like they did. Now we are all truly sisters, in life and death. Am I going to jail? I don't want to go to jail."

I assured the pathetic little creature that she was too young to go to jail, and hoped I was right. With Judge Faulkner now permanently off the scene, no longer alive to pronounce the death sentence or a lengthy stretch of imprisonment, I thought there was a good chance of leniency, if we ever pressed charges and got a conviction. Right then I didn't think any of them had committed murder, and if D'Eath was correct in his findings, no one had.

There remained only one person I needed to question—the servant, Awang. When I asked to speak to him, I was told that he had retired to his room with a migraine headache. Nervous tension, I assumed, as the jaws of the vise that is the law closed around him. One of the household servants took O'Toole, the sergeant and me to the man's room at the rear of the house. He came to the door in response to O'Toole's knock and opened it. He took a couple of steps back and sat on his bed, looking like a prize fighter who had been badly beaten on points.

"*Saya perlu bertanya beberapa soalan*," I said. "I need to ask you some questions."

Awang's face and eyes registered terror as he looked from me to the sergeant and back. He nodded and held his head in his hands.

"*Adakah anda api pukulan yang pertama?*"

He struggled to his feet and looked straight into my eyes. He swayed. He held out his arms to balance himself and opened his mouth to say something. It sounded like "*Saya*," the Malay for 'I', but before he could say the all-important, 'did', or didn't', he collapsed in a heap at my feet.

"Probably fainted, Sir," O'Toole said. "Whatever you said to him most likely put the fear of Christ into him."

"I hope I asked him if he fired the first shot. This could be the reaction of a guilty man, thinking he'd be accused of murdering his employer. He'll come round in a minute."

I stood back as O'Toole felt for a pulse in the man's throat. He looked up at me with consternation on his face. "There's no pulse, Sir. And he's not breathing. I think he's dead."

"Are you sure?"

"Pretty sure, Sir. Feel for yourself."

"I'll take your word for it, O'Toole." I turned to the sergeant. "Call for an ambulance."

"There's no question he's dead, Masters," Dr. D'Eath said, when he examined Awang on the stainless-steel table in the morgue in the presence of O'Toole and me. "All that remains is to determine the cause."

"He was Tukurahman's personal servant and a potential witness in the case of the mysterious death of his employer," I said.

"I've told you before, Masters, there's nothing suspicious, mysterious or otherwise unexplained about Tukurahman's death. It was heart, plain and simple. You can take that to the bank. Don't waste any more police time on it. Now, let's have a look inside this man's head." He picked up a small circular power saw and switched it on. In moments the top of Awang's head lay on one side and his brain in a stainless-steel bowl.

"As plain as the nose on your face, Commissioner." The pathologist pointed to one side of the grey mass on front of him. "Burst artery causes a brain haemorrhage, an aneurism. Death is swift. Nothing could have saved him. Did he complain of a headache, by the way?"

"Yes. And he was really groggy when we first spoke to him. We thought he had fainted until we couldn't find any vital signs."

"Don't blame yourselves. There was nothing you could do. It was irreversible since the onset of the headache."

I hadn't actually thought of shouldering any of the blame for the man's death, but it was of some comfort to know that I needn't. We left the pathologist humming softly as he dissected Awang's corpse, as happy as a clam at high tide in his work, and returned to the police station to file my report. The deputy commissioner called me into his office.

"Someone behind bars for this, Masters?"

"No, Sir." I was about to expound, when he gave me an icy look.

"And why not? A man is murdered, execution-style, according to your interim report. Half a dozen suspects questioned and no arrest?"

"I didn't want to go off half-cocked, Sir. I felt it important to gather all the evidence possible before I promulgated a theory, rather than devise a hypothesis and then search for facts and evidence to support it. Putting the cart before the horse, as it were."

"No. Quite. A pity more don't see police work in that light."

"Anyway, according to the pathologist, death was from natural causes, a heart attack which only just preceded death from multiple cancers."

"But the bullets to the brain. How do you explain those?"

"He was already dead when the first shot was fired. I was initially surprised by the absence of blood from six gunshot wounds. But if the heart stops before the first shot, little or no blood flows, particularly from the brain. It's all in the path report, Sir."

"And the servant? What about him?"

"We'll never know, Sir. Awang, the servant, was about to tell us something but he collapsed and died before he could get it out. By all accounts he was devoted to his master. I suspect he may have fired the first shot to show Tukurahman's wives, who all despised their husband, how to work the gun. Or he may have fired the first shot without realizing there were five others who were perfectly happy to see their husband dead. Knowing his master was on the point of death, perhaps Awang shot him to save any further pain and suffering, a mercy killing. And perhaps Awang didn't fire the shot at all, but someone else did, someone who remains unknown at this time, and left Awang to discover the body. Or perhaps Awang and the wives are all lying and he fired all six shots. Who knows? I certainly don't, and I don't think the Force can justify spending the time and manpower on a wild goose chase when the path report says it was death by natural causes."

That little speech, my first verbal murder/non-murder report to my deputy commissioner, left me exhausted. He didn't offer me a chair but left me standing at ease in front of him, cap under my arm, as if I were still in the army.

"Let me have your written report before you go home tonight,

Masters. That is all."

I turned and marched out of his office. I spent the next few hours writing my report, counting down the time before the deputy commissioner usually left for the day. With ten minutes to spare I knocked on his door. "My report, Sir, as requested." I handed him the file.

He took it and placed it unopened on his desk. He tapped it a couple of times before looking at me.

"It's all in here, is it?"

"Yes, Sir."

"Good."

"If you need any further explanation I would be happy to give it."

"If it's all here." He tapped the file again. "No further explanation would be needed, would there?"

"No, Sir."

"Good." We seemed to be back to the beginning. He eased his bulk in his swivel chair and set it creaking. "I've spoken to the Commissioner about this case. He agrees we should not spend any more manpower chasing a will o' the wisp. The man was only a native and of little consequence. I'm marking it 'Case Closed.'" He took a rubber stamp from a collection hanging from a circular rubber stamp stand, and in true Civil Service fashion, pressed it on an ink pad and thumped the stamp on the front cover.

I never discovered if he, or anyone else, ever read the report, nor why the Force was only too happy to see the back of Tukurahman. It would probably turn out to be a case of one villain down and several more fighting a turf war to take his place.

I saw Fatima the next morning as the official bearer of the news. She met me at the front door. She did not seem the least upset at my presence and only a little down at the mouth over the death of Awang.

"He was a good man and totally devoted to my husband. He was like a big brother to him while Abdul was growing up. They were together for over fifty years," she said, quietly, over coffee in the small drawing room. "I will miss him. We all will. And now that he's gone I can confide in you, if you promise it will go no further."

"My final report is in. The case is officially closed. No amendments allowed."

"I saw Awang fire the shot. I think I surprised him. He turned the pistol on himself but he was old, slow and weak, and I was quicker and stronger. I took the gun from Awang and shot Abdul. My sisters ran to the room. I swore them to secrecy and made them shoot Abdul in turn so that we would be forever linked in an unbreakable chain. Does that surprise you?"

"No. It's much along the lines I suspected. The most unfortunate thing about his death as far as the Police are concerned, is that there will be a war between rival gangs to take over control over your late husband's business empire. It might not be safe to stay here."

"My sisters and I will move. I will marry Imran once these clothes become too tight and uncomfortable. He has already agreed. I understand you didn't get along too well with him."

"Unfortunately not. It was entirely my fault and I must apologize to him."

"I have already intervened. Pressure, tension, the need to satisfy your superiors balanced against uncovering the truth. He understood. You will be invited to the wedding. I hope you will accept."

"Gladly." I rose to leave.

She stood and walked to the front door with me.

"There is one more thing you should know, Commissioner Masters."

I was somewhat taken back. "And what is that?"

"Abdul. My late husband. He really was the grandson of King Mongkut." She paused. "As are so many others."

7. THE HEADLESS BOOTHLEGGER

It was mid-December 1940 when the Commissioner summoned me to his office as we were shutting up for the day.

"Just had a call from Ernest Pengilly, the British Resident in Brunei. It seems that the Sultan's estate manager has blown his head off with a shotgun. Literally. Pengilly seems to think the local Inspector's young and isn't up to this sort of thing and would we help?" He dropped his voice. "Just between us, I think he's a bit of an old woman but I wouldn't want his job for anything." He brightened. "Nothing on your desk that won't wait?"

I shook my head and watched my two days off go up in smoke. One of the inevitabilities of investigating a death, however it arrives, is that we, the police, invariably arrive on the scene after the event. We are left to gather evidence in determining the cause and, in the event of an apparent suicide, the state of mind of the deceased immediately prior to his demise—in other words the Who, What, When, Where, Why and How of the matter.

The second of the inevitabilities of police work is what I have long called 'The Friday Rule'. Although in the police force tragedies requiring our intervention happen all the time, there seems to be a fascination with calling for our help on a Friday afternoon. And unless I was swift in completing my investigation, Christmas leave sat squarely in the crosshairs.

"The Sultan's a powerful wog," the Commissioner said. I suppressed a wince. A common enough word in Malaya as well as in England, but nonetheless one my father had forbidden me to utter. 'You will respect everyone,' my father hammered into me the first time I said the word in his presence. 'Even those who have shown they don't deserve it.' I think I was about seven. I took the rebuke, and the accompanying spanking, to heart.

"He pretty well owns the country," the Commissioner continued without missing a beat. "The Sultan, I mean. They discovered oil there in twenty-nine. He's rolling in money so we can't afford to upset him. Pengilly wants someone to conduct an investigation into the death and file a report. Sounds like a pretty straightforward suicide, but just in case…" The Commissioner raised his eyebrows. I'd known him long enough to know that raised eyebrows signified an order, not a request. And that 'Just in case' was a reminder not to stir the water in the event that there really were crocodiles lurking in the shallows of an apparently placid lagoon.

"On my way, Sir."

"I can get you a seat on an RAF cargo plane to Singapore. Flying boat to Brunei. Leave you to make your own return arrangements when you're done."

Before I left the office, I placed a call to the police station in Brunei and was put through to Inspector Williams. "Is the body still where it was discovered or has it been removed?" I asked.

"Given the temperature I had it taken to the mortuary. I've had the scene secured with a constable on the door and another outside. The window was open when it happened so I left it like that. I didn't want to disturb the scene and the last thing I wanted was anyone climbing in and snooping around for souvenirs."

"Good. I should be there in the morning. Keep the guard on the door until I get there."

"Will do, Sir. Probably nothing to it, but Tajuddin—that's the Sultan, well, he's easily agitated. I'm sure if the estate manager hadn't been a white man he'd be buried by now and nothing more said. Still, we need Tajuddin and his oil probably more than he needs us. Especially now there's a war on."

"I got the impression I was to hold the Sultan's hand, figuratively speaking, and keep him reassured that nothing unpleasant will land at his feet."

"That's about the sum of it. Tajuddin can be touchy at times."

I threw a few odds and ends into a holdall and headed for the RAF airfield. After an uncomfortable, bumpy ride in a metal seat in a Dakota, I landed at Singapore. Bad weather kept the flying boat to Brunei in the harbour overnight so it wasn't until shortly after seven that we took off. Three hours later we arrived in Brunei in a shower of spray. After we taxied to a dock I disembarked, hot, perspiring and irritable after a night in as uncomfortable a bunk at the naval dockyard in Singapore as the plane rides had been. If it were possible, Brunei was even hotter and more humid than Singapore.

The red-haired and generously freckled Inspector Williams met me on the dock.

"Glad you could make it so quickly, Sir," he said, snapping up a salute before he took my bag. I returned it immediately.

"At ease, Williams," I said quietly. "If you want to impress, save the salutes for when the Sultan and Pengilly are around."

"Sir."

"You can fill me in on what you know on our way to the scene of the incident."

"We don't have a police driver, Sir," he said, sounding most apologetic. "It's not far from the police station to almost anywhere in Brunei. I usually drive myself if there's no one else available."

He held open the passenger door of a Standard Flying Eight that still had that distinctive new smell to it. I tossed my holdall on the back seat and settled into the most comfortable ride I'd had since leaving K.L. the afternoon before. Within ten minutes we pulled up at the bungalow of the Sultan's estate manager and me none the wiser about what had happened to the man, other than that he had blown his head off with a shotgun. That much I learned in Kuala Lumpur.

We crossed the strip of grass that separated the driveway from the front of the bungalow. I wrinkled my nose. The all too familiar smell of death wafted through an open window, enhanced by eighteen hours of heat and humidity. Williams glanced in that direction. A native constable stood guard outside the window with a kerchief covering his nose and mouth. It must have offered scant protection from the foul stench wafting through the window and which reached us several feet away.

Williams fished a key out of a trouser pocket and turned it in the lock. The door opened and we stepped inside.

"What can you tell me about what happened and the people involved?" I said, as I pulled my pipe from my pocket and stuffed it with Indonesian shag tobacco from my oilskin tobacco pouch. I struck a Swan Vestas and lit the pipe, sucking and tamping the burning plug until I was satisfied it was drawing well. Williams looked at me with a puzzled frown.

"I know," I said. "Definitely not in the manual. But I'm no stranger to violent death and my stomach usually rebels at the stench." I drew on the pipe and exhaled the smoke. "This helps a little. Come on, let's get it over with." I headed off in the direction of the smell with Williams in my wake.

The spacious bungalow had a steeply sloping roof of thick thatch in the native style which was supposed to insulate the interior from the heat. It didn't work. It was hotter than Hades inside and the stench almost overpowering. I glanced at the native constable guarding the door to the room. If it were possible for his skin to turn green, I'm sure it would have. To his credit he had not thrown up.

"Anda boleh pergi sekarang," I said.

The constable smiled and almost bolted down the corridor in the direction of the outdoors.

"You speak Malay?" Williams said, sounding astonished.

"Fifteen plus years out here. You get to pick it up, especially if you put your mind to it. It's amazing the degree of cooperation you get when you use it. You've no doubt discovered the Malays don't really like us much. But we need them to help us with our enquiries, as they say at Scotland Yard, so every little bit helps."

"What did you say to him? He seemed happy."

"I told him he could go now."

Williams pushed the door open. The smell hit me like running into a wall. I drew heavily on my pipe, breathing clouds of blue-grey smoke into the room. My stomach churned at the sight in front of me. I turned to Williams. He took his cue and opened his notebook.

"This is all that's left of the head of Erik Braaten, the Sultan's estate manager. Age sixty-two. Born in Montreal, Canada of Dutch parents. Jews. Married. Two children, a boy and a girl. The boy, Martin is twenty-one, the girl, Greta is fifteen. The wife is Adriana Braaten, age forty-one. It's his second or third wife. I'm not sure which. I think she's originally Italian but naturalized Canadian. With the Eye-ties now in the war we'll need to see where her true sympathies lie. At present, we don't have an extensive file on him or his family."

"Have you had any cause to come here, to the bungalow or the Sultan's palace on official police business in the past?"

"No, Sir. There's never been any trouble, no calls for police service, nothing like that since they arrived six or seven years ago."

"Have any eye witnesses to the shooting come forward?"

"None. The Braatens have a small staff but apparently none

present when the gun went off. I've refrained from questioning any of the family members at this time. The British Resident told me that Kuala Lumpur was sending a senior officer to conduct the investigation. I thought it best if you started and finished rather than taking over half way through. Besides, the wife and daughter were hysterical and the boy not much better. All three spent the night sedated on the doctor's orders."

"I see. Not much to go on, then. What else?"

Williams furrowed his brow. "I've met Braaten a few times. It's a small European and American community here. There's a club, of course. Bridge tournaments, canasta, that sort of thing. There's a swimming pool and a bit of a sailing and rowing side that comes with the social group but nothing too serious or competitive. He and his wife are members, which is where I've met them. They're quiet, respectful but they don't mix that well. Understandable, really, given that they're kikes."

I rounded on the unsuspecting young man. "If you want to keep your job, Williams, rather than taking your chances in the army, don't ever use such derogatory language in my presence," I snapped. "I won't have it."

Williams took a step back and felt for the wall behind him. His face turned white beneath the greenish tinge that overlay his pale complexion. "I'm sorry, Sir," he stammered. "It won't happen again."

"A good copper is one who buries his dislikes and prejudices. Both cloud clear thinking and sound judgement and get in the way of a proper investigation." I cleared my throat and sucked on my pipe again, sending a cloud of smoke towards the ceiling. "We'll say no more on the subject. Who heard the shot?"

"I think they all did."

I took another couple of steps forward. I imagined the body when discovered ending at the shoulders with the neck and head missing entirely. Fragments of bone and dried brain tissue, cerebral fluid and blood splatters stuck to the walls and ceiling and were now festooned with flies. "Has the photographer been?"

"Yes, Sir. Yesterday. The photographs should be developed and printed by now. They'll be at the station."

"Were you present when he took the photographs?"

"Yes, Sir."

"Do you know if he photographed the blood spatter or just the body?"

"Everything. I insisted. I made a note of the victim's appearance when I found him and before I had him taken to the mortuary."

"Go on."

Williams consulted his note book. "He wore tropical weight cotton khaki trousers which could have used a press, and a leather belt. The trousers looked as if he had probably worn them for a few days. He was a big man, over six feet tall and with the build of a heavyweight boxer gone to seed. The shirt seemed clean on the day he died. The shirt collar bore the marks of powder burns and blood. The rest of his clothes were unmarked by any sign of a struggle. His hands were clean and smooth, not those of a man who did much manual labour. His finger nails were clean and manicured rather better than most men's."

I glanced at my own nails, splintered, cracked and flaking and rebuked myself, again, for chewing them when under stress.

"Do you have any photographs of him alive on file?"

"I don't think so, Sir. But I expect his wife will have some."

I straightened, eased my sore lower back with a hand and turned to Williams. "So, any thoughts?"

"Nothing out of the ordinary, Sir."

"A clear case of suicide, don't you think? He blows his head off with a shotgun, which I see is no longer at the scene. The gun has undoubtedly been contaminated by whoever has handled it since it went off, thereby obscuring or removing useful fingerprints and adding several other sets."

Williams looked around the room then back at me. "I took custody of it, Sir. It's back at the station in the evidence locker. With my fingerprints on it." He hung his head. I noticed his pallid face had twin red spots over his cheekbones.

"So, you handled it, as probably did Braaten, a constable, the station sergeant, and Uncle Tom Cobley and all. It's probably been wiped clean of useful prints by now. What kind of shotgun is it?"

Williams flipped open his notebook again. I glanced at his face. His cheeks and ears were now even redder than a moment ago, whether shame or anger, I didn't enquire. No need to belittle the man. "A Browning twelve bore, double barrelled side by side." He closed his notebook and slipped it in the breast pocket of his shirt.

I hid the exasperation in my voice. "Did both barrels discharge?"

"I… I believe so, Sir. Unless there was only one shell in the breech when he pulled the trigger. When I examined the gun, both barrels had powder residue and looked as if they had been fired. So I think there were two shells and both were fired simultaneously."

"One would do the job quite adequately, don't you think?"

"I suppose so, Sir. Unless he wanted to make sure."

"Or someone else wanted to make sure."

Williams' mouth gaped. He snapped it shut. "Do you mean he might have been murdered?"

"We haven't established a motive for suicide, so the death is not only sudden, but suspicious until we can definitively rule out foul play. I suspect they impressed that upon you while you were in Police College."

"Yes, Sir. But it never occurred to me that it was anything but suicide. While the balance of his mind was disturbed. That sort of thing…"

I took one final look at the room, at the carnage a gunshot can wreak, and turned my back on it. My pipe had gone out but the stench did not seem as overpowering now as it had when I first entered the room. Nevertheless, I decided not to take a deep breath until safely out of the bungalow and upwind. Williams closed the door behind me.

As far as anyone knew, Braaten had not left a suicide note, which is something many who have a deciding hand in their own death are inclined to leave behind. For that reason alone, I was not satisfied he had blown his own head off and I had no intention of writing this incident off as a suicide simply to satisfy the Sultan and the Commissioner. Repercussions there may be but at forty-six, being a bit too old for service in the army, (and definitely once bitten, twice shy on that score), I was in the Colonial Police until death, dismissal or retirement interrupted my service and forced to live with the consequences of my decisions.

We spent an unproductive hour in the police station munching on stale sandwiches, going over the slim file they had on the Braaten family, and reviewing the police photographs of the scene. Then Williams drove us to the hospital, a long, single story building near the centre of the town. The pathologist, Dr. Horsham, an elderly, white-haired man, had received the body of Erik Braaten the day before. When we arrived, the corpse was on a stainless-steel table with the body cavity already opened.

"When I heard they were sending a senior officer to investigate I delayed the post mortem as long as possible," he said. "We normally do them as soon as they come in. No basement, no cooling." He pointed to the ceiling fan. "Just these and basic refrigeration. I couldn't keep the corpse waiting any longer. He'd already overstayed his welcome."

He stood back, placed the back of a rubber-gloved hand in the small of his back, and straightened. "Arthritis," he said. "Bending over anaesthetized patients in the O.R. or here in the mortuary. It's the same."

I detected a strong nasal twang. "Australian?" I said.

"Brisbane. Been here almost since I graduated nearly fifty years ago. I'm the only doctor. I expect I'll die here unless someone, anyone, who knows anything about tropical medicine comes to take my place." He glanced at me. "I won't hold my breath." He uttered a short, hoarse laugh and busied himself with removing the organs.

"I knew him, Braaten." He pointed at the corpse with a scalpel as if he wasn't sure if I knew to whom he was referring. "Not well. Met him a few times at the club. Always seemed a jovial type. I'd never have suspected he'd blow his head off. Still, you can't always tell from first impressions."

One by one he placed the heart, liver and kidneys on a scale and made a note of the numbers. "All within the normal range," he said cheerfully. "No sign of cirrhosis or any other damage. A pity about the brain being missing, but you can't have everything."

I wondered if he might break into a whistle or hum a tune while he worked. I gave him a few more minutes. Eventually, tiring of the lack of communication, I raised my eyebrows and said, "In your opinion, the cause of death?" No sooner had I uttered the words than I realized they qualified as the stupid question of the month. I'll give him his due—he could have called me a clot, but he had manners.

"See for yourself. Massive head injury. Probably caused by a firearm." I detected a hint of exasperation in his voice. I felt my face grow hot.

"That much we have be able to determine. Both barrels of a twelve-bore shotgun."

"That'll do it. I saw plenty of headless bodies at Gallipoli."

"Bad show, that," I said.

Horsham scowled and grunted.

"The Western Front for most of my time," I said.

"Mesopotamia and Egypt mostly. Not much call for a specialist in tropical diseases in France."

"I suppose not."

He returned to the task at hand. "Some powder burns present on both hands and on the front of his shirt. To blow his head clean off the blast probably entered under the jaw in an upward trajectory."

"Suicide?"

"One of three possibilities. Another is accidental. The third is where you come in. We don't get a lot of gun related suicides around here." He looked up from his work. "The Sultan doesn't approve of firearms, except for the military and the police, and I'm not sure how far he trusts them. From the residue I'd say he had his hand on the trigger when the gun went off. More than that I won't hazard a guess. That's your bailiwick."

I thanked him and we left Dr. Horsham to his work.

"Back to the bungalow, Williams," I said once we were in the car. "We still have some questions to ask and some answers to obtain."

"Don't you believe it's suicide?"

"All the indications point in that direction. Still, one can't be certain until we've asked all the relevant questions and satisfied ourselves with the truthfulness of the answers." I made a mental note. Christmas Day was still four days away. That should give me plenty of time to conduct a thorough investigation, write up the report and be back in K.L. in time for leave.

When we arrived at the bungalow, Martin Braaten sat slouched and stoop-shouldered in his bamboo chair on the raised verandah, squinting as we approached. A half-finished cup of coffee rested on a rattan table in front of him. A cigarette smouldered untended in an ashtray full of butts. Up close I saw that his face had an ashen hue. His hands shook as he rose and he extended one to greet me.

He mumbled something incoherent to go with a limp handshake and collapsed back into his chair. I drew up its companion and lowered myself into it. Williams stood by at my side. He made to take his notebook out of his shirt pocket. I shook my head. "No need for that, Inspector. Just an informal chat."

I turned my attention to Martin Braaten. "I'm Assistant Commissioner Masters of the Colonial Police in Malaya," I said. "I'm here to investigate the surroundings of your father's death."

I didn't receive a reply or even an acknowledgement that he had heard me. A fan above my head stirred the turgid air in the afternoon heat. Only its rhythmical clank with each revolution broke the still silence. Braaten picked up the burning cigarette, drew hard on it and stubbed it out with angry stabs before exhaling forcefully.

"I was probably one of the last to see him alive," he mumbled.

"Tell me about it," I prompted as gently as I could, given that in the few seconds I had spent with Martin Braaten I had taken a dislike to him. I'm not normally one to rush to judgement but there was something about the young man that set my teeth on edge. He looked as if he had slept in his clothes and smelled like he hadn't bathed that morning. He clearly hadn't bothered to shave. A yarmulke perched on the crown of his head, attached to his short hair by two flat clasps. His red-rimmed eyes seemed unnaturally bright and watery and a filigree of veins wove a spider's web through the yellow cast of the whites. I wondered if he had been drinking excessively though I could not smell liquor on his breath. I noticed the pupils in his dark brown irises were small, almost pinpricks. The sunlight was intense and glared but not bright enough, I thought, to cause that degree of reaction. My immediate thought was drugs, heroin or morphine most likely. He had his sleeves rolled down and buttoned at the cuff so I couldn't see any needle marks to confirm or refute my diagnosis.

He must have seen me inspecting him. "We're Jews, Commissioner. And male Jews in mourning don't shave for a week while we keep s*hiva.* The house is also shuttered and in darkness."

"Your mother is Italian, I gather, but a naturalized Canadian."

He nodded.

"Catholic?"

"Probably. I don't think she's been inside a church since she married my father. They had a Jewish wedding ceremony. I was there. So was my sister."

"Your mother…"

"She's my adopted mother," he snapped. "And before you ask, she's not Greta's mother either. Greta was four when my father married her."

I raised my eyebrows.

"My father insisted I call her my mother rather than by any other name. For Greta it came naturally." His shoulder again twitched. "That's life in some families. You probably wouldn't know."

I took the insult without comment and wrote it off to an overwrought reaction brought on by his father's death.

"When did you last see your father alive?"

Martin stared past me without blinking. I looked over my shoulder to see what held his attention. A slim woman – dazzling was the word that sprang to mind – and a younger woman, not much past the days of her girlhood I guessed from a distance, approached us. I looked back at Martin.

"My mother," he emphasized the word mother, as if to make his point, "and Greta," he said in a flat voice.

I rose as they stopped by the table and extended my hand. "Mrs. Braaten," I said.

"Commissioner," she replied. She looked directly into my eyes and held my gaze for a couple of seconds. "It's Adriana. It's only Mrs. Braaten if you insist on being formal."

Adriana Braaten could easily have passed for thirty. Her dark, wavy hair touched her shoulders and a bright red lipstick accentuated her full lips. She wore a sleeveless white sun dress and sandals. A thin gold necklace with a small crucifix hung around her neck. She looked down and touched the crucifix briefly before she looked back up. She must have seen me looking at it.

"For my first communion," she said, as if I needed to know. "It feels comforting to wear it today, under the circumstances. And, as you can see, neither Greta nor I are dressed for mourning." She stared at Martin with her lips in a narrow, straight line. Martin turned his head away. "Black is ridiculous in this heat."

I uttered a light cough. "Yesterday," I said, serving up an opening for my investigation.

"Yesterday was traumatic for all of us but we will all get over it eventually. Those who are left behind always seem to find a way of coping with the aftermath of such a tragedy, as devastating as it was." She touched her crucifix again. I thought, perhaps rather uncharitably, that she was laying it on a bit thick for my benefit.

I glanced at Greta who immediately looked away. Like Adriana, she wore a flimsy cotton sun dress, smocked across the front and belted at the waist, and a pair of sandals. Her long pigtails tied off with light blue satin bows rested over the top of her small bust making her look younger than she was. I saw her glance at Martin. He ignored her.

I cleared my throat. "I'll need to speak to all of you before I leave. I have to make sure I have everything covered before I write my report." I offered what I hoped they would interpret as an encouraging and sympathetic smile. Greta eased her weight from one foot to the other and ran the tip of her tongue over her lips.

"Me, too?" she said. "I don't know anything. I was in my room. All I heard was the sound of the gun going off. It scared me. I hid under my bed until mamma came and told me what had happened. I never saw anything." Her voice shook as she spoke. She burst into tears and covered her face.

"I almost had to drag her out from under her bed," Adriana said and wrapped an arm around Greta's shoulder.

"I thought the Germans had invaded," Greta sniffed. "And they were going to kill us all. It was on the radio."

"It's true. It was on the radio yesterday that the Germans had invaded England," Adriana said. "A false report, obviously, but enough to scare an impressionable young girl out of her wits."

I looked from one to the other. It sounded pat, rehearsed, but a hunch is a dangerous thing in an investigation, all too often leading to all kinds of wrong conclusions. Besides, it was something easily checked with Williams. I let it drop. I turned my attention to Adriana. "Have you any idea why your husband might take his own life?"

"None, Commissioner."

"Had he been acting strangely, out of character recently"

"Not that anyone noticed." She glanced at Martin and Greta—seeking confirmation. She received it from both with shakes of the head.

"I take it he didn't leave a note."

"We've not found one. It came as a complete shock. None of us was expecting it."

"Had he had a falling out with the Sultan recently? Anything that might jeopardize his job here?"

"Not that he said. Erik didn't have a great deal to do with Tajuddin. They met on a weekly basis, sometimes more frequently, but very rarely daily unless there was a major flap."

"Such as?"

"A cyclone. Or unrest upcountry. That sometimes happens. Once, the British Malayan Petroleum Company threatened to stop drilling. That didn't go over too well but it blew over quickly. All Tajuddin wants is his royalty money. He left pretty well everything else of the day-to-day running of the estate to my husband."

"Did your husband hire and fire staff? Could anyone hold a grudge against him?"

Adriana paused, then looked as if she were about to say something of importance. She raised her arms from her side for a second then let them drop. "Let's take a short walk around the grounds, Commissioner. They're really quite lovely. Then we'll come back for some iced tea with the others."

She looked at Martin and Greta and smiled. I thought it a bit forced but I held my tongue. I assumed I was about to learn something, something she regarded as important and which she didn't want to share with Martin or Greta.

"Let me take you back a long way. Maybe you will understand where we're coming from," she said, once we were well away from the bungalow. "Do I have your word you won't spread it around? It's not for publication under any circumstances. There are things Greta and Martin know, and things they don't."

"Of course. I am the definition of discretion."

She dropped her voice. "Ours is not a conventional family."

As we'd only just met, what I took to be the start of a confession of some sort surprised me. I put it down to me having the type of open, honest face and doctor's bedside manner that almost complete strangers feel compelled to confide in when they to get something momentous off their chests.

"Oh." It wasn't much of a response but the heavy pause that followed encouraged the sluice gates to open a crack.

"Erik, my husband, was a whisky distiller and bootlegger back in Montreal. Thanks to the stupid Americans and their prohibition, they made him quite wealthy. He made the whisky in Montreal, shipped it to the Mohawk reserve on the St. Lawrence and they smuggled it across the river into New York. Eventually, Erik decided he wanted in on the distribution side as well. Some of my fellow countrymen had no intention of diluting their profits and warned him off. Erik wouldn't listen. Then the F.B.I. became interested in his activities and the American Internal Revenue Service started sniffing around for unpaid taxes. The Mafia put a price on his head. So did the Jewish mob. He beat a retreat to Montreal. The Americans wanted him extradited to face charges. In a matter of months he became Public Enemy Number Eight on America's Most Wanted list, some distance behind Al Capone and Bugsy Siegel." She laughed. "To his dismay, he never made it any higher."

"What happened then?"

"He shut the distillery and laid off the workers. It was the early spring of nineteen thirty-two and the worst of the depression was biting. We managed to sell out lovely mansion in Westmount—that's the best part of Montreal—for about twenty cents on the dollar and left on a ship as soon as the ice cleared from the harbour. Erik was smart, though. Before we left, he converted almost all our money into gem quality diamonds as a medium of currency.

"The next problem to overcome was where were we going to go? When we eliminated all the countries with extradition treaties with the United States and cozy relationships with others, the rest of the world didn't hold much appeal. We drifted around the seas for the best part of six months before we ended up here. The British Resident was most helpful. The Sultan needed someone to run his estate—not the household but the business side of the property—and Erik knew how to run a business. Ernest Pengilly—he's a dear man—made the introduction. The rest is history."

She seemed to have come to the end of her tale at that point. I waited a few seconds for more to come forth but my silence was greeted with hers. "So," I said, "Essentially your husband was involved in bootlegging and got on the wrong side of the American authorities and the Mob."

"At first he didn't take the threats seriously. I begged and eventually he listened to me."

"In spite of what you say, I don't see that as being a particularly unconventional family."

By this time, we had wandered into a glade among a plantation of palm trees. Adriana stopped and looked around. "Let's sit here," she said. "There is more as you guessed." She sat on the grass and patted a spot next to her. I took the hint.

She smoothed her dress over her thighs and tucked a leg beneath her. "Erik was taken hostage at gunpoint by the local police in Panama. I don't know how they found out about the diamonds. Maybe it was a lucky guess. It cost a ransom to get him out of custody. We couldn't leave South America fast enough. We didn't have much left after we were able to get a passage to Singapore. The ship had to divert to Brunei with engine trouble. It's still in the harbour with the bottom rusted out and the water over the cargo deck. Erik decided we may as well stay here as look for a better spot. He got the job working for the Sultan and it paid reasonable wages."

"The long and the short of it is, you floated ashore and here you are. And I'm no wiser why you consider yourselves an unconventional family or what should prompt your husband to take his own life."

She gave me a doe-like look and fluttered her eyelashes. I thought that was a bit much. I didn't fall for it. We hadn't known each other half an hour and in twenty-four hours' time I'd be on a flying boat heading for Singapore with my report neatly typed.

"Erik and I have an open relationship," she said.

That one caught me unawares. "Go on," I said.

She bared her chest, figuratively. She was fourteen, she said, little more than a year younger than Greta was now. Her father was a prominent member of the Italian Government, a Cabinet Minister as well as numbering among the wealthier members of the aristocracy, a Count. A summer holiday at their clifftop villa on the Amalfi coast with house guests, among them the eighteen-year-old son of the President, led to a late-night walk along the shingle beach after everyone else had gone to bed. And in the moonlight, with the sound of waves gently lapping the shore, they kissed. Three months later she miscarried and the foremost gynecologist in Rome told her she would never be able to have children. At the time she wasn't sure whether she was upset, or pleased but, relieved of the need to be extremely careful, over the next fifteen years she had had more lovers than she could name. Her father knew of them—most of them at least—and seemed neither to approve nor disapprove of her behaviour. He had merely shrugged, acknowledging that his daughter now enjoyed more reproductive freedom then he did. And the steady stream of beautiful women who came and went through their villa in Amalfi and their *palazzo* in Rome only served to reinforce in her mind the old dictum, 'like father, like daughter.'

She certainly didn't love Erik, she said. She never had. It had been her decision to marry him after he had pursued her across several countries and two continents. He was twenty years her senior and good looking enough, though she had not been tempted to add him to her circle of friends and former lovers until he proposed. Her father's dwindling wealth played a prominent part in her decision to marry a few weeks before her thirtieth birthday. As his part of the bargain, Erik got an Italian Count's beautiful daughter, a trophy wife to show off, in exchange for more money that she could dream of, coupled with unimaginative and not over-demanding sex. She could not call it lovemaking. It was sex, for him at least, and for her a duty which she had accepted as part of the marriage bargain.

"From the night before my wedding until two years ago I never slept with another man." She fluttered her eyelashes at me again and I wished she wouldn't do that. "Then Ahmad, the Sultan, came into my life. I'd seen him before, but only from a distance. He invited Erik and me to a reception at the palace one evening. He was exotic and good looking." She hesitated. "Something Erik no longer was. And Ahmad was a man who always got what he wanted, which proved to be me, on his terms, which did not include Erik."

For the past three or four years she and Erik slept in separate bedrooms, she said, leaning closer as if she had no wish to be overheard. Erik had seemed to lose interest in her as a wife and the decision to sleep apart had been tacit and mutual. She didn't miss him. He had gone from snoring softly at her side almost as soon as he climbed into bed to simply not being there. There really hadn't been that much difference.

The Sultan had several properties scattered throughout the palace grounds. They met secretly in one of them during the day when Erik was busy in another part of the estate, and at night once everyone had gone to bed. These trysts continued undiscovered for two years until a palace servant told Erik. Erik flew into a rage but he could do nothing—the Sultan provided him with his only means of employment and housing. Once the Sultan discovered that their secret was no longer a secret, he had the servant flogged to death. The novelty of their affair wore off, and the Sultan discarded her. She hadn't spoken to him since.

It was around that same time that she had become concerned about Martin. He had been at a boarding school in Sydney since he turned sixteen, returning to Brunei for the holidays. Then he spent three years at university. In that time, he had become a man and she had to admit it was almost as if they had become strangers.

"Martin's like Erik in many ways, though he'd probably never be a patch on his father as a businessman. Perhaps that's a good thing," she said, almost as she were speaking to herself. "While he was at school and later at university, Martin had become interested more in his religion. Erik had no real interest in his Jewish roots. To him being Jewish was merely something he inherited from his mother, though his father was observant too. And Erik didn't look Jewish. He even had hazel eyes." Then, only last month, she told me, Martin had announced his intention to return to Sydney to study to become a rabbi. Erik had only shrugged. 'If it's what you want,' he said, 'go ahead, but don't expect me to support you while you're there. I had an uncle who was a rabbi. He was a schmuck.'

The flow of information petered out. So, she had married Erik Braaten for his money and the security it could buy. She had committed adultery with the most powerful man in Brunei, not once, but over a two-year period. Now, here she was, a widow who once had everything, about to be cut loose to fend for herself and her two step-children. I tried to feel empathy for her. It didn't work. I saw her regarding me and I couldn't read the look on her face.

"I've never been in this position before, or even contemplated it. Now I don't know which way to turn." She plucked a blade of grass and studied it as if she had never seen grass before. Knowing that there is no pressure like silence, I waited until she was ready to continue with the revelations. I didn't have to wait long.

"Family secrets, Commissioner are even more titillating than palace intrigue. If I tell you ours, perhaps you'll understand where we're all coming from."

"I'm listening."

"Martin was home for the holidays. It was this time two years ago but I remember it as if it was just last night. He and Greta were on the verandah after dinner. I had gone to bed but I'd left my window open. I could hear every word they said. I was about to ask them to keep their voices down when Martin said, 'what are you hiding, Greta? You've got a smug look on your face. You look as if you're busting to share a secret.' I crept as close to the window as I could without being seen. The shutters were half closed. I could see out but with the hurricane lantern lit on the verandah and it being dark in my room I was pretty sure they couldn't see in.

Adriana told me what she heard…

"What do you think about mamma?' Greta said, sounding excited. "Haven't you noticed ever since you came home she's been looking and sounding very happy? I've even heard her humming. And smiling a lot. Do you think she could be having an affair? She went to bed early. Do you really think she went to bed? Or did she sneak off to meet her lover? Wouldn't that be a turn up for the books?"

Martin glared at Greta.

"What?" Greta spluttered. "Why are you looking at me like that?"

"Sometimes, Greta, you sound like a schoolgirl with a smutty secret you're dying to share. It's not becoming of a young lady. People in glass houses shouldn't throw stones.'

"What do you mean by that?"

"I've heard about you and Faisal."

"What about me and Faisal? There's nothing to it if you must know. And I'm no more a young lady than you're a gentleman."

Martin put a hand on Greta's shoulder. "So maybe mother is having an affair with someone. Get over it. As long as our father doesn't find out she should be safe with her secret. If she even has one. Besides, you've got nothing to go on, only a female suspicion. That's not enough to hang anyone."

Greta refused to give up. "She's obviously been carrying on an affair right under our noses because no one could bring himself to believe she was capable of it."

"Just like you?"

"That was only kissing. Christ, I'm only thirteen, Martin. It's not what you're thinking."

"And only once?"

Greta didn't answer.

"Twice?"

"A few more than that, if you must know."

Martin looked her straight in the eye. "All right. I believe you. But if it's still going on between you and Faisal, for God's sake, don't get pregnant."

"It's not… We didn't… you know. I've known about the facts of life for ages. Mamma and I have had the chat. Don't worry about me.

I know how you get pregnant."

"But you're…I mean, thirteen's pretty young to be, you know…"

"I told you, we never got any farther than kissing. Anyway, it's over. I called it off a month ago. I doubt I'll see him again. Besides, he wasn't that interesting, or much of a kisser."

"Still that's pretty bold of you. With the Sultan's son?"

Greta smiled. "Even bolder of mamma. I bet she's gone a lot farther than a few kisses."

"If you're right, I'd call it brazen, almost. Worth a round of applause."

"And maybe she has motive, too," Greta said. "More than an itch to try something new and exciting. I suspect father's ignored her for quite some time. Maybe years."

"They don't seem to be particularly close, do they?" Martin said. "He trots her out for formal occasions, dressed to the nines with a fixed smile on her face. Then, like you say, when they come home they seem to live separate but parallel lives in the same house."

"Who do you think it might be?"

"I couldn't begin to guess. How about a very small bet on Dr. Horsham?"

"Could be. He's the only white man around, apart from the oil men, and they only leave their camp on Sundays. But I can't think it'd be him. He gave me my boosters a few months ago, so I got a good look at him close up. I can't say I was impressed. He's no Humphrey Bogart, that's for sure."

"Perhaps he's exactly what mamma needs at this time in her life."

Greta frowned. "A man even older than father? I know they don't sleep in the same room anymore. If it's sex she's looking for I can't imagine it's with Dr. Horsham. But I'm sure she's having an affair."

"And if she is, good luck to her. Do you think that's a bit bold of me? I assume it would be to satisfy a basic need, that's all. Like you."

"That's so unfair," she snapped. "And so not like you." She turned her back on him. "I told you I didn't go that far with him."

"You're right. It was unfair," he mumbled. "I'm sorry I hurt you like that. Forgive me?" He put an arm around her shoulder and pulled her to him.

Greta pulled away. "If it's more than that, then good for her. I hope she'll be happy, at least for a while. I almost feel like giving her a big hug."

"I wouldn't go overboard, if I were you, Greta. If she has a secret, let her keep it to herself. It's hers. She's entitled to it. And I really don't think you want to know what's going on between them, do you?"

Greta shook her head. "I don't even want to imagine it. They're both so old."

Martin squeezed Greta's hand. "And I'm pretty sure that Dr. Horsham, if it is him, won't be tempted to spill the beans."

They sat in silence for a moment before Martin looked at Greta and gave her a wicked smile. "Time to go looking for a successor to Faisal?"

She gave him a dig in the ribs. "He'd have to be a better kisser."

"There's only one way to find out."

She linked an arm through Martin's. "Knowing this about mamma makes us co-conspirators, or something. Like in Julius Caesar." She giggled, then turned to face Martin. 'Why the long face?"

"It's a night for secrets, Greta."

"Isn't it?"

"More than one."

"What do you mean?"

Martin took a deep breath and exhaled noisily. "In spite of what you've been told and led to believe, you're not my sister."

"I've known that for ages. Mamma told me years ago. It's no secret I was adopted."

"Let me finish. I've seen our birth certificates. The man we call our father isn't my father either. It's all documented. It's in a file in a filing cabinet in his office. He left it unlocked one day. I don't know what made me do it, but I looked when he was out. My real father was a policeman who was killed on duty during the conscription riots in Montreal back in March of nineteen-eighteen. My mother worked in the typing pool in father's office. She was expecting me when my father died. She died in the Spanish 'flu epidemic a year later. I was an orphan. He took me in and adopted me." He fell silent.

"What about me?"

Martin hesitated. "She didn't tell you?"

"No. Only that I was adopted when I was a baby."

Martin took a deep breath. "Erik Braaten is actually your uncle.

Your mother is his youngest sister, Sarah. She wasn't married. On your birth certificate your father is down as 'Unknown'. You can guess what that means. Apparently, your mother had been a bit odd for years. As soon as you were born she was placed in an insane asylum and you came to be with us rather than going to an orphanage or put in a foster home. I remember you arriving, only a day or two old. I was six. I don't know where your mother is now, or if she's still alive. I'm sorry, but that's all I know."

He turned to face Greta. In the harsh white light of the hurricane lantern her face looked ashen. Her lips trembled and her breath came in ragged gasps, as if she had been running. Tears filled her eyes and plopped down on her hands folded in her lap.

It was several minutes before she regained control of her breathing. "Are you sure this is all true?"

"Cross my heart, Greta. It's in black and white in his office filing cabinet. I didn't know whether to tell you or not. For better or worse, now you know as much as I do."

"So there's not a drop of common blood between any of us."

"Not quite. The only connection is that Erik Braaten is your uncle, and I have absolutely not a drop of Braaten blood in my veins. So no, we're not related. But I still think of you as my sister."

"And you'll always be my brother. And my best friend, at least until I get married. If I ever do."

Martin laughed. "Do you really expect me to believe you only went as far as kissing with Faisal?"

She nodded vigorously. "I promise."

Martin hugged her. "Good. Let's hope Faisal doesn't let anything slip and the Sultan never finds out…"

Adriana stopped at that point. "I don't doubt that Faisal would have been flogged," she said. "And maybe Greta as well. Anyway, it didn't happen. Martin and Greta went off to bed after that and I never heard another word on either subject again."

"How does Greta get along with you? Does she look to you for guidance still, or is she her own woman now?"

Adriana took a deep breath and exhaled loudly. "Do you promise never to say a word of what I'm about to tell you to anyone?"

I wondered what she was getting at. I hedged my bet. "Doesn't that really depend on what you're about to tell me?"

"No. And I won't say another word without your unconditional promise."

Was what Adriana about to tell me relevant to the case? Or merely background? I hesitated then took the plunge. "All right. You have my guarantee."

"As a gentleman?"

I wasn't sure that the rank of gentleman extended down as far as the middle classes. I hoped it did. "As a gentleman," I said.

"You've seen Greta?" I nodded. "She's quite the young woman now, but when she reached adolescence I could see several things were bothering her. She confided in me. She'd known for a long time that I wasn't her mother, which in some ways made things easier for her to open up. She told me she was in love with Martin." Adriana bit her lip. "That really caught me by surprise. I didn't know what to say. I hoped it would turn out to be only a temporary crush that would blow over before anything happened."

"And did it?"

Adriana hesitated before blurting out, "Not long after that they became lovers."

I snapped my gaping jaw shut before I appeared a drooling imbecile.

"They know I know. I can't be a hypocrite. By the time I was Greta's age I'd had more than a couple of lovers."

I tried to imagine Adriana Braaten at fourteen or fifteen and decided she would probably have looked a younger version of what she was now—quite stunning. I dragged my mind back to the present.

"Erik found out about them a week before Martin went back to university for his final term in September. He went berserk. He laid a real beating on Martin. I thought he was going to kill him. Greta and I were powerless to stop it until I fetched the shotgun. I shoved it in Erik's face and told him to stop. He snatched the gun from my hands and broke it open. 'If you're going to threaten someone with a gun,' he snarled, 'load it first.' He threw the gun on the floor and stalked out of the room. Only the three of us, and now you, know about that. Greta has hated Erik ever since. So has Martin. And I could have cheerfully blown his head off then if I'd known how."

So, I reasoned, if Greta or Martin had pulled the trigger, Adriana could be relied upon to lie to protect them. And naturally she'd lie to me to protect herself as well. I really, truly hoped it was suicide. It would be so much easier if it were. 'Everyone a winner,' as the fairground barker shouts—the Sultan, Pengilly and the Commissioner. Only now it was beginning to look like anything but.

"Does either of them know how to use a shotgun?"

"The same as most of us. Load it, aim it and squeeze the trigger. But I doubt if either of them has actually seen it done. None of us has had any cause to. While we lived in Quebec Erik hunted, deer and pheasant mostly, but he never took Martin with him, not that Martin was interested. When Erik went out in the palace grounds he had no need to carry a gun, but in the rest of the estate, which is several square miles, he carried both a shotgun and a hunting rifle."

"Why?"

"The Sultan has a phobia about vultures."

"Not my favourite bird either."

"Nor mine. But Erik had authority to shoot any vulture he saw, anywhere."

"And the hunting rifle?"

"Wild pigs. The Sultan won't allow them anywhere in Brunei. He ordered Erik to shoot them on sight. Unfortunately, the carcass is too heavy to carry away and the locals, being Muslims, won't defile themselves by touching them. The ones he shot were left where they fell until the vultures arrived. It's a vicious circle. I don't think he enjoyed that part of the job much." She shuddered.

I waited a while for more water to surge through the sluicegate. Eventually, when there was no more forthcoming, I broke the silence. "Tell me about Greta. You said she hated Erik. Did she hate him enough to kill him?"

Adrianna whipped her head round. "No! She's a sweet young girl without a mean bone in her body. I defy anyone to say different."

Which, I thought could be true just as easily as it could be a lie.

Adriana looked away at the palm trees, then up at the sky. Thunder clouds were building. The afternoon rain would be here soon and unless we found shelter, it wouldn't be long before we would be soaked. "There's a small bungalow around the corner," she said, and I wondered if she and the Sultan had met there on occasion. "We won't have time to get back to the main house before the rain comes, and what I have to say is in private." She stood and I eased myself to my feet.

The bungalow was not more than a couple of hundred yards away and we made it just before the downpour arrived. We sat on the verandah with me perspiring from the exertion of the brisk walk and Adriana looking cool in her sun dress.

"There's something else, Commissioner."

I raised an eyebrow.

"Greta's three months pregnant."

"Oh." It happens from time to time and it wasn't hard to understand how and why in this case.

"Dr. Horsham has refused to do anything to terminate the pregnancy and herbal remedies the locals swear by haven't worked."

"I see."

"Martin's only been back from university a couple of weeks."

"So he's not the father, then?"

"No."

"Does he know?"

"Yes. Greta told him yesterday. She couldn't keep it from him any longer. She's slender. If you saw her without any clothes on, you'd know she was starting to show."

Which in one way explained the loose-fitting sun dress. "Did she reveal to you or Martin who the father is?"

"Yes."

"Are you going to tell me?"

"No."

"Why not? You've told me everything else."

"It no longer matters."

"In what way?"

"He, the father, can't hurt her any longer. He's off the scene permanently." Adriana hesitated then turned to me with tears in her eyes. "You promised," she gasped.

I didn't know what to say. "And I'll keep that promise," I said, and I know it must have sounded lame to her.

"It was Erik."

The thunderstorm that rolled in at that moment made any further conversation in a normal voice next to impossible, so we gave up. We sat in contemplative silence and watched the rain fall like a theatre curtain a few feet in front from us. An hour later the rain stopped as abruptly as it had begun, the sun broke through the clouds and Brunei became a Turkish bath in a matter of minutes. We made our way slowly back until we came within sight of the family bungalow, when Adriana stopped. Goosebumps ran up and down my arm when she touched me. We turned to face each other.

"Martin went back to university for his final term in September," she said. "Almost as soon as he was on the plane Erik beat Greta unconscious. I tried to stop him but he punched me in the face and knocked me down." Adriana put her fingertips to her cheek. "Then he raped Greta in front of me. He called her a little whore and me a bigger one for condoning it. He said Greta was only getting what whores want and he told me that if I breathe a word to anyone, he'd kill me. He'd already laid a savage beating on Martin when he found out about him and Greta. I never doubted he meant it."

"Does Greta know what happened to her?"

"When Greta came to me a month ago after she missed for the second time, she knew something was wrong. Dr. Horsham examined her and told her she was pregnant. She had no idea until that moment. She and Martin have slept apart since Erik beat him. Neither wanted to risk another beating."

I patted her arm in what I hoped she took to be a reassuring manner. "I promised. I take your word for what happened. There's no need for her ever to know you told me anything about her."

Adriana burst into tears once more.

"Which leaves me to believe one of four things, Mrs. Braaten," I said, once she composed herself.

"What are they, Commissioner?" We seemed to be back on formal ground and I felt more comfortable for the return.

"Either your husband committed suicide while the balance of his mind was disturbed, distraught perhaps over raping his niece, an appalling act of incest."

"Or?"

"Greta was angry over your husband's beating of Martin. That, coupled with her hatred of Erik for beating and raping her, drove her to shoot him, thereby gaining revenge for the wrongs both she and Martin had suffered."

"Or?"

"Greta told Martin that your husband had beaten and raped her while she was unconscious. Martin, possibly still smouldering from the humiliation of the beating inflicted upon him earlier, took revenge."

"Or?"

"Or you killed your husband. You obviously didn't like him. You slept apart. You'd taken a lover for a while, a dangerous liaison at best. You were angry about Martin's beating. Your husband hit you. You witnessed him rape Greta. By now you probably hated him, that hatred festering in your heart enough to take the shotgun he had shown you how to use, load it and, when you confronted him, you fired both barrels at his head. All of which, except the first scenario, amount to murder."

To her credit, Adriana did none of those things women do in Hollywood films when confronted with the truth about a crime. Instead, she stood her ground and in a firm voice said, "It was the first option, Commissioner. Unless someone, a complete stranger, broke into the bungalow and killed him for some unknown reason, Erik took his own life out of remorse for all the things he had done to us. He may have been a ruthless businessman at one time, but he had a human side to him too, one which he managed to keep suppressed most of the time. Now, shall we join the others?"

I followed her down the path to the bungalow. Williams was sitting under the verandah with his back to us when we arrived, sipping iced tea with Martin and Greta.

"Must be nice for some," I said, pointing to the half empty tumbler with perspiration beading on the glass and dripping onto a cork coaster. Williams leapt to his feet.

"Sir!" he barked. His right hand twitched. I think he was about to salute. I forestalled him.

"At ease. Carry on. Perhaps you'd care to pour Mrs. Braaten and me a glass while you're on your feet."

We sat in a semi-circle around the table. Right then, an ice-cold beer would have gone down without touching the sides. I made do with the only thing on offer in the heat of the late afternoon. I cleared my throat. In the silence it sounded a trifle dramatic.

"I have learned a great deal about the death of Erik Braaten since I arrived," I said. "As we all know, he died from a shotgun blast to the head. In Dr. Horsham's medical opinion, the trajectory was upwards, from beneath the jaw. That is consistent with a decision to take one's own life if using a shotgun. Given that he was a tall man with long arms, he would have been able to reach the triggers and depress them with his thumb. In my experience, if someone else had decided to kill him, a blast from close range to the chest would have been the most efficient way. Walk into the office, point the gun and fire. Mr. Braaten would probably still have been sitting behind his desk when the gun went off. An assailant is highly unlikely therefore to have placed the barrels of the gun beneath the victim's jaw before he fired. If an assailant had got that close, Mr. Braaten would probably have struggled and there is a fair chance that the attacker would have missed or become disarmed completely. And quite possibly shot instead."

I looked around at their faces. Adriana watched me intently without blinking. Martin refused to make eye contact. Instead, he looked past me, almost serenely I thought, at some unseen object in the distance. Greta's face was white, her eyes wide open, staring at me and breathing heavily through her mouth.

"I need to know exactly where you all were when the gun went off, and what you did. Let's start with you, Greta." I turned and looked steadily at the one whom I considered the weakest link. "You said you were in your bedroom. You heard the gun go off, thought it was the Germans invading, and hid under your bed."

Greta swallowed. Her lower lip quivered and tears flooded her eyes. She covered her face with her hands. "Yes," she sobbed. "That's what I did. I didn't see it happen. I only heard the gun go off. I was terrified."

"And you were in your own bedroom? Not somewhere else?"

She nodded vigorously. "In my own bedroom."

I fixed her with a penetrating stare. "Surely there wouldn't be enough room for a fully-grown woman to hide under the bed?"

She howled. "There is. It's a high bed. There's lots of room."

"All right." I turned my attention to Adriana. "Mrs. Braaten, I haven't heard from you as to where you were."

"Because you haven't asked, Commissioner," she replied in a measured voice. "I was in the drawing room arranging flowers in a vase when I heard the gun go off. I immediately ran to my husband's office and found him, or what was left of him, on the floor quite a way from his desk. His office chair had been tipped over and there was blood and bits of…" She hesitated and gulped. "Of bones and brains over the walls and ceiling. It was ghastly. I never want to see anything like it again." She looked so deathly pale that I thought she might vomit at any moment.

"Weren't you afraid?"

Adriana collected herself and hesitated before answering. "I don't think I had time to be afraid, Commissioner. I reacted instinctively. It was only after I found my husband's body that shock set in."

"Did you see anyone leave the office?"

"No. It would be most unusual for my husband to receive a visitor here. I don't recall it ever happening. He had a reception room at the palace if he wanted to impress visitors with his importance."

I turned to Martin. "You've been very quiet about the whole affair. Where were you when the gun went off?"

He looked at me as if he hadn't a care in the world. "I was in the lavatory. I came as soon as I could." He turned his head away and resumed his study of the middle distance.

I looked from one to the other, then at Williams. Williams pulled a face which I interpreted as indicating he hadn't a clue how Erik Braaten had died, other than by a shotgun blast to the head. I felt like Hercule Poirot in one of Agatha Christie's detective novels. I had gathered all the suspects together for the purpose of unmasking the murderer, yet I still wasn't absolutely sure it was murder rather than suicide. The latter seemed highly unlikely: No odd behaviour, no suicide note, and no signs of stress or depression. It didn't seem as if the balance of his mind was disturbed at any time before the gun went off. If it really were suicide, and I'd made an arrest, I'd have a lot of egg on my face, some serious backtracking to do and profound apologies to offer. I also had a promise to keep.

"I am aware that Erik Braaten is not your biological father, Martin." I turned to Greta. "Nor yours, Greta. As is required of non-British citizens, he provided that information when you arrived in Brunei several years ago." That wasn't strictly true. It wasn't in the slim file and I hadn't checked, but it seemed plausible. Besides, Braaten wasn't there to deny it. "I have also been able to determine that you have all suffered ill treatment of one sort or another, physical, psychological or emotional, at his hands. You all have reason to resent him for that treatment, and I can't say I blame any of you if that's the case."

I looked at each of them squarely and saw Williams doing the same. I took a deep breath. Here goes, I said to myself. "One, or two of you, or all three decided to end your individual and collective misery once and for all. But only one of you squeezed the trigger. We have examined the gun and determined that both barrels were fired, and there was no evidence of pellet scatter on the walls or ceilings to suggest that the first shot missed and a second was necessary."

I hesitated, letting the short ensuing silence sink in and put pressure on them. Greta squirmed in her chair. Martin wouldn't make eye contact. Adriana had the faintest of smiles playing with the corners of her mouth.

I turned to Greta. "I don't believe you were in your bedroom at all. You were in the office when the gun went off, weren't you? You had motive, anger and hatred enough to kill your step-father several times over."

Greta covered her face with her hands and burst into tears. "No," she wailed, shaking her head. "I was in my bedroom." Had I overplayed my hand with Greta? I turned my attention to Adriana.

"You weren't in the drawing room arranging flowers like you said, Mrs. Braaten. You were in the office. You confronted your husband. He had harmed you, but not in the way he had Martin and Greta. But you wanted to be in at the kill, to see your own version of justice done. You didn't squeeze the trigger, but you conspired with Martin and Greta. You provided the loaded gun and gave them their alibis." Her face turned pale under her olive complexion. "And that makes you an accessory to murder and in the eyes of the law, equally guilty of the offence."

I turned to Martin. "You hated him with a passion, for all the put-downs you had to endure over the years, for his attitude towards your desire to become a rabbi, for the way he treated you, and Greta and your step-mother. It was you who fired the gun that killed Erik Braaten and made it look like suicide."

Martin stopped gazing into the distance. His pupils were pinpricks, his face an unhealthy grey made darker by his day's growth of beard. He turned to me and sat with a calmness I had never seen in someone who had just been accused of murder.

"You're almost right," he said. "A little off in some of the minor details." He nodded in turn at Adriana and Greta. "They're telling the truth. Neither Greta not our step-mother had anything to do with it. I was alone when I killed him. Not quite how you think but close enough. I hated him for many reasons. When I decided to kill him, I took the shotgun from the cupboard where he kept it. It's never locked. The box of shotgun shells was on a shelf. I loaded the gun, took it to his office and confronted him. He stood up, lunged at me and grabbed the barrel of the gun and tried to snatch it away from me. His hand closed over mine on the trigger and it went off. I admit I had intended to kill him. I failed. I hadn't intended him to do the job for me. Then I went to my room and shot myself full of heroin. I thought it would be enough to kill me but I even failed at that." He rolled his sleeve up and I saw the track marks of needles that confirmed my suspicions.

"He scorned my desire to become a rabbi. He had no faith of his own yet he belittled mine. It was what I wanted to do with my life. Now I'll never be able to. I'm a failure, just like he always said."

Greta was on her feet. She lunged at Martin and clung onto him as if he were a life raft. Adriana regarded me in a way I couldn't decipher. I don't think she liked Martin particularly but he had helped her by covering for her and I had no way to prove she was lying.

I turned to Williams. "Do the honours, Williams." The young Inspector dug his handcuffs out of their leather pouch. Martin held his wrists out and sat without emotion while Williams clicked them shut. "We'll take you back to Singapore as soon as we can arrange transport. They have jurisdiction over Brunei. Then we'll run it by the Crown Prosecutor and see what he has to say. I won't make any promises, but a plea to manslaughter means you won't hang."

The last time I saw Adriana and Greta was with a backward glance as we were getting into the police car. Adriana had her arms around Greta, hugging her. Greta had her head buried in Adriana's shoulder, sobbing loudly. Adriana looked at me and mouthed something I couldn't hear over the noise of the engine, but I doubt it was complimentary.

After a night in the cells at the police station, I loaded a gaunt, haggard and handcuffed Martin Braaten into the RAF flying boat. Having come down from the effects of his last heroin injection by this time, he looked terrible, his skin greyer than ever, shivering and twitching as he sat in his seat, leaning forward, hands in his lap.

We reached cruising altitude and headed on a compass bearing for Singapore. My mind drifted to Tajuddin, the Sultan, whom I had managed to avoid meeting while I was in Brunei, then to Pengilly, the British Resident, and lastly to the Commissioner. I wondered how they were going to take my report. They had all wanted a finding of suicide. How would they take to a prisoner and a charge of murder? In my mind I started working on the delicate wording.

Half an hour into the flight Martin turned to me. "I have to relieve myself," he said, the first words he had uttered all morning. "I can't hold it any longer."

The flying boat only had an Elsan chemical toilet, little more than a bucket for the use of the crew, and its use was discouraged except in emergencies. I took Martin aft to the toilet and removed his hand cuffs. He completed his business and turned back to me with his hands outstretched, ready to receive the handcuffs again. I never saw the blow coming.

When I regained consciousness with a sore chin and a bleeding mouth from a broken molar, I saw the co-pilot bending over me demanding to know what had happened. I started to explain as best I could before he waved me off.

"He jumped," he said, pointing to the open door, which explained the cold wind howling around me. The co-pilot slid it closed. "They should put a lock on these things. You're lucky he didn't take you with him." He helped me to my feet and we threaded our way past boxed stores towards the cockpit.

I watched my Christmas leave go up in smoke: I would without doubt spend the next several days composing and writing a report that would not only have to be full, complete and accurate, but pass muster with the Commissioner, Pengilly and the Sultan. I hoped Martin Braaten had told me the truth, that he hadn't lied to protect Greta or Adriana. Either way, his version was all I had and would have to do for my report.

"The bastard jumped," the co-pilot told the pilot.

"It wouldn't be the first time," the pilot said, and shrugged. "They should put a lock on the door." He turned to me. "Are you all right? You look a bit pale." He reached into a canvas holdall by his seat and produced a flask. "This should help," he said. "But leave some for the rest of us."

8. THE COMMODORE'S SEA CHEST

With the teetotaler Police Commissioner's funeral over and, in accordance with his expressed wishes a decent wake only a pipe dream, I returned to my office in Kuala Lumpur to find Chief Superintendent Sutcliffe of the Straits Settlements Police waiting for me in the anteroom, clutching a briefcase on his lap and looking uncharacteristically agitated.

"Is this a bad time, Masters?" he said, after I shut the door and had the office for the two of us without interruption. "I heard about the Commissioner, but that's not why I'm here. And congratulations on your promotion."

"Temporary Acting Deputy only, unless Whitehall confirms it, and they've got more urgent problems on their hands."

"The German invasion and now the Blitz? There are times when a nice quiet little backwater like Singapore is just what the doctor ordered."

"We did our bit and then some in the last one. We're both getting a little long in the tooth to be volunteering for a second go round."

"I'll say. Still, acting or permanent, the pay's the same. Mark my words, the rank will be confirmed once the new Commissioner takes over the reins. In the meantime it might be wisest to keep your head down and try not to rock the boat."

"Sounds ominous, Sutcliffe. Pull up a pew and make yourself at home. Then you may enlighten me as to the real reason for this visit." I glanced at the Government Issue wall clock and noted the hour. "Scotch?" Without waiting for an answer, I pulled a bottle of single malt and two glasses from my desk draw.

"My father's," Sutcliffe said, indicating the black leather case after I passed a generous double tot of whisky across the desk. "He was at my place for dinner a couple of nights ago and he had it with him. I can't think why, and least of all why it wasn't locked away in a safe or a bank vault. He left in a bit of a rush to board a light cruiser for a short sea trial after a refit, and she was due to sail at midnight. I'd not heard from him by first thing yesterday morning, so I presume he made the ship in time. When I opened the case and found what was in it, I decided it was not the sort of thing we should investigate in Singapore." He stifled a yawn.

"Am I keeping you up?"

"Sorry. I was up all last night, going through his private office in his house."

"And here you are and you've still not told me why."

"If my father knew I was here, and why, he'd be in a frightful stew, probably at panic stations."

"You can unburden your conscience about going through your father's private correspondence, if that's what's bothering you."

Sutcliffe placed the heavy briefcase on my desk and clicked open the clasps on either side. He turned the case to face me and pulled up the lid to reveal papers—documents and files with the Admiralty crest on the topmost. Mystified by this almost theatrical show, I raised my eyebrows but said nothing, waiting for the gems of information to pour forth.

"Admiralty papers, as one might expect given my father's position. Nothing highly classified. But beneath them is another matter." He pulled the top few files from the case and set them on my desk top. Beneath them I saw a sheet of paper which I recognized as a bearer bond. I looked up enquiringly and inclined my head slightly. Sutcliffe got the message.

"United Kingdom Government bearer bonds with a maturity value of one thousand pounds sterling each. They're all short term, maturing in the next year or two. I counted them. There are eight hundred of them here, which is why the case is so damn heavy. They're as good as cash at any bank." He held up a wad of money in his fist. "And five wads of one hundred, five-pound notes."

"And I take it you're suggesting your father has no legitimate right to be in possession of any of these?"

"I think it highly unlikely on a Commodore's pay, don't you?"

"Your father has no private income and no legacy that could account for eight hundred thousand pounds?"

"A small income which he inherited from my grandfather. Barely enough to pay his wardroom account. But this isn't all. It's merely the tip of the iceberg."

"You mean there's more?"

Grim faced, Sutcliffe nodded.

"I think we need another one of these," I said, pushing the Scotch bottle across the desk. "A stiff one." Three fingers of The Macallan found their way into each glass. "Then you had better start at the beginning."

We each took a sip of the whisky and held onto the glasses, as if reluctant to let go in case the truth would slip through our fingers as easily as the Scotch slid down our throats. Sutcliffe had been my best friend all the way through grammar school. He had been gassed at Ypres, not badly, but enough to be invalided out. His lungs had been a bit weak ever since. Like me, he joined the London Metropolitan Police and as soon as he was fit enough to pass the medical, made Inspector rank. Then chronic bronchitis drove him to a warmer climate, which turned out to be a transfer to the Straits Settlements Police in Singapore.

"Everyone's surprised I'm not following my father into the Navy," he told me once when we were thirteen. "If I ever have to serve, it'll be in the army." When I asked why, he told me, "I have a morbid fear of drowning and I get seasick in my bathtub." We had a good laugh over that one. Then he turned serious. I remember my stomach lurching when he told me in strictest confidence, "My mother drowned when I was eight. She and my father were out sailing. A fog descended and their sailboat was rammed by the Isle of Wight ferry. My father swam to shore. My mother couldn't swim. I'm sure he abandoned her. I've lived with my aunt ever since while my father was away at sea."

Sutcliffe looked at me over the rim of his glass. "You know where I stand with my father, Masters. What you don't know is that later on he was the gunnery officer on a cruiser at Jutland." He took another decent swig at his Scotch. "His ship was torpedoed and sank. The official story is that he was thrown overboard by the explosion and later rescued. I'm sure it was a whitewash, but like with my mother, I can't prove it. Oddly enough, he only ever got shore jobs after that, never a sea command. That's probably how he ended up in Singapore as Second in Command to the Vice Admiral commanding the shore establishment."

"So, the question is, how did he come by all this money?"

"He's been in Admiralty procurement for years. He buys everything from jam and toilet paper to battleships and ammunition. Bribes? Threats? Payoffs? You name it." His account dried up. A little encouragement was called for. Three more fingers of The Macallan helped lubricate the vocal cords.

"Companies that want to do business with the Royal Navy went through him and his department while he was at the Admiralty in London. A little bit from each contract quite possibly stuck to his fingers, oiling the wheels of industry—his industry and theirs. Over time it added up. How much I don't know, but I have a guess that what's in this briefcase isn't a tenth of what's in his sea chest in his private office. I went in there last night after I was sure he wouldn't be back for a week. You might want to see for yourself what else I found in his sea chest, or at least send someone down to head up an investigation. Obviously I can't do that and I can't fob it off any of my Inspectors. The dirt's too close to home and in any case there's protocol to follow."

He leaned back in his chair and closed his eyes for a moment, seemingly exhausted by the enormity of the corruption that apparently ran through his father and spread its tentacles throughout British industry. If his suspicions were correct, it might possibly implicate others within the Admiralty and even to members of Boards of Directors of some of the biggest and most prestigious companies in the country. And many of those Board members sat as Cabinet Ministers in Churchill's government and the House of Lords. The Blitz might be remembered in history as a storm in a teacup in comparison.

I glanced at the wall clock. "There's a train to Singapore tonight, a sleeper. I'll be on it with two of my best men. Hopefully we'll get to the bottom of this before your father gets back from his sea trial. Then we'll see what he has to say."

"I can't thank you enough, Masters. It's a huge weight off my shoulders. I can't be seen to have any part of the investigation but I'll make sure you have free rein. I'll have you and your men booked into Raffles Hotel and I'll get the warrant to search under way as soon as I get back. There's a train early this evening that will get me in late but I'll manage a cat nap." He stretched and yawned.

I stood and held out my hand. "One thing before you go, Sutcliffe."

"What's that?"

"How did you gain entry to your father's private study?"

"Really!" He laughed for the first time. "We were both on the

Met as I recall. I've still got my tool kit."

"Say no more," I said. "As long as you didn't kick the door in with your size twelve boots."

He grinned. "See you off the train tomorrow morning. I can see myself out."

Sutcliffe met us off the overnight sleeper and drove us to the hotel for a wash and a shave. He then had us taken to his father's house. Fortunately, Commodore Sutcliffe lived off base, in a pleasant community of whites only, upper class homes in an almost parklike setting near the centre of Singapore.

"The Admiralty owns this house, and the Admiral's," Sutcliffe said. "One of the perks of being in the upper echelons of the Service. It's rent free and comes fully furnished and staffed. My father's been out here a couple of years and I've visited him a few times at his invitation. Reluctantly, I assure you."

The head of the household servants, and unusual for Singapore, was a tall, bearded and turbaned Sikh who met us at the front door. "Chief Superintendent," he said, addressing Sutcliffe. "I was not informed that you would be here today. We were not expecting you. The Commodore is away at sea for several days. We have taken the opportunity of his absence to thoroughly clean the house."

"These gentlemen are here on police business, Mr. Malhi. They have a warrant to search the house for certain things and to seize them as evidence should they find what they are looking for."

I read surprise and consternation in Malhi's face before the Sikh regained control of his features. "Of course, Chief Superintendent," he said, and bowed as he gestured to us to enter.

"I'm no stranger to my father's study—far from it," Sutcliffe said when Malhi unlocked the study door for us. "It's set up very much like his old study in Portsmouth and the one later in London. Old naval habits die hard, no different from the rest of us, I suppose, Commissioner."

I noted that he had reverted to a formal way of addressing me in the presence of Inspectors Barnes and Jessop who had accompanied me. As we were there on business, a strictly business relationship was called for. And as Sutcliffe said, old habits die hard, and ours had been ingrained by the military, polished by the London Metropolitan Police Force, and further reinforced by our time in the Colonial

Police. I saw him glance around the study, as if searching for something. He shivered as his gaze alighted in turn on the globe, then the astrolabe, the sextant on the desk, the telescope in the window and the binoculars on a bookshelf.

"Everything's here as I remember from the last time I was here," he said. He turned to the Sikh. "Thank you, Mr. Malhi. You may leave us now. We do not wish to be disturbed. We will lock the door. Make sure none of the servants enters this room, including you, without our permission." He held his hand out. "The key to the study, if you would." The Sikh bowed and without a word handed the key to Sutcliffe who slipped it into his pocket. He turned back to me once Malhi had shut the door behind him. "It doesn't look as if anything's been moved since the day my father brought these things into his study." He swept a hand around to indicate the naval paraphernalia on display. "I sometimes wonder if he even touches them. He told me that the sextant once belonged to the young Horatio Nelson and the astrolabe by one of the first explorers of Quebec. I think he said Champlain, but I can't be sure. Old, anyway. I think he regards them almost as religious relics."

He took a couple of steps towards the long wall of the study. "Here's what you're looking for, Commissioner, my father's old sea chest. He claims it survived the Nile and Trafalgar. It's got a light layer of dust on the lid. It doesn't look like it's been dusted in days. I'm sure my father will have a word with the servant responsible for cleaning this room when he gets back."

Yes, I thought, the training on the job in the Met had been more than thorough. Sutcliffe hadn't left a trail of fingerprint evidence behind him in the dust during his clandestine, and almost certainly illegal search of his father's study after the servants had retired to bed two nights ago.

Sutcliffe shook his head. "This room, and all its predecessors," he said quietly, "have always left me uneasy. I remember his Portsmouth study being like this before my mother died. Every square inch is as familiar to me as my bedroom, yet today, more than any other, I have a sense of dread, as if an invisible hand is strangling my throat." He shivered again. "It's stuffy in here," he muttered. He crossed the floor and flipped the switch on the wall. The ceiling fan purred into life. "When I come in here it somehow feels like I'm walking past a graveyard in the dark, at every step anticipating a ghost would jump out and scare the life out of me. I should never have read all those horror stories by torchlight after lights out at my aunt's house." He laughed, but it sounded forced and brittle.

He picked up the phone and placed a call to his office at the Hill Street police station. He spoke quietly but authoritatively to whoever answered, then put the receiver down and crossed over to the sea chest. He selected a skeleton key from the ring he pulled from his pocket. Three seconds later the lid of the sea chest was open. He stood back to allow me a look at the content. What I saw didn't surprise me, and I wondered why I was in Singapore on some cockamamie wild goose chase. Lying in the sea chest were rolled up charts. I pushed them aside. Beneath them lay several aquatints of etchings, the margins now mottled brown with age and seawater, probably done decades ago. I picked one up and recognized the Great Gate of India in Bombay and another of the Taj Mahal.

I gave Sutcliffe a stern look. "You didn't bring me all this way to show me the Commodore's etchings, Chief Superintendent."

Sutcliffe gave what I interpreted as a wan grin and bent over the chest. He pulled away the last of the charts and etchings to reveal wads and wads of bearer bonds. Detective Inspectors Barnes and Jessop leaned over my shoulder. I heard one of them whistle softly behind me. Sutcliffe grabbed one of the side handles and lifted the chest an inch off the floor before setting it down again. "Try it, Commissioner," he said.

I accepted the challenge and nearly wrenched my back. I set it down gently on the floor and straightened. Sutcliffe's hands trembled as he lifted a canvas sheet separating the top layers from whatever lay beneath. I gasped at what I saw.

Beneath the bearer bonds, United States Treasury bills in thick wads and dozens, perhaps hundreds of stock certificates lay neatly stacked. I recognized the names of British and American companies. Some certificates, I saw on closer examination, were no more than a few months old; others much older, well predating the start of the war. I picked up the papers and placed them on the floor next to the chest. Beneath, and covered by another layer of canvas, what I saw when I peeled back the sheet turned my stomach: photographs, most of them I guessed from the quality and the enlargements, professionally taken; dozens of them, possibly a hundred or more, of what I took to be Sutcliffe's father engaging in sex acts with children, some boys but mostly girls, and none apparently over the age of twelve or thirteen.

"I'd rather not look, Commissioner," Sutcliffe said. "If the rest are in a similar vein, I never want to set eyes on them." He turned his back on the three of us. "I have children of my own."

Sickened, I thumbed through them. My mind went numb with the same kind of shock I experience every time I viewed a body on a steel table in a hospital morgue, or a blood-drenched corpse in a back alley, already buzzing with fat bluebottles. Most of the children in the photographs, I noted, looked Indian or Oriental.

"Where was the Commodore stationed before here?" I said.

Sutcliffe turned to face me. "Before the last war he spent time on the China Station, Malaya, Singapore, Hong Kong and Shanghai. And other places like Ceylon, Burma and Siam." He gripped the top of the large wooden desk in the study and steadied himself. I noticed his heavy, ragged breathing and read anger and loathing in each breath. "I think his last foreign posting was the Bermuda station which covered the Atlantic coast of the United States as well as the West Indies. I think that ended about ten years ago."

I forced myself to delve deeper into the chest, afraid of what else I might find.

"I've known fear, Commissioner," Sutcliffe said between clenched teeth. "It was my close and constant companion at the front, but what lies in this chest is the sum of all my fears, compounded. It's not a fear of dying or of losing my sight or a limb. Nothing in my life or training as a soldier or a police officer has prepared me to confront the consequences of this loathsome discovery, my father's basest secret. I wish I'd never embarked on this course. Where ignorance is bliss…"

"'Tis folly to be wise," I finished. "But not as coppers." I clamped my jaw shut.

I ran my hands over the bottom of the chest. My fingers brushed against something cold and hard. I closed my fingers over coins, spilling out of my hands even as I clutched them. I picked one up and stared at a gold sovereign. I threw the photos out of the chest, pulled back a second canvas sheet and gaped at the floor of the old sea chest littered with gold sovereigns several layers deep. No wonder the chest seemed heavy when I lifted one end a couple of inches off the floor.

When I finished scooping the last of the coins from the chest, I piled the sovereigns in columns ten high and counted them; one hundred and forty-one columns, one thousand, four hundred and ten gold sovereigns. I inspected the top coin and found the mint date: 1794. I checked several more at random. The earliest was dated 1772; the latest 1887. I could not begin to guess their worth, other than their face value, nor speculate why or how Sutcliffe's father came to possess them.

"When I made this discovery," Sutcliffe said, in a hoarse voice, "I tried to collect my thoughts but the sound of my blood rushing past my ears in a continuous hiss almost drowned them out. I can tell you my temples throbbed in time with every heartbeat. My knees trembled with a kind of dread different from and more debilitating than any I knew at Ypres. This fear reached out and held me in a suffocating embrace. I felt a terror such as my mother must have known when she could no longer prevent the sea from rushing into her lungs."

He tottered over to the desk, grabbed hold of the edge and almost collapsed into the chair. He rested his forehead on his forearms for a moment before looking up at me. "I'm sorry, Commissioner. That was a bit melodramatic."

"Completely understandable."

"With all the thoughts swirling through my mind I had to force myself not to be physically sick at what I'd uncovered."

He slumped over his folded hands again and remained like that for several minutes. When the clock on the wall struck eleven Sutcliffe pushed himself into a sitting position and surveyed the scene before him. "Your choice, Commissioner," he said with a grim expression on his face and in his voice. "We can go through everything here and post a twenty-four-hour guard on the door until we've finished tabulating the inventory, or we can take it back to Hill Street and do it there."

The phone rang before I could arrive at a decision. Sutcliffe waved me away and picked up the receiver. He listened for a moment, said, "Thank you," and replaced the receiver. "The sea trials are going well. She should dock back here in three days. It looks as if we have seventy-two hours at the most to decide what we're going to do."

I came to my decision. "We'll do it here. Either way we'll have to get a magistrate to come out and verify we've executed the warrant to search. It's not something we can whip in through the back door of his office. Once we've got everything sorted you can arrange for a police photographer take photos of the evidence. Then we'll have to decide on what charges to lay and what to do with the evidence that we won't need for the case."

Sutcliffe placed a phone call. "Chief Superintendent Sutcliffe here. I want a guard here every eight hours for as long as I need him." He gave the station Sergeant the address and put the phone down.

"Let's get to work," I said to the two Inspectors. "We have three days to gather all the evidence we need. And then we have to make sure we have all our ducks in a row to make the charges stick. If heads don't roll over this, we can watch our pensions float downstream and we might as well sign up for the poor bloody infantry."

"I don't know how much is there," Sutcliffe said. "It staggers me why this isn't in a bank vault in Switzerland or somewhere safe rather than in an old sea chest with a rusty lock a child could pick with a paper clip."

"My father was a bank manager, don't forget, Chief Superintendent. He once told me crooks never make bank deposits. Too much paper and the trail pointing back to them like an arrow. Best to stick it under the mattress where no one asks questions."

Sutcliffe's mouth narrowed in a tight line. "I'd best be going. There's no point in hanging around here, getting in everyone's way. Besides, protocol dictates I should play no part. I'm not sure how I'm going to hide this from my wife. She has a nose for my moods." He shrugged. "This is the last thing she needs to know about."

When the three of us finished totalling the values of the bonds, a little over £10,000,000, we decided on an estimate of ten shillings per share for the stock certificates. We came up with a value of £5,000,000, but we could have been well over or under. On a policeman's pay we don't very often see stock certificates, let alone buy them. Then there was over $1,000,000 in United States Treasury bills, not counting the value of the contents of the briefcase.

I pushed the chair back and put my hands on the desk top. My next move was but a telephone call away. My hand reached for the telephone, then stopped before I could pick it up. Who on earth could I, should I call over this? I was way out of my depth.

I checked the stock certificates again for clues. Of the companies whose names I recognized, many I knew to be suppliers to the Admiralty for equipment, armaments and provisions. Even two major shipbuilders. Surely these stock certificates and bonds had to be the payoffs in secret commissions, of bribes, of coercion in exchange for awarding contracts worth tens of millions of pounds or more over the course of the rearmament and thus far in the war? Could Sutcliffe's father truly be, not only a criminal but one of this magnitude? Logic denied any other reasonable explanation for these stocks, bonds and largely untraceable sums of money and cash equivalents easily approaching, and probably exceeding £20,000,000. Only one question remained: is this all? How could it be?

I came to the same inescapable conclusion as Sutcliffe had—that his father was a common criminal dressed in a Commodore's uniform, who used his position to turn other powerful and wealthy businessmen, Directors of some of the country's largest and most successful business empires, into criminals as well. How willing were these men to participate in a criminal conspiracy, conniving to make personal fortunes out of the war? Were they all, many of them Peers of the Realm with family histories dating back centuries, no more than morally bankrupt opportunists? Were some coerced and strong-armed by Sutcliffe's father? Or did they come to him unbidden?

Then there were the photographs. None appeared to be recent, but I could be mistaken. I had never met the Commodore, so I had no idea what he looked like now, or two or three decades ago. But Sutcliffe said the photos showed his father and I had no reason to doubt him. The man looked to have been in his early fifties at the latest when some were taken, and much younger in others. Besides, Sutcliffe had said his father's last foreign station was a decade ago. Nonetheless, the thought sickened me, probably less than it would have sickened Sutcliffe, but as much as it ought to revolt any sense of decency and morality in a man. I could not prevent bile and acid from reaching the back of my throat. I felt sweat beading on my brow and dabbed at the moisture with a handkerchief.

I did some quick mental calculations. Sutcliffe was only a few months older that I, both of us born in 1896. He was eight when his mother died in the summer of 1904, thirty-seven years ago. Was it possible that the earliest of the photographs could have dated from the time while she was alive? Very possibly, though I decided to spare Sutcliffe the embarrassment and probably disgust of verifying this unless absolutely necessary. But one thing these photos did was to provide clear and damning evidence the Sutcliffe's father had a perverted and depraved sexual appetite and was a man unfit to hold the King's commission.

I turned my attention to the gold sovereigns while Inspectors Barnes and Jessop ploughed through the bonds and stock certificates, sucking indelible pencil tips and making notes. There was no law against holding gold coins, though bullion was another matter. Absent an explanation for having the coins, I had to assume the Commodore had acquired them legally, though I doubted it. The U.S. Treasury bills were another matter and could have come from the time spent on the Bermuda Station. But $1,000,000 worth? I thought it hardly likely he had acquired them legitimately, though I could not absolutely rule it out. However Commodore Sutcliffe had gained possession of the gold and the Treasury Bills, he clearly did not trust his London bank to keep his secret. That could be the only logical reason not to have this fortune in a Swiss bank vault where no one might accidentally stumble across it. Criminals, in my experience, are rarely among the most intelligent of life forms. Unless I was wrong, the Commodore was no doubt an intelligent man to have advanced as high up the naval ladder as he had. That begged the question, therefore—how absolutely stupid could he be?

I stared out of the study window at the formal gardens with clipped hedges and manicured lawn. The hibiscus by the window was in bloom. I imagined the smell drifting in through the closed window and wished for a moment it was open to allow the fresh air in. But it was hot and sticky, as Singapore always was, and the house was shut up to keep it as cool as humanly possible. The gravel drive, I noted, had already been swept clean of our tyre tracks. A pink-flowered oleander which I could see if I craned my neck bloomed near the front door. From my vantage point with my back to the room I briefly contemplated Sutcliffe's future in the Straits Police if his father's crimes came to light. Disgrace by association would fall on his shoulders. He may have to resign. It could cost him his marriage, not to mention his pension and his employment prospects back in England even without Herr Hitler's other plans for the foreseeable future.

I turned my back on the window and paced around the study, clearly getting in the way of Jessop and Barnes who had to work around me. I stopped pacing and turned back towards the window, staring first at the massive mahogany and brass desk, then at the telephone, vacillating between one option and the other. I knew I had to protect the good name and reputation of the Police Force and somehow of Sutcliffe and his wife, Amanda. Sutcliffe could easily have confronted his father, told him what he knew and threatened to go to the authorities unless his father cut him in on the deal, past, present and future. By coming to me he had turned his back on a vast fortune, one beyond the comprehension of most people, the existence of which no one knew and which for all intents and purposes did not exist, officially or otherwise, in any ledger anywhere in the country. It was of some comfort that Sutcliffe had done the right thing by coming forward, but that was the nature of the man I had known since I was eleven. The quandary I faced, however, was that if this discovery came to light, half the biggest names in England could fall under scrutiny, especially if I handled this imprudently. And almost certainly they deserved to be placed under a police microscope.

I told myself to place the call. But to whom? I knew no one in the Admiralty, here or in London. I didn't even have a telephone number for the Port Admiral's office. And besides, whom could I trust there? Who else within the Admiralty hierarchy might be an accomplice, or at the very least, implicated? The Admiral in charge of Singapore? Far East Command? The Cabinet? How deep did the plot extend?

To the annoyance of Barnes and Jessop I resumed pacing the study while I thought. I stopped in mid turn in front of the large window and, hoping for inspiration, stared at the rose gardens on the other side of the driveway. Their colourful display lit up the blank, distempered wall which served to keep burglars and gawkers alike at bay, and Singapore's vehicular traffic out of sight. I marvelled at how the gardeners maintained their domain so clean, neat and tidy, obviously in keeping with the Commodore's no doubt standing orders of 'Shipshape and Bristol fashion.' I wondered if the grounds at the Admiral's house were as impeccably ordered. I wrenched my attention away from the garden to the matter at hand and decided only one viable option presented itself.

I picked up the telephone. When the operator responded I told him where to place the call.

"Commissioner Harwood." The gruff voice on the other end of the phone did not sound pleased at having his morning interrupted.
I glanced at the clock on the wall and noted the time. The Acting Commissioner was not a teetotaller and, now that he was in charge, no doubt anxious to take advantage of the relaxation of the rules around what constituted lunch in Kuala Lumpur.

"Masters, Commissioner, calling from Singapore."

"And how is Singapore? Hot and sunny as usual?" The voice was still grumpy.

I decided to cut to the chase before the Commissioner cut me off. I let out the breath I hadn't realized I'd been holding in since the Commissioner answered the phone.

"I have reason," I began slowly and deliberately, "to believe there is bribery, corruption and possibly other offences being committed at the highest levels within the Admiralty, both in Singapore and possibly as far away as London. I have what I believe is evidence to back this up."

"Why have you not spoken of this to the Admiralty?"

"Because I don't know how high up this conspiracy extends, nor whom to trust."

"I see."

At the word conspiracy I sensed a change in the Commissioner's interest level, almost as if he sat up in his chair and stopped drawing doodles on his blotting pad with the pen from his desk set. "But I do know," I continued with renewed hope my information would bear fruit, "at least one Commodore has received bribes and these bribes come from members of the peerage and other individuals at the pinnacle of British industry. I can't conclude at this time if this is ongoing or strictly in the past tense."

I spoke at length about Sutcliffe's discovery and I could hear the Commissioner grunting on the other end of the line while I presumed he jotted down notes.

"Is there any suggestion of a breach of military security, or of an offence under the Official Secrets Act or the Defence of the Realm Act?"

"Not as far as I can tell, Sir. But money buys many things, including information on upcoming contract proposals which are matters of military and state secret and could be of use to our enemies."

"I shall need to see and weigh the evidence before I can make any decision on what action to take, Masters." From the Commissioner's tone of voice, I could almost hear him add, "If any."

"I can provide some evidence within twenty-four hours, possibly less. The rest will have to stay here until we can complete its examination."

"Why?"

"It's too heavy to move by one person. I can have a paddy wagon take it to Hill Street Police Station if needed, but we have a police guard posted outside the door where the evidence lies in a sea chest."

"I see. One thing you haven't told me is how much you suspect is involved. A few hundred pounds? A few thousand?"

"As the one-time mess president and battery adjutant my bookkeeping was more estimate than fact, but we are talking in the range of twenty million pounds, Commissioner. And a million American dollars." At my end of the line I heard the Commissioner's sharp intake of breath and realized I had probably diminished his appetite for lunch.

"There's close to a million in a briefcase which started the investigation. I can have that hand delivered to you by the next train from Singapore, but I don't think that would serve any practical purpose."

"Perhaps I should be the judge of that." His new tone of voice confirmed that I had definitely ruined his appetite for lunch, liquid or otherwise. "How did this come to light?"

"Chief Superintendent Sutcliffe's father is Commodore Sutcliffe, the second-in-command to the Port Admiral in Singapore. You probably remember Sutcliffe from your days on the Straits Police. His father does not yet know we have his briefcase or that we've searched his study. The study is secure twenty-four hours a day and I have the key. The Commodore is at sea for another three days conducting sea trials unless for some reason he returns early."

"I see." I felt like saying that I doubted if he did but stopped myself just in time. We never really had seen eye to eye. I'd had my eye on a promotion when the Commissioner had been transferred from the Straits Police and leapfrogged me. Still, no point in sour grapes and I had to admit he generally left me alone, which in police parlance amounts to damp praise.

"I'm not prepared to allow the briefcase out of my possession until either I or Chief Superintendent Sutcliffe hands it over to you in person. It's hard to trust anyone with that kind of money."

I heard another sharp intake of breath. "I meant no disrespect, Commissioner, but a lesser individual than Chief Superintendent Sutcliffe may be tempted to take an early retirement."

"You have Barnes and Jessop sifting through the evidence. You have executed a lawfully obtained warrant to search the premises. As long as we can find a link between the money, the Commodore and directors of British companies, you can place your life savings on someone hanging for this… this treason. Perhaps many somebodies. Does anyone else know about your discovery?"

"Five individuals, now including you. Sutcliffe I can trust. I've known him for more than thirty years. We were at school together. And Barnes and Jessop I picked personally for this job."

"Could the Commodore have ordered the ship back to port as soon as he realized he'd left his briefcase behind?"

"I don't know how much authority he carries, Sir. But possibly."

"He could possibly be back in Singapore at any time? Before you've gathered all the evidence you need?"

"It's not out of the question. It's also possible he doesn't know he left the briefcase behind. If he suspects he has, he can only pray his son hasn't opened it. He could hardly risk a ship to shore message over a missing briefcase without gathering suspicion, or at the very least drawing attention to himself. And if he ordered a return to base he'd be here by now." I hesitated. "If you want my best guess, Sir?"

"What's that?"

"He's shitting his pants as we speak and has been for three days."

"Do you need me there?"

"No, Sir. But perhaps you might get in touch with the Admiralty in London, tell them what we suspect, and have them start a very discreet enquiry of their own. Is there anyone you know there who you can trust absolutely?"

"I'll have to think about that one. The Home Secretary and I were at school together—different years, but we knew each other. I might have a quiet word in his ear. It might be best to keep this away from sailors. You know what gossips they can be."

"Worse than policemen, I've heard."

I heard a grunt from his end.

"Do you have enough to arrest and hold him, Masters?"

"Yes, Sir. We can arrest him as soon as he comes ashore. We won't involve the military or naval police. We'll wait for him at his house once we know the ship has docked. There's nowhere for him to run in Singapore. We'll question him and remand him in custody. I don't know if any of the offences were committed in Singapore. If London wants him, extradition should be a rubber stamp. Three days in an RAF flying boat and he'll be cooling his heels in the Naval Prison in Bodmin."

"I'll get on it right away." I imagined the Commissioner rubbing his hands at the prospect of the highest profile arrest of his career and confirmation of his Acting rank being made Permanent.

"Thank you, Commissioner."

"Before you go, I have one further question for you, Masters."

"Which is?"

"Why did Chief Superintendent Sutcliffe bring this to you?"

I hesitated before choosing my next words with care. "Sutcliffe says his father is not the most agreeable of people. He doubts if many people care much for him. He certainly doesn't. I doubt if it took much for him put aside bonds of family and do the right thing." I felt like reminding the Commissioner that Sutcliffe was an Englishman, after all, but remembered in time the Commissioner was a Welshman.

"I see."

"There's more, Sir. He's not doing this because of his distaste for his father. He has a personal history with his father dating back to childhood and his father is a constant reminder of that history. He suffers through his father's presence in Singapore only in the knowledge that his father will be transferred or will retire in the next couple of years. Sutcliffe took on this responsibility which a lesser man might care to shirk."

The Commissioner didn't say anything, which I took it as my cue to continue. I took a deep breath and told myself to slow down. "If that were not enough, while our army and air force have been decimated in France and over the South of England, and while our civilians die under German bombs, men like Sutcliffe's father make millions out of the war from criminal activity. We have an obligation to do what is right, and proper." I stopped, weary of the need to justify Sutcliffe's actions. "And even if we didn't have a professional obligation, we would still have a personal moral obligation to do so." I cleared my throat noisily. "It's not simply enough to catch and prosecute criminals then move onto the next case. Sutcliffe believes his father failed to meet a level of integrity demanded by his position, both personally and professionally. I agree with him. I don't believe he has any other motive, Commissioner."

And if that little, self-righteous speech didn't seal my fate to return to the rank of Assistant Commissioner from which I had only been temporarily promoted on the death of the Commissioner a few days ago, nothing would. It was out, like the Genie from Aladdin's bottle, or lamp, or whatever it was, and no shoving it back behind the stopper. I hoped I could depend on the Commissioner to do his job with the Home Secretary and that the reprisals by the henchmen of a large number of very angry, powerful and almost certainly guilty men would not be the physical death of either Sutcliffe or I, or our professional deaths as policemen.

It took all three full days to finish going through the contents of the sea chest and tally the inventory. The amount involved was much as I anticipated – in the region of £20,000,000. I suppressed a momentary inclination to applaud the enormity and barefaced boldness of the scheme. Then Sutcliffe phoned to inform me that his father's ship had just docked and that the Commodore had called him from the Port Admiral's dockside office.

"I told him I'd realized the next morning he'd left the briefcase behind at my place and that I'd taken it back to his house for safekeeping under lock and key. I think he bought it. He should be there in less than half an hour. Do you want me to be there when you make the arrest?"

"Not unless you have any particular reason. I don't doubt he'll see you in terms of Judas once he discovers it was you who tipped us off. No point in making a bad situation worse."

I heard him exhale at the other end of the line before I hung up. I pushed aside the sandwich I had been eating for supper and glanced at the clock. It was just after nine o'clock. We could anticipate an arrest in minutes and with luck a confession before midnight.

Jessop, Barnes and I did not have long to wait in the Commodore's study before the crunch of tyres on gravel alerted us to the arrival of his staff car. The head bearer, Malhi, loped down the steps to greet the Commodore as the car drew away. We followed. The Commodore looked startled and half turned to look over his shoulder at the departing staff car.

"Commodore Sutcliffe?" I said.

"Yes. What is the meaning of this? Who are you?"

A moment later Barnes and Jessop stepped forward and put their hands on the Commodore's elbows. "Commodore Sutcliffe," I said. "I'm Deputy Commissioner Masters of the Malay Police. These gentlemen are Detective Inspector Barnes and Detective Inspector Jessop. You are under arrest for conspiracy to commit offences contrary to the Theft Act of Great Britain. Please place your hands behind your back."

"Take your filthy hands off me, you ruffians," the Admiral hissed, and pulled his arms away. "I shall have your jobs and your pensions for this outrage. How dare you!"

A simple police hold later and Commodore Sutcliffe found himself in handcuffs. A moment later a Black Mariah of the Straits Settlement Police pulled up by the front door. A Sergeant got out and opened the back door of the paddy wagon. The Commodore was bundled inside and shackled to the floor.

The Commissioner himself, who had arrived earlier that afternoon from K.L., watched the proceedings from the shadows of the Commodore's partially lit house. "I just wanted to make sure no one changed his mind at the last minute, or absconded with the evidence," he said.

"As you see, we did neither," I replied coldly.

"We needed to make sure, Masters. People sometimes have a change of heart when it comes to shopping family. It's a pity the Commodore chose to make something of a scene."

Ten minutes later the Commissioner was on his way to the railway station and the sleeper back to Kuala Lumpur, and Commodore Sutcliffe was in a secure, soundproof cell in the sub-basement of the Hill Street Police Station.

The three of us took it in turns to grill the Commodore for the best part of three days and nights. We tried everything we knew about police interrogations short of beating him which, by the end of it I'm ashamed to admit, I seriously considered. We played good cop, bad cop. I threatened life in prison if he didn't cooperate. When that didn't work, I bargained, dangling the prospect of leniency in front of him in exchange for a confession. I could sense him weakening with each interrogation but he would not break. I smelled sweat, fear sweat, flooding his armpits in the cool, dank cell and watched perspiration trickle from his temples and run down his stubbled face whenever I seemed to be getting close to the truth. He received food and water but I refused to let him shower or shave or even wash. I deprived him of sleep, waking him at irregular intervals to continue the interrogation and to keep him off balance. He had no watch. The cell was without windows. He did not know the time of day, or day of the week, or how long it had been since the last time I grilled him. By the time three days and nights were up, I must have been almost as exhausted as he was. I had nothing more in my arsenal.

He met every line of questioning with the same response: "I acquired everything legally over a period of years." Nothing more; no expansion on how, or from whom he had accumulated enough money to build a battleship.

The Commodore steadfastly refused to co-operate in any way beyond providing his name, rank and serial number as if he were a prisoner of war. In the end, around breakfast time on the fourth day, as exhausted as he must have been, we stopped the interrogation. I phoned Sutcliffe at home. He was about to leave for the police station so I asked him to stay. I thought it would be appropriate to put his wife in the picture. Twenty minutes later I was in his teak furnished drawing room with the ceiling fan swirling warm air overhead.

"I don't know what Graham has told you, Amanda," I said, "but I think you should know what's been going on this past few days."

"Graham's been acting very odd, Commissioner," she said, sounding anxious, "but he wouldn't tell me what was bothering him, which is most unlike him. It must be something serious for him to behave like this."

"It is, and I asked him not to mention what was going on to anyone, including you. I need you to keep what I'm about to tell you completely under your hat, probably forever."

She looked first at her husband then back at me. Her hand went to her mouth and I could see she was on the verge of tears. "Perhaps you had better sit down," I said, and she took a seat at one end of the settee with Sutcliffe at the other. I remained standing.

"We have arrested your father-in-law for a number of very serious offences."

She looked wildly at Sutcliffe for confirmation.

He nodded. "It's true," he said. "As soon as he returned from the sea trials."

"He's in custody at the police station as this is not a military or naval matter," I said. I glossed over the more lurid details of the discovery, including the part her husband played in the investigation, and the arrest.

"The sea chest was the biggest surprise of all, Amanda," Sutcliffe said, as we reached the end of the story. "If it's all bribe money, I can't get to grips with the scale of it. Millions of pounds, and a million at least in American dollars. I can see no reason for deceit on such a scale, other than pure greed and a lust for the power that sort of money brings."

I thought she took it rather well, considering. She put her hands around Sutcliffe's neck, drew him to her and kissed him.

"Am I forgiven?" he said when they broke apart. She linked her arm through his.

"Absolutely not! There's nothing to forgive you for. If you have a fault, it's being intensely loyal to what is right and just. I don't count that as blameworthy."

"The Old Testament says the sins of the father shall be visited upon the sons, even unto the tenth generation." As we had already agreed not to mention the photographs, I was wondering where that comment might lead. I saw him tremor and ball his hand into a fist to stop it.

"I don't believe it for a moment, Sutcliffe," I said hurriedly. "That would be silly."

"Perhaps I'm being overdramatic, Commissioner," he said, then turned to Amanda. "But I wouldn't blame you for one second if you packed your bags and went back to England on the first boat."

"Why on earth would I do such a thing?" She pushed Sutcliffe away.

"Because you discovered your husband's father is a criminal. I wouldn't blame you if you felt the same revulsion as I did once I found out."

"Graham Sutcliffe, I married you, not your father. I'm not leaving your side, today or ever, even if it affects your career. But we won't have to tell the children, will we?" She sounded worried even as her hand covered her mouth.

"No. They hardly know their grandfather in any case and never ask about him. Perhaps one day, when they get older and ask questions. It wouldn't do to lie to them."

Sutcliffe broke away from his wife's clinch and turned to me. "We should say something to Amanda's mother before the story hits the press. A letter home. Perhaps a telegram." He stopped. "No. A telegram would only alarm her. Leave it to the Commissioner to be circumspect and do his job without interference from us. A letter to your mother can wait another day or two."

Unfamiliar as I was of the intricacies of finding the right balance in married life, I left them to their scene of domestic harmony and returned to Hill Street Police Station, there to interrogate Commodore Sutcliffe again, more thoroughly after his spell in solitary.

I placed the phone call shortly after noon and came straight to the point. "The Commodore is proving most uncooperative, Commissioner. No names, no confession. He won't even admit ownership of the briefcase, the sea chest or its contents."

A lengthy silence greeted this news. "Does anybody know he's in custody?"

"Only the Port Admiral, Commissioner. We had to inform him. I told him the minimum necessary and swore him to secrecy. The Commodore's bearer saw the arrest, but we made certain he knew he would serve a very lengthy prison sentence if he as much as breathes a word. We notified Chief Superintendent Sutcliffe's wife this morning. Sutcliffe's with her now. She took it well and seems very supportive. There was nothing in the morning papers or the stop press."

"What else?"

"We took the Commodore in through a back door and straight to a cell in the sub-basement. The Commodore's not officially here. No booking. Nothing."

Another lengthy silence followed this snippet. "The Home

Office," the Commissioner said slowly, "very occasionally grants extraordinary powers in circumstances such as these, authorized only by the Home Secretary himself. That's for your information alone. I trust you will not repeat what I said."

"Of course not. Fully understood. I don't need to follow the Commodore into a special dungeon."

"Bear in mind, Masters, you can't hold him forever without charges."

"We can remand him in custody without bail once we've charged him and brought him before a magistrate but given the likely range of charges and the high-profile nature of the Commodore, such an appearance might have to be *in camera*."

"I have been in touch with the Home Secretary. He has made it clear to me the Government cannot risk this becoming public knowledge. Those are Churchill's words."

"We'll do our level best to keep this entire episode under wraps, Commissioner. What we need is time, and a full confession. Then we can decide what to do about proceeding with charges."

"See to it that you get the confession, Masters. It's still early in London. I have a phone call scheduled with the Home Secretary again in an hour. I hope he'll be out of his bath by then." I heard the Commissioner almost laugh. "We'll map out a strategy. I'll call you later this afternoon, but you can take it that the Home Office regards this as officially a police matter, not an Admiralty one."

There was a lengthy pause from the other end of the line, one I chose not to interrupt.

"When I next speak to the Home Secretary," he eventually said, in a strained voice, "I have your word, Masters, that as the police officer in charge of the investigation, you assure me you will not treat this as a routine police matter. I can further assure the Home Secretary that, for his own safety and protection, you are keeping Commodore Sutcliffe away from the rest of the people in custody. It is essential that he not be ill-treated in any way. These are matters of national security."

"I can assure you, Commissioner. Given the totality of the evidence against him, I can't see us releasing Commodore Sutcliffe with a caution."

"You've got a week, Masters. *Habeas corpus*."

There was nothing more to be said. I replaced the handpiece.

Later that afternoon the phone rang in Sutcliffe's office. I answered it.

"The Commissioner is on the phone for you," the female voice of the switchboard operator said.

"Masters here."

"Masters," the Commissioner said, "I have only just put the phone down after my call with the Home Secretary. In a word, the Home Secretary is worried."

"About what in particular, Sir?"

"If we can prove the allegations, namely that the Commodore was taking bribes in return for placing Admiralty contracts, the implications are enormous."

"I agree. And…?"

"As you no doubt know, Cabinet Ministers sit on many of the Boards of Directors of the larger companies, as do most members of the House of Lords. If any might be implicated as being even indirectly involved in this conspiracy, the Prime Minister could lose the confidence of the House."

"Then perhaps he deserves to."

"Allow me to continue, Masters." The tone of voice did not convey a request. "Scandal is one thing. In politics it is to be expected from time to time. But should a whiff of this become general knowledge, not only would the Government likely fall, but faith in the Government would have a severe undermining of the morale of the British people." He paused, then continued. "And the morale of the British servicemen fighting in North Africa and elsewhere for the preservation of the Empire and the British way of life. If that were the case and we are defeated in the field, Herr Hitler might come marching up Whitehall any day, or something similar to another Russian revolution might occur."

"What you're saying, Commissioner, is that the criminal conspiracy must be allowed to go unpunished in order to preserve the greater good?"

"Not exactly, Masters."

"Then what exactly, Sir?"

"Bad apples will be found at the Admiralty. Careers of any who have stood to gain in any way will end in tatters. Cabinet Ministers can and will be replaced. Those in the ranks of industry will see their companies undergo financial audits. And the Commodore, who has not yet seen fit to co-operate with your enquiries, will be the first to feel the wrath of the Prime Minister. He will, of course, be sacked and disgraced when charges of buggery and having sex with minors are brought to bear. He will face a lifetime in prison, possibly a short and extremely unpleasant lifetime, if you understand my meaning. You have the word of the Home Secretary on that."

"We have gathered all the evidence we require to lay suitable charges. There only remains the matter of a full confession and the return of the Commodore to England to face charges, unless the Home Secretary wishes the Commodore to face the courts here."

"I will let you know what the Home Secretary's position is once you have obtained the confession. See to it, Masters."

In a despondent mood, I hung up. This was a case with implications that reached further than the confines of Malaya and Singapore. If the Prime Minister was involved, who knew where it might end? And whose careers might vanish as if they had never occurred?

"A few careers will end in ignominy," I told Sutcliffe. "Many guilty men will escape criminal justice. There'll be no massive scandal. The Government won't fall. And the British soldier and sailor will never be the wiser."

"That hardly sounds fair," he said.

"Perhaps not, but Governments have ways of emphasizing in its senior members the need to see things in the larger picture. Heads will roll, quietly and without fanfare. Your father will most likely rot in solitary confinement in Bodmin or Dartmoor prison for the rest of his life."

"If that happens, I for one won't shed one tear at his conviction or his sentence or visit him in jail."

"That sounds a very harsh thing to say about one's own father, Sutcliffe," I said.

"Nevertheless, it'll be a fitting end to an otherwise unremarkable life and a death I regret did not come about in some valiant way. I despise my father, Masters. Prison, even Dartmoor, is too good for him, if that's where he ends up, though perhaps rotting in jail might be a more fitting, longer lasting and more meaningful punishment than the gallows. What will happen to the others, the men who escape prosecution?"

"They'll undoubtedly find themselves the subject of personal income tax audits and minute scrutiny in their business and financial dealings for decades to come. The tax authorities have ways of making life very unpleasant if they choose, and I'm sure the Prime Minister will make certain they do."

"Is what you're saying, Masters, that, instead of going to jail for a long time, a lot of influential people are going get a telling off and a tax audit?"

"That's about the sum of it, Sutcliffe. You know as well as I do, in real life the crooks usually win."

I heard a cynical laugh from the other end of the line. "I'm glad it's almost over, Masters. Do you know what I need right now? A stiff drink."

"I'd join you but I have a confession to obtain. The Commissioner's particularly anxious about a written confession, as apparently is the Home Secretary."

"My father will come around to seeing things your way in the end. He is a coward. He will do what serves his best interests. I have great faith and trust in your methods, Masters. The secret is to find the key that unlocks the treasure chest. Meanwhile, a large Scotch calls my name and I must respond."

The key that unlocks the treasure chest… That conundrum consumed my thinking all afternoon. I was at a loss as to which line of questioning might provide the answer when I remembered an interrogation I had conducted some years earlier. It had worked then. It might work now.

"Tell me about the photographs," I said to the Commodore.

"What photographs?"

"The ones of you engaged in sex acts with minors that we found under lock and key near the bottom of your sea chest."

I saw his face pale. He swallowed and licked his dry, cracked lips. "I don't know what you're talking about."

"Would you like me to show you a few? Would that refresh your memory?"

His shoulders slumped. I sensed the sluicegates cracking open.

"Bodmin jail's not a very nice place to spend the rest of your days, Commodore. If the existence of these photos should somehow get leaked to the inmates, I'm sure your time there will be short and extremely unpleasant. I wouldn't want to be caught in the showers with the guards looking the other way."

He swallowed again and his face turned almost alabaster. "What do you want, Masters?"

"A full written confession, names, dates, everything about each and every transaction."

"And you'll promise to keep the photos out of evidence, as if they never existed?"

"You have my word. Once I have your signature on the bottom of the confession you can watch me destroy them."

He sighed and leaned back, relaxing for the first time since his arrest. "Where would you like me to begin?"

I phoned the Commissioner in K.L. with the news. He greeted me warily with, "*Quid nunc*, as the Romans used to say, Masters?"

"I have what you need, Commissioner. Names named, in writing and without duress. I believe the powers that be will be satisfied with the results of our investigation thus far. We've done our bit. All that remains is to carry out London's instructions. I can keep this under wraps a little longer but eventually someone is going to say something and word will get out. The Port Admiral knows to keep this buried for as long as it takes for the good of the Service."

"Good work, Masters. I'll let the Home Secretary know. I'll be back with further instructions in due course. Best say no more for now. You never know who might be listening."

He hung up. The silence on the other end of the line left me drained, physically, mentally and, yes, emotionally. I needed to sleep for a week, by which time I would be in a fit state to carry out the Home Secretary's instructions, put the Commodore on an RAF plane and fly him back to England where he would spend the rest of his days in a prison cell.

Chief Superintendent Sutcliffe came into his office as I was preparing to leave.

"Congratulations must be in order if you're packing up to go home," he said.

I smiled weakly. "A few hours in a bed between sheets, followed by a shower, a decent shave and a change of clothes first. Barnes and Jessop have already returned to K.L., lucky devils. I'm awaiting instructions from further up the tree."

"He confessed eventually?"

I nodded. "He finally broke down. He could brazen his way through his criminal wrongdoings, justify them perhaps, at least in his own mind. Perhaps even claim them as a source of pride and boast of them, as some criminals do. By that point he didn't seem to care who knew. But that's not what turned him."

"What was it, then?"

"It was the photographs that proved the tipping point."

Sutcliffe made to interrupt, but I held up my hand as if I were directing traffic back on the Met in London. "Allow me to finish, if you would. I suspect the photos were something he could never live down if their existence were to come out at trial. Things wouldn't go down too well with the rest of the prison inmates wherever he serves his time. As you well know, they can be far less forgiving in their judgement than any court."

I gave Sutcliffe time to absorb the information.

"I see. And you're satisfied as to the truthfulness of his confession?"

"I am. Your office telegraph bill will be enormous the next time you receive it, but it was authorized by the Commissioner. I cross-checked every name and company. It pieced together like a jigsaw puzzle."

Sutcliffe remained silent for several moments. I could see from the way he was fidgeting with his hands something was on his mind. "Would it be possible to see my father before he's shipped back home?"

"I don't see why not. It might be your last chance. Do you want to see him now?"

He nodded. I stood and motioned for him to follow me. We threaded our way along several corridors and down two flights of concrete stairs to the building's sub-basement. I closed a heavy, soundproofed door behind us, took a few steps and opened another similar door. Without circulation and proper ventilation, the air smelled musty down there. The short corridor was dimly lit. I shut the second door behind me and locked it. We stood in front of a single steel door. I slid back the covering to the screen. In the light of the single bulb high above his head, the Commodore sat on a narrow raised concrete sleeping platform staring dully into space.

"A visitor, Commodore," I said through the screen.

Sutcliffe removed his service Webley revolver from the holster on his Sam Browne belt and broke it open. He ejected the bullets and handed them to me before closing his revolver and returning it to the holster. I unlocked the door and Sutcliffe stepped inside. I closed the steel door and slid the screen covering closed.

I waited for several minutes, then a single gunshot rang out. I hastily unlocked the door and pushed it open. The Commodore lay on the concrete floor with a small pool of blood gathering beneath his head. I counted the bullets in my hand—five, and looked at Sutcliffe. He broke the revolver open. He held his hand out and I gave him the five bullets. He reloaded the gun and holstered it. Then he turned to me.

"I gave him a choice—him or me. That may have been the only time in his life he did the honourable thing."

I detected more than a tinge of sadness in Sutcliffe's voice.

I sucked in a deep breath of air laden with stale sweat and cordite. "I think there will be many in Westminster and the Admiralty who would share your sentiment," I said. "And many, many more who would appreciate his sacrifice if they were ever to know of it."

I had the Commodore's body secretly removed to the hospital morgue. The pathologist, Dr. Morton had his habitual mournful, undertaker's look on his face and the personality to match. He shot me a quizzical look followed by a sigh of long suffering. I had first run into him back in 1924 over the death of Charles Richardson, the concert pianist, and had clashed swords with him on that occasion over the cause of death. I doubt if he had ever forgiven me for proving him wrong.

"I need to speak to you in strictest confidence, Morton," I said quietly. "And what I have to say does not leave these four walls unless the four walls you next see will be on account of a breach of the Defence of the Realm Act and the Official Secrets Act."

I laid it on thick but it served to focus his attention. I had no idea if either of those Acts of Parliament applied. To be frank, I had never read either. He inclined his head towards his small office in one corner of the morgue. I followed and shut the door behind me.

"This comes on the authority of the Home Secretary himself." That was the first lie. I had no idea what the Home Secretary may, or may not have told the Commissioner, or indeed whether the Home Secretary had the authority to order a certain course of action half way around the world.

"The deceased has been charged with offences against both the Defence of the Realm Act and the Official Secrets Act." That was the second lie. I had yet to complete the paperwork charging the Commodore with offences contrary to the Theft Act. In any case, that paperwork was now redundant.

"On the instructions of the Home Secretary, the cause of death on the report will not indicate suicide or any other form of violent death." That was the last lie. To the best of my knowledge the Home Secretary had no knowledge of the Commodore's death and even less interest in the cause. That he might be relieved at the convenience of the death was yet to be seen, though I doubted if he would ever let his feelings be known.

The pathologist took his time in responding. When he did, he surprised me.

"I'm retiring very shortly, at the end of the month to be precise. I had hoped that my final few days here would pass without complication, or even incident. I see that my hopes are to be dashed. However, I know the Home Secretary, not well, but it's a small world at the top. We were at school together almost fifty years ago. Please let the Home Secretary know that I shall accede to his request as a personal favour and he can rest assured that nothing further will be said on the matter. Then perhaps you, and the Commissioner, the Home Secretary, the British Medical Association, the Prime Minister's cat and Uncle Tom Cobley and all, will let me alone for the rest of my days."

"I'm glad we can rely on you, Morton. And I wish you well in your retirement. Back to England, is it?"

He offered a rare smile. "Tasmania. It reminds me of my home county of Devon, which I've not seen since before the last war, but it has one priceless advantage over Devon."

I swallowed the bait.

"Tasmania's not likely to be in any Luftwaffe Heinkel's bomb sight any time soon."

I didn't get my sleep. Instead I caught the overnight sleeper to Kuala Lumpur and presented myself at the Commissioner's office after a shower, a shave and a change of clothing first thing the next morning.

"I felt it the right thing to do to bring you the news in person rather than telephoning," I said.

He raised his eyebrows. "What news, Masters?"

"I must inform you, Sir that Commodore Sutcliffe died yesterday while in police custody. However, as he was never officially in our custody, the customary inquiry might not be appropriate. I can assure you there was no wrongdoing on our part."

"How did he die?"

"I'll come to that in a minute, if I may, Sir. Given his confession, a guilty plea would be the best outcome for all concerned. However, it seems what the Commodore had in mind was a different, and perhaps in hindsight, more proper course of action. The Commodore was duly provided with the means to redeem himself. There was only one round in the chamber."

The Commissioner raised his eyebrows but remained silent.

"To his credit the Commodore did not hesitate. The post mortem will list the official cause of death as a cerebral haemorrhage."

"'Will', Masters? Are you sure?"

"The post mortem had not yet started when I left Singapore, but I imagine it will be finished by now. I swore the pathologist to silence under the Official Secrets Act. I suggested that his finding of the cause of death will be a cerebral haemorrhage. He agreed."

"You have a wonderful way with words, Masters. A cerebral haemorrhage would be the natural outcome of a point four fifty-five caliber bullet through the brain."

"From the stress of overwork, perhaps. They tell me it happens to some of the most successful men. The Commodore was close to retirement age and not in the most robust of health. There will be no suggestion there was any other cause of death."

"Or that anyone ordered it, encouraged it, provided the means or in any way was involved or implicated?"

"Unless you personally tell the Home Secretary, only the pathologist, you and I know the truth." I deliberately omitted Graham Sutcliffe's name on a need to know basis.

"Perhaps it's the best outcome we could have hoped for. I'll notify the Home Secretary immediately. I imagine he'll be quite pleased, as will the Prime Minister I'm sure."

"I've left Chief Superintendent Sutcliffe to make the private funeral arrangements. Cremation followed by disposal of the ashes at sea seems most appropriate. I must say, he took his father's death quite well, all things considered." I took a step back from his desk. "Unless there's anything else, Sir I have some paperwork to complete."

"Just one more thing, Masters. Your Acting rank has been replaced by permanent status starting forthwith." He offered a rare smile. "Carry on."

AFTERWORD

When the Japanese invaded Malaya, Loretta Ingles and I managed to get away before the surrender, as did Graham Sutcliffe and his family in Singapore. The Sutcliffes made their way to Australia and I lost touch with them for a while. Loretta and I spent the war in Ceylon, she up in the hills outside Kandy where she married a tea planter, and I in Colombo as a major attached to Military Intelligence. After the war I returned to the Colonial Police in Kuala Lumpur. There was much work to be done with only the skeleton force that remained after the Japanese occupation and a British officer corps that had virtually no experience of colonial policing.

Over my nearly thirty years as a policeman I was fortunate to meet and become enchanted, beguiled even, if that's not too strong a word, by many women of varying beauty and charm—Evelyn, Millie, Fatima and Loretta Ingles among them. Fatima and Dr. Aziz chose to remain in K.L. rather than escape to India. I know only that the Japanese were not kind to Fatima after they executed Dr. Aziz for reasons that remain unclear to this day. I have had no contact with Evelyn or Millie, the Donaldsons or Adriana Braaten and her daughter since I last saw them.

After the war Loretta and I became better acquainted, mostly during local leave in places like Singapore where we could spend time away from the scrutiny of the Commissioner. In this way we managed to keep our relationship undetected until my retirement. As far as Loretta knows, she is probably still married to the planter in Kandy, although she has neither enquired nor received a letter from him since her return to Malaya in 1946.

Unlike so many of my former colleagues, I avoided relying on the bottle to see me through my final years in K.L. The day I retired from the Colonial Police, forty years and two wars after first donning a uniform, I moved into the hillside bungalow I rented for Loretta in George Town, Penang. We continue to live there in a happily unmarried state now that the morals clause in my terms of service no longer applies. My only regret is that distance, the exigencies of the service, and a second husband kept us apart for so long.

We have no intention of returning to England. Loretta is Malaya born and raised. For her, England is not home. Ashton-Browne was right: I've been away too long and without family or friends there, England no longer seems like mine. When I took Loretta with me on my last home leave before retiring, we found England, and especially London, cold, dreary and rather grubby. It's a shame. I remember fondly how it used to be there, though I suspect those memories are coloured by the passage of time and distance.

The Club in Penang where Loretta and I met was taken over by the Japanese during the occupation and used to house local 'comfort women' for their officers. It has never reopened and, given its more recent history, I can't say any of us is sad. These days, while the sun sinks behind us into the Strait of Malacca and distant Sumatra, Loretta and I sip a locally made gin and tonic on our verandah before dinner. I wish it were The Macallan single malt whisky like I used to enjoy when I was on the job but, without an expense account these days, having to pay for my own on a policeman's pension can stretch the monthly budget uncomfortably thin.

B.H. Masters,
Penang, December 1956.

ABOUT THE AUTHOR

After forty years in the work force, including almost thirty spent in courtrooms, Michael Joll turned to writing, which many people do not consider a real job. His first offerings, four radio plays, three of which somehow came to be broadcast on Canadian Public Radio were, by his own admission, terrible, and mercifully buried and forgotten years ago. A steep learning curve followed and subsequently bore fruit in a series of award-winning short stories, many of which have appeared in anthologies and collaborations.

His first collection of short stories, *Perfect Execution and Other Stories*, also published by MiddleRoad Publishers, came out in 2017. For *Persons of Interest*, the author drew on his experience as a former police officer in Canada.

Born, raised and educated mostly in England, he has lived in Brampton, Ontario for more than forty years. He currently serves as the Chair of the Brampton Writers' Guild.

He no longer writes plays.

LOOK FOR UPCOMING WORKS FROM MICHAEL JOLL THROUGH MIDDLEROAD PUBLISHERS

MORE BOOKS FROM MIDDLEROAD PUBLISHERS

"Making literature see the light of day."

RACING WITH THE RAIN

Ken Puddicombe

available on Amazon

"Ken Puddicombe's brilliant novel Racing with the Rain evokes not only personal consequences of an historic political conflict in Guyana, during the Cold War, but also the cold cynicism and tragic irony of a small, defenseless Caribbean state being sacrificed to super-power hegemony." -Frank Birbalsingh, author of Novels and The Nation: Essays in Canadian Literature.

JUNTA

Ken Puddicombe

available on Amazon

"After a first novel—"Racing in the Rain" (2012)— introducing a Caribbean, steaming in post-colonial turbulence, Ken Puddicombe follows up with Junta, another suspenseful tale of churning political chaos..." –Frank Birbalsingh author of Novels and The Nation: Essays in Canadian Literature.

DOWN INDEPENDENCE BOULEVARD AND OTHER STORIES

Ken Puddicombe

available on Amazon

"Ken Puddicombe's brilliant collection of stories tells the tales of people forced to leave their homes and while enjoying freedom in a faraway country, they crave the past, the known and predictable...it is the universality of their destiny that comes across, escaping from racial conflicts or dictatorship of any kind from anywhere in the world." —Judith Kopácsi Gelberger, author of *Heroes Don't Cry.*

PERFECT EXECUTION AND OTHER STORIES

Michael Joll

available on Amazon

Brampton Author Michael Joll has written an appealing and diverse first collection of short stories that span several continents and encompasses the gamut of human emotions.

PEOPLE OF GUYANA

Ian McDonald and Peter Jailall

available on Amazon

Guyanese poets Ian McDonald and Peter Jailall have turned out moving poems about a diverse mix of Guyana's colourful characters, folk lore, and history. From Berbice to Essequibo, and Demerara in-between, these poems traverse the geography of Guyana with startling insights into its people and culture.

WITNESSES AND OTHER SHORT STORIES

Raymond Holmes

Armin Negossian's vintage violin is stolen from his car. In the year 2338 the Lagomarsias purchase their first Androbot. Taxi driver Paul Wilkins picks up a young woman at a street corner and gets more than he bargained for. Arthur Lovacs is sentenced to death for a murder he claims he didn't commit. Rebecca Fraser feels that Death is lurking outside her door. Eight-year old Alvin is convinced he's contracted polio. Daniel Burchard has just found out he has six months to live. Successful lawyer Sarah Richmond uses her ring as an instrument to reveal the circumstances of her death. These are some of the intriguing stories in the first collection from Raymond Holmes.

Made in the USA
Monee, IL
17 September 2019